Tell Me Where You Are

Moira Forsyth

W F HOWES LTD

This large print edition published in 2012 by
W F Howes Ltd
Unit 4, Rearsby Business Park, Gaddesby Lane,
Rearsby, Leicester LE7 4YH

1 3 5 7 9 10 8 6 4 2

First published in the United Kingdom in 2010
by Sandstone Press Ltd

A CIP catalogue record for this book is available
from the British Library

ISBN 978 1 47121 341 0

Typeset by Palimpsest Book Production Limited,
Falkirk, Stirlingshire
Printed and bound in Great Britain
by MPG Books Ltd, Bodmin, Cornwall

MIX
Paper from
responsible sources
FSC® C018575

For Malcolm and Esmé

PART I

NOT JUST THE TURKEY
IN THE DREAM

CHAPTER 1

On Christmas Eve, Frances dreamed about the turkey. In the dream it was not yet dead. It had turned itself over, staggered onto drumstick legs, and emerged from the butcher's white plastic bag. When she went down the garden to the summerhouse, boots crunching on frosty ground, and opened the door, it tottered across the wooden floor towards her, its skin mottled and bluish, but not completely bald: a few tufts of feathers adhered to its body and its head was the head of a live turkey, complete with beak, beady eyes and dark purple wattles quivering on the neck. Its beak opened and closed, and Frances understood that it was talking to her, telling her something. Of course it spoke Turkish, so she couldn't understand a word.

In the dream she made this little joke and smiled at it, all the while paralysed by dismay which ran underneath her freezing feet like an electric current. For she knew the turkey must, if still alive, have suffered horribly in its journey from farm and butcher to Frances's summerhouse. Was still suffering. She stood shivering in the dark December dawn, torn between fearful pity and anxiety about what on earth they were to eat for Christmas dinner instead, since there was no longer any question of it being the turkey. Somehow, she had to rescue and rehabilitate it.

Then, with a heavy flap of its naked wings, it hurried past her, down the steps and out of the summerhouse. She must have cried out and her own cry woke her.

The bedroom was dark and cold. Too early for the heating to have come on, much too early for daylight. Frances lay on her back, waiting for the dream to fade.

Of course, the turkey really was in the summerhouse, which was suitably cold and out of reach of the cats. Nothing could have been more dead than that lump of flesh, weighing her down on one side as she walked back to the car, the handles of the bag cutting into her fingers through woollen gloves.

She turned in bed with a sigh, tugging the duvet round her. After a moment, she realised she was not going to get any more sleep, so she flung back the covers and stood up, the bones in her legs creaking. She bent and stretched a few perfunctory times, then put on an old pullover of Jack's she used as a dressing gown, and went down to the kitchen.

The cats in the basket chair looked up as she came in. The grey tom stretched, paws reaching across the little tabby, so old now she took her

4

time waking and getting up for breakfast. The grey cat jumped down and rubbed himself against the backs of Frances's legs as she filled the kettle. A few yards from the kitchen window were the woods, and she became aware of an unusual whiteness beyond her own reflection. She switched off the light and looked again. Snow, a fine powdering, the first white Christmas for years. She remembered the dream now, rising up in her with a rush, a taste almost of fear. Soon she would have to go down the garden to fetch the bird. She switched on the light again, and filled the kitchen with reality. The cats mewed round her, asking to be fed.

Upstairs, her sons stirred but did not wake as Frances carried the radio up to the bathroom. She looked in on both of them. Andrew's room smelled of beer and more strongly of the rank aroma of young maleness. Jack's room also smelled of unwashed clothes brought home from Halls and left in a heap on the floor. As Frances went into the bathroom and turned on the shower, the water pipes rumbled and the central heating heaved into life. Half conscious that his mother had been there, Andrew turned over, kicking at his duvet, so that the red climbing sock, filled by Frances late the night before (while the boys were in the pub), rolled off his bed and landed on the floor with a thud.

At sixteen and eighteen they were too old for Christmas stockings but still had them, still had a tree with decorations kept since childhood, and the traditional dinner she had always cooked. It would have been the same if they had gone on being a family of four instead of three. Then, they might even have been five or six. She had meant to have more children; she had meant to have a daughter. There you are, Frances thought, vigorously rubbing herself dry, that's how it goes. She could switch off the past now as swiftly as she turned off the shower: a second's delay and it was gone.

In his bedroom next to the bathroom, Jack emerged from heaped-up covers, annoyed to find himself awake so early. His feet stuck out, cold at the bottom of the bed. Everything here was too small for him now. It was bloody freezing in this house. In halls, you lived in a fug of stale heat twenty-four hours a day. His mother said it was unhealthy but you got used to it, used to wearing a tee-shirt all year round. No-one wears jumpers he had explained to Frances, going through possible Christmas presents for his grandmother to give him. He pulled up his knees, pretending to be still asleep, in the hope that soon he would be. Then, with a suddenness amazing to him, he realised it was Christmas morning.

When they were kids they were up at four, tearing open parcels. Were there any parcels here? He had his present already, having gone with his mother to buy an I-Pod in Inverness several days ago.

There must be parcels though. He kicked to feel the heavy stocking at the foot of the bed, the mysterious weight of it creating an echo of childhood excitement. Something rose in the air, and thrust itself off the bed with a thud. He had dislodged the tabby which had sneaked in, believing, like Jack, it was too early to get up. There was something else; he felt the weight of it between his feet. Satisfied, he turned and settled again. In a moment, the cat jumped back and nestled behind his knees, where she had a quick wash and then, like Jack, sank back into sleep.

Outside, the clear sky paled and the moon faded to a papery hemisphere. Frances went downstairs to light the oven before venturing out to fetch the turkey. The dream skirted the edge of her thoughts but it seemed ridiculous now.

Her breath clouded the air in front of her and the snow sparkled in the light from the back door. The summerhouse was dark, smelling of soil and damp wood. The deck chairs were stacked in the corner and terracotta pots, cleaned out ready for spring, lined one wall. On the potting bench, scattered with dried geranium leaves and a few crumbs of compost, was the butcher's bag with the turkey inside. Frances snatched it up and went out, tugging the door shut behind her. Usually the bird was stuffed and trussed by this time, indeed, actually cooking. She would never have the meal on the table by two at this rate. She blamed the late finishing of term and the weight of work her new job had given her, that she was so far behind. Not that it *mattered*, but her parents would fret, not being used to eating at what they called 'odd hours'.

As she began work in the kitchen, mug of tea and half eaten toast on the table beside her, the telephone rang.

'I've got my hands covered in oatmeal – *Jack?*' A rumbling from someone's room, a stirring, not urgent enough. She wiped her hands on her apron and went to pick up the phone.

It was Gillian.

'Happy Christmas! You all set? We're leaving in about five minutes. We've got snow, would you believe it – real snow! The folks are in a state of course, fussing about weather forecasts and dangerous roads. It's not much – a covering. How is it up in the frozen north?'

'Running late,' Frances said, 'so I'm not hurrying you. You really should have come yesterday Gill. I knew they'd panic about travelling on Christmas morning.'

'I know, but I truly couldn't get here till last night. Work. Better than letting Dad drive, eh?'

'We've got snow too, but it's a lovely morning. How are you?'

'Fine, apart from hating Christmas. The price you pay.'

The price his wife pays too, thought Frances, though she may not know it yet. There was no point in saying this, since it was an old story and

8

when you have only one sister left, there is no sense in falling out with her. So Frances said merely, 'Go easy on the road.'

About twelve, when she was still in the kitchen, the room redolent of roasting fowl, Jack appeared barefoot in tracksuit bottoms, hair ruffled. He needed a shave and his chin and neck were scabbed with dried out spots. And yet, she thought with an impulse of love, he is a good looking boy. She could not see, as she still did with Andrew, the child's face shadowing the adult's.

'Happy Christmas, Mum.' He went to the sink and ran the cold tap, filling himself a mug of water and drinking it off. 'Nice smell. When are we having dinner?'

'About two. When Gill gets here with Granny and Grandpa.'

'Who's driving?'

'Gill – that's why they're so late. She was working till yesterday afternoon.'

'They'll make it today then. In about five minutes, probably.'

Frances was amused by the way he had managed to comment on both his grandfather and his aunt in the same breath, but chose to defend her father. 'Don't be cheeky about Grandpa.'

'You're the one who says he's lethal behind the wheel.'

'Gill's probably more lethal,' Frances admitted, 'but I'm sure she won't terrify them by going at her usual speed. Is Andrew awake?'

'Don't know. You want me to chuck him out of bed? Throw cold water on him or something?' He sat on a stool and stretched out his long legs.

'Go and have a shower – mm?'

'In a minute. Cosy in here.'

'You could light the fire in the living-room.'

'I could open my presents.'

'Or wait for Andrew?'

'Wait for everybody?'

'You wouldn't have suggested that a few years ago.'

'I'm not suggesting it now, I'm still going to empty my stocking first.' He sloped off upstairs. In a few minutes, she heard Radio 5 Live and the sound of the shower.

Frances made a fresh mug of tea and took it to the living-room, where she set a match to the fire and stood looking out of the window at the bare winter garden. Grass showed patchily through the thin covering of snow, and the weak sun rising gleamed on the summerhouse windows. A robin perched on a clothes pole, his breast bright against the grey and white around him. She was captured by the peacefulness of the moment. There were no tractors out today, no traffic on the road at the bottom of the lane. Then she heard the tha-thud, tha-thud of hooves on frozen ground as John Ramsay came down from the farmhouse at the top of the hill to feed his cattle in the field adjoining the end of Frances's long garden. If she went up to the back bedroom where her parents would sleep tonight, she'd be high enough to see the black stirks crowding the wire manger, and John in wellingtons and flat cap heading back to his Land Rover. She was grateful every time she paused in this way that she lived here, and was content.

Her thoughts drifted back through the years and she began to think, as she always did on Christmas morning (like touching an old sore), of the last Christmas they had had with Alec.

It was no different from the ones before it, all the years they lived in Northumberland. She and Alec always had the neighbours in on Christmas Eve. It was a sociable street full of young families who went in and out of each others' houses all the time.

They had mince pies and mulled wine, the house festive with holly and tree and tinsel. At ten they said their good-byes, ushering excited children out into the frosty air to sweep them off to bed at last, where they would, for once, try to get to sleep. At eleven, she and Chris from next door put on coats and scarves for the walk to church and Alec poured what he called his last drink. As she wound her scarf round, leaving, she said,

'Remember to get the kittens from next door. Better do it now, before Irene Soutar goes to bed.'

'Oh, she never goes to bed – sits up with the TV all night.'

'*Don't* forget, Alec,' she said, going out on this last word.

When she came back an hour later, full of good wishes and the choruses of familiar carols singing in her head, she found him on the sofa, drink in hand. The kittens were still in their basket in Mrs Soutar's kitchen. Irene Soutar was an elderly widow: she had agreed to take delivery of the kittens for that one evening. Alec was to fetch them in when the children were in bed, to sleep in their basket till morning.

He had become engrossed in an old film or he had dozed off with too much wine. What did it matter? He had forgotten, and jumped up guiltily when Frances, coming in with a breeze of cold air, said, 'Where are they?'

He had been drinking since lunch-time, so she knew she should have gone herself. It was daft to rely on him.

'It's after midnight!' she snapped, flinging on her coat again. 'I just hope she's still up, that's all. You've ruined it – as usual.'

He shrugged his apology, his eyes glazed with prolonged drinking.

'Aw, hey, I'll go round first thing in the morning. I'm sorry – c'm'ere, forgive me eh? It's Christmas, after all.'

Looking back when it had all changed, she acknowledged the marriage must already have been disintegrating. Perhaps what happened only cut short an inevitable end. Still, she did not think he would have gone so soon, left to himself.

In that dark first hour of Christmas morning, the kittens still next door, the boys asleep, her husband contrite but not sorry, she was angry. So she turned on him, not caring what she said.

'You're useless, Alec, bloody useless.'

'I know,' he said, with a shrug, and filled his glass again, since there was no reason why not, and he needed another drink after all this drama. 'You love me anyway!' he called after her, sinking back onto the sofa. He changed channels, looking for something else to take his mind off whatever it was he had to take his mind off.

Mrs Soutar was still up. 'Come away, hinny – I was beginning to think you'd changed your mind.' She let out a gasp of throaty laughter. 'Thought you'd landed me wi them for a Christmas present.'

There they were, the black one for Jack, the tabby for Andrew, asleep in a basket by the radiator. They raised their faces to Frances as she knelt beside them, and when she carried the basket into the hall, woke and looked round in surprise, nosing the cooler air.

'I hope they settle,' she said, as Mrs Soutar opened the front door. 'I'm really sorry to disturb you so late.'

'Nae bother to me.' Mrs Soutar began coughing. 'It's a bitter night. Heh – mind the step now – it's slippy.'

Frances paused on the path. 'Happy Christmas,' she said.

'Aye, and the same to you and the bairns.' Even after the door was shut, Frances could hear the harsh coughing, and music loud from the television.

Alec had had an attack of conscience and was washing up glasses in the kitchen. He began making coffee for both of them.

'You get the beasties then?'

'I did.'

'Told you she'd still be up. Happy now? All your plans in order?' He grinned at her, and came to see the cats.

They were wide awake. When Frances put the basket down they got out and began tentatively to explore their new place. They were twelve weeks old, and Frances was relieved to find them confident, even – after a few minutes – lively, and ready to play.

She and Alec sat up an hour longer keeping the kittens company, watching them discover the Christmas tree, the heap of presents around it crackling beneath exploring paws, and laughed when one of them was tapped on the nose by a shiny bauble swinging back.

Frances moved away from the window and swallowed the last of her cooling tea. Probably they had ended by making love. Friends again, as of course they had to be for the next morning, the

14

excitement of the kittens, and the whole, long, festive holiday. It did not seem so long these days, slipping past uneventfully. Her break would be over, and Jack back in Aberdeen before she had got used to his being at home again.

She heard her sons' gruff voices and the sound of wrapping paper being torn. Why on earth had she let old that old stuff flow into her mind? There was no point.

As she began to climb the stairs, the telephone rang. When she picked up the receiver she had no inkling that anything was about to change, none of the premonition women are supposed to achieve, being so intuitive. 'Frances?'

She did not pick up his voice in those first seconds. 'Yes.'

'Hello there. How are you? Sorry this is a bit of a bolt from the blue. It's been a long time, I know, but I thought you wouldn't mind, since it's Christmas. And it's important, or I wouldn't.'

In all this polite preamble, he had not bothered to announce his name.

'Alec,' she said.

CHAPTER 2

Jack came upon his mother sitting on the stairs, half way down. To see her doing nothing was in itself surprising, but there was something about her back, the way her head bent forward, that made him pause instead of rattling past ruffling her hair. Instead he came and sat beside her.

'You OK, Mum?'

'What? Fine. Did you open the stockings?'

'Thanks for the sugar mice.'

There was always some childish sweet in the stockings, as well as socks, after shave, and a satsuma destined never to be eaten, but discovered weeks later, shrivelled under a bed. 'Andrew's gone back to bed. Did I hear the phone?'

'I told you – Gill called.'

'No, again. A couple of minutes ago.'

A pause. Then she said, her voice carefully neutral, 'It was Alec. Your father.'

'Good grief. What did *he* want?'

'I really don't know. He just asked if he could come here.'

'What, come and *visit*?'

*   *   *

He had never done that, or Frances would not let him. Jack had seen his father only twice since Alec left. The first time it had been evening, and he and Andrew sat at the top of the stairs in pyjamas, listening to their parents' voices below. Soon, they knew, Daddy would come up and see them, as he always did after a trip away. When he eventually came up and chased them into bed, he had brought them no coming-home present, not even sweets. He had looked and smelled different. Only later did they realise he had left them for good. Jack had been six, Andrew four, so the memory was blurred.

The second time, years later, Alec had been curiously familiar, like a television actor, and yet a stranger. Jack had no particular feelings about him now. He suspected Andrew was interested; he was more defensive when fathers were talked about. Of course they had *missed* having a father, Jack supposed, especially when they were younger. There had always been Grandpa, however, and later John and Albert Ramsay, to help out, take them to football matches . . . whatever it was fathers were supposed to do. People made too much of it, Jack thought.

'What did he say?' he asked.

'Well, not much. Could he come for Christmas.'

'He rang this *morning*? To ask—'

'He seemed to mean . . . He wanted to come today.'

'He wants to drive up from Newcastle on Christmas Day? I thought Gill was cutting it a bit fine, from Aberdeen. You could keep him some cold turkey, I suppose.'

Frances got to her feet and followed Jack downstairs. 'Maybe I got it wrong, and he didn't mean actually *today*. I was so taken aback I couldn't think straight.'

'What did you say – did you say he could?'

'No, of course not. It would be ridiculous. Awkward, to say the least. I suggested he come the day after Boxing Day, if he really wants to.'

Jack stopped and looked at her in surprise. 'Right. So he's coming?'

'Well, Granny and Grandpa will be away in the morning. They won't even meet. I'll change the bed in the spare . . . He sounded very keen, as if he needed to talk about something, though I can't imagine *what* after all this time. I couldn't very well say no, could I?'

'You did before.'

'I know.'

'It's Ok, Mum, it's cool. Don't worry about it.'

'I didn't think you'd mind, now you're both grown up.'

'I said – it's cool. Maybe he's come to see Andy and me, maybe he's been left a fortune and he wants to divi it up with us.'

Frances laughed. 'He did inherit a bit. It wasn't a fortune, and I think he got through it pretty quickly.'

'The swine – and we were eating porridge and using string to tie up our boots.'

18

Andrew appeared at the top of the stairs in pyjama trousers long outgrown, revealing hairy calves and large feet bruised by rugby. His black tee-shirt had a skull on the front, and the name of a rock band Frances had definitely heard of.

'What's going on? Can't get back to sleep for the racket you two are making.' He came downstairs two at a time. 'Thanks for the presents Mum. Happy Christmas.' He hugged her then headed towards the living-room. 'You want *your* presents? They're under the tree.'

'That would be nice.'

Jack said, 'Dad's coming. He just called.'

Andrew, standing by the tree with a neatly parcelled box, looked blank. 'How do you mean, *Dad?*'

'As in father, blood of our blood, etcetera . . . person not to be mentioned in front of Grandpa.'

'What, like, he's coming for *Christmas?*'

'No, no. In a couple of days,' Frances took the parcel from him, since he looked as if he might drop it.

'Right. Remind me to go out to the pub or something.'

'You're underage,' Jack said. 'You'll just have to stay here and be polite.'

'Shut up you.'

'Oh lovely,' Frances said hastily, unwrapping first the salad bowl she had asked for, then a pair of earrings. Not quite the ones she would have chosen, but pretty, and she knew plenty of mothers whose sons never bought them anything.

She tidied away wrapping paper and directed Andrew to the bathroom. 'Remember I need to change your bed for Gill to sleep in tonight.'

'Is there anything I can eat now that's not part of Christmas dinner?'

'Help yourself. I must get on.'

She left them standing in the hall. They looked at each other in silence for a moment, then Jack said, 'Don't ask me. Maybe she's just in the Christmas spirit or something.'

'She could have asked us what *we* thought.'

'I think she was kind of stunned.'

Andrew turned and went upstairs.

From time to time during the rest of the morning, Frances heard the echo of Alec's voice in her head. Her whole day was given a nervous edge by that call. She did not say to her sons, 'Don't mention it to Granny and Grandpa'; there was no need. She would tell her parents, but not yet.

Christmas Day was easy, if you simply gave in to it: the rich food, the stupefying afternoon in front of the television, the box of chocolates going round too many times. After the meal was over, Frances's father bore the last of the dishes to the kitchen, determined to do his bit. With difficulty, Frances and Gillian wrested plates from him to load in the dishwasher.

'Don't worry, Dad, there's still plenty for you to

do. I can't put these glasses in, and there's no room for all the pots.'

'Right then – clear a space you girls. Let the dog see the rabbit.' At eighty he was fit and active, his silver hair smoothly brushed, his sleeves rolled up. Briskly the pots and glasses and serving dishes were assembled in their proper order.

'Now then – who's chief dryer? Where are those boys of yours?'

They were in Andrew's bedroom in front of a computer.

'We can dry,' Gillian said.

'Nonsense. Man's work this. One day in the year, eh?' This was a tease (*you liberated women!*) but they suspected he meant it.

Their mother hovered in the doorway. 'I suppose I've to keep out of the way?'

'You sit in front of the fire with the girls.'

Frances went up to Andrew's room and leaned on the door jamb, listening for a moment to their discussion of European football, of tactics and players. On the screen was their invented league table. Andrew, she saw with amused dismay, was selling a player he had named Alecis Uselessowski. Have I missed something, she wondered.

'You've to go and help Grandpa with the dishes.'

They groaned.

'One day in the year it's men's work, apparently.'

Jack grinned. 'Tell him we do it all year round.'

'I'm not perjuring myself like that. Come on,

he'll only get irritable, then Gill and I will have to do it.'

'No sweat, Mum.' Jack rose to his feet and prodded his brother. 'We're between games anyway.'

'You want a walk?' Gillian asked when Frances came back downstairs.

'We should keep Mum company – what do you think?'

'She might come with us.'

'I doubt it.'

'Oh well. I wouldn't have minded some fresh air, that's all.' Gillian looked sullen. 'I drove for three hours this morning, remember.'

'Go out then – nothing to stop you.'

'Not on my own.'

Frances thought, she wants to talk, and if there's no new drama (though there usually was) I'll end up telling her about Alec. 'I'll ask Mum,' she said with a sigh.

Grace had fallen into a doze, the Radio Times askew on her lap. She opened her eyes as Frances came in.

'Oh dear,' she murmured. 'It's that heavy meal making me sleepy. Lovely, though, dear. Very nice.'

'Would you mind if Gill and I went for a quick walk before it gets dark? Would you like to come?'

'No, you go ahead. We've all day tomorrow to catch up on the news. The boys are looking well. Jack's still enjoying the university, is he?'

Frances perched on the arm of the sofa. 'He loves it. Now Andy can't wait to get there too.'

'What is it you said Jack's doing? A science subject, isn't it?'

'Microbiology.'

'My goodness, what kind of job will he get with that?' She shook her head, not waiting for an answer. 'Your Dad thought he should be a lawyer, did you know that?'

'Mm.' Frances rose to leave, aware of Gillian hovering in the doorway. 'We won't be long.'

Outside, the air was clear and frosty but the light was going already at half past three, the landscape greyish white, misty over the fields.

'Careful,' Frances asked, as they began to walk up the lane. 'It's slippy in places.' Gillian was walking quickly, impatient to be clear of house and family.

'I'm telling myself that next year is the year I'm going to change everything.'

'Your love life, you mean.'

'Not just that.'

'But that too.'

'Oh yes.'

'You're going to give him the heave, are you? I seem to have heard that before.'

'I'm thirty six!' Gillian declared, as if Frances might not know. 'I thought I'd have a party next birthday. Well, a sort of wake. For all the hopeless relationships I've been in.'

'You could have married Michael.'

'It wasn't ever *right*.'

'But if you had, you might have children. Isn't that what you're saying you want?'

'Oh yeah, but not with – anyway, don't *preach*, Fran, just because you've got everything sorted in your life. You don't mind being on your own, but I'm not strong like you. If I were, I wouldn't be saying this, year after year, about changing my life. My God, I'll soon be *forty*.'

'It seems quite a nice life to me,' Frances commented. 'A well paid, interesting job, a beautiful flat in a nice part of Edinburgh . . .'

'Oh I know.' Gillian dismissed this with a wave of her hand. 'But you don't really understand the feeling of waiting for something to happen, for your sort of real life to begin.'

It was almost dark by the time they neared the house. A car coming towards them stopped in the lane by Frances's driveway. The headlights dazzled.

'Visitors?' Gillian asked.

'Not today – I wonder who—'

The engine died, the headlights dimmed and went off, then doors opened and slammed shut. Frances blinked, looked again. There were two people standing on either side of a low silver car. It was the woman she focused on first. Her heart leapt so fast it was like a pain, and she thought, *Susan*. But of course, Susan was not young any more, not thin, and her hair did not fall straight on either side of her face, as this girl's did.

'My God,' Gillian sounded breathless, but she was not as fit as Frances and the walk had had a good deal of uphill in it. 'Is that Alec?'

24

'Yes.' They stopped, instinctively side by side, as if Gillian meant to square up to him too. 'It's Alec. I think that's Katy with him. It *must* be.'

'Just for a minute I thought—'

'So did I.'

Gillian held Frances's arm. 'Are you Ok?'

'Yes. He phoned me this morning.'

Now they were within earshot of the two by the car, who stood waiting for them. Alec moved forward, his city shoes uncertain on the unmade road. He wore a long overcoat and in the almost dark looked still young, though his hair, brushed back, had receded in the five years since she had last seen him.

'Hi there. Gillian – *hello*.'

He might have been the host himself, embracing them in turn, Frances stiff in his arms, Gillian giving back a bewildered, hasty hug. The girl stood apart.

'Sorry, I know we agreed day after Boxing Day, but Kate didn't want to wait, did you Kate, and I thought . . . well, thought you wouldn't mind really.' A slight dip of his head, as if in apology, was followed by a smile.

'Come in,' Frances said. 'Hello Katy, how are you?'

The girl did not speak, but she allowed herself to be ushered into the house through the back porch, where Frances opened the door to the kitchen, and she and Gillian took off their boots and coats.

The kitchen was empty, everything as neat as if no dinner had happened at all today. Only the turkey carcass and the covered leftovers of the Christmas pudding remained as evidence.

'Take your things off,' Frances said. 'You can hang them here.'

'Ah,' Alec breathed, 'the hallstand,' greeting it like an old friend. In the light, his face had the worn tiredness of someone who sleeps badly, but he was still lean and well-dressed, a good-looking man.

Gill said, 'Will I put the kettle on?'

Frances looked from Alec to Katy. She must be fourteen. The girl was as tall as she was herself. She was dressed entirely in black, a fair wraith of a girl, with dark shadowed eyes, pale lips, and rows of ear-studs. Frances glanced at Gillian, flushed with fresh air and exercise, frowning, full of how terrible all this was, and earnestly trying, for Frances's sake, not to enjoy it.

'Yes, just put the kettle on. That seems simplest,' Frances said. She turned to Alec. 'Well, since you're here you'd better come through, I suppose.'

Then she opened the living-room door and went in to face her parents and her sons.

CHAPTER 3

Alec was awake, stiffly supine on the camp bed, like the effigy of a knight in some medieval church, and almost as cold and disregarded. The boxroom was so small his feet touched a bookcase along one wall, and his head pressed against the one behind. He fancied to himself through the night, not quite conscious, dozing, that this must be what your coffin was like: a limited space, enough but no more, and of course, no room to move. But he was not dead, however lacking in life he had felt over the last few months. He stuck his elbows out to prove it, to remind himself there was at least an armslength on either side, but it was too cold for experiments, so he eased onto his side and curled up a little, in the hope of growing warmer.

Frances had thrown a sleeping bag and rug onto the camp bed with a brisk 'Sorry, this room has no radiator.' She turned on a small fan heater. 'You'll have to put this off when you go to bed – it costs a fortune to run.'

He did not know if recognising this ancient

heater, which emitted a flow of dusty air round his ankles, made him feel better or worse. He opened his mouth to say, 'Isn't that the one your grandmother gave us?' then changed his mind and said only 'Thanks. Sorry to be such a nuisance.'

Frances said, 'I'll put Katy in with Gill and give her the pullout bed. Why don't you get your things out of the car while I make it up?'

'We don't have much.'

'Then it won't take you long.'

There was to be no quarter here. He acknowledged it with a suppressed sigh, and went downstairs. He recognised other things in Frances's house, of course: pictures, a bookcase – the hallstand. In thirteen years she had bought new furniture and pictures and books, and he was interested in her taste. A certain clutter, which she would not have allowed in those early years, seemed to have gathered comfortably around her. The bookcases were untidy, with small heaps of books lying on their sides on top of others. On the kitchen window sills pot plants jostled with china cats given to her by the children, and also with pens, a sheaf of cutout recipes and a fat bulb of garlic. He was curious, and would have liked to prowl about opening drawers and looking in cupboards. The house however was full of people, all of whom must be hostile to the idea of his being there at all, let alone nosyparkering about in their beloved Frances's home.

His sons thudded downstairs in stockinged feet. He felt himself whiten, with that pinched feeling

28

round his nose. Frances was flanked by them. He tried not to mind Jack's guarded coolness, his 'Hi there', when Frances said 'It's your father', as if they might not otherwise recognise him. Catching Andrew's embarrassed flush, he knew there was no question of that. Andrew knew him. Then Frances said 'Come in,' and pushed open the living-room door. That was it, the moment of reunion come and gone. The boys followed their parents into the room.

Frances's family closed like a shield around her. In the warm living-room, with newspapers, chocolate boxes, and unwrapped presents scattered about and a jigsaw just begun on the table by the window, Jim and Grace Douglas sat side by side on the sofa. They looked up in astonishment over the tops of their spectacles, their jaws not dropping, they were too much in control of themselves for *that*, but taken aback, oh yes. There was a small measure of satisfaction in the utter surprise of his arrival. He could tell Kate did not feel the same and his instinct when the first moment was over, everyone getting to their feet, Jim even shaking him by the hand (his an old, dry hand now, but just as firm a grip), was to protect her. He stepped back to where she hesitated by the door and put his arm lightly round her shoulders.

'I've brought Kate with me,' he said. 'Frozen stiff I'm afraid – car heater wasn't working too well.'

Whatever they might have said to him on his

own, they would be nothing but welcoming to Kate, their lost third grandchild whose birthday presents, perhaps they now realised, were always a year or so too young for the age she had reached.

'Come away, Katy,' Grace Douglas said, using the name she had when she was removed from them. 'Get yourself nice and warm by this fire. Would you like a hot drink?'

'Cold drink would go down well too, I think,' Jim said, lifting the bottle of malt whisky. His demeanour suggested there were occasions when it was called for. Alec was no longer in any way their responsibility, so they need not mind whether he had a drink now.

In this festive room all green and gold, by a log fire, they might have been old friends having a dram.

Kate huddled silent on an arm-chair, still wearing her black coat, hair falling forward over her face in two soft concealing wings. She'll think I've been lying to her, Alec realised with amusement. I've been telling her how much they all hate me. 'Expect to be met with a shotgun,' he had said. 'On Christmas Day?' she had protested, scornful. 'Especially on Christmas Day.'

While the whisky pouring was going on Frances retreated with Gillian to the kitchen. Jack eyed Kate but Andrew stared at the floor, glancing up now and again at the little group his grand-parents and father made as they talked about the weather and the journey, the state of the roads.

'Well,' Grace said, bewildered but determined to keep a conversation going, 'Are you staying? I don't know where Frances can put you – she's got a full house.'

'The floor would be fine,' Alec said. 'We can sort something else out tomorrow – a pub maybe.'

'A pub?' Grace raised her fine eyebrows.

'You're planning to stay a while, then?' Jim asked, raising his glass and swirling the whisky round.

Alec gulped his, grateful for the injection of alcohol. 'No fixed plans. You know how it is,' he said, realising they did not.

They sustained the evening with remarkable composure. Everyone behaved well. Only Frances had let him see the edge of her anger, if that's what it was. The boxroom, the cold, the sleeping bag smelling stale from long storage in the loft, her curt 'Goodnight'. What else could he expect, landing without warning? Frances liked to be well prepared and in control, which was why he had done it like this. Well, *he* had been left with no choice in the end.

Along the hall, Kate slept in the pullout bed in Andrew's room. On his own bed, made up with fresh linen but still somehow redolent of Andrew, Gillian lay awake for a long time. Kate had taken the first opportunity to go to bed, disappearing into the bathroom for half an hour, then being found asleep when Gillian eventually retreated from Frances's room where they had been talking for an hour. Perhaps tomorrow she would have the chance to get to know her niece. At first when she lay down her head was full of what was happening, her reaction to seeing Alec, *everyone's* reaction, the keen excitement of the utterly unexpected. She thought Alec had worn well, he was that sort, thin and dark, looking gaunt as they get older but still attractive. It was odd, she reflected, curling herself up cosily in the single bed, seeing Alec again in this objective way. All the old emotion seemed to have evaporated. Not that much of it had been hers, beyond the hurt she had felt for Frances. What she had felt for Susan was more complex. She had only a sense of emptiness now, thinking of her other sister.

Alec was not Gillian's type, that was one good thing, so she could be objective. Anyway, you didn't have to see *every* man as a potential lover, surely to God. She had been telling herself that for years.

She had followed Frances up to bed, and Frances had gratefully welcomed her in so that they could huddle together side by side under the duvet, talking.

'Of course I don't mind,' Frances said. 'I'll never get to sleep anyway.'

'Are you Ok? What a shock, eh?'

'You could say that.'

'Everybody's behaving so well, aren't they? I suppose Dad's past socking anybody on the jaw now.'

'It's a bit late for that. Not that he'd ever have done such a thing.'

'Mm. He felt like it once. How long is it – fifteen years?'

'Thirteen. Katy wasn't even two years old.'

They focused on Kate.

'Why has he brought her with him, did he say?'

'Only that he wants to talk to me when you've all gone home. I got the impression it was about Katy.'

'Not . . . Susan.'

'I don't know.'

'She didn't come. She hasn't changed, then.'

'I said – I don't know.'

'So is he staying for a while?'

'Not with me,' Frances said firmly.

'It is a bit much,' Gillian admitted, 'turning up on Christmas Day out of the blue. I mean, you couldn't very well turn them away, could you?'

'I did think of it.'

'Not Katy—'

'Well, there you are. Maybe that's why he brought her.' Frances shook her head. 'Oh Gill.'

'You're *not* Ok. How do you feel – about him?'

'Numb.'

'Do you still hate him?'

'No, not for years. Just numb, as I said.'

'He'll go away quite soon, he'll have to. Then everything will just go back to the way it was.'

They contemplated the fatuousness of this in silence for a moment. That was like Frances, to leave the idiotic thing you had said hanging in the air. Maybe, thought Gillian with such force it seemed like an insight, she did that to Alec too. Maybe she made him feel inadequate. I wonder if he's still such a drunk? She stopped, conscious of Frances in blue pyjamas beside her, hugging her knees. Then Frances reached up and began to take the pins out of her hair, so that its dark blonde and silver coil unfolded slowly and spread over her shoulders and back. Her face seemed to alter as she did so and in the lamplight grew softer and younger.

'I must do something about this,' she said, pushing her fingers through her hair. 'It's all right when I have it up, but old women with long hair . . . very unattractive.'

'You're not old,' Gillian protested, 'and your hair is beautiful.'

'My face isn't!' Frances gave a rueful laugh. 'Oh dear, what does it matter? Usually I don't even think about that sort of thing.'

'I do,' Gillian sighed.

Frances contemplated her darker, slighter sister, the cropped hair and stylish clothes, the pretty, smooth face, eyes mournful and large at the thought of youth sliding away from her. Gillian always wanted to be thought young, and was lucky she looked it.

'I wonder what he wants,' Gillian mused, reverting to Alec.

'Goodness knows,' Frances said, cool now.

'Nothing he does ever quite adds up, or it never used to. I doubt if anything's changed.'

'What about tomorrow – we were all going up to the Ramsays, weren't we? Will we take Alec and Katy with us?'

For the first time, Frances looked nonplussed. 'I'd forgotten all about it. I suppose we'll have to.' She laughed. 'Oh dear, Gill, I'm glad you're here. Don't leave me alone with Dad, will you?'

Gillian smiled. 'Don't worry, I'll protect you all day tomorrow, then whisk them away early on the 27th.' She nudged her sister. 'Hey, what if we get snowed in and have to stay for weeks? All of us?'

Instinctively, they both turned to the curtained window. Gillian got out of the bed and went to draw the curtain back, looking down into the lane. The roof of Alec's car glittered with frost, but it was a dry night.

'No more snow. Panic over.' She dropped the curtain.

'You'd better go to bed,' Frances said, lying back on her pillows. 'Heating's off – it's getting cold in here.' Gill paused by the door, as if she was trying to say something else. 'Go to bed,' Frances repeated. 'Enough talking for one day.'

Going over this in her head, listening to Kate's snuffly breathing, Gillian grew drowsy, and fell into dreams.

⋆　　⋆　　⋆

35

In the small spare bedroom, which held only bed, dressing table and chair, Jim and Grace Douglas talked in low voices for a long time.

'Well,' Grace said in the end, 'after all these years maybe we should give him the benefit of the doubt. He seems to care for Katy at any rate. And Susan – well, she was always a very strong willed girl.'

'Ach.' Her husband turned away from her, preparing to sleep. 'Are you putting the light out, or what?'

Grace sighed, rearranging her pillows (beds away from home were never quite right) and switched off the bedside lamp.

Alec woke at four, thoroughly chilled, and thought immediately, 'Frances is still stunning. Still a beautiful woman.'

CHAPTER 4

On the morning of the 27th Gillian set off to drive her parents back to Aberdeen. While she packed, Jim went out to remove all traces of frost and ice from the car windows. He refused lock de-icer and warm water (Frances's usual shortcuts) and it took him some time to get the doors open. The air was misty with cold and Dingwall below was lost in a greyish haze, but overhead the sky was brightening to blue.

Frances stayed outside to help her father. The boys and Kate were still in bed; her mother was nursing a cold; Gill was in the shower. Alec had not appeared, from tact or nervousness.

'Now then,' her father said, wrenching the driver's door open at last, 'we'll get the engine warmed up.'

'What about windscreen wash?' Frances asked. 'Maybe we should check that first.'

He paused, thwarted. Instead of answering, he said, 'So what's he up to?'

'Who?'

She had avoided being alone with her father till now. Boxing Day had been eased by the long buffet lunch at the Ramsays, an annual event gathering of neighbours. The Douglases had an old connection with Pat Ramsay's parents, and felt welcome there and comfortable.

'Alec. Your once-upon-a-time husband. What's he up to?'

'He's not *my* anything now, Dad.'

'He's here, though. Shot out of the blue, was it?' He glowered at her, suspicious.

'Yes. He rang on Christmas morning. I said not to come just yet, but he turned up anyway. Because of Katy, it seems.'

'What's wrong with Katy? Nothing a good talking-to wouldn't cure. Why do they wear black, these girls? You'd think they were forever going to funerals.'

'It's just the fashion,' Frances said. She leaned past her father and released the catch for the car bonnet. 'I'll check the water.'

'But he's after something, don't tell me he's not. When's he ever made an effort before? Brought Katy to visit you? Never.'

He did not mention Susan, Frances noted. No-one said her name. Even Gillian and she, out of earshot of everyone else, had shied away from talking about her. It was a measure perhaps of the force she still exerted. Or was it like naming a curse, bad luck?

I might have some of that screenwash stuff in the shed,' Frances said. 'I'll look.'

When she came back, her father was polishing

38

the back window, unnecessarily, since he had already cleared it, and the sun was shining now, softening the film of frost on the bodywork. A moment later, Frances slammed down the bonnet and he got into the car. The engine started without protest so he got out, leaving it running. Behind the car, the exhaust emission condensed in the air. They stood side by side, Frances with the bottle of screenwash in one hand, the kettle in the other.

'They're good cars,' she observed. 'Gill says it never lets her down.'

'Prefer British made myself. Or French,' he conceded. 'Auld Alliance. But not German, not Japanese.'

What an unforgiving crew we are, Frances thought, the irony not lost on her.

'You take care of yourself and the boys,' her father said abruptly. 'You can't have him waltzing back now. Even if he is their father.'

'Oh there's no question of that.'

'Maybe not. Let me know, Frances, you hear me? Any help you need . . .'

'I know, Dad. Thanks.' She sighed, leaning her head for a moment towards his shoulder. 'It's a bit awkward, that's all. Not for me. He's like a stranger, thank God. But the boys and Katy. I feel for them.' She bit her lip. 'Dad, Susan hasn't been in touch, has she? With you and Mum?'

'Not a word. Ask your mother. There's usually a Christmas card but *he* signs it. Not her.'

'You get a card?'

'Not this year I think. Ask your mother.'

Even this, so small and harmless a thing, gave her a stab of – what – jealousy? Of course not. She wanted Susan to be in touch with her parents. It was Susan who had made contact impossible.

'Let's go and see if Gill's ready.'

'And when is *she* going to settle down?' her father grumbled. 'Left it a bit late for having a family. Though they don't care nowadays – wait till they're middle-aged, some of them.'

This was an old grievance, hardly meriting a response. 'Oh well,' she murmured, 'Gill's happy the way she is.' Not true, though.

Dressed but unshaven, Alec appeared just as they were leaving, to shake hands and be polite. As the car crept down the icy lane he vanished into the bathroom.

Frances meant to strip beds and restore her home to order but the house was still full of other people, so she found herself wandering about distractedly, achieving nothing. In the end, she stuffed some towels in the washing machine and abandoned all other pretence at housework. Instead, she made coffee and stood for a while at the living-room window, looking down the garden and across the fields to Dingwall, clearer now in the distance. Behind the long building of the Academy and a scatter of houses on the hillside, rose Ben Wyvis, snow covered. For a while she went on watching this stillness, where all that moved were specks of flying gulls or crows, to and fro across the landscape.

'You've got a great view.'

It was Alec, shaved and wearing jeans and a fine-knit pullover. He joined her by the window at a cautious distance.

'I love it,' she said.

'Your mother says you're a headmistress now, is that right?'

She told him the name of the school. 'It's tiny,' she said, 'just two and a half teachers. The head teacher's post came up before the summer, and I was ready for a change.'

'You like it?'

'It's a lovely wee school. Nice kids, very rural. A change from Alness.'

'That was a bit grim, was it?'

'No, just a tougher place to be. To be a child in.'

'Right.'

'What about you?' She turned to face him with such directness she surprised herself, and he, startled, was compelled to meet her eyes. The rush of recognition, the electric charge of it, her blue eyes, his brown, the naked knowledge they had had of each other once: these things made the blood well to her face and to his, so that unable to bear it, they turned to look at the view again.

'Oh, I'm doing all right. Dryburn's made me redundant years ago – did I tell you when you came down that time with the boys? Anyway, I

41

was ready for a change. I've a part share in a restaurant now, in the centre of Newcastle.'

'A restaurant?'

'Nice place – hard work though.'

'What do you do in it – not cook?'

He laughed. 'No, not that. Manage. Finance, staff, marketing, the works.'

Frances was silent, finding it hard to imagine his life.

'Any chance of a coffee?' he asked.

'Sure. Would you like some breakfast?'

'Coffee's fine.'

As she rinsed mugs and filled the kettle he said, 'It's very good of you to have us here.'

'I didn't seem to have a choice.'

'I do appreciate it.'

He was much less sure of himself these days, she realised as a shaft of sunshine caught his face, showing the pitiless lines, tired round his eyes, the skin dull with being indoors too much. The life had gone out of him. Was he drinking still, she wondered. Hard not to, in his business, but he had not drunk much since his arrival, even yesterday at the Ramsays when it would have been easy.

'Sit down,' Frances said. 'I'll make some toast.'

While she did this he rested his elbows on the table and leaned into his hands, rubbing them over his face, emerging bleary-eyed, the flick of dark hair which still fell over one side of his forehead, shoved aside.

'Sorry,' he said. 'I'm not in good shape.'

'I can see that.' She pitied him, relieved to feel so little. 'So what is it that's brought you here with Katy? Kate.'

'Susan's missing.'

Of all the things he might have said, she had not thought of this. In her surprise she did not even feel the sense of shifting discomfort that always came with the sound of her sister's name.

'*Missing?*'

'She went away a fortnight ago.'

'How do you mean *went away*? Are you saying you don't know where she is?'

'She's done this before.'

'Gone *missing*?'

'Wait. Let me tell you.'

'Alec, what am I supposed to think?'

'You said my name.'

'Of course I did!'

'No, first time since I phoned. You said it when I phoned.'

Frances swept this aside. 'What's going on with Susan?'

'About three weeks ago she went to the Retreat. It's a place she goes, for women, a kind of zen-ny place.'

'Say that again?'

'Zen. Buddhism. A retreat.'

'Heavens.'

'It's OK, not cranky, really, not more than these places usually are. Nice people . . . She always

43

came back a bit *spaced*, but friendlier, if you know what I mean. More settled.'

'You mean she's usually *not* . . . friendly? Settled?'

Frances had spent thirteen years not wanting to know anything about Susan, not wanting to hear her sister's name, or see her face or hear her voice, nor so much as sense the shadow of her, dark across the lives they had now. She was realising for the first time that she might have shut off more than her own agony.

'No,' Alec answered, cradling his coffee. He still took it black with one spoonful of brown sugar. Nothing changes, Frances thought, distracted, everything changes.

'Susan?' she prompted. Alec put the mug down on the table.

'She's had some bad times. Anyway, the Retreat helps. Better than drugs.'

'Drugs. Sorry, I seem to be turning into some sort of demented echo. You mean medication, she was on medication sometimes?'

'Anti-depressants, but that was ages ago. She was due to come home the week before Christmas, but she didn't. I thought I must have got the date wrong, so I rang them but they don't always pick up the phone if they're, you know, meditating. At least they have an answering service now so I left a message. One of the women there, Karen, called me back.'

'So was Susan not there?' He was going so slowly,

she wanted to urge him on to whatever terrible revelation he was going to make.

'She'd never been there. About two days before they expected her, she rang and cancelled. She said, listen to this, her *parents* were coming for Christmas and since it was the first time for years she wanted to spend the time at home getting ready for them. Karen knew about the break with her family. She said Susan sounded really upbeat, she said *I told her I was so happy for her.*'

'But Mum and Dad—'

'I know. They hadn't even been in touch. They never wavered, did they, after they sided with you.'

'Oh Alec, that wasn't—'

'I'm just saying they're consistent, you've got to give them that. They sent Kate money, presents . . . never made a difference there. Well, in that way. Never saw her though.'

'That wasn't my choice,' Frances protested, conscious that of course, it might have been, had she made a choice. 'Anyway, never mind that. You went to the police, I assume?'

'Not at first. I rang one or two other people she might have been with. Nothing. Then I started ringing hospitals and after that, the police. Still nothing.'

'What did the police say?'

'They weren't very interested. She'd taken clothes and her passport and cheque book and she'd drawn out money. Two thousand quid. They quite naturally assumed she had left me. When I told them she'd gone missing before, it was obvious they thought she'd turn up again.'

'Maybe she will.'

'It's different this time. She never made plans before, never took much money. What she'd do is kind of disappear and turn up after a few days at the Retreat. Eventually they would persuade her to call me.'

'I don't know what to ask here – there seems to be so much. What about Katy?'

'Well, no hiding it from her this time. I've tried not to let her see I think there's anything seriously wrong.'

'You think there is, though?'

'I don't know.' He looked up, seeming to plead with her. 'You can't imagine what it's been like—'

'No, of course not. To be honest Alec, I don't want to know.' She sighed. 'Sorry. All that matters is finding Susan and making sure she's safe. She's probably just gone to a friend or something, don't you think?'

'Possibly.' He hesitated. 'There was a letter. Came about two days after I expected her, when I was seeing the police, all that.'

'From Susan?'

'All it said was not to worry, she wanted some more time on her own. It was a bit scrappy. Then Kate decided everything for me. She said let's not hang around, let's just go and see the rest of the family.' He smiled, rueful. 'Family. Are you sure, I said, do you know what you're suggesting?

But she was quite definite. I want to go and see them, she told me, they send me presents and money, they don't hate *me*. It's not my fault none of you speak to each other.'

Frances bit her lip, dismayed. 'That's awful.' She got up abruptly from the table then stopped, sharp again,

'Did you show Katy the letter? What did *she* think?'

'The letter!' He looked startled. 'Oh no, I tore it up. Ground it up in the waste disposal, actually. I suppose I was angry.'

'But you told Katy about it?'

'Oh yes.' His eyes slid away from her. 'After a while . . . I began to think she was right, we should come. So here we are.' His voice dried up and Frances saw Kate was standing in the kitchen doorway.

'Sorry,' she said. 'I just wondered – could I get a towel?'

CHAPTER 5

When they sat down to a lunch of leftovers at half past one it was impossible not to picture the parallel life they had not had, Frances and Alec: the two of them, their sons, their daughter, eating cold turkey and salad after the relatives' departure, finishing the Christmas pies and the box of chocolates. If they had stayed together there could have been another child. We might be any normal family, France thought, catching the reflection they made in the kitchen window as the day darkened early outside, the sky heavy with snow.

Then, turning with a fresh pot of tea in her hands, she saw Katy raise her head, which was usually dipped down, avoiding contact. Her face, luminous with the past, was Susan's face. Frances moved the hand that balanced the spout, it slipped, and recoiling from the sudden heat on her fingers, she let go. The teapot, narrowly missing her feet as she leapt back to avoid the splash of scalding water, smashed to the floor. The pool of hot tea seemed to spread for yards around her.

Alec jumped up and Jack shoved his chair back out of the way. 'You all right Mum? What happened?'

'My hand must have slipped – stupid thing to do.'

Andrew and Kate went on sitting at the table while everyone else mopped up, and retrieved scattered shards of china. Covertly, the two of them glanced at each other; Andrew looked away first.

Later, alone in the kitchen, Frances wondered what had shaken her most: the sight of them all round the table, Alec at the head, or that terrifying glimpse of Susan at fifteen. She prided herself on her composure. This is different, she thought, excusing herself for once as she smoothed a damp tea-towel over the radiator. But if anything had happened to Susan . . .

'What about a walk?' Alec asked from the doorway.

'I think it's going to snow.'

'We'll go now, then, before it does. It's just – there's more.'

'More what?'

'To tell you. Ask you.'

'All right. Let me get my things.'

She looked in on Andrew and Kate in the living-room.

'Where's Jack?'

'On the computer.'

'Is he doing any work?'

'Don't ask me.'

'I'm just going for a walk with your – with Alec. We won't be long.'

'Ok.' Andrew was hunched over the table in the bay window, gazing at this year's giant jigsaw. His grandfather brought one every Christmas. This year, it had been a godsend. For two impossible days, there had always been something to talk about, do, share. It was not quite finished, despite Jim Douglas's urging: blue sky and green field were still patchy. Kate was curled in a chair with a book.

'What are you reading?' Frances asked.

'Jane Eyre.'

'Oh, I loved that at your age.'

'I think it's crap,' Kate said. 'You can't understand half she's on about. But I couldn't find anything else I'd heard of, and I read all my magazines yesterday.'

'There's another bookcase in my room,' Frances offered. 'Thrillers and so on are mostly there. Why don't you have a look?'

'I'll just read this. I might as well.'

Perverse girl, Frances thought as she unhooked her jacket from the hallstand. Alec was waiting by the back door.

'All set?'

'Haven't you got gloves? You'll freeze.'

'In the car, maybe.'

'I'll get you some.'

Jack's gloves looked large on his elegant hands. He gazed at them for a moment.

'Up the hill? Frances asked.

*   *   *

50

Below them the lights of the town were pricking like glowworms already, turning the air to dusk. The sky glowered slate grey and there was a scent of snow. The ground was hard underfoot, the morning's frost, which had never dissolved, crunching faintly. They walked side by side along the track to the wider, smoother road which led to the farm if they turned uphill, or down into Dingwall, if they turned left.

'We'll go up to the Ramsays,' Frances said. 'There's another path takes you behind the farm and back to our house.' She glanced at Alec's shoes. 'Ground's quite hard so it shouldn't be muddy.'

'That's fine,' he said. 'Whatever you think.'

He did not care where they went, wanting only to be on his own with her so that he could say what he had come all this way to ask. For a moment or two they walked in silence, and she slowed her usual pace. He was not used to exercise.

'Could I ask you to do something for me?' he began. 'Not really for me. I wouldn't ask a favour for myself. It's Kate—'

'You said she knows about Susan. You don't want me to tell her something about her mother?'

'No, no. She's had to cope with her mother for years, so she's not as upset by it as you're probably imagining.'

Again, Frances had a glimpse of someone else's past, like a wound opening up. 'Do you *want* to talk about Susan? I don't mind. I'm not saying I was wrong then, but so much time has gone past and I have a different life now. I'm happy, I'm all right.'

'I can see that. I could tell you plenty, God knows, but I've talked enough. It's a wonder I've any friends left, frankly. No, I wanted to ask if you would have Kate?'

Frances said these words over to herself but they made no sense. 'Have Kate?' she echoed. 'How do you mean?'

'Just for a week or so till I get something sorted out. See the police again, see if I can bloody *find* her.'

'But Kate will want to go home, won't she?'

'Maybe. Maybe not.'

'What's going on? Is there something I don't know about Kate?'

'We've had a few problems,' he said, picking his way across a stony part of the track, a minefield of words.

'She seems all right to me. Teenage girls are often a bit sullen, aren't they?'

'She's been skipping school.'

'I see.'

'It's a good school, we've made sacrifices to send her there.'

'But she doesn't like it?'

'She used to come home on her own. Susan left work at lunch-time one day, feeling ill, and found her there. There's a crowd of them now, some from another school, the comprehensive. They go into town, hang about. Go to somebody's house if it rains.'

'Have you contacted her school?'

'We threatened to speak to the Headmistress after we discovered Kate had intercepted a letter from her. It's an all-girls school, we were so *careful*.'

'You've got to tackle the school. What on earth could *I* do?'

'It's this business with Susan. All things considered, I think she's better here for a while – at least till the end of the holidays.'

'I've no experience of girls. None past puberty, anyway. The ones I teach are into Barbie dolls and making friendship bracelets out of coloured thread.'

'Sorry. It's not your problem. I shouldn't have asked.'

After a moment Frances said, 'She can stay here for a while, of course she can. On one condition.'

'What?' His air of anxiety deepened.

'She must agree herself. No coercion. That's all.'

'It was her idea to come.'

'Ask her.'

'I will.'

They walked on in silence but Frances guessed Alec wanted to say more. As they came down the last part of the track to her house again and saw the lights in the uncurtained windows, he said,

'I'm bothered about the people she goes around with.'

'Oh, bad company,' Frances scoffed. 'I thought that was essential at fourteen. A way of asserting your independence.'

'Like taking drugs?'

'Ah. Are you sure?'

'Pretty sure.'

'What sort of thing?'

'Oh God, how would I know? It was cannabis and a bit of LSD when we were at uni, wasn't it?'

'Speak for yourself.'

'I was. It could be ecstasy. Not sure what else. Not often – or maybe it's just the effect of too many vodkas with lemonade or blackcurrant – these drinks with silly names – breezer, hooch, whatever. She's come home with her eyes blurry, unfocused. Been sick.'

'I'd have thought you'd find it easy to recognise the effect of alcohol.'

'I don't drink much now.' He sounded defensive. 'That's a whole different thing and she's young, not used to it. She'd have no idea if someone had slipped something else into the glass.'

'What are you really worried about?' Frances asked, pausing as they reached the house.

'That I'm losing control here, if I ever had it. And if I let her drift away now – what if she turns out like her mother?'

'Oh, Alec.'

'Susan hasn't taken drugs for years of course – or only the prescribed kind.'

54

'Are you saying she's mentally ill? And you're afraid Kate could end up like that too.'

Alec hesitated. 'I suppose that's what I meant.'

Frances put her gloved hands over her face. 'I need to think,' she murmured. 'I must *think*.'

He put a tentative arm round her shoulders, but she took her hands down and moving away, opened the door.

'Sorry,' he said.

'I'll have her here, but she has to agree. All right?'

'I really appreciate this, Frances. I'm sorry.'

He followed her into the warm kitchen.

In the living-room, left on their own, Andrew and Kate had remained silent for ten minutes, Andrew leaning over the jigsaw, Kate pretending to read. Eventually, she shut the book with a sigh.

'Should I put more logs on the fire?' she asked. 'It's going out.'

'Yeah, go on then.' Andrew did not look round. Kate got up and took a couple of logs from the basket beside the fire. She dropped them on the red ashes, then jumped back at the show of sparks.

'My God, that's dangerous.'

'It is if you do it like that.'

'All the flames,' she went on after a moment, watching them curl greedily round the new wood, 'they're different. Keep changing. We have this gas fire at home that looks real but it's not. The same flame comes up, the same shape, all the time.'

She drifted across the room, arriving beside the jigsaw as if by accident.

'You've nearly finished the field,' she said.

'There's a piece missing. Where it joins the plough handle. See?'

'I think so.'

'Should be brown on one corner. But there's not a bit like that lying here.'

Kate shuffled the loose pieces that were left. 'Maybe it's fallen on the floor.' She dropped suddenly to her knees and looked under the table, lifting the edge of a rug and peering round.

'See it?'

'It's all the same colours as that down here. The rug's brown and green. It wouldn't stand out. Hey – here's a bit of sky though.' She brought it up to him, flushing with the effort.

'Is your mother working or what?' Andrew asked suddenly.

'She had to go away.'

'Oh.'

'She does that sometimes, just for a break. You know.' Kate was leaning over the jigsaw and he could not see her face.

'So where does she go?'

'This place called the Retreat.'

Andrew had found the place for Kate's piece of blue sky. 'Magic – I've got the whole of this bit now.'

'It's just a place for people to go for a rest. It's totally, like, quiet. No music or TV or radio. Hardly any talking, even.'

'Sounds boring.'

'It's for people who're stressed out.'

'Freaked?'

'My mother doesn't freak. She just gets tired.'

He thought about this. 'My mother goes for walks.'

'When she's tired? *That's* freaky.'

'Well, she comes back in a better mood, anyhow.' He grinned. 'I think she gets so she's had enough of little kids. She's a primary teacher. She's the head now, but she teaches as well.' He was trying to remember what Kate's mother did. Had they been told? We weren't told much, he thought, she's my cousin and I don't know anything. 'What does your mother do?'

'She used to be a nurse. She hasn't had a job for a while.'

For a few moments they concentrated on the jigsaw.

'It's annoying about this bit – it's kind of crucial,' Andrew said. 'I'll have another look on the floor.'

He knelt down. Beneath the table he was facing Kate's long legs in black trousers and her feet in pink socks. She had long narrow feet. As she had done, he lifted the edge of the rug, then ran his hand over the carpet, feeling the grittiness of scattered crumbs and finding a small green button, which he put on the window sill. He tried again. Kate's foot moved, and his hand brushed her toes, so that the foot drew back sharply.

'Sorry.'

'It tickled.'

'Sorry.'

'It's Ok.' She came down beside him. 'You have to sort of smooth your hand over – like this.'

'That's what I was doing.'

They were both under the table.

'Did you play like this – with a rug over the table like a tent, you know? When you were little.'

'No.' She looked at him. 'Did you?'

'Me and Jack.'

'I don't have any brothers or sisters.'

'You had friends though.'

'Oh yes.'

'It's not the same, I suppose,' he offered.

'I never even had cousins.'

'I suppose we didn't count.' He tried to think whether his father had any nieces or nephews. He did *know* that, of course.

Kate was digging in the pocket of her trousers. She turned to sit with her back against one of the table legs, knees bent.

'I'm gasping for a fag,' she said. 'You want one? We could go outside if it bothers your Mum. Or blow it up the chimney, eh?'

'I don't smoke.'

'Everybody does in my school. Nearly everybody.'

'I play rugby,' Andrew explained. 'You can't smoke if you play rugby. I know one guy that does, but he's shot.'

'I don't play rugby,' Kate pointed out and for

the first time, the faint ghost of a smile flitted across her face.

'Obviously.' He watched her take a cigarette out, and from the half empty packet, a blue plastic lighter. 'You'd better go outside. My mother'll go mental if she smells it in the house.'

Kate put the cigarette and lighter away again. 'That's what I reckoned. I've been going outside. It's bloody freezing though.'

'Where d'you live exactly?'

'A sort of suburb of Newcastle. Like a small town, with its own shops. Totally dead, believe me.' She shrugged. 'We go up the Bigg Market Saturday night but you don't always get into the clubs. A lot of them ask for IDs now.'

'I thought you were only fourteen?'

'Nearly fifteen.'

For a moment Andrew felt as if he were younger than she was. Trying to be hard, he thought, but I bet she's not.

The door opened and after a few seconds, Jack said,

'Hide and Seek eh? Can anybody join in?'

'Air raid warning,' Andrew said, coming out. 'Whole of Ross and Cromarty destroyed. This is the only house left standing.' He was doing a Second World War project for Higher History.

Kate emerged after him, tucking her cigarette packet away again. She retreated to the chair she had been sitting in earlier, and the abandoned book.

Jack studied the jigsaw. 'You've nearly finished.'

'Bit missing. Thought it might be on the floor.' Andrew pointed out the gap.

'It's here,' Jack said, picking up the piece with the brown corner, and fitting it to the handle of the plough, completing it.

Andrew glanced at Kate but she was flicking through her book. He nudged Jack out of the way. 'Pure luck,' he said.

'Powers of observation.'

'Big head.'

'Entirely justified.' Jack fitted three pieces in quick succession.

'Fuck off – I was getting on fine without you.'

'Language, language, in front of ladies.'

Andrew nudged again, Jack nudged back, and they elbowed each other round the table, kicking at knees and ankles, each trying to knock the other off balance.

Jack stopped suddenly and moved away towards the fire. He dug at it with the poker. 'Where's Mum?'

'Out with him.'

'Where?'

'A walk.'

'It's dark.'

They looked up together at the window. The garden was so dim now they saw only their reflections, and Kate's. She was watching them.

The back door opened and they heard voices. Something tensed in both boys. Kate saw it and felt something tighten in her too, the old familiar clench of anxiety.

'That's them,' Andrew said.

'You going out tonight?' Jack asked.

'McGhee said he'd come round if his Dad would give him a lift.'

'That geek.'

'You went out with his sister, didn't you?'

'Yeah, but the older ones always get the brains. Natch.'

They both laughed. Kate glanced from one to the other. 'Who's McGhee?' she asked.

'His best mate.' Jack grinned, shoving at Andrew again. 'Old friend of the family.'

'You're not very nice about your friends,' she said.

They looked at her blankly. 'Who isn't?'

Frances came in and was struck again by how all three seemed to belong together. Kate was flushed with the heat of the fire and for the first time looked animated instead of sullen. I will have to talk to her, Frances thought, but she dreaded it. 'Anyone want tea?' she offered.

'Go on then,' Jack said. 'Christmas cake as well?'

In the kitchen, Frances hunted fruitlessly for the teapot for several minutes before remembering it had got broken at lunch-time. She would have to find her grandmother's Coalport pot, kept in a cupboard and never used. She could not for the moment recall which cupboard so began dropping tea-bags in mugs instead. Around and between her legs the grey cat wove in and out, asking to be fed. Absently, she bent and picked him up, and he nestled against her, purring, pushing his head under her chin.

On the edge of thought, Susan hovered. 'I wonder where she is?' Frances murmured to the cat. Beneath her heart, a thin line of uneasiness hardened and she longed for Alec to be gone.

If they had stayed together, there could have been another child.

CHAPTER 6

Frances had moved up to the house at Finnerty five years earlier. Before that, she and the boys lived in a small house with a patch of garden in the centre of the market town of Dingwall. She had saved up for this second house, wanting it for a long time. When she inherited some money from her grandmother, the house became possible. Buying it, she felt she had almost regained the status she would have had as a married woman. Two incomes make it easier to buy a good house but she had done it on her own.

It was not that she had kept her eye on any particular house, only on the idea of one away from the town on a hill, with a view of the Firth. The one she found was old and shabby and some of the 'improvements' made by the previous owners had to be undone. But it was a comfortable roomy place, and the garden was mature and sheltered.

'I won't move again,' Frances told people who seemed surprised she had taken it on, when the Dingwall house was so 'handy' and her boys likely to leave home in a few years.

Finnerty Farm, whose land surrounded her

house (the original farmhouse), was owned by two brothers, one of them unmarried. You don't meet many men as a primary teacher and her friends thought how nice it would be to see Frances fixed up. She deserved it, the married ones said, at least those who did not know Albert Ramsay. None of them knew about Kenny, just then hovering on the edge of her life. She had met him through a hill-walking club she briefly joined in an attempt to get herself away from the narrow circle of teachers.

Kenny did not do much more than hover at the edge even now, her friends observed, wondering if they might live together when Andrew left home. Goodness knows, it would be the making of *him*.

After Alec left, Frances drove to the supermarket and met there (as you always did in such a small place), half a dozen people she knew, including Christine, her senior teacher.

In the Station Café over a pot of tea and scones, they exchanged Christmas stories. Christine had daughters at the Academy and was Frances's informant on the habits of teenage girls.

'You put Don's sneezing fit over the pudding into perspective,' Christine said, when Frances had told her about Alec's and Kate's arrival on Christmas night.

Frances laughed. 'Everyone behaved with great restraint. Even my father.'

'How long is it since you've seen your ex?'

'Five or six years. *That* was the first time for nearly seven years before.' France buttered her scone. 'It was the only time really, after the first year or so, when I tried to do anything about our situation. It must have been when Jack went up to the Academy. I suppose since they were becoming teenagers I thought I had a duty to let them see their father.'

'What happened?'

'Nothing much. I took the boys to Glasgow for a long weekend, to a hotel with a swimming pool and fitness room. The weather was foul so we didn't do any of the things I had planned. They weren't much interested in the Burrell or Kelvingrove anyway. We got tickets for a match at Ibrox, through someone Albert Ramsay knew. I thought if Alec came up and met us, he could take them to that. I saw myself going to the Galleries then, but he didn't even arrive till the Sunday. Let us down as usual, and me sitting in that hotel room feeling absolutely a fool. Still, the boys enjoyed the game, though I was terrified we'd go to the wrong end or something and get involved in violence. But there was nothing like that. Everyone was so nice, making room for us, lending Andy a scarf, buying them pies at half time. I thought, my God, there are some nice men in the world after all.'

'So Alec turned up on the Sunday?'

'He was like a stranger. He *was* a stranger. He had made an effort, he'd brought them presents and he left them with an enormous amount of cash. But despite all I'd said in my letter, he seemed to have the idea they were younger than they really were and the presents weren't quite right. Well, Andrew liked Jack's. I can't even recall now what they were.'

'How were the boys with him?'

'Polite. I felt I'd made a huge mistake and upset my kids for nothing. They were very quiet that night, just watched TV in their room and said they were glad we were going home next day.'

'Did Alec say anything about seeing them more regularly? I mean, you always gave me the impression he wanted to, you were the one who cut him off. It doesn't sound like it.'

When Frances didn't answer, Christine poured fresh tea for them both.

'That's what everyone thought,' Frances admitted after a moment. 'I let them. After all, there was some truth in it. Anyway, we set off home the next morning, and Jack said, when we were about half way up the A9, he said *it's OK Mum, I'm not bothered about seeing Dad.* I thought Andrew was asleep in the back, but he wasn't, he sat up and said, *we don't know him, do we?*' She shrugged. 'I didn't bother after that. No contact, nothing. I guess Alec must have felt the same.'

'So he didn't—'

'No.'

'Oh well, if that was his attitude, after you'd made such an effort—'

'I don't think it was ever *his* attitude, to be honest. It was Susan's.'

Frances was dismayed to find herself talking so much about this, however safe she felt Christine was as a confidant, her oldest friend here, who knew more of her life than anyone but Kenny. She stopped, then just as Christine was about to change the subject, added,

'Anyway, it appears Kate's been in a bit of bother at school so he wants her to stay here for the rest of the holidays. God knows what *I* can do. I'm hoping you can give me a few hints about dealing with teenage girls.'

'Frankly,' Christine said with a smile, 'I'd advise you to have as little to do with them as possible!'

By the time Frances drove up the hill again it was dark. Jack and Kate were watching television; Andrew and his friend Ross McGhee were in his room in front of the computer. Frances put her head round Andrew's door.

'Are you staying for tea, Ross?'

'Yeah, he is,' Andrew said, not looking up.

'Would that be all right?' Ross asked.

'Fine.'

How polite other people's children were. Did that mean Kate would be polite with her too? There was something about the girl Frances did not trust. I don't know her very well, I must try to be fair, she thought. Perhaps what troubled her was the heart-stopping likeness to Susan. Or perhaps it was the impossibility of reconciling this Kate with the infant who had been taken away from her.

When the telephone rang in the evening she assumed it was Alec, who had promised to call Kate regularly, but it was Kenny, just back from spending Christmas with his former wife, her present husband and his grown-up son and daughter-in-law.

'How are you? Good Christmas? Survived it?'

'Yes, survived,' Frances said. How about you?'

'Missed you. Missed Jock. Calum and Gail don't give him enough to eat. He's looking terrible.'

'Rubbish. That dog's far too fat. Like you. I expect you've put back all the weight you lost on your diet.'

Kenny sounded momentarily gloomy. 'Oh I dare say. But it's enough to drive you to it, staying with your ex-wife. *My* ex-wife, at any rate.'

'It didn't drive me to it. Or drink either. I know you've been drinking a lot, Kenny, you always do.'

He had picked up her allusion and brushed aside this reference to his drinking. 'How do you mean? You didn't spend Christmas with your former spouse, did you?'

'I did.'

Silence, while Kenny put together all the facts he could muster about Frances's marriage.

'What happened?'

'He turned up on Christmas night.'

'On his own – or with—'

'Oh no, but he had her daughter with him, my niece Katy who's about fourteen. She calls herself Kate now.'

'Well, well.'

'Why don't I come over tomorrow? Or you come here? We can catch up then.'

'You come to me. It sounds as if your house is full of people I'd better not meet.'

'Only Kate, now. She's staying over New Year but Alec's gone back south.'

'Right then.' He paused, and she could hear his slightly asthmatic breathing. 'Tomorrow. When?'

'I'll come after lunch. We can decide what we're doing about Hogmanay, if anything.'

'I was hoping to drink myself into oblivion as usual. Only joking,' he added hastily.

'I wish you were. See you tomorrow.'

As usual, he left her feeling an odd mixture of exhilaration and dismay. The dismay, of course, was constant: that she should choose only two men in her life of any importance to her, and both were drunks. Or who, at any rate, she thought, trying to be fair, are much too fond of drink.

The next day, when she came back from Kenny's at five o'clock, she asked Jack if Alec had called.

'No, don't think so.'

'Where's Katy?'

'McGhee's Dad took Ross and Andy and her up to Inverness. Said they'd get the bus home.'

Frances was taken aback. 'She won't know her

way around! I hope she sticks with Andrew or he makes sure she knows where to get the bus—'

'Don't worry, Mum. She's well used to looking after herself, I'd say.'

'Do you think so? Should I make supper at the same time as usual?'

'Call Andy and ask which bus they're getting.'

'As long as Kate's with him . . .'

Jack drifted back to the television and Frances began to prepare the meal, half listening to the radio news, but really thinking about Kate, remembering her as a baby and remembering Susan too. After all this time it was impossible to see Susan straight. None of them knew her now, had not known her for thirteen years. Even then, given what happened, they had obviously not known her as well as they should have done.

Frances felt that old combination of anger and frustration. They could still be prodded into life, the emotions that had created a breach lasting years. Looking back, Frances did not blame her father for his reaction. She had been grateful for her parents' support after Alec and Susan left, sheared off from the family like branches from a lightning struck tree. She had imagined them flourishing elsewhere, rooted in a different soil, but perhaps they had not. She was beginning to see them differently.

What had happened to Susan? How was she *unstable*? She recoiled from the word, standing by the sink, her hands in cold water, a potato in one hand, knife in the other. She was lost now to the kitchen and the reasonable radio voices.

She was in the house where she had grown up, she and Susan and Gillian. There, in the comfortable West End of Aberdeen, in a stable home with two fond parents, they had lived through their childhood and adolescence. They had gone out every weekday morning in navy uniforms to walk a mile and a half to the High School. They had come home at half past four to television and tea and homework, to a life so safe and ordinary there were no excuses at all for oddness.

'It's because she's the middle one,' Frances had once heard her mother say to their Aunt Barbara, a childless school-teacher. 'Don't you find it's the middle ones that are awkward?'

'They're all awkward at thirteen,' Barbara had answered. 'In my experience.'

'Oh, I don't know,' Grace protested. 'Frances was no bother at all. No doubt Gillian will have her moments, but she's an easy bairn. She and Frances both, easy bairns.'

'Susan's like her father,' Barbara said. 'Same quick temper.'

Barbara was their father's sister so could say what she liked about him, or thought she could.

Here was Susan now, the front gate banging behind her as she came up the path, the last one home from school as always, tie undone, beret stuffed in her bag, skirt tucked up at the waist to make it shorter, with her long legs and the blonde swing of her hair as she turned back for a moment to wave to the friend going on up the street without her.

'She has his looks too, even more than Frances,' Barbara said, dropping the net curtain and moving back from the bay window as Susan neared the front door. Not that Susan was looking at the window, she was seeing something that was no longer there. Susan the dreamer. That was what her father said, banging his spoon on the table at tea-time, making her jump. *Dreamer!*

'Where have you been all this time?' her mother accused when Susan came an hour after the others.

'Nowhere – just to the Pelican.'

'For goodness sake, what's that?'

Barbara knew. Barbara liked showing how much she knew about what you did after school, reminding them she was a teacher so they couldn't pull the wool over *her* eyes.

'It's a coffee bar,' she informed Grace. 'All the young ones go there after school to *hang about*.' She added, as if this made it even more dubious, 'They drink Coca Cola.'

'Thank goodness she doesn't teach at the High, that's all I can say,' Susan said as she trudged upstairs behind Frances.

The three of them settled in the room Frances and Susan shared; Gillian still occupied the little nursery bedroom, full of toys and children's books. The three of them: Gillian on the floor, Frances

72

and Susan on the single beds, facing each other, swinging their legs back and forth, just touching toes. But what had they said to each other, upstairs away from their parents and Barbara, at five and nine and thirteen, or at nine and thirteen and seventeen, year after year in that house?

It was impossible to go back and see it clearly, now that so much stood in the way. When Frances tried, the picture froze, and she could no longer hear the voices.

'Mum!'

Startled, heart jolting, Frances turned. Jack said, 'That was Andy.'

'What was?'

'On the phone. He wants somebody to pick him and Kate up from the station. They got off the bus there and he said they'd start walking up. You want me to go?' He was dangling the car keys from one finger.

'The bus. Yes, off you go. Sorry, I was miles away.'

Miles and years. She put her cold hands back in the cold water, to scrub potatoes.

A little later, Alec called.

'I'm in the middle of cooking,' she said, to let him know it was a bad time. 'We're just about to eat.'

'She's not here,' he said. 'She hasn't come home.'

'You didn't expect her to, did you?'

'No.'

'Sorry,' Frances said. 'I should have asked you.'

'I just wanted to tell you in case Kate asked.'

'You'd better speak to her yourself.'

While Kate stood in the hall, hunched over the phone, Frances went back into the kitchen and shut the door. She was shaking. She had not asked about Susan. It was not the first thing she had said. Yet it was Susan she'd been dreaming about. She wanted to say to Alec, *you cannot bring the dead to life*. Because it was all dead between them, Frances and Susan. Susan and all of them. Or she had thought it was. Now, standing in her kitchen, Alec's voice reaching into her house, her life, she wondered if she had been wrong about that. Not dead but waiting. She gripped the back of a chair with both hands.

Susan.

CHAPTER 7

Frances usually liked the week after New Year. It was quiet, and she was able to prepare for next term with no pressure. She caught up on the jobs in the house which had been waiting for her attention. She cooked substantial meals for the boys, and went walking for an hour every afternoon.

This year there was an edge of discomfort to all of it that she resented, but which also made her feel guilty. She was conscious that Kate was bored, and though there was nothing she could do about this, she felt she ought to try. Kate slept late as the boys did, which was something of a relief. She pecked at her food, fussily disengaging the vegetables she did not like (a wide range) and leaving them on the side of her plate. Then she would be found eating crisps and chocolate in front of hours of television. Frances could see she did not know what to do with herself. Jack and Andrew lived their separate lives. Ross McGhee made more of an effort to be friendly than her sons did. The jigsaw, completed, lay on the table till after Hogmanay, when Frances broke it up and swept it back into its box, to join the others in the hall cupboard. Seeing the stack of them, given over many years by her father, she picked one out and took it into the living-room.

'If you fancy doing another,' she suggested to Kate and Andrew, 'there's plenty of choice.'

Andrew groaned, but Jack coming in, said, 'Oh yeah, we must have rakes of them.' He took the box from her. 'Not this – is there not one with boats in a harbour and a row of houses?'

'They're in the hall cupboard – go and have a look.'

Jack found the one he wanted, and began building edges. Andrew made a few sporadic attempts but Kate ignored it.

'What about work?' Frances reminded Jack, coming in to help him with the row of houses that evening.

'I've done hours. Hours and hours. When you were out.'

So she helped him with the jigsaw and they were companionable together. She was driving Jack back to Aberdeen on Saturday and she might not see much of him again before Easter.

There was no word from Alec until the Friday night.

'Any news?' she asked him.

'Not really.'

'Well, there is or there isn't – which?'

'I haven't tracked her down but one of her friends thought she saw her at the station.'

'When?'

'Christmas Eve. Judy – that's the friend – was meeting her son off the train and she said she was sure it was Susan. Getting *on* a train.'

'Where was the train going? Did she speak to her?'

'Judy was kind of caught up with her son so she wasn't paying much attention. Then when she heard from Karen at the Retreat she called me. I went down, and the platform she must have been on is where the trains go north, so she could have been heading for Aberdeen.'

Frances was both angry and relieved. 'She's all right then. I must say, this is like the way Susan behaved years ago. I don't feel I can care any more.'

There was silence for a moment.

'How's Kate?' Alec said at last.

'She's bored but she's fine. Do you want to speak to her?'

'May I?'

'Of course – she's your daughter. Step-daughter.'

'Sorry,' he said. 'I know it's not the easiest situation.'

'She seems to be getting on all right with the boys. In some ways, you'd think they'd been used to each other for years. She's bored though.

77

They're so *embedded* here. I think she should be at home with her own friends.'

'That's not a good idea.'

'But you are coming to take her home in time for school?'

'Could we leave it a week or so longer? I'll square it with the school.'

'I'll be back at work next week, Jack will have gone and Andrew will be in school. If she's bored *now*—'

'Let me speak to her, eh, see what she thinks.'

Frances opened the living-room door. 'Kate, it's your – it's Alec. He wants a word.'

Kate uncoiled herself from the sofa. When she had lifted the receiver in the hall, Frances shut the door again.

'You were going to say "it's your father", weren't you?'

'Well, he is. Her step-father.'

'Weird. More her Dad than ours.'

Andrew was lying on his back on the rug, making different shapes from an intricate web of copper wires and beads, a puzzle she had put in his Christmas stocking.

'Do you mind?' she asked.

Jack looked up from the jigsaw. 'Why would we?'

'She's welcome to him,' Andrew said. 'And it sounds as if her mother's a total fruit cake.' He glanced sideways at his mother, wondering how she would take this.

'We got the best deal,' Jack said, grinning at her.

Frances had an overwhelming desire to tell them how it had been, explain herself and Alec, and all that had happened. She swallowed it back: they were all right as they were, and she was all right. Then, hearing the low murmur of Kate's voice from the hall, she thought no, *she* was not all right. As if he had picked up her thoughts, Jack said, 'When's she going home?'

'I don't know. When Alec comes for her.'

'Where *is* her mother?' Andrew asked, sitting up.

'Alec doesn't know,' Frances admitted. 'Apparently she's gone off before without telling anyone. She turns up eventually so he's sure she's all right.'

'Don't *you* do that,' Andrew warned her. 'Who would make my tea and give me a lift to the pub when Jack's gone back to uni?'

'Don't worry,' Frances told him. 'There's no fear of that.' Leave her children and go off without a word – why would she do such a peculiar thing? How could any mother? Susan seemed more than ever alien and lost. Or ill, she thought with a spasm of guilt and anxiety.

'Poor Kate, eh?' Jack said as the door opened and the girl came in.

'All right?' Frances asked.

Kate looked at them for a moment, as if taking in the whole family. 'Yes,' she said. Behind its mask of make-up her face looked pinched and afraid. She turned and went out leaving the door open and they could hear her going slowly upstairs.

'Is she all right?' Andrew asked.

'I doubt it.' Jack sounded sarcastic. 'Disappearing mother, abandoned in the frozen north with relatives she hasn't seen for years . . . What do you reckon?'

Frances went upstairs. The door of the spare bedroom, where Kate was now established, was shut. She tapped on it lightly: 'Can I come in?' – not waiting for an answer. 'How are you?'

Kate was lying on the bed, her face turned towards the window. 'Go away,' she muttered. 'Just go away and leave me alone.'

So Frances, being unequal to this, did.

She called Alec again, annoyed to find herself trembling. He was a long time answering.

'What did you say to Kate? She's gone up to her room in a mood.'

'Nothing – nothing you don't know. Is she upset?'

'She won't speak to me, but maybe I don't have the knack with girls. I'm used to boys and they're very uncomplicated.'

'I asked her if she wanted to stay, and she said yes, she seemed fine about it. It's her mother, she's worrying about her mother. I can't seem to reassure her this time.'

'Did you tell her someone had seen Susan at the station?'

80

'Yes – d'you think I shouldn't have done? Try speaking to her again, you're so patient and calm, it's bound to help.'

He had made no personal remark to her for thirteen years and it stung that he came out with this, glibly. How dare he, he didn't even know her now. She said more sharply than she meant, 'There's nothing I can say to reassure her – is there?'

Silence. He cleared his throat.

'All right, I'll try.'

'What's up?' Jack asked as Frances laid down the receiver.

'Kate's upset about her mother.'

'Send McGhee in,' Andrew suggested, joining them in the hall. 'He gets on with women. They like him.'

'He's a nice lad.'

Andrew snorted. 'I'll tell him you said that.'

'So what's happening?' Jack asked.

'She's staying on for a while. Not indefinitely of course. She's Alec's responsibility, not ours.'

'Is she?'

'Let's leave her in peace for now. I'll talk to her tomorrow.'

'You're taking me to Aberdeen tomorrow.'

'So I am – I completely forgot. I wonder if it's wise to leave her with Andrew.'

Andrew was indignant. 'I'm perfectly capable. I'll force her to listen to some heavy metal – teach her to appreciate good music. Buy her a beer. Pity

County's not playing at home tomorrow, I could take her to the game.' He sauntered out, pleased with his own wit.

Frances plunged into ironing, packing, getting Jack sorted out. Blithely, he let her do it, making a show, at last, of studying while she bustled round him.

'I'll be back on Sunday night,' she told Andrew. 'The freezer's full of food and remember to feed the cats. Don't go off and leave Kate on her own.'

'I'm going to a party tomorrow night. Maryburgh – Mark's house.'

'Oh Andrew.'

'I could take her with me. I don't mind.'

Frances hesitated. Surely she could go away for one night? Ridiculous even to worry. She went to check what was in the freezer.

In the spare bedroom, Kate sat up and gazed out of the window. The garden was still snow-covered, though no more had fallen since New Year. The trees and the roof of the summerhouse were bare. A robin hopped from one apple tree to the other. Kate turned her head and saw herself in the dressing-table mirror, head and shoulders. I look terrible, she thought, tweaking at her hair. And there was another spot! She felt the angry little lump rising on her chin and worried at it till there was a red mark. 'I hate everything,' she told her reflection, and lay down again. She heard Andrew on the stairs and expected his feet to thud past her door, but they stopped and he banged on it twice.

'C'n I come in?'

She could hear his breathing. 'All right.' She sat up and swung her legs over the side of the bed, still fingering the red spot as if that would wipe it away.

'You fancy coming to a party?' He seemed to fill the doorway in his baggy sweatshirt and the loose trousers that hung down over his feet in white socks.

Kate shrugged. 'I don't mind. Where?'

'Maryburgh. We'd get a lift from a guy I know. Taxi back.'

'Is Jack going?'

'It's tomorrow. He'll be back at uni. Mum's driving him down in the morning.'

'Might as well, I suppose.'

'I'm doing you a favour here,' he pointed out. 'Wild entertainment, free booze. If you stay here you'll have to watch reality TV and keep the cats company.'

'I said *all right*.'

Andrew hesitated in the doorway, feeling he should do more. 'Is your Mum still away then?'

Kate flushed. 'Yes. Not that it's any of your business.'

'I'm sure she's all right,' he offered. 'I mean, not hurt or anything.'

'I know *that*.'

He turned to go, giving her up.

'When's she coming back?'

Momentarily confused, Andrew thought she meant her own mother, then realised she meant his.

'Oh – Mum. Sunday night.'

He did think of adding, it's all right, *she* doesn't go off, but decided this would sound more like mockery than reassurance. If that was what she wanted. On an impulse of pity, he said, 'It'll be a great party. Mark's got this pure fantastic house. And his folks are away for the whole weekend.'

She only grimaced at this, as if he had said something stupid. But what?

When he had gone, Kate got out her mobile phone and read her latest text messages. Several a day came from her friends at home, throwing her a line to her real life. She keyed in her friend Sara's number.

'Going 2 a party,' her fingers tapped rapidly, 'w Andrew. Jack the neat 1 goes back to uni. Staying here a wk more. Help.'

She lay back on her bed with the phone on her chest, holding on to it. Sara, Jackie, Hannah, they all kept in touch. But not her mother. She knew it was stupid to go on thinking that every time a message came in, it would be from her mother, every time it rang, it would be her mother speaking. Alec had told her Susan did not have her phone, he had found it lying on the bed. But Susan could get another phone, couldn't she? She'd taken plenty money, Alec had said.

'Get in touch,' she said aloud, and repeated her number. 'Come on Mum, you know it, you memorised it soon as I got the mobile, you said you would always remember it. *Call* me.'

She lay back, waiting, holding the phone close, so that the beat of her heart was up against it, pulsing its own message.

CHAPTER 8

Frances and Jack had a good day for travelling to Aberdeen. The temperature had risen a little, the sky clearing to pearly blue by half past nine. Frances was uneasy about leaving Kate, but promised herself she would make more effort when she came back.

Kate was still in bed when they left.

'We're off now,' Frances murmured. Kate turned and raised her head.

'Ok,' she said sleepily, then as Frances began to close the door, 'Sorry I was rude yesterday.'

'I never thought anything about it,' Frances lied

Kate flopped back on the bed. 'I'm moody. I can't help it.'

'I'll see you tomorrow. Don't feel you have to go to the party with Andrew if you don't want to.'

'I don't mind going. It's something to do.'

'Take a taxi home. There's money in the drawer in the hallstand.'

'Alec gave me loads of money.'

When she said goodbye to Andrew, still buried beneath bedclothes, he muttered, 'Say hi to Granny and Grandpa,' then called after her as she closed the door. 'Oh hey, did you leave me any money?'

Frances went on fretting about Kate as they drove down the road. 'She's very young,' she said to Jack. 'I keep forgetting how much younger she is than either of you.'

'Come on, Mum – you'll be home tomorrow. Can we have some music?' He put on one of his tapes, more or less obliterating thought, so Frances turned her attention to her parents. After a while, in a break while Jack sorted out what he wanted to listen to next, she said,

'It's odd we haven't heard from Gillian since Christmas.'

'Is she still at Granny's?'

'She's been back in Edinburgh for ages. But she's so caught up in her social life down there I suppose she forgets she hasn't been in touch.' She glanced sideways at him. 'Like you. Try and phone now and again, Jack.'

He grinned. 'Don't worry.'

They had lunch with Frances's parents in their unused dining room, with the electric fire smelling of scorched dust and the second best china.

'A bowl of soup would have done us fine,' Frances said, watching her mother tip a pan of potatoes into a serving dish. Jack sat talking to his grandfather, waiting to be served.

'We'll just have soup and a sandwich at night.' Grace put pork chops on plates, the largest allocated to the men. 'I thought Jack would like a proper meal. I'm sure the food where he is doesn't amount to much. He's awful thin, Frances, does he eat enough?'

'Constantly and enormously,' Frances reassured.

'Oh well.' Her mother lifted the men's plates. 'Bring the veg Frances. He'll have a good meal at our table, at any rate.'

Jack was in favour. He looked respectable because Frances had washed and ironed all his clothes, and he ate everything put in front of him, following rhubarb tart with a wedge of cheese and a heap of crackers.

'Now then,' his grandmother beamed, 'that's what I like to see.'

Behind her back Jack grinned at Frances and signed to indicate that he was about to burst.

Frances suspected her parents were keeping their questions about Alec until the evening, when Jack would not be there. She wished she had said she would go home the same day. The niggle of anxiety about Andrew and Kate started up again.

She planned to shop in the town centre once she had settled Jack in Halls. 'Do you want me to get you anything?' she asked her mother. Grace was in her arm chair with spectacles and news-paper, the dishes cleared and the dining room swept of crumbs, abandoned until the next time she had visitors who merited more than a sandwich in the kitchen. She looked over her glasses at Frances. 'No, dear, I'm fine.'

Her father was in what he called his 'business room', where he had once employed himself with work taken home from the office. On the walls there were drawings and photographs of some of the buildings he had designed or been involved with. The place retained the impersonal air of a working space but all Jim was doing was making up the golf fixtures for the Spring season at his club.

'I'm taking Jack back to Halls,' she told him.

He put down his pen. 'Has he kept in touch?' He meant Alec.

'He's phoned a couple of times.'

At lunch they had talked briefly about Kate. It was weighing on her conscience that they still knew nothing about Susan.

'I was wondering if you'd heard from Gill,'

'She telephoned to say she'd got home safely, as I recall. But nothing since, now that you mention it. No call on New Year's Day.' He frowned. 'That's remiss. Your mother likes to hear.'

'She'll be back at work now. You know how busy she gets.'

'Ah well. Your own lives to lead, I suppose.' But he did not sound as if he thought this much of an excuse.

Jack was pleased to be back in his small hot room in the Hall of Residence. Students and their parents were unloading cars all round them, carrying in CD players and computers, refurnishing the rooms which had had been stripped before Christmas. Frances hugged him quickly before any of his friends appeared. Already he was separated from her, and from home.

'Phone me,' she reminded him. 'Now and again.'

'Yeah, yeah. See you Mum.'

In town the shops were crowded, the sales in full swing. Frances fought her way through department stores still glittering with Christmas decorations. She tried on clothes in cramped fitting rooms and eventually bought a jacket which seemed a bargain because it had started life with a terrifying price tag and was still expensive. Exhausted, she went for tea in John Lewis. Coming out again onto the down escalator, she glanced across at the one going up, every step with shoppers on it. A red coat caught her eye, then a dark blonde head, so that she went swiftly from admiration of the coat to a sickening lurch of recognition. So shocked was she, it was several seconds before she managed to call, her voice hoarse, 'Susan!'

The red coat had gone. Now she was not so sure and besides, she had not seen her sister for thirteen years. But you always know your own sister. She got off at the next floor and went round to the up escalator. Susan must be in the shop somewhere. Surely she would find her; the red coat was like a flag.

As the escalator rose with infuriating slowness (and too crowded to push past the people in front), she began to think she had been mistaken. At the top she hesitated, blocking the way, apologising, moving aside. In the crowd on the floor spread out in front of her, amongst the sparkle of crystal and china, there was no red coat. She glanced at her watch. After five already. Now she really did feel exhausted, as if she didn't even have the energy to get herself back to the car park and drive to her parents' house in the West End.

'You idiot,' she scolded herself, going out into the wintry streets where thin flakes of snow had begun to fall. And yet, there had been something so *like* Susan in the tilt of the head, the movement of the body.

'She's put on weight,' Alec had said.

'Oh we all have.' She had tossed this aside, not really listening, not wanting to be able to picture Susan.

'A lot more than you,' he had added, pointedly, it now seemed.

Susan unbalanced, going off on her own, Susan taking anti-depressants, Susan *overweight*. It was as if Alec was feeling something that could only be interpreted as regret. A tiny flame of triumph licked up for a moment, female and selfish. Frances turned her collar up and set off for the car park. She had begun to think about Alec differently; she had begun to pity him.

As she turned the car into her parents' street,

she thought of Gill again, who had not phoned on New Year's Day. I will call her tomorrow, she decided, I'll make sure she's all right.

In Ross-shire, there was no more snow. A clear moonlit night saw Andrew and Kate get into a car full of boys and head off to Maryburgh. The two of them had dined on pizza taken from the freezer, since this seemed the easiest thing to cook, with fewest dishes. They had eaten it together in the kitchen, talking about school. Andrew thought Kate's school sounded weird.

'Why would anybody pay money to go to school? Who wasn't a toff, I mean. Not Eton or anything.'

'You haven't seen the other schools where I live. The ones you don't pay for.'

'So, have you all got to wear uniform?'

'Shirt and blazer, tie, the works.' She shrugged. 'It's all right, I suppose. Leaves you all your gear for the weekend, going out.'

'Mum said you were skiving off. Bit of a problem there, if you wear a uniform?'

Kate smiled, looking smug. 'Got a friend lives near the school. We leave our stuff at her house, go in for registration, then head back there and get changed.'

'Cunning plan, right.'

'Her mother goes off to work early, so it's fine.' She cut another wedge of pizza. 'What about you?'

'No, it's only the divvies skive like that. Regularly.'

'Divvies?'

'You know – they're all going to leave school at Christmas and work in the fish factory.'

'Everybody does it at my school. Nearly.' Kate got up and tipped the remains of her pizza into the kitchen bin. 'I'm going in the shower.'

Andrew put their plates in the dishwasher, conscious of remembering all his mother's instructions.

When Kate came down he was taken aback by the scantiness and transparency of her top and the visibility of the black lace bra underneath. Her make-up was more thickly coated than usual, her eyes black-lashed and lined. She might be anyone, under such a mask. The trouble was, she wasn't anyone, she was his cousin and associated with him tonight. But there was nothing he could do about it. Her expressionless gaze unnerved him.

At the party she did not hang around as he had feared she might, clinging to his side. Very quickly, after brief introductions, she vanished. He was taken aback to find her some time later wrapped round a sixth year boy he knew by reputation, but he had had a few beers by then and shrugged off the responsibility, only kicking her on the ankle as he went past, and saying, so that Roddy Macallister would at least register it, 'I'm supposed to be keeping an eye on you, remember?' Her face being well chewed by Roddy, did not emerge, but she flapped a blue nailed hand at him, dismissively.

*   *   *

Later still, two people were sick (one of them in the bathroom) and someone fell out of a first floor window, but landing on the coal bunker slid off into snow, and was found to be unharmed. Mark, whose party it was, had a fit of conscience at one o'clock, and got the vacuum cleaner out, banging it into ankles and calves as he manoeuvred it round the living-room. The noise competed with the stereo. Andrew lost track of Kate.

In Old Finnerty Farmhouse, the telephone began ringing again, as it had done from time to time all evening. Finally, whoever was calling decided to leave a message and Alec's voice, surprising the tabby curled in a chair by the phone, said, 'Call me, Frances, please. As soon as you can.'

Shortly after half past three, a taxi crawled up the frosted track and stopped at the house. Andrew got out, followed more clumsily by Kate. She staggered after him on high heels, squealing as she skidded on ice, wildly waving her arms to right herself. Andrew was sober, having eaten a lot of food in the kitchen at two o'clock when someone decided to make toasted sandwiches. Kate was very drunk, her eyes unfocused, and it took her quite a while to get her upstairs, holding on to the banister with both hands, Andrew patiently following behind in case she tipped back and came crashing down,

At least his mother wasn't home. He saw Kate into her room, where she fell onto the bed and lay without moving. With some difficulty, he tugged a good part of the duvet out from under her, and wrapped her in it. She lay with her eyes shut, breathing noisily with her mouth open.

'Are you Ok?' he asked. In answer, one blue tipped hand emerged from the duvet and waved tremulously. He left her and went to bed.

While it was still dark he was disturbed by noises coming from the bathroom, and realised she was being sick. He waited, listening. The lavatory flushed, there was running water, then Kate made her way back to bed. Andrew lay cocooned in his own warmth, one cat over his feet and the other behind his knees, making it difficult to move. He went back to sleep.

When he woke again it was daylight, but the light behind his curtains did not have the brightness of the clear frosty days they'd had all week. He was cold now, the cats gone and the duvet slipped sideways. He lay listening to silence, until the pressure on his bladder forced him to get up. He saw Kate's door was closed.

Downstairs in jeans and sweatshirt, he stood by the kitchen window watching the snow, great fat flakes falling straight through windless air. The ground was already covered. He thought he might have breakfast. It was a meal he rarely had much interest in, but he felt hollow and it was, he realised, after twelve.

He took his toasted roll and glass of milk to the living-room, so that he could lie on the sofa and watch television. Going through the hall, he saw a light was flashing on the answerphone. He put his plate and glass down for a moment and pressed the 'play' button. Six calls, and three of them had left messages. The three were all from Alec, asking Frances, with increasing urgency, to call him. 'I'm not ringing him,' muttered Andrew. 'Mum can do it.' He picked up his plate and glass and headed for the television. As he did so, the telephone began to ring again.

CHAPTER 9

In Edinburgh, Gillian had already been back at work for three days. Once the flurry of Christmas and Hogmanay was over, the parties at an end, the foray to the Sales successfully made, what was the point of the holiday? If she stayed off work she would only lie in bed in the morning; drink too much coffee and get light-headed; watch television and despise herself for it; open a bottle of wine well before supper-time. No, better to be at work where it was still quiet, her email box unusually empty and the plants in need of watering.

She had brought her filing up to date, made notes for her next project and tried to phone people who were all still on holiday, or if they were not, behaved as if they were, going for long lunches and leaving at four o'clock. Gillian felt virtuous: she had at least made a start on her New Year workload.

She did not want to acknowledge any other reason for going back to work, but of course it was there. She was not having a good time just now. For all the boldness of her declaration to Frances that she was going to change her life for the better, she was miserable when she thought of having to do it on her own. Into the open sea again, and it harder to swim year by year. How many New Years had she greeted like this, joining the party in the flat downstairs (if you can't be with the one person you want to be with, what does it matter where you are?) singing Auld Lang Syne and kissing people she hardly knew. How many more? She did not want to think about that.

On the Saturday morning when Frances drove Jack back to university, Gillian went to Princes Street for a final hunt round the Sales. She would go to Jenners, where you could sometimes get designer stuff at bargain prices. Gillian spent a lot of money on clothes. As long as she paid her mortgage, she could do as she liked with her money. She had no responsibilities.

She dithered for a long time over a black evening jacket with sequinned flowers. She admired herself in it, pulling in her stomach as she turned. Too much food and drink – back to the gym this afternoon, and *twenty* lengths of the pool. Regretfully she replaced the jacket on its rack. The party season was over and by next Christmas she would want something new.

Later, she did find some bargains and in higher spirits went off with them to a coffee house. It was a bright windless day and she even enjoyed the climb up the Mound. Edinburgh was graceful and gay in the sunshine and she loved the whole city.

Coming back through Princes Street Gardens she felt the caffeine surge ebb away, her good humour with it. The gym, the pool at the Health Club – then what? Get a video, a bottle of wine. That was a good enough Saturday night. On her own. Coming up the steps out of the gardens, she saw the crowds surging along Lothian Road and decided to head straight home. Ahead, her eye was caught by a red coat. Now that was nice – great swing at the back. She stopped. Then began walking again, trotting to catch up with the red coat, carrier bags bumping against her legs. It couldn't be, *of course*, but just in case.

Whoever it was wearing the red coat, she moved faster than Gillian, and now she had vanished, perhaps into a shop or restaurant. At any rate, Gillian couldn't see her, so she slowed again. She would call Frances tonight, that's what she'd do, and her parents. They would all be at home on Saturday night. Why then, shouldn't she be at home too? Frances would say *fancy you thinking you saw Susan in Edinburgh*. It would be all right, just a mistake. Feeling giddy she hailed a taxi and sank into it, longing to be back in her flat. It's no good, she thought, it's no bloody good, the three of us in different places, hardly ever speaking to each other, and Susan *never* speaking. What did she ever have against *me*, she never went off with *my* husband. I didn't cut her off, the way Dad did. I was just part of the family, and that wasn't my fault. *We were so close, when we were young.*

The flat smelt stale, in need of a good clean and the windows opened. She flung herself onto the blue sofa that had cost so much money and sat there, still in her jacket. I'll phone Frances in a minute, she thought, I won't wait. Instead she began to cry silently, heavy tears rolling unchecked over her face.

After a few minutes, she wiped them away with both hands like a child, and got up. What she must do was contact Susan. She did not need permission from her father or Frances. Alec's reappearance meant, surely, that he at least wanted reconciliation. Perhaps he had even been paving the way for Susan. After all these years of stubborn silence (thirteen unanswered Christmas and birthday cards) she could not do it directly, and by herself. Alec had gone to Frances first of course, but she could call him now.

This tremendous insight had much the same effect as the new clothes, the frothy Cappuccino: she was filled with energy again. Shrugging off her jacket and throwing it on the sofa, she went straight to her address book.

She trembled, though, picking up the receiver, and could not help but taste again the horror of the last time she had called Susan. She didn't know now why she had thought she could make any difference. But she had always been closer to Susan than Frances. Frances was so much older – almost eight years – and as remote as an adult. But Susan had told her secrets to Gillian, who had hoarded them as she had hoarded the half finished bottles of pink nail polish and the cast-off clothes, crumpled from lying at the bottom of the wardrobe. Susan wearing them looked like a model, and Gillian remembered wondering help-lessly why she – tugging them this way and that – never did. She just wasn't *with it*, as everyone said then, and Susan was. Later, she realised Susan abandoned clothes simply because they were no longer *with it*, but abruptly out of date.

At any rate, as Susan's bearer of secrets, clothes, hidden life (hidden from her parents and Frances), she had gone on believing she could still be the one to reach her. She had left home and moved to Edinburgh in the wake of the row over Susan's going off with Adam, ten years older than she was, and divorced. Not *quite* divorced, as it turned out. The repercussions, it seemed to Gillian, had all been hers: *Where are you off to, now? What time will you be home? We want to know where you are.*

In Edinburgh, alone and nervous, she was at least able to begin living an independent life. It was sublimely fresh and innocent to her in retro-spect, that life: her first flat shared with Chloe and Mags and Anne (where were *they* now?) and her first job in House of Fraser, selling tights and socks. When news of Susan's far more terrible betrayal reached her she felt, naturally, that she could be the one to whom Susan would turn. She might even *listen* to Gillian now that they were both grown up.

'Oh yes, I have a number for them,' Frances had said. It had taken far more courage to call Frances and ask for this, than to pick up the phone to the ostracised Susan. 'Naturally I have a number – so that I can let Alec know if one of his sons is at death's door.' How cold Frances was. There was no way through to *her*. Perhaps she cried on her own and was broken and hurt, but you would never have guessed from the way she spoke.

She expected more warmth from Susan, even gratitude.

'Oh,' Susan had said, on the breath of a laugh, incredulous. 'Gill – hi.'

And Gillian, stumbling onto something she never did – never could – fathom the depths of, offered friendship, support, trying to say it was possible Susan could still undo the damage. But Susan, mocking, scornful, had told her to *fuck off, who did she think she was? They've all had a go at me, did you think they wouldn't? Not Fran of course, trust Fran, she knows how to twist a knife. But all the rest – even Aunt Barbara. And now you think you can as well – that you can tell me what to do? What do you think, eh, that I'm going about for the rest of my life full up to here with guilt? Well, I'm fucking not. They had a rotten marriage, he was miserable. You didn't know that, did you? He was only too glad to get out. Now sod off wee sister and get a life of your own.*

It was years before she got over it. If she had. When she had at last grown closer to Frances than

102

she ever had to Susan, she repeated all this and
Frances said, 'She was drunk. They were always
drunk. Why do you think I cared so much? Not
for her. Not for him.'

'Oh,' Gillian said, a weight lifting, a barrier
falling. 'Because of Kate.'

'Yes. Because of Kate.'

Now it would be different. They were all older
and time had revealed Susan's heartlessness as
drunken hysteria. Guilty? Of course she had been
guilty but now, years later, she could give her
another chance, open the door a little. The red
coat on Lothian Road had been a sign.

Alec answered after several rings.

'Hi, Alec,' she began.

'Frances – I was just going to—'

'It's not Frances, it's Gill. Gillian.'

'Gillian – *hello*. How are you? Happy New Year.'

'Alec, look, I know this is sudden, it feels so
strange to me you can't believe, but – is Susan
there? I really want to speak to her. Do you think
I could? I thought maybe if you were in touch she
must want to be as well.' She was shaking, her
hand tight round the receiver, damp with sweat,
but she was glad she was doing this.

Alec's silence went on too long. 'Alec?'

'Sorry – Gill – when did you last speak to
Frances?'

'Actually, not since Christmas, I've been a bit
busy. Anyway, this is nothing to do with Frances
– well, not directly, I just wanted to—'

'Susan's not here. She left before Christmas and I haven't had a word from her.'

'What do you mean, *left*?' She felt stupid, his words jammed together in her head, making no sense.

'Disappeared. I don't know where she is.'

The red coat whisked away up Lothian Road, past office blocks, among crowds.

'Had you fallen out or something, what happened? I mean, she's all right, isn't she?'

'Oh I think so. She needed a bit of a break, but it's gone on rather longer than usual.'

'Usual?'

'She's not always very well. If you see what I mean. She needs a lot of space. I told Frances all this, it's why I went up there, why I wanted Kate to stay.'

'Kate. Oh God, this is awful, I should have phoned Frances, shouldn't I. Look, I've got to tell you, this morning, I'm coming up from Princes Street Gardens, right, I'd been shopping, and I come out onto the street and I see her – honestly, I saw Susan. I thought I *had* to be mistaken. I couldn't manage to catch up with her, but maybe she's actually here, in Edinburgh. What do you think, could she be?'

'Gill, you haven't seen her for a dozen years, and she was – how far off?'

'My God, Alec, you always know your own sister.'

'Do you?' he asked, his voice so low and tender Gillian's eyes filled with tears.

'Look can I do anything, can I help? What about Kate – you said something about Kate.'

'She's staying on with Frances for a while.'

Absurd to feel jealous. Absurd. Frances was the capable one who ought to be in charge, if anyone was.

'It's really good of you to call,' Alec went on. 'As soon as she – well, as soon as she's home, I'll make sure she gets in touch.'

'You have reported this to the police?'

'Oh yes but they're not interested. Look, I'm absolutely convinced she's fine.'

'You don't think she could be in Edinburgh?' Why did she want so much to believe it was Susan she had seen? Because then, it would not be too late. She would not have left it too long to make the telephone call and say, *Susan, speak to me, let's talk again. Please.* What was Alec saying? She tried to concentrate.

'It is possible. But she doesn't have a red coat, she doesn't even wear red.'

'Oh, men. You might not even know. And the sales are on, she could have bought it here.'

'Gill, don't feel you have to do anything. If anyone should *do* something, it's me. And I am, I'm doing what I can. So don't worry.'

Later, making herself supper in her tiny kitchen, Gill found she was not at all hungry. *She doesn't have a red coat.* Something nagged at her about that. Then she saw Susan at fifteen coming up the path in scarlet, in red ski pants and a striped jumper. Loud, red stripes. She *liked* red. Away from Alec, she was wearing it again.

Gillian sat down with a mug of herbal tea. (Enough caffeine for today, she needed to feel calm.) When they were young, their mother had made most of their clothes. As their father became more successful, and Frances and Susan as teenagers wanted to buy clothes in *Dorothy Perkins* and *Girl*, she stopped. But the year of Aunt Barbara's marriage, they had all still been young enough, Gillian remembered, to wear dresses made by their mother.

Aunt Barbara married late, and the bank manager who became her husband died within five years, so Gillian hardly remembered him. Aunt Barbara, who had given up teaching to become what she called a 'lady of leisure', went back to it with renewed vigour, so that really, the only effect of her marriage had been to turn her from Miss Douglas to Mrs Simpson, and provide her with the bank manager's pension.

Gillian, while forgetting the husband, did remember the wedding, or at any rate the preparations, which seemed to go on for months. And the dresses. Each of them was supposed to have a favourite colour, and at the time of the wedding, Gillian's was yellow. (And now it is black, she thought, how dreary.) Frances wore blue; indeed, she still wore blue, serene and soft, Wedgwood or dove. Susan wore red.

Gillian tucked her feet up on the sofa. Her flat with its modern furniture and pictures, simple and primary coloured, the pale walls, the clever lighting, all gave way to the crowded living-room in Balmoral Terrace, where Frances turned slowly in front of the cheval glass, her mother on her knees beside her, pin cushion in one hand, the other raised to say 'Stop!' And Frances did stop, grave in her blue dress, while Grace pinned the hem. Then it was Susan's turn and she twirled in scarlet, unable to stand still. Grace waited for her to calm down: 'For goodness sake, child, stand at peace.'

'I'm beautiful, amn't I?' Susan asked, twisting and turning, admiring herself all the way round. 'This is a beautiful dress – the *most beautiful* – isn't it?'

'Now Gillian,' her mother said, 'last but not least. Come away.' Then she saw what a crumpled heap Gillian had made of the yellow dress. 'What *on earth* have you been doing?'

'I want a red one like Susan. I don't want this yellow dress. It's horrible, I hate it.'

'Too late,' Grace sighed, tugging the hem straight. 'You chose it yourself, Gilly, you said you liked the white daisies – remember?' The tug and pull of the skirt, and Gillian made to turn slowly, then keep still. Her frowning face in the mirror.

When the others had left and their dresses were on wooden hangers, hems sticking out stiffly with pins, Grace whispered to Gillian, 'Never mind, when Susan grows out of it, you'll have the red one.'

'*And* the blue one,' she had agreed, seeing possibilities here, a future Gillian dramatic in red then graceful in blue. Her mother got to her feet, and helped her carefully out of the despised yellow dress.

'Well, you're a bunch of bobby dazzlers, aren't you?' Aunt Barbara had exclaimed, coming in during the final trying-on to show them her new hat. It was pink, with a black and pink spotted veil. Gillian thought it beautiful; perhaps her favourite colour was pink, really. Behind Aunt Barbara's back, Frances and Susan giggled, calling it 'hideous' and Gillian knew they thought the yellow dress was hideous too. 'It scratches me,' she complained, 'it makes me hot.'

As it turned out, she was incubating chicken pox and missed the wedding altogether. Mrs Baxter from next door stayed with her till her mother came home, earlier than everyone else. It was almost dark, and she woke with sticky eyelids, itching all over despite the calamine lotion so liberally applied in the morning. There was her mother in the doorway, in blue like Frances, and she looked and smelled of some other more exciting world, so that Gillian began to cry. Close up, Grace was familiar again, with her special scent of face powder and her arms cool and comforting when she helped Gillian to sit up. 'I'll just get out of my finery,' she said, 'and then I'll get you some calamine, and a drink.'

When Gillian eventually got up again, she had magically grown and the yellow dress no longer fitted.

Gillian opened her eyes. The itching, the dim bedroom, the yellow dress unused on its hanger, her soft-spoken mother, had all gone. Her I am, she thought, grown up, and far, far away from all that. It was still there, of course, there to go back to, the house, and her mother and father, and Frances. *How could Susan turn her back on all of us?* Gillian's eyes filled with tears again and she let them spill over, not sure whether they were tears for herself or for Susan.

CHAPTER 10

Frances reached home on Sunday afternoon. Andrew and Kate were watching television, and both were still in the tee-shirts and leggings they slept in. Frances, coming into the room, had a moment's uneasiness. Both smelled sweaty and there was a whiff of cigarette smoke. The room was cold and the fire black with last night's ashes. There were used mugs and plates scattered on the floor.

'Hi Mum.' Andrew waved a hand. 'Could you light the fire? We're freezing.'

'You could do that yourself,' Frances pointed out. 'Did you get on all right, on your own?'

'Yeah, fine.'

Kate looked up. Her make-up had vanished overnight, though not with any appearance of having been properly cleaned off. She was pale with black eyeliner smudges under her eyes.

'We had a late night,' she said. 'Sorry we haven't tidied. I didn't actually get up till about one.'

'Was it a good party?'

'Duncan and Mark were *lathered*. Mark started *hoovering* about two o'clock. You should've seen the food – there was more on the floor than the table.'

'Thank you, Andrew, for reminding me why I won't let you have parties here.'

'Oh yeah, well, that's Mark. I wouldn't let people trash my house, no way.'

'You can't have known a soul, Kate.'

Kate shrugged. 'Didn't matter.'

'Right, what about food?'

'Can we have chips? I'm starving.'

Kate shuddered. 'No thanks, *I* couldn't eat chips.'

'I'll unpack, then I'll get us something to eat.' Frances paused by the door. 'Any phone calls?'

'Ehm . . . *He* phoned about fifty times.'

'Alec,' supplied Kate.

'What did he say?'

'*I* never spoke to him,' Andrew said, offended. 'We were out, anyway. He phoned again this morning. Kate got it, didn't you?'

Frances turned to Kate but she still did not look up.

'He just said would you ring him.' Reluctantly, drawn by Frances's waiting figure, she glanced up briefly. 'He hasn't seen Mum.'

'Auntie Gill phoned as well,' Andrew added. 'She said something about a red coat.'

Frances stopped where she was. 'What did you say?'

'Auntie Gill phoned.'

'No, you said – what was that about a red coat?'

'*I* don't know, do I? Just she'd seen this red coat or something.'

In the kitchen, the cats greeted Frances with relief. She fed them, cleared out and made up the fire, sent Kate off for a shower, and went to telephone Alec. If he had not found Susan, there was no urgency. As for Gill, this red coat would be some bargain she had got in the sales.

Alec's telephone switched over to an answering service. She left her name, then dialled Gillian's number instead.

'Hi, Gill. Andrew said you'd called.'

'Hi, yes, I did.'

'Mum and Dad were just saying we haven't heard from you since Christmas.'

'You've still got Katy, haven't you?'

'Yes.'

'What's going on?'

'Is that what you rang to ask?'

'Alec says Susan's missing. He says he told you, you knew at Christmas. Is that right?'

A beat, two beats. 'When did you speak to Alec?'

'Today. I was actually trying to speak to Susan—' her voice defiant here. 'I did it because I thought I saw her.'

'*Susan?*'

'Going up Lothian Road. I mean, it sounds mad, but—'

'When was this?'

'Day before yesterday.'

'Saturday?'

'That's what I said. I was on my way—'

'When yesterday?'

'About lunch-time, if you'd let me finish, Fran, I'm trying to explain.'

There was the flash of a red coat, going up the escalator. 'What was she wearing?'

'That's what I'm coming to – she had on this red coat, very bright – and I remembered—'

'Lunch-time?'

Gillian sounded really annoyed now. 'What on earth difference does it make? I wish you'd just listen, honestly Fran, I'm sorry I rang her, I knew you wouldn't be pleased, but after all these years, surely to God I can choose whether to contact her or not?'

'No, no, you've got it wrong. Hang on, I'm just going to get hold of a train timetable, I'm sure there's one here somewhere.' Frances reached into the drawer of the hall-stand, and rummaged till she found what she wanted. 'Listen, I don't care if you contact her, how on earth could you think it had *anything* to do with me.' She flicked over pages, trying to read the tiny figures. 'She was on Lothian Road, that's the one beyond Princes Street Gardens, right, about fifteen minutes from Waverley?'

'Fran, what are you getting at?'

'I saw her. I saw her yesterday too. Only she was in Aberdeen, in John Lewis of all places, about five o'clock.'

Gillian took a deep breath; Frances heard her taking it.

'Did she have on—'

'Yes. A red coat.'

'You know your own sister,' Gillian said softly, 'don't you? I mean, even after years and years.'

'Oh yes.'

A shiver ran between them like an electric current, and for a moment neither spoke. Then Frances said, 'I know this is awful, but I still can't like her. Not hate, jealousy, anger – all that went a long time ago. I'd have told you if you'd asked.'

Gillian did not say, you made it impossible. Perhaps Frances knew, for she went on, 'It's all in the past. What she's doing to Kate now though – I can't forgive that.'

There has been a lot of not forgiving, Gillian thought. After a moment, she suggested, 'Susan's ill?'

'That's the other thing. You shouldn't blame someone who's ill. But I do, I suppose, I can't help it. We don't know her any more.'

'Except physically.'

'What?'

'We both recognised her yesterday.'

'It couldn't be. Two cities, a few hours apart. I must have been mistaken.'

'It was early lunchtime, it was about twelve. She could have got there.'

'I don't know.'

Gillian tried again. 'It's like a signal, isn't it? A sign to us that we've got to do something about it.'

'Well, I can't think what,' Frances retorted. 'I'm looking after her daughter, that seems to me quite enough.'

Gillian did not take this amiss: she was ahead already, speculating and planning. 'We should meet in Aberdeen. Maybe even tell Mum and Dad. Family's so important.'

'Gill, you've *never* thought that.'

'Oh I have. I've just been side-tracked, the last few years.'

'So what's changed?'

'It's over with Steve. Like I told you – a whole new start.'

Had Gillian said that? But Frances knew she had not listened. She had stopped hearing Gill's troubles, simply because they were always the same. 'Good for you,' she said now, making an effort, though without faith. 'You're really not going to see him any more?'

'It happened before Christmas but I never said anything in case I couldn't stick with it. I know you think I'm weak.'

'I never said that!'

'You've got very high standards. Anyway, this time it is over.' She sighed. 'It's not easy though. So – will you meet me in Aberdeen?'

'I've just got home from Aberdeen, and Kate's here. Anyway, I'm back at work tomorrow.'

Gillian sighed. 'I'm getting carried away, I suppose.'

'No, it's all right – I'm worried too. Maybe once Kate's gone home – let me think about it.'

'It is weird, isn't it – both of us thinking we saw Susan?'

'Very odd.'

'She's still our sister, no matter what she's done.'

'Oh yes,' Frances said, but not as if she meant it.

After supper, Frances drove over to Kenny's house and spent the evening with him, mainly in bed.

'I mustn't doze off,' she said eventually, rousing herself.

'Stay a bit longer.' He tugged her back into the comfortable nest of his arms.

'Ten minutes.'

'This was a nice surprise,' he told her. 'Thought you'd be too tired to bother.'

'Back to work tomorrow,' she reminded him. 'Things are rather difficult at the moment. I needed a treat.'

He laughed. 'Glad to oblige.'

She slipped from him so easily he sensed he was no more than that: an interlude, a bit of cheer in her life. Calmly, she put up her hair in front of his mirror, still naked, but no longer vulnerable and tender as she had been in his bed.

'Your beautiful hair,' he murmured.

She considered her reflection. 'I was thinking I might have it cut.'

'Why?'

'Oh, we all need to change, don't you think? I've been stuck for a long time with this image.' She turned to him as she pulled on her clothes with swift economy. 'I'm not mad, am I?' she asked, as if this were a reasonable question. 'Noone in our family has ever been anything but sane and sensible. And yet—'

He propped himself up on one elbow. 'Is something wrong?'

Frances dipped her head first to one side then the other, fastening earrings. 'I was thinking about my sister Susan. Somewhere in our childhood, or more likely adolescence, there must have been clues, something to indicate she would become the way she seems to be now. Odd, at least. To go and leave your daughter without a word . . .'

'But she left all her family years ago, didn't she, without a word?'

'I suppose she did,' Frances admitted. 'Was she ill then, I wonder. Poor Alec. What a vengeance for Fate to take.'

'What – to find you've left a beautiful sane wife to go off with an inferior model who turns out to be crackers?'

Frances flushed 'Well, I wouldn't put it like that myself. Anyway,' she countered, 'Susan was stunning.'

She crossed to the bed and leaned over him, to kiss the top of his greying head, where the springy hair was thinning. She patted his stomach. 'Back on the diet,' she suggested.

'Aye, aye.' He reached up and pulled her close, his hand warm on the back of her neck. 'See you soon, eh?'

Driving home, she thought how lucky she was to have him there, undemanding and kind.

Alone in his cottage, Kenny got up and pulled on his old corduroy trousers and a jersey, and went to make himself a mug of tea. Changing his mind, he poured a dram instead and settled in front of the television, the dog at his feet.

'Lucky Kenny,' his friends said. 'Beautiful woman, plenty of sex, no going round Tesco on Saturdays.'

'Aye,' he agreed. 'A fine life.'

Later, going out with the dog to let it have its last pee of the day in the lane, he had no memory of what he had just been watching. The sky was clear and full of stars and he smelt the sharp tang of frost in the air. Briefly, turning indoors after the dog, which felt the cold now in old age and was hurrying back to the fire, he longed for a warm woman still to be in his bed, and company that would last the whole night through.

After her unsatisfactory conversation with Frances, Gillian could not settle. Always before, in this sort of restless empty space, she had turned to Steve, even on Sundays when he was with his wife and children and not supposed to be contacted. She had left messages on his mobile phone and he had often picked them up when he strolled along to the pub in the evening. Sometimes he even came round to see her. Then, if he had forgotten to switch it off, the mobile rang again while they were in bed and it was Carol, asking him to bring her something from the corner shop on his way home. When this had happened two or three times they realised she had guessed what was going on, though she had never known who Gillian was, or (thank God) where she lived. For several weeks their affair became much more intense and passionate. Then that too changed and Gillian knew there must have been some kind of confrontation. Carol had used the children against him, Steve said.

She knew it had to end; he would never leave his family. For months, they went on without even mentioning Carol or his children. They existed in a vacuum. Perhaps he had reached some sort of accommodation with his wife. Some kind of payoff had been exacted, Gillian guessed. Her own bargain with him, which she had always felt left room for change, closed in, and she lost hope.

'End it,' her friends advised. Eventually, two weeks before Christmas, she did. He took it well. Rueful, he gave her a silver bracelet she put at the back of her dressing table drawer. 'I'll miss you' he said, 'so much. I wish it could be different'

She realised now that he had expected her to relent after a while, as she so often had before. Eventually it would all start up again. They'd had several passionate 'last nights' together; this time, determined it would be the last, she abandoned caution, making the most of it. She had a pinch of anxiety about it. The last time. So evocative, the ache of loss before it has happened.

So here was Sunday evening again with no Steve, no phone calls. She must turn to something else, call a friend, go for a drink. Instead she went to the cupboard in her bedroom and began to delve into the boxes and papers heaped on the bottom shelf. She was sure she had an album of photographs from their childhood. Five years ago she had gone to a school reunion. Everyone had been asked to bring photographs of themselves at school so she had raided her parents' collection.

'Bring back that album,' her mother had reminded, more than once. She had not mentioned it for a while so perhaps she had forgotten Gillian still had it. It was full of photographs of all three of them.

As she hunted, the telephone began to ring. Steve. In her haste to answer it, she knocked her ankle on the door frame without noticing the pain, wondering next day what had caused the bruise. It was not Steve. It was nobody. Silence, and a click, then the dialling tone. She dialled back without recognising the number, an Edinburgh one. It rang sounding hollow, but no-one answered.

She hung up and went back to the cupboard. The album had fallen onto the floor. She took it into the living-room and poured herself a glass of wine. The telephone rang again, but again there was no-one. She checked the number and it was the same. If this kept on happening, she would call the police. Two women had been attacked by an intruder in their own houses in Edinburgh recently. She put the chain up on the door then went back to her glass of wine and the photograph album.

There were a number of loose pictures stuffed between the pages. She tipped them onto the sofa beside her and they spread to a fan of memories.

It struck her that Susan was rarely set in the middle as she was in the family, and in the studio photograph she had picked up first. There, they were all facing the camera, smiling. There was something stiff about the pose and the smiles held too long, the neatly arranged dresses, skirts spread out with a glimpse of net petticoats and the hair brushed smooth, held by ribbons tied in perky bows. Susan looked particularly wooden.

The snapshots taken in the garden, on beaches or in parks, during weekends and holidays, were less clear, the faces tiny, eyes screwed up as they faced into the sun, but they were full of movement. We are real in those, Gillian thought, our ribbons undone, socks slipping down, caught for a moment, but fidgeting to be off again.

It was Susan who seemed to move furthest and fastest, to be least in evidence, her face turned away or obscured by tangles of fringe. She slipped to the edge, almost out of the frame altogether.

Later, black and white changed to Kodacolour.

121

They had longer legs and hair, shorter skirts. That was on the last few pages. If there was in their parents' house another, later album, Gillian knew that Susan dropped out of that one at the same time as Frances, but not because like Frances, she had married. She had dropped out of their family life. Several years of escalating rows over cigarette packets found in her room, the smell of drink on her breath as she came in later and later every weekend, had climaxed in her abrupt departure to live with Adam. The unreliable, still married and ultimately absconding Adam. At the same time she had abandoned university and taken a series of short-lived jobs in shops and cafes. All of that was jumbled together in Gillian's memory, since now she could hardly remember what triggered the moment of despair when she realised she had to leave home too, if she was to have any life at all.

Why on earth do I want Susan to turn up again, Gillian asked herself. She caused me nothing but misery.

This was not quite true. What neither the vague family snaps nor the storm of Susan's leaving home revealed was that Susan had been the kind of girl in whose shadow you would gratefully fall. She was always surrounded by other girls when she was a child, and by girls and boys when she began to grow up. She was the one they all flocked round and longed to be noticed by. There was something magical about the aura she cast, something magical about Susan. And Gillian, the little sister growing up behind her, had basked in Susan's brief bursts of affection, her generosity, her confidences. *You're the only one who knows. Don't tell anyone else, promise. Swear.* So she promised, she swore fidelity, and was left, when Susan had whirled off on another adventure without her, with a sense of excitement so enervating it was like lust or shame. She had gathered Susan's secrets to her like jewels.

Susan had not told her everything about Adam. It had been as much of a shock to her as to Frances when they discovered Susan was living with someone five years older, a man who had left his wife.

Gillian turned over the photographs, dreaming. When the telephone rang again she did not hurry to answer. When she eventually picked it up, she was sure she heard breathing.

'Who is this?' she demanded, then called loudly, as if to someone else in the room. 'Steve – it's that crank again. Come here, would you?'

The dialling tone. She was shaking. Some crank, some pervert. And yet, as if compelled, she dialled the number again. It rang and rang, sounding hollow and far away. As it went on ringing, she turned slowly towards the sofa, and saw lying, face up, a clear photograph of herself with Susan and Frances on either side. The three Douglas girls.

On and on, in an empty call box on the other side of Edinburgh, the telephone went on ringing.

✶   ✶   ✶

As Frances let herself into the house, her telephone was ringing too. She struggled with boots and coat, hurrying through the kitchen from the back door, but it stopped as she reached it. Then she realised someone had picked up her bedroom extension. Andrew appeared at the top of the stairs.

'It's him again,' he said.

'I'll take it upstairs, I'm going to bed in a minute anyway.'

'I want to see a film that starts at half past ten,' Andrew said.

'You'll never get up in the morning.'

'It's one of these teacher training days tomorrow,' he reminded her. 'We're not going in till Tuesday.'

'Where's Kate?'

'In bed, I think.'

He *thought*. They were living separate lives in the same house. Of course they were – Jack and Andrew had different friends and interests. She wondered if Alec was calling to say he was coming to take Kate home.

'Any news?' she asked.

'Not really. Gill called me.'

'I know, I've spoken to her.'

'Did she say—'

'I think we've got Susan on our minds, that's all. *I* thought I saw her in Aberdeen. Wishful thinking – we both want to believe she's all right.' He began to answer but she interrupted. 'When are you coming for Kate?'

'Well . . .'

124

'Alec, what is she supposed to *do* here?' I'm back at work tomorrow, then Andrew will be at school – it's no use.'

'Could she enrol where Andrew is? Which school does he go to?'

'Dingwall. As you ought to know.'

'Oh yes, sorry—'

'Are you going to take Kate home or not?'

A pause lengthened to uneasy silence. Frances waited.

'She's better with you. I'm at the restaurant all the time. You've no idea, it's a twenty hour a day job. I just can't keep an eye on her, and she needs it. Needs a mother, but – look, I'll send money, it needn't cost you anything—'

'For God's sake. It's not the cost, it's just that it's *wrong*. She's your responsibility.'

She halted, aware of the ambiguity of this, the fragility of his relationship with all of them, not just Kate. If he had run from his own sons, what was to keep him with Kate, if Susan was no longer there?

'Why don't you ask Kate?' he said, meek now, as he could well afford to be. He knew Frances. She would not say no, in the end.

'I will. She's not a child, she has to decide for herself.'

She was a child though, that was the trouble, a minor, and if anyone had to take responsibility for making the right decision, it was not Kate.

'Give me a ring when you've spoken to her.'

'She's in bed. I'll call you tomorrow night.' She put the receiver down, not waiting for a response.

When she tapped on Kate's door there was no reply, only a stillness that seemed like absence. But when she pushed the door open, the light from the landing showed the girl on her back, eyes shut and mouth open a little, hair spread on the pillow. She looked much younger in the vulnerability of sleep, and with a rush of tenderness which she could not prevent, she went in and quietly straightened the bed covers. Kate moaned a little, rolling away from her, curling up tight. Frances went out and closed the door.

PART II

THE RIGHT TO CHOOSE

CHAPTER 1

'How are things in the far north? It's freezing in Edinburgh. How's Kate – does she like the Academy?'

'Do teenagers ever like school? She's out at some girl's house tonight, so that's a good sign I suppose.'

'What's happening at Easter? Are Mum and Dad visiting?'

'They haven't mentioned it, and Spring still seems a long way off.' Frances looked out of her bedroom window. Gillian's call had come while she was half-heartedly getting ready to go out. It was still light after six but the sky was overcast and a sleety rain had been falling for the last hour. The grey garden with its corners of banked up snow was fading from sight.

Six weeks of the New Year had passed. Work had claimed Frances. Susan had not come home. Alec called weekly and Frances's conversations with him, at first about Susan, and Kate's welfare, had begun to stray into other, neutral, subjects in a perfunctory but amicable way. Sometimes Kate was out when he called but Frances always knew, or believed she did, where she was. As far as she

129

could tell Kate was at school during the hours she was supposed to be.

'Anyway,' she said to Gillian, 'how are you?' Gillian's voice was brave and bright, a bad sign. Still, better to ask. Who else was Gill going to turn to? Frances could hardly imagine the people her sister worked with, her frenetic world. She was always building up to some conference or seminar, or rushing around during it, or suffering the anticlimax afterwards and fretting about what had not been perfect.

'I'm all right.'

'You're not, I can tell. Has Steve resurfaced?'

'No, you should be proud of me. Still single.'

'Nobody new?'

'I did go out with this guy – but no, nobody new.'

'You probably need some time on your own.'

Gillian did not answer this so Frances felt rebuked. I'm not sympathetic enough, she thought, I don't make allowances for people being different.

'I think I might come up next weekend. I've got a clear Monday for once, so I could take a break. Would that be all right?'

'Here?'

'You've got a spare bed, haven't you, if Jack's not home?'

'Yes, but you're usually so busy.'

'I need a break.'

Jack's bed was stripped, the room clean and aired. 'No trouble', Frances always said, when

130

people came to stay, though of course it was, but she did want to see Gillian. Between them their missing sister hovered and must be caught. Only they could do it, only between the two of them could she be understood.

Kate was to call when she was ready to come home. Frances had said she would collect her from a village about four miles away where the new friend lived. 'Not later than ten,' she had warned, 'since it's a school night.' It was after ten already.

Andrew reached the phone when it rang, since he was passing at the time. He had hung up by the time his mother got there.

'Was that Kate?'

'She's at 6 Mackenzie Place.'

'Do you know where that is?'

'I think so.'

'You'd better come with me.'

'Do I have to?'

'Yes.'

'What's she doing over there?' he asked as they drove down the lane.

'It's where some girl in her class lives – Amy, I think.'

'What's she want to hang out with that crowd for anyway?' he muttered, fiddling with the car radio.

'Turn that down – it's earsplitting. What do you mean, that crowd?'

She remembered Jack saying disdainfully, when

he was still at the Academy, 'Nobody goes about with anybody from *there*.' He had been winding Andrew up, since his friend Kevin lived in the village.

'I think it's up here on the left,' Andrew said as she drove slowly along the High Street past the fish and chip shop, where a small group of teen-agers had gathered. Turning right, they were in a warren of council housing, all the streets looking the same.

'Where now?'

'Not sure. Keep going.'

Frances turned a corner and there it was. She drew up at number six. 'Go and knock, Andy.'

'*I'm* not going.'

'Don't be silly – just go and ask for Kate.'

'No way.' He slumped in his seat.

'For goodness sake—'

As Frances got out of the car the front door opened and two girls appeared. One of them was Kate.

'Can we give Eilidh a lift?'

They were clones in black with their cropped tops, hip-tight trousers and straight hair. They got in the back of the car together, ignoring Andrew and not meeting Frances's eyes.

'Where do you live, Eilidh?' Frances asked.

'Robertson Drive in Dingwall. You can drop me at the bottom of your road, if you like.'

'Nonsense – it's dark. We'll take you home.'

She negotiated another council estate, this time

with directions. Even Jack admitted to friends here, so it was half familiar.

Later, she said to Andrew as she made herself tea and he ate two bananas one after the other, 'She seems to be making friends, so perhaps she's settled all right.'

'Yeah, but she's not *staying*?' He dropped banana peel into the pedal bin and let the lid bang shut. 'I can't see the point in her going to Dingwall, what's the point in her getting to know people here? She'll be back in Newcastle soon, won't she?'

'That's the idea.'

'Well then.'

'You don't mind, do you? She's not disrupting your life. She watches *Eastenders*, granted, but you still get all the sport you want.'

Frances had resigned herself to Kate being here for the whole term. Alec, always elusive, had been impossible to pin down. As long as I don't get involved, she told herself, or care too much, we'll be fine.

Andrew shrugged. 'I just thought she was leaving soon, that's all.'

'Is something wrong?'

'No.'

If his mother couldn't see for herself, Andrew wasn't going to say anything. She had no idea who her mates were, the huddle round the back of the drama studio, the loud laughter, the swagger of them, coming back for afternoon school coughing and smelling of smoke.

'She seems quite popular,' Frances persisted. 'People are forever ringing her up.'

He did not even answer this. Depends who you want her to be popular *with*, he thought. That useless lot, who'd never pass any exams and would stay in the same place all their lives? Though they were careful never to be *caught* studying, the attitude his own crowd took was that without being, of course, a swot, you passed what you needed to. You were cool, you knew where you were going. Out of Dingwall.

Kate was popular with boys, all right. Was that what his mother wanted to hear? There were two academic years between them, but he heard the sniggers about Kate and he was beginning to fear that he might soon have to decide whether to defend her (*You keep your dirty mouth shut, Mackay . . .*) or disown her. He kept hoping she would just leave, and solve the problem.

As for Kate, she had gone the only way she could. The girls Frances probably wanted her to be friendly with, had shunned her. Politely, after a few weeks of hearing Kate's stories, they cut her off, so that there was only one thing to do if she did not want to be isolated. She needed a circle of admirers to be impressed by her air of sophistication, her reminiscences of skiving off, of smoking and drinking, and taking Es at raves her parents never knew she went to: the world she had been torn from, glamorous and daring in memory.

Had she played other cards – the missing mother perhaps – she might have attracted sympathy, but she always said *my mother's away for work. She has this job where she has to travel a lot. The States, Europe.* Sometimes she almost convinced herself.

It was as if half her real self had been left behind in Newcastle, the half with her own computer and Facebook page. She had been dismayed to find the only computer here was in Andrew's bedroom; Jack took his laptop with him to Aberdeen. When Frances wanted to check websites or buy online, she did it at work, or used Andrew's machine.

'Of course you can use the computer,' Frances had said, early in her stay. 'Just tell Andrew you need it.'

That was no good. How secure was that? She could just imagine Andrew and Jack on her Facebook, spying. The only consolation was the girls she went about with were not into all that; they didn't have their own computers either. She could ask Alec, she could tell him he had to get her a laptop or an i-phone. She hadn't asked him yet. What was the point? As soon as her mother came back, she was going home.

She could hear Andrew and Frances in the kitchen, talking. She shut her bedroom door. There had been no message from Susan, but that did not stop her constantly checking her phone. There were fewer messages from her friends at home now. Sometimes she called them in the evenings, but to get any privacy had to use the mobile in her own room, and it needed topping up again. There was no branch in Dingwall of the building society where she had her account, and she had only a fiver till she could get into Inverness for more money. She would ask Alec to get her a contract phone and pay for it. He owed her that.

Meanwhile, she turned the mobile over and over in her hands, willing it to ring. After a moment she lay down and set it aside. She put both hands on her stomach. She had cramps coming and going, so probably her period was on its way at last. She could not remember when she had her last one. Not in this house. Ages then.

She had not had many ordinary conversations with her mother in the last few years, but there were times when it was easy: Susan was good about female stuff. She was a nurse so nothing like that fazed her. You could ask anything when she was in a good spell.

'They'll settle down,' Susan had reassured,

'I never know when it's going to start. It's not fair.'

'Oh, I wasn't regular until after you were born.'

'That's a bit of a drastic cure,' Kate scoffed and her mother laughed uneasily. Kate could guess why.

She could not remember the time before Alec was in her life, but he had always been Alec to her, never Dad. 'He's not my real Daddy, is he?'

she asked her mother when she was very young. Susan turned, her voice sharp, 'What did you say?' Kate was afraid even then of the way her mother could switch from kind and ordinary to angry and breathless.

Once when Kate was six or seven they were in the park, the one near their house they called the swing park. It was raining and the park was deserted. Only Kate and Susan were there, for some reason out of the house, defying weather. Susan put a plastic carrier bag on one of the swings so that Kate's bottom would stay dry, but the chains of the swing were wet and slippery in her grip, cold metal, greasy with rain. Beneath the swing was a puddle with a rainbow in it. Kate looked down at the puddle trying to identify all the colours as she was pushed on the swing, to and fro, a little higher each time. The rainbow vanished as she swept over it, reappearing as she reared back, her mother's hands on the small of her back, giving another push to send her flying forward. She flew so high she could see over the railing, over the trees, and in the distance the main road, cars and a bus with its windows misted by rain.

'That's enough, that's enough!' Kate shrieked, holding tighter and tighter to the chains, and Susan stepped back. Little by little, its momentum gone, the swing slowed and Kate let her legs drop.

'Another push!' she cried, but her mother did not answer and when she looked behind her Susan was not there. She stumbled off before the swing had stopped, slipping on the carrier bag, her feet splashing in the rainbow puddle. All around her was the empty park in the rain, the slide gleaming silver, the bushes behind a dense green mass and the only sounds the swing creaking and a rook cawing insolently in a tall tree. There was no-one else there.

For years afterwards, if she really wanted to scare herself, she could conjure that moment of terror, her sense of loss so overwhelming nothing could ever match it. She experienced all over again the not-being-there of her mother, the emptiness left behind, the helplessness of her own trembling self, crying and crying in the deserted park.

'Katy!' There she was on the path, emerging between two rows of trees, her arms full of yellow flowers. 'Look,' she said, 'I picked some daffodils. They'll never miss them.'

Their house, like so many in Northumberland, had no garden, just a small square yard with a coalhouse and dustbin. Daffodils. It must have been Spring, a wet April. Throughout her childhood, Kate dreamed this, and now and again still did. Sometimes she wondered if it had only ever been a bad dream. Susan denied it had happened. 'Leave you? Steal a huge bunch of daffodils from the park? What an imagination you've got. I'd *never* have gone off and left you alone – even for a minute.'

Kate knew it was true, in her heart she knew

that. It was on their way home that day, one hand tucked into her mother's, the other holding a bunch of the stolen daffodils, the stalks wet and slimy in her cold fingers, Kate was told about her father.

'He was called Adam,' Susan said. 'The first man. Well, more or less.' She laughed the wild laugh that meant she was laughing at something she hadn't told you. 'I was madly in love with him. I thought we were going to get married, but he went off to Canada, so there you are. He never knew about you. I went to stay with Auntie Frances after you were born. She adored you but she wasn't very nice to me. Maybe *she* wanted a little girl, she just had the boys. Anyway, that's when I met Alec, and I fell in love with him instead. He liked *both* of us. So we got married.'

Had Susan really told her the story like this? It was years before Kate knew more. Now that she had met Frances, she realised there were still gaps.

The real Frances was not at all as she had imagined. Or Gillian either, though she had heard even less about her, discovering her existence only when she was ten and found a letter from her grandmother tucked inside a Christmas card, one probably of many chatty, but desperate, unanswered letters. *My Dear Susan, perhaps this will be the Christmas you write back to us. I hope you are well, and Katy too.*

'Who's Gillian,' she asked her mother, bold in

Alec's presence, 'and what does it mean her engagement's broken?'

Kate lay with her hands over her stomach, pressing on the cramps till they faded, and drifted into sleep, to a dream that was confusion of past and present. Her mother with her arms full of daffodils, the creak of the swing, Frances's firm voice, Andrew coming round the corner of the gardener's shed, catching her smoking with Amy and Eilidh. Then Dave Prentice laughing at her, so that she had that burning, shameful feeling she had when he made such a fool of her. She wished, *wished* she'd never got off with him, what an idiot she was to fall for him. Never mind, never mind, he was miles away, couldn't touch her now and her mother must be home after all, her arms full of flowers.

She woke breathing in the smell of them, wet and green and bitter, woke suddenly, and found herself alone in Frances's spare room, the smell fading to nothing in the dark. Turning her face into the pillow she let the tears soak into cotton, cool on her hot skin.

CHAPTER 2

By the end of January Gillian knew she was pregnant. She had suspected it sooner but pushed the idea away, not wanting to think about it. She had never been pregnant and as the years went on had grown a little careless about preventing it, as though her luck was bound to hold. Now she was well through her thirties it would probably never happen.

She bought a testing kit from Boots and put it at the back of her underwear drawer, telling herself it was too soon to tell for sure, even to visit a doctor. Yet she knew she must not just let time drift by.

Such a huge anxiety fills up the days. At work, people said, 'Are you OK?' or 'You're very quiet – anything up?' Everything was under control at work; if anything, she was more efficient, not less. Fear can concentrate the mind.

In February she made an appointment with her doctor and came home early one afternoon so that she could keep it. She went into the local super-market for groceries on her way and stopped off to unpack them. On the window sill of the ground floor flat the Fletchers' ginger cat sat gazing in, mewing now and again. Hearing Gill he jumped down and came to rub against her legs.

'I can't let you in,' she told him as she put her key in the front door. Pam Fletcher worked from home but the car was not there, so she must be out. The cat had the eagerness of an animal shut out for longer than he liked. Swiftly, he took advantage of Gill's fumbling with bags and keys and shot past her into the hall, to sit hopefully by his own front door. She would put him out when she came back down in a few minutes.

As she reached her flat on the first floor she realised he had followed her up and was coming in with her instead. The Fletchers had had this cat for about a year; he was young and slender, adopted as a kitten from the cat rescue home. He came into Gill's kitchen and sniffed around, delicate and cautious, then strolled into the living-room and sprang lightly onto the window sill, sitting down to take in a different view of the street.

'You're going back out very soon,' Gill said, closing the fridge door and coming to join him. He pushed his head up under her fingers and rose as she stroked him, arching against her hand. His fur was silky, electric, sparking a little against her dry skin. 'What do you see, eh?' she murmured, as they both gazed down at parked cars, dry leaves rustling along the gutters and a man on a bicycle, in helmet and lycra, pedalling fast, low over the handlebars. In a window of the flat opposite there was a vase of flowers, so pink and flourishing Gillian thought they must be artificial. In winter she was never in her flat in daylight during the week. Everything looked a little different, as if surprised to see her. Some sort of life went on without her, even in the empty flat.

'I could have a cat like you,' she said, 'if I worked at home.' Or a baby, her conscience whispered, or a baby. 'You know what,' she went on, still stroking the cat, rubbing him gently under his chin. 'I'm pregnant. What do you think of that? You're the only one in the world who knows.'

The cat jumped down and padded swiftly to the door, asking to be let out. 'You just came in to look at the view, didn't you?' Gillian said. 'Not to start any kind of relationship.'

When she came out of the bathroom he was still sitting there. Gillian put her jacket on again, and they both left. At the front door, Pam Fletcher was just coming in.

'I've had a visitor,' Gillian said.

'Oh, he's a pest. He wants to sleep inside all day just now.'

'He saw your car,' Gillian said, realising this, 'and he was off like a shot.'

As she walked to the surgery she was absurdly pleased about this. The cat had only wanted to leave because he saw Pam's car. You won't clipe, will you, she thought, the old childhood word coming back to her, you won't tell.

The doctor was a woman about her own age, but married with young children, brisk and pragmatic. She could be relied on to deal with problems in a sensible fashion, presenting her patients with the possible options and letting them choose. Why then, as she stared at garish magazines, surrounded by the really ill with their coughs and crutches, was Gillian so reluctant to tell Dr Andrews what was wrong this time?

'Hello there, how are you?'

'Fine.'

Why did doctors always ask you that before you'd even sat down? You were lying already, before the interview had begun.

'Well, I *feel* fine, but—'

Bridget Andrews gave Gillian her full attention. She's attractive, Gillian thought, in a way, though her clothes are so dowdy. I know I look a heap better. Yet there she is, with her good career and her husband and children, and here I am. In a mess.

'I've missed a period, nearly two now. I think I might be pregnant.'

The doctor turned to Gillian's notes, and began leafing through them. 'Didn't you have an IUD fitted?'

'I had it taken out again. I was bleeding a lot.'

'Right, I'd forgotten. You didn't go back on the pill?' She was still reading the notes.

'It was an accident,' Gillian blurted out. She felt like a schoolgirl, caught out. Perhaps the doctor would say, eyebrows raised, 'So you took no precautions at all?' But of course she did not. Instead, they talked symptoms, dates.

'Have you done a pregnancy test yourself?'

'Yesterday. It was positive.'

'I don't want to examine you internally – not a good idea at this early stage, but from what you say, it seems very likely. If you want to wait a couple of weeks, we can leave it and do a urine test here.'

'A couple of *weeks*?'

Dr Andrews went smoothly on, 'I gather you don't want to proceed with the pregnancy?'

'No. I don't know how I *could* in my circumstances.'

'You're not in a stable relationship?' She smiled gently. 'I'm sorry, but I do have to ask questions like this.'

'I know, I do know. Look, the relationship is over, I'm on my own. I have to think about the future. I could get a termination, couldn't I?'

'I should think so.'

They talked about dates again, explored the options and discussed procedures. Dr Andrews asked Gillian to leave a urine sample and said she would arrange an appointment for her to see a second doctor. Then as the interview came to an end Gillian felt suddenly desperate, more trapped than ever.

'I can still think about it?'

'Of course. You're committed to nothing yet,

nothing at all. Let's make sure you *are* pregnant first. Then it's very important that you do think about it, that you feel absolutely sure about what you want to do.'

Gillian nodded, submitting to this good advice from this other woman who had her two children – or was it three – and who did have a stable relationship. What did she really think of Gillian, with her carelessness and her failed relationship?

Out in the street, dark now and cold, Gillian turned up her collar and began to walk slowly home. She must talk to someone. She couldn't do all this thinking and deciding on her own. Not Steve, never him.

It was her women friends she needed, except that for months Steve had taken up her free time, or she had kept it free for him, and she hadn't recovered her old habits of friendship. Finding her unreliable, other people had drifted away. She could ring Carol tonight, why not? Or Ros, or Steph. She had heard Carol was heavily involved with a new man. Telling people, though, would make no difference. The truth remained, immovable.

A cold sleety rain had begun to fall, so that by the time she was indoors her hair and trousers were soaked and her hands frozen. She towelled her hair, changed out of office clothes and went to make herself coffee. As she filled the kettle, she said aloud, 'Gin – that's what I need. Gin and a hot bath.' There was no-one to share the joke, if that's what it was, so she began to cry instead. 'Stupid woman,' she muttered, 'get a bloody drink.'

So she did. While the coffee was brewing, she poured herself a large gin and went to check her answerphone for messages.

'Hi, Gill, it's Lynn – call me quick if you get in before six.'

Work. What was that about?

'Guess what?' Lynn's clear young voice was full of excitement. 'You know the environmental conference we did in the EICC last year? Remember those guys from the States that were from some sort of think tank in San Francisco? The fair one was neat – he fancied you.'

Gill laughed. 'Aye, right. What about them?'

'Well, they emailed Richie today, and they want us to do this thing in the States for them. Kind of international think-in. Lots of guys getting together and thinking great thoughts about the future, global warming, mankind's survival, stuff like that. We're going to do the international bit. And get this: they asked for *us*, for you and me. So how do you fancy San Francisco next Spring?'

'You're kidding.'

'More than a year away I know, but we'd need maybe two visits over there first, and some other trips too. They want us to liaise with Sweden and Australia as well. Apparently that's where guys who do all the, like, craziest thinking hang out.'

Gillian laughed. 'Wow. *Australia*.'

'Fantastic, eh? It's a big contract, Richie's chuffed

as hell. We're the golden girls, Gill. We impressed them.'

'We did, didn't we? Next Spring.'

'April.'

'That's amazing.'

'Are you Ok? You sound a bit subdued. Oh God, you were at the doc today, weren't you?'

Lynn was probably imagining terminal illness.

'I'm fine. Minor female problem. I'm thrilled, really. A bit stunned, that's all.'

'Worth a drink though. Celebration after work tomorrow?'

'Sure. Must go, I put something in the oven. Cheers, Lynn.'

Gillian reached for a chair, overtaken by such a wave of fatigue she was unable to stand. This was what it was then, what it meant: a woman's right to choose. She had to choose, choose now, between work, her future, *life*, and motherhood, someone else's life.

Successful career women had babies all the time and went on working. They even went on organising conferences in San Francisco, flying abroad and keeping up with people like Lynn, who was twenty seven and never seemed to sleep. But not me, she thought, not me. What kind of mother had a high powered career and put it first, her children second? Besides, she thought with the honesty of lonely thinking, I haven't the bloody energy.

Then there was Susan who took a man from his

two small sons and later left her own fourteen year old daughter. What kind of mother was that?

Frances was a single mother and she had managed. But she had no choice, and her children were anyway not babies when she moved back to Aberdeen and began teaching again. She had her parents for support till the boys were older and she moved to the Highlands. Her parents would have followed her there if she had let them, but Frances had coped on her own.

I'd have no-one here but some paid child-minder, Gillian thought. It would just be a long slog of doing everything by myself. She put her face in her hands, unable to bear this heroic and painful image of herself, full of pity for the imagined life she knew she could not face, and would dislike more than anything.

This could be your last chance, a demon voice reminded her, as she blew her nose and got up to go and make supper. *Your last chance to have a child*. Yeah, and wreck my life, and probably any chance of getting married. *Selfish cow*, the voice mocked, *selfish stupid cow*.

She made herself scrambled egg, invalid food, as though she needed special care, then ate two chocolate biscuits and made more coffee. She felt fat now, ugly and tear-stained. She hated herself in every possible way.

The smell of the coffee made her feel sick so she poured it away and lay down exhausted on the sofa, unable even to think. She would not call anyone. The charge of excitement Lynn's news had given her was dissipated in confusion and misery. Her hands crept over her belly. A collection of cells, that was all. Like a bit of jelly. No, it had to be this way. Her job, the flat, her future all depended on being free and childless. It was the moral choice, surely it was. If she could only think straight she would be able to prove that.

Something was sticking out from underneath the sofa, a piece of card. She felt with one hand, and pulled it out. It was the photograph she had kept aside, the studio portrait of herself with Susan and Frances. Frances at sixteen, Susan at twelve, herself at eight: the three Douglas girls. She sat up and put on the lamp beside the sofa, to look at it again. The three Douglas girls. Then she got up and went to call Frances. She would go to Dingwall, sleep in Jack's room and walk in the fresh air with her sister. That would clear her head.

Chez Louis was quiet, as it usually was on a Thursday night. Alec had anticipated when they opened that Thursdays would be busy with people coming in after late night shopping, but although they had a flurry in the Bistro section between five and seven, the main restaurant was never booked up. People went home tired after late night shopping, feeling they had spent enough money already. It was the Bistro which was keeping them going. Lunch-times and after work were the busy times, but the profit margins on the food they sold then – soup, sandwiches, baked potatoes – were low. The main restaurant did well at weekends, but not well enough.

He went to tell Graham, the chef, that he might as well go home. 'I'll cope with anybody coming in now. Not that there will be since it's nearly ten. We'll close up when Table 6 is cleared, eh?'

Graham was Alec's partner. In the first few months they had often sat down late at night with glasses of red wine and planned their future, working out menus and marketing, but these days they simply worked side by side, avoiding each other and avoiding debate.

In the empty restaurant, when the evening clear-up had been done, Alec went to lock up and switch on the burglar alarm. The cleaners would be in in the morning when the warm smells of garlic and spices, tomato and fresh coffee, had staled, and the window sills and pot plants were dusty in morning sunshine.

In the dark street it was raining again as he turned up his collar and made for the car. Behind the driving seat, he thought about going to Lizzie's place. Lizzie was the woman he was seeing, had in fact begun seeing before Susan left, though nothing had come of it then: it had been only a few drinks and friendly chats. Her easy nature attracted him.

He was tired and indigestion sent shooting pains through his gut. Better to go home, have a brandy, lie down.

The house was in a Victorian terrace in Gosforth with large square rooms, a patch of grass in front, and a small yard behind. From the outside it looked the same, but it had altered in some indefinable way since he had been living in it on his own. Everything was always exactly as he had left it, and it smelled of neglect.

This time, when he walked into the hall, there was a smell of burning. Not fire, nothing dangerous. It was the charcoal smell of burnt toast. He stood for a moment in darkness then headed for the kitchen and switched on the light. Under the glare of the fluorescent tube he saw a plate smeared with toast crumbs and a china mug with a ring of brown tea on the bottom.

'Kate?' he called, turning. 'Kate!'

He ran upstairs, switching on lights and throwing open all the doors. The house blazed, but it was empty. Here the smell of burnt toast had been replaced by something subtler and sweeter, a scent once as familiar as his own body. He went into Kate's room. The bedcovers were pulled straight, the debris of the life she had left behind untouched. Not Kate then, not Kate. He went into his own bedroom, his and Susan's. The bed was unmade, but he had left it like that. A shoe lay in the middle of the floor as if kicked aside but it was one of his own shoes.

The doors of the long fitted wardrobe were open. A few things had been pushed along the rail to the end. The rest was empty.

Alec sat on the bed, heart pounding, gazing at the empty spaces. He breathed hard, trying to keep calm. How had he left it this morning? He tried to remember the morning, but it would not come clear, it merged with all the other mornings of this week. Last night, then. He looked at the whisky bottle on the bedside cabinet, the empty glass. He remembered those, of course he did, they came to bed with him every night. He didn't get hangovers; that was why he had been able to drink heavily for so many years. Frances had been angry about it, as if it was a fault he should have corrected. Susan had been envious and resentful. But for years he had thought himself lucky, someone who could handle drink. There was nothing to make him feel remorse.

He hardly ever started drinking through the day, and never at work, but these last few years and especially lately, there was a vagueness about his mornings. He was not an alcoholic, nothing like it. He was coping all right, he got up and washed and shaved, maybe even had breakfast. It was just that he couldn't remember doing it.

The scent was still there. It was as if the wardrobe doors, left open, had released it. He got up and pulled the sliding doors across, their rumble and thud alarmingly loud. Steadying himself, he crossed to the dressing table. The top drawer on the left was open and he stood gazing down at the jewellers' boxes lying there higgledy-piggledy, as if they had been tumbled about in a rough search. Some were empty; others were missing.

Aloud, he said, 'You're all right, aren't you?' She was not in the Tyne after all, or down a mineshaft, or deep in a dark wood, buried under leaves and pine needles. 'Not you, Susie. You're not so far away.'

She did not answer. The house ached with emptiness, the not being here of Susan. He reached for the telephone then changed his mind and went downstairs to get a whisky since the bottle in the bedroom was empty. The griping pains in his stomach had begun again, worse this time.

He felt the burn of the whisky in his throat and stomach. He gulped it down and poured another. Around him, silence thickened like a reproach.

CHAPTER 3

They had tried the Ouija board, but after a while Roxanne said it was spooky so they stopped. The glass had been flying about like crazy, spelling out names they had never even heard of. Kate had definitely heard of Zebedee: she thought he was a character in a children's programme years ago, but Eilidh thought it was a name for the devil. They decided to try levitation instead.

'If it doesn't work we'll just put on the video, right?'

'Right.'

Through the five of them ran a delicious frisson of fear.

Roxanne was small and light so they decided to try with her.

'You won't drop me or nothing?' she begged. She lay on the coffee table, with one of a nest of tables at her feet, the second table and a pile of cushions at her head. The others surrounded her, two at her shoulders, two at her hips.

'Now,' Kate said, 'just put the tips of your fingers under her.'

Kate had done this before so she was the expert.

'Did it work?' Michelle kept asking her. 'Did the girl really, like, move?'

'She went up nearly a foot, I'm not kidding.'

'Wow.'

They each put both hands lightly under Roxanne, who giggled. 'You're tickling me.'

'Ssh.'

They became solemn, waiting.

'Do we like, push her or anything?' Amy whispered.

'No – *ssh*. Think about air, about lifting, think how light Roxanne's getting. Concentrate.'

Kate had become their leader. They were docile for all their hard shells, the smoking at school, the cheek they gave teachers, the vodka breezers at weekends. Kate could hardly believe how easy it had been to take the lead. She would rather have impressed a different crowd but that but got nowhere.

Inside the house, the room, all was still. Sounds from the early evening street – a child calling, a dog barking, a car moving off – faded and grew as faint as sounds echoing in another village, another world. The sun had gone down over the horizon of rooftops, the light almost gone at seven o'clock, and it seemed to grow darker in Roxanne's living-room. On the sideboard two coke cans trembled; inside the cocktail cabinet, bottles shivered, clinking faintly against each other. The electric fire hissed as if dust was being burned off.

Supported by forty fingers Roxanne became weightless and rose unsteadily by an inch, two inches, above the coffee table. She tilted slightly, rose again. Michelle shrieked, Amy yelled, she was down and they had all broken apart, hysterical. Roxanne scrabbled to her feet.

'It worked!'

'Oh my God, that was *so scary!*'

Kate sat back and smiled. 'I told you,' she said.

By the time they had talked it over twenty times, they were convinced Roxanne had risen a foot at least.

'I'm not doing it again,' she declared. 'What if I just kept going, and couldn't get down? Can you see me, eh, floating up at the ceiling—'

'Imagine your mother,' Amy said. 'She comes home, right, and she can't see you, so she shouts "Roxanne!" and your voice is, like, right above her?'

'Don't tell my Mam! She might tell my Granny, and my Granny goes to church. She'd go spare!'

'What's it got to do with the church?' Kate asked, mystified.

'It's against the teaching of the Bible, isn't that right?' Eilidh explained.

'It's spooky, anyhow,' Roxanne decided. 'I'm not doing it again.'

'Put the video on then.'

'Yeah, put the video on.'

It was a teenage horror film.

'I wish we'd got something else.'

'What time's your Mum home, Roxanne?'

'About midnight.'

Hours away. They watched quiz programmes on television instead, and cheered themselves up toasting marshmallows and drinking Coke, cosy together on the long sofa.

Later they revived, and with the television off went over again the success of Roxanne's mysterious rise into the air. They agreed it was weird, but—

'It doesn't mean nothing, really, does it?' Michelle consoled.

'My Mam's boyfriend comes back onshore tomorrow,' Roxanne said. 'I'm not telling him. He'd make a real fool of me.'

'Do you like him?'

'He's OK. He's younger than my Mam.'

'My Mum's going out with this guy I really hate,' Michelle sighed. 'I said to her, if he moves in, I'm moving out.'

'You wouldn't really.'

'I fucking would.'

Eilidh moved off the sofa and sat toasting her feet by the fire.

'What's the best and the worst things that have ever happened to you?' she asked.

Kate waited to hear what everyone else would say. After a moment, Amy began.

'The best was when we got Jasper.' She turned to Kate. 'That's our dog. He's a Labrador and he was this tiny black puppy with wobbly legs, really cute. You should've seen him.' She laughed. 'He wee-ed all over our kitchen floor, my Mam was mad, but he was so cute.' She paused, thinking. 'He's kinda fat now, he's quite old.'

As they told their stories Kate realised their best things were all childhood memories, Christmas and birthdays, theme park holidays, pets, surprises. They had happened in easier times. Now of them all, only Eilidh's parents still lived together.

'You haven't said *your* best thing,' they reminded Kate.

'Can't think.' She shrugged. 'There were loads of things when I was little. Holidays and that. We were always going on holiday.'

What could she tell them that did not seem, in the light of all their remembered joys, either pathetic or trivial? Her mother turning round and smiling when she had been afraid she was still in a black mood and saying, 'Kate, let's go to the sea.' They had gone to Amble, a long way in her mother's rickety car. They had seen Freddie the dolphin leaping and diving, following a boat in. Her mother had bought them fish and chips before they drove home and they had been happy all day. This would seem dull to them. How could they understand the lightness in your heart when your mother, for such a long time unhappy and strange, behaves like anyone else's mother?

'Nobody's said their *worst* thing, have they?' she countered.

'My Dad moving out,' Michelle said at once.

'That was OK for me,' Roxanne said. 'I was

expecting it anyway, when my Dad went to live in England. That's where he was born and he was always like, away, working there. The worst bit was when he was home, then they was always fighting.'

'My Dad hit my Mam once,' Michelle volunteered. 'Don't tell nobody, right?' She looked as if she wished she had not said it. 'It was years and years ago, I was just a little kid. I hid under my bed I was that scared.'

'Did he *hurt* her?' Amy asked. 'There's this women's refuge in Dingwall, for battered wives.'

'I wouldn't let any guy beat me up,' Eilidh announced. 'No way.'

'My Mam never either. He only done it once so you don't need to say it like that.' Michelle turned her back on Eilidh. 'She had a black eye, though,' she added, after a moment. 'She wouldn't go down the street for ages and I had to get the milk in and that. I had to go to the shop. I was only six.'

'Women can't help it, it's the man's fault,' Eilidh offered.

This sounded pretty bad to Kate, as bad as having your mother go crazy. Not that Susan was *crazy*, or not often. Still, she wasn't going to tell them. What was the worst thing that had happened to her? She could say *my mother's left me, disappeared. Nobody knows where she is*. Saying it would undo the other things she had told them about her mother, and she wanted to cling to those. Lies lead to more lies, that was the trouble with them.

160

The rough edge of her fear caught at her like a ragnail.

She realised the others were all talking about their mothers.

'The first time, right, my Mum brought her boyfriend here,' Roxanne was saying, 'the first time he stayed over. Don't tell nobody this, OK? I'm in bed, right, and the two of them, they're having a drink and watching telly, then they go to bed in her room, next to mine. I knew they were in there. And then they're doing it, right, I can hear them, what a bloody *racket*! So you know what I did? I bang on the wall, really hard, and I yell 'Shut up!' They went *totally* silent.'

They all collapsed, laughing helplessly.

'God, the *embarrassment* – what did they say when they saw you, did you see them in the morning?'

'I got up before them. I just went to school. When I come home he's out, and she goes, "Had a good day, what would you like for your tea?" Stuff like that, like, trying to get round me.'

'He move in after that?'

'Soon. He's not bothered now if I bang. He just bangs back. Du'n't care.'

'Oh my *God*.' Michelle raised her eyes to the ceiling. 'I hope my mother's not doing it with Carl. He's *gross*, my God. *Disgusting*.'

'They're old, I don't know why they want to do it anyway,' Eilidh said, ripping open a packet of crisps. 'Anybody want one?'

'I don't like pickled onion. Any salt and vinegar?'

'Really old people do it as well,' Michelle said. 'I seen this programme on telly about it. Like, I mean, *pensioners*. Gross.'

Kate sat back on the sofa, joining in the laughter, but uneasily. *What was the worst thing that could happen to you?*

'The worst thing ever,' Amy said as they gathered cosily again, 'was when I thought I'd – you know – caught on. I was late, I was in a right panic. But it was OK, I wasn't.'

'You thought you were *pregnant*?'

'Yeah, I did. I was in a *state*.'

'Who was it?'

'Was that when you were going out with Kieron?'

'Might have been.' Amy got up, smug.

Kate's heart was beating fast. *What was the worst thing that could happen to you?*

'We only done it the once,' Amy pointed out as she sprang open a can of coke. 'Would've been really bad luck, eh?'

'Remember that girl, Annabel, that left in the middle of fourth year, right before the exams? She was pregnant. I saw her in the High Street, she was huge. Then I think they moved away, I never saw her after that.' Michelle turned to face Kate. 'She came up from England, like you. She was posh as well.'

'I'm not posh!' Kate laughed, reddening.

'Posher'n'us at any rate,' Eilidh muttered.

'That's not difficult, eh?' Michelle shoved her,

162

laughing. Kate said nothing, keeping apart. But then, leaders were always apart.

She was much more at ease here though, than in Frances's house, trying to be whatever it was Aunt Frances expected: a grateful niece, a forlorn motherless girl, something like that, with Andrew ignoring her, muttering about 'watching herself'. None of his business who she went about with. It was cosy here, it felt safe, to bed down at midnight in Roxanne's room on quilts and sleeping bags, squashed together, talking half the night.

She woke at five, Eilidh's elbow poking into her side, Michelle's long hair spread over her arm, tickling. Across her feet Roxanne's mother's cat lolled, digging his claws in if she tried to move. Her mind was as clear as if in sleep all the rubbish had been washed away, and she had only one thought left.

She was late, that was all. She was always late. They hadn't even done it properly. He'd been so mad at her – *you've been leading me on, slag*. She shuddered every time she thought of him saying that, saw again the way he zipped up his trousers with difficulty over his swollen penis. Men were so ugly. Were they all like that, their balls hairy, the skin purplish?

It must be all right. It wasn't all right *then*, the way he never spoke to her afterwards, though he spoke *about* her all right. 'We could go to Scotland,' she had said to Alec. 'Go and see my real family. They don't hate *me*.'

Alec, surprised and pleased, said, 'yes, why not, why not for Christ's sake?' He had thought she was upset about Susan, but she had not had time to get upset about that yet. It was Dave Prentice who'd made her feel so terrible.

'I wouldn't let any guy beat me up!' Michelle had declared. But she did not know anything, none of them did, none of them had any idea how somebody else could make you feel like rubbish. *Cockteaser, fucking cockteaser, that's what she is.*

She had panicked, pushing him away, saying she didn't want to, please, not now, please stop. Her mother had said once 'Make the first time special.' It was the only advice she had ever given Kate on the subject. At the last minute, *during* the last minute, she had panicked, not wanting this to be her first time, Dave Prentice to be the first guy. At first he'd begged, *please please, just let me, please,* but when she eventually managed to shove him off, he got angry.

Afterwards, she told herself it had not *really* been her first time, in someone's mother's spare room, at a party with people being sick all over the place, a window smashed, some guy crazy on ecstasy, so that a neighbour seeing him in the garden had called an ambulance.

It couldn't have done any damage. She was just late, she was always late. She shut her eyes and tried to think of other things. What? *What's the best thing that's ever happened to you?*

Just last night Frances had said to her, as they

164

cleared away the supper dishes, 'I looked after you
when you were a baby, but you won't remember
that.'

Kate stopped, drying cloth in hand, surprised.
'What?'

'When you stayed with us, you and your mother.'

'Oh, yeah, so we did.' Kate flushed, thinking of
her mother's version of this story, which would
not be Frances's.

'Your mother was working and I was at home.
She got relief work at one of the hospitals in
Newcastle. We had two cats then. Mimi's one of
them, still going strong, and there was a black one,
Hector, but he died. They were still young and
playful when you arrived and you loved watching
them. You didn't speak, not a word, but one day
Mimi jumped up on the window sill in front of
you. You were on the floor with some toys, and
she leapt up waving her tail. You put your hands
up – right up, like this – and shouted 'Oossy!' For
pussy, you know.' Frances let her hands fall,
smiling. 'And you laughed,' she added. 'It was
lovely.'

Kate smiled back, embarrassed. 'I don't remember
that.'

'Oh well, you were only fifteen, sixteen months.'

'How long did we stay with you?'

'Nearly a year. Then, after your second birthday
. . . you left.' Frances looked straight at her. 'You
and your mother. And Alec.' Startled, Kate looked
back. She wasn't going to start about *that*, was

165

she? But Frances said only, 'Don't worry, it's so long ago I don't think about it now. It hurt at the time of course.'

'I was staying with you at Christmas?'

'Yes, for one Christmas.'

'You had a tree, didn't you, and lots of decorations?'

'We always did, when the boys were little. Now we just put up the tree.'

Kate thought hard until the half forgotten images rose again. 'Did you have a snowman made of sort of frilly paper, hanging up?'

'Yes, in the living-room doorway. He got torn, that snowman, I had to throw him out after a few years. He had a black top hat the way they do in picture books.'

'I remember,' Kate said.

Huddled in her sleeping bag, borrowed from Andrew and smelling cheesy, she closed her eyes and pictured herself lifted in someone's arms, reaching for the snowman and touching his paper stomach, so that he swayed a little. She had wanted to say something to Frances that would exonerate her mother, and she also wanted to show she remembered living there. Now it was as if Frances had opened a door that could easily stay ajar between them. She was trying hard, Kate admitted. Suppose her mother came back now. Would Frances speak to her? Kate could not imagine it, but neither could she imagine her aunt being spiteful and cold. She had thought there must be something bad about Frances for Alec to leave, for her mother to go with him, but there was not. She wasn't very easy to get to know but Kate wanted Frances to like her. How could that happen though, without betraying her mother?

A weight shifted in Kate's chest like a pain waiting to happen. She shivered, trying to turn on her side and get comfortable and sleepy again. Maybe the worst thing had not happened yet. You couldn't know the awful things lined up in the future, looming.

CHAPTER 4

'I thought I might come up for a couple of days.'
It was Alec, interrupting mealtime preparations as usual. Why was he not busy, for goodness sake, in a restaurant of all places?

'Could you leave it till Easter? I'm run off my feet just now.'

'Busy time for me, the holidays. No, I'd rather come this weekend, if possible.'

'I've got Gill this weekend.'

'I won't land on you – is there a good B&B in Dingwall?'

Ring the Tourist Information Centre, she wanted to retort, but did not. 'Well, I suppose if you're not staying here . . .'

'I need to see Kate.'

'Are you taking her home?'

He hesitated, which meant no. 'How is she?'

'Fine. So you're not taking her home?'

'If she's settled it would be best not to disrupt things. I thought I could reassure her.'

'About what, exactly?'

Alec was vague, slipping as usual from her grasp. This time, however, what she felt was relief that he was leaving Kate with them. He had taken her away before with no warning. The teenage Kate, lank and sulky, was nothing like the rosy cheerful infant Frances had looked after so long ago, but her presence had touched a wound she had thought healed over.

'It's a long time ago,' she had told Kate. 'I don't mind any more.'

She did mind. However little she allowed herself to think of it she still had a vivid memory of that dark February morning when Susan, instead of sleeping late as she usually did on her day off, got up at eight. Dressing Katy she said, 'I'm taking her to Aberdeen to see Mum and Dad. I've got three days off, then it's the weekend. I'm on nights next week, so it'll give us a good break.' She smiled at Frances. 'You too, eh?'

'A bit sudden isn't it? Katy's no bother,' Frances said. Hearing her name, Frances's voice, the child ran towards her. Only last week, they'd had a tea party for her second birthday with cakes and candles and three other toddlers, children of Frances's friends. Susan had been working so Frances had done it all. Andrew was home from nursery at lunch-time and Jack out of school at three o'clock, so they had joined in, raising the pitch of excitement much too high, the little ones shrieking in delight as the boys showed off, inventing dangerous games.

Susan packed up with remarkable thoroughness

169

for someone who had only just decided to go away. Perhaps she was actually thinking of moving back to Aberdeen, and this was the first step. It would be a relief if she did. Frances longed for her house, and her marriage, to be clear of Susan. She and Alec got on well, that was not the trouble. They liked the same television programmes and music and they both liked to drink. That was where the trouble lay. Too much money, and time, in Frances's view, was spent on drinking.

If Susan left, things would settle down and Alec would turn more of his attention to the boys again and to Frances herself. Had it not been for Katy, she would have asked Susan to leave months ago.

She watched Susan pack up with mixed feelings, but drove her willingly to the station, Katy wide awake and chatty in the child-seat.

'Just drop us off, no point in your waiting,' Susan said, as she got herself and Katy onto the pavement, She put up the buggy then hauled her bags out of the boot.

'I'll find a parking space, then come and give you a hand—'

'Don't bother. I'm fine.'

She headed off, laden but confident, the lone parent struggling bravely, through the station entrance. Frances watched her go, her bell of shoulder length hair brightly fair in contrast to her dark jacket, jeans and boots. Frances's heart jolted at the sight of the tiny figure in the push-chair, sitting still, overawed by the vastness and echoing sounds of the station concourse.

The last of Susan.

Not, as it had turned out, the last of Kate. This time, Frances did not intend to miss her so much when she went away.

Susan had not been going to Aberdeen and Alec had not gone to work. They had met and gone away together. Alec had almost nothing with him, so perhaps he had still been swithering. How had Susan persuaded him? Frances did not let herself speculate about that.

It had not been the last of Alec either. He came back to collect clothes and other belongings, and make financial arrangements for them all. It seemed he had the offer of a job with a branch of his company in Leeds. They would live in Leeds together and Susan would get a part-time job nursing.

'And Katy?' Frances asked, her voice trembling.

'We'll get a childminder.'

'A childminder!'

She almost said, *leave her with me*. Of course that was impossible. She was a single mother with no income of her own. She was going to have to survive, and make sure her boys did too. That was enough to cope with. Sometimes she wondered if Alec might have stayed if she had given him the slightest opportunity, if she had pleaded with him. But she had turned her back on him in disbelief and contempt. Later, she understood that she had been in a state of deep shock and in that state she had focused painfully on the loss of the child. Not her own miscarried baby, but Katy. She missed with a profound physical ache the weight and warmth of her in her arms, her presence in the house. With Susan and Alec at work, or as she now realised, in the pub together, Jack at school and Andrew at nursery, she had spent many hours of many days alone with Katy.

Eventually she came to terms with the loss, knowing she must. What choice had she? Lying awake one night next to Andrew who'd had a nightmare and was restlessly taking up most of the double bed, she reached this stark conclusion. Dry eyed, she waited for daylight. I won't cry any more, she decided. What was the point?

It was a pity her parents couldn't be so pragmatic. Her father's anger against Alec and Susan blazed as far as Northumberland and gave her no peace. In the end, she gave in to his demands and moved to Aberdeen, partly to reassure him she had survived, partly to make it easier to go back to work and become independent of Alec. It had been the right thing to do, even if she had not done it for the best reasons. In taking care of their grandsons, her parents had to keep silent about Susan at last. Frances sometimes thought as she accommodated her life to suit them, taking responsibility for the future on her own shoulders, her life would have been easier if she had been alone.

★   ★   ★

The coming weekend, with both Alec and Gillian in the house, filled Frances with gloom. There was parents' night to get through and two children in the school had been put on the 'at risk' register, so there was a meeting with Social Workers tomorrow. She had more on her mind than *family*, she thought, frustrated.

In the evening she spoke to her parents on the telephone. Still no-one had told them about Susan, but Frances felt this could not go on much longer. Her mother said, when she told her Gillian was coming for the weekend, 'That's nice she'll be there for Katy's birthday. You've still got her staying with you?'

'*Birthday?*'

'She's fifteen on Sunday.' Grace kept a birthday book; she was always on time with her cards and presents and attached more importance to this than either Frances or Gillian could bear, having other things on their minds.

'Sunday! Right, I'll have to get her something on Saturday, there's no time before then. But I'll have Gill and Alec on Saturday. What a nuisance. What do girls want at that age – clothes?'

'You've such a busy life,' her mother said reproachfully. 'It's very hard on you to be landed with Katy as well. What on earth is Susan thinking of? Don't say anything to your father but I thought I might try and speak to Susan. What do you think?'

Frances heard the pleading note in Grace's voice. She wanted Frances to give her blessing.

'It's up to you. It always has been. Nothing to do with me. Except—' She hesitated.

'Is Susan all right? There's *something*, I know that, what with Alec turning up out of the blue.'

'Maybe now's not the best time to try to speak to Susan.'

'Have they fallen out, is that it? I knew it wouldn't last, I'm surprised this hasn't happened before now.'

'Not fallen out, exactly. Susan's away from home.'

'Away where?'

Frances backed off, unable to have this conversation by telephone. 'She goes to this retreat for women, for meditation, that sort of thing.'

A pause, while Grace took this in. 'So she abandons her daughter to you again.'

Her mother had not forgotten; for a few seconds, thirteen years vanished. Frances's anger against Susan and Alec revived suddenly, a flame of pain burning as hard as ever.

'I don't know,' Grace went on. 'It seems a funny business. All we ever wanted, your Dad and me, was a quiet family life. It doesn't seem much to ask.'

All these years, her mother had probably felt like this: resentful and annoyed, as if she had been the one betrayed.

'We can talk about it when you and Dad come up at Easter, if you like,' Frances said, weary of it now, longing to put the phone down.

'I don't know that there's much to say. It's very hard on you, dear,' Grace said, her voice softening. 'I'll speak to your father. Are you sure you want us at Easter?'

'Of course I do.' What else could she say?

Grace had decided to change the subject. 'How about Jack? We never see him, but I suppose student life must occupy him full time.'

By the time this terrible conversation was over Frances, wrung out and hopeless, had forgotten Kate's birthday. Over the evening meal, she thought of it again.

'You're fifteen on Sunday, aren't you?'

Kate looked surprised. 'How did you know?'

'I just do.' I ought to, she thought, recalling suddenly a cake with two candles, a toddlers' party. 'I wondered if there was anything special you wanted to do. Go to the cinema or something? What sort of present would you like? Andrew always wants money.'

'I like presents too,' he said, grinning, 'if there's any on the go. Like a Ferrari or a Rolex watch, or maybe a round the world ticket?'

'You're hopeful,' Frances retorted, getting up to clear the dishes. 'No chance of any of those.'

'It's Ok,' Kate said. 'I don't want any of them.' She smiled and Frances, her heart turning over, thought, *how pretty she is sometimes*, and smiled back.

'So, any ideas?'

'Clothes?'

'Better give you money and you can choose your own.' Frances sighed. 'I'd take you up to town on Saturday myself but we're going to have visitors.'

'Who?' Andrew asked as he cut himself another chunk of cheese.

'Gill's coming, and Alec.'

'Nobody important then.' He sloped off with the cheese and a glass of milk, disappearing up to his bedroom and computer.

'Ignore him,' Frances said.

'I do,' Kate answered.

'Would you like anything else to eat?'

'No, I'm fine.'

'You haven't had much, are you all right? You look a bit peaky.'

'I'm tired, that's all.' Kate pushed some crumbs around the table, poking them into heaps with one finger. 'What's Alec coming for?'

'Just to see you.'

Kate looked up. 'Does he want me to go home?'

'It's probably better if you finish the term here. What do you think?'

'I don't mind. Probably.'

Frances got up and began to pack the dishwasher, closing it with a rattle of china. Kate went on sitting at the table. Then, remembering it was time for a programme she wanted to watch, she got up and headed for the living-room.

Frances stood alone in the kitchen. 'There you are, Susan,' she said aloud. 'Life goes on without you. Your husband runs his restaurant, your daughter goes to school and watches TV. So no need to hurry back, eh?'

She closed her eyes for a moment, reminding herself Susan was ill. *How ill was she thirteen years ago, when she took my husband and Katy and left?* Susan had been all right before that. Self centred, yes, careless, but lucid and sane – until she went off with Alec. Perhaps she had a conscience after all, and it drove her mad. For the first time, a quiver of pity encroached on all the other emotions Susan had aroused.

CHAPTER 5

Gill arrived by train late on Friday evening so Frances left Kenny at ten to go and meet her.

'What about our curry tomorrow night?' he asked as she put on her jacket.

'Oh help, I'd forgotten. Let's still do it. Gill can come with us and Alec can look after himself.'

'Alec?'

'Remember he's coming tomorrow as well, though just for one night, thank goodness. He's taking Kate out in the afternoon, so maybe he'll give her a meal. It's her birthday on Sunday. If Andrew's free, he can come out with us. You wouldn't mind, would you? He'd be aggrieved if he thought we were going for a curry without him.'

Kenny looked doubtful. 'Sounds to me as if you should be having a family party,' he said. 'Leave me out of it, eh? You all go for a meal for Kate's birthday instead.'

Frances was dismayed. 'Can't you come with us?'

He laughed. 'No thanks. Keep your family dramas to yourself. I have enough of my own.'

'What's happened?'

'I'm going to be a grandad again.'

'Not Nicky?'

'No, Neil and Anne again, so no surprises there.'

'That's lovely. There's no drama in that.'

'I suppose not.'

She pulled on her gloves. He looked downcast and she felt guilty. She did not give him enough attention. He demanded so little; that was the great attraction of Kenny. She kissed him. 'Poor you,' she said. 'Does it make you feel out of it, that's there's a step-grandfather on the doorstep?'

'Oh no, he's a nice enough chap, and a much better match for June than I was.'

'That's not the point.'

'I know.'

'I have to go or I'll be late for Gill's train. I'll ring you tomorrow. You know I'd rather spend the evening with you, don't you?'

'Do I?'

'Now stop it, you're getting despondent. Not like you.'

'I'll have another whisky when you've gone,' he warned her, teasing. 'Several.'

'Ach,' she said, going out, 'that's nothing new.'

Gill was unusually silent on the way home.

'You must be tired,' Frances said, 'with the journey on top of a full day's work.'

'I am.'

'You're not ill, are you?' Frances asked, sounding sharper than she meant to. Encouraged, Gillian was too open, telling you things you wished she would keep to herself.

'Just tired.'

They drove the rest of the way in silence, Frances's thoughts reverting to work problems. She should go into school tomorrow: there were things she had not had time to do in the week. As they climbed the hill to the house, Gillian said, 'How's Kate? I meant to ask.'

'Quite at home now. It's her birthday on Sunday.'

'How old is she? I can get her something tomorrow but I wish you'd said before.'

'I've only just found out myself. Guess who told me.'

'Mum.'

'She was asking about Susan.'

'Did you tell her?'

'I couldn't, somehow, on the phone. I just said Susan's away for a while, on Retreat. I could tell Mum didn't think much of that. We've got to tell her the truth soon. Kate might say something at Easter, then where would we be. The *thought* of it.'

'She'll say we've been deceiving them.'

'We have.'

They drew up at the house and got out, Gillian lifting her bag from the back seat. She stood for a moment looking up at the clear sky.

'You can never see the stars like this in the city. Lucky you.'

★　　★　　★

In the morning, Frances rose early, and leaving a note for whoever got up next, drove to school. She did two hours solid work and left feeling better. She shopped at Tesco on the way back, joining the long Saturday queues so that it was almost one by the time she got home. Andrew, hearing the car, came out shuffling his feet into trainers. 'Want a hand?'

Gillian was reading the local newspaper in the kitchen and drinking coffee.

'When's Kate coming back?' she asked, as Frances began to unpack groceries.

'Not sure. Her friend's mother is dropping her off sometime today.'

'When will Alec get here?'

'Early afternoon, probably.'

They were eating lunch when Kate rang.

'We slept in,' she moaned, 'and now Amy's Mum's gone to work. Can you come and get me?'

'What a bore,' Gillian said when Frances told her where she was going. 'Can't she catch a bus?'

'In about an hour and a half, maybe. This isn't Edinburgh.'

'It's hassle all the way with kids, isn't it?' Gillian asked, getting up to help Frances clear dishes. 'You have to keep running after them.'

'I'm a *great* asset,' Andrew protested, in mock indignation. 'Brought in hundreds of mega-heavy bags, didn't I?'

Kate, when Frances collected her, was white and lethargic.

'What time did you all get to sleep?'

'I dunno. About four.'

'No wonder you look tired.'

'We slept hours. I feel sick.'

'Oh dear, what did you eat last night?'

'Loads of popcorn. Then we had a Chinese.'

'You deserve to feel sick, in that case.'

Kate groaned. 'Drive more slowly,' she said. 'I feel terrible every time you go round a corner.'

'That will be nice for Alec. He said he was planning to take you out somewhere.'

'In the *car*?' Kate looked appalled.

'I think so.'

'Oh God, I'm going to bed, I don't care.' Kate sat upright, lips pressed together, keeping as still as possible.

Alec's long silver car sat outside the house.

'Any better?' Frances asked, as they went indoors.

'A bit,' Kate admitted.

'You can go and lie down in a minute, Alec won't mind. He can talk to you later.'

'Talk? What about?' Kate's white skin coloured suddenly. 'Is Mum—'

'Don't worry, nothing's happened. I think he just wants to spend some time with you.'

Alec got up from the sofa as they came in. Gillian had made him coffee.

'Hello, Kate, my lovely.' He made to embrace her, then seemed to change his mind and held back, smiling.

'Hi,' Kate said.

'She's not too well,' Frances told him. 'Late night, Chinese food.'

Andrew, behind her, muttered something and Kate said, 'Shut up you.' She slumped on the sofa. 'I feel *awful*.'

Frances nudged Andrew out of the room. 'Gill and I are going for a walk. We'll leave you in peace.' In the hall, as the living-room door closed behind them, she said to Andrew, 'What was that about?'

'What?'

'You know.'

'No, I don't.' He escaped upstairs.

Frances and Gillian walked up the hill past the farm. The air had the scent of early Spring, fresh and balmy, giving the illusion winter was over.

'Look, will I tell Mum and Dad?' Gillian offered. 'Tell them nobody knows where Susan is. You're right, somebody's got to do it. I could take the train down to Aberdeen tomorrow and spend Sunday night with them. They're always complaining I never go and see them.'

'Would you?'

'Easier for me than you, eh?'

'I know, but—'

'You don't have to be the one who does it all.'

Gratefully, Frances gave in, feeling she had been unfair to Gillian. 'That would be such a relief. And then we could discuss it at Easter if they wanted to, but it wouldn't be a shock any more.'

They stopped at the brow of the hill and looked

over the fields to Ben Wyvis beyond, still snow-capped.

'It's lovely here,' Gillian sighed. 'You're so lucky to live in a place like this.'

'You'd hate it. No shops, hardly any pubs.'

Gillian did not laugh, or answer. She seemed to lose all at once the energy that had taken her up the hill. 'Can we go back now? I'm so tired.'

'Has it been a hard week?' Frances could not understand what was tiring about Gillian's job. How could being in an office and going to meetings (which was what she imagined her sister did) compare with running a primary school? Gillian began telling her about the San Francisco contract.

'What an exciting life you lead.'

'I spend most of my time in hotels and conference centres, and they're all alike really. I'm looking forward to this, though.'

She seemed anxious rather than excited, Frances thought.

'Have you ever been sorry you had kids? Of course not, stupid question. If, say, you had your life to live over again, would you still have them? Children.'

Frances looked at her in astonishment. 'Of course.'

'You think it's worth it then, the expense and the worrying and all that?'

'What on earth has brought this on? I think every time you come here you imagine the life you might have had with Michael if you'd married him. Odd,

184

when that's been over for years. I've noticed that every time there's a change in your working life, even if it takes a turn for the better, you can't quite believe in it. You start wondering if maybe you'd have been happier if you'd made a different choice. You're frightened you missed something.' Frances found her voice rising. 'We all have these alternative lives but you can't waste time fretting about them.'

They had almost reached the house again.

'I know that,' Gillian said, her voice cold, as she went indoors. Frances followed with a sigh. Despite her good intentions, she had failed again to be sympathetic.

Alec was on his own in the living-room, standing by the window looking into the garden. Andrew had gone to the Ross County game; very faintly, sounds of cheering floated up from the town.

'Where's Kate?'

'She's gone to lie down.'

'Is she OK?'

'Hung over.'

'Oh surely not. All she did was spend the night with some other girls her own age . . .' Frances flushed: she should have recognised that.

'Never mind, she seems OK.'

'I'll have to speak to her.'

'Might be better not.'

This was what had been wrong before, Frances was sure. She felt a fool, and was angry with him, as if he and not Kate were the cause. Before she could argue the point he said,

'I need to have a word with you.'

'What is it?'

'Can we sit down?'

Gillian had come in. 'What's wrong?'

'You'd better hear this too,' Alec said. The women waited, but he did not seem able to begin. He sat looking down at his hands, twisting his long fingers together. 'Susan's been home.'

Frances and Gillian exclaimed aloud, cries of surprise. He put up his hands as if fending them off.

'I haven't seen her.'

'Then what—'

'A couple of weeks ago when I came home from the restaurant, I discovered there had been someone in the house.'

'How did you know it was Susan?' Stupid question, Gillian thought, as soon as she asked it, but Alec did not seem to think so.

'The wardrobe's nearly empty.'

'She took clothes?' Frances asked. 'Was anything else missing?'

'Jewellery. Not all of it. Quite a valuable pendant is still there. She had something to eat as well. There were dishes used.'

'You do know it was her?' Frances persisted.

'It was Susan. I could smell her scent all through the house.'

Gillian shivered. 'Did she leave a message?'

'I didn't find one.'

They were silent, trying to imagine Susan hauling clothes from the wardrobe, piling them into—

'Did she take suitcases?' Gillian asked. 'What did she put the clothes in, do you think?'

'I've no idea. We keep the big suitcases in the loft. I never checked. My own bag was in the cupboard as usual. I've got it with me.' He frowned. 'I don't think she'd gone into the loft. She always had trouble putting the Ramsay ladder away so she wouldn't have gone up there.'

'Someone could have helped her,' Gillian suggested.

'A lover, you're thinking.' He gave a wry smile. 'That's obviously what the police believe.'

'But you don't?'

'No'.

That's cocky of him, Frances thought. If she'd steal one lover, why not another? No, not fair to think like that. Susan was ill. Or maybe not. It was harder to believe in Susan's illness now. To come back for clothes and jewellery, but not all of it, not anything you disliked, looked calculating. Then she stayed to eat. A sense of unreality crept over Susan's sisters. Somewhere else she wore her usual clothes, clasped on her watch and bracelets, slept, ate, made plans. They looked at Alec, knotting his fingers.

'Have you told Kate all this?'

'It's what I came for. 'I thought it might reassure her to know her mother had been home.'

'What did she say?' Frances rose, wanting to go to Kate.

Alec bit his lip. 'I didn't do it. I couldn't, somehow.'

Frances let out a breath of relief. 'I think you were quite right.' She moved to the window, too restless to sit down again. 'Quite right,' she told the garden, where birds were singing and sunshine lay across the grass.

'Don't you think she's got a right to know?' Gillian asked.

'Think about it,' Frances said, turning towards them. 'Her mother comes home but makes no attempt to contact her. Takes her clothes, but doesn't leave a message. How would that make *you* feel, at Kate's age?'

Gillian was not sure. She had no knowledge of teenage girls; they were a mystery to her, as children were. I am a childless woman, she wanted to say, what would I know?

'Oh well,' she sighed. 'I'm sure you're right.'

We'll all go out together tonight, Frances thought in the silence that followed. I can see Kenny after they've gone. If we close in like this and care for each other, Susan will still be outside, excluded, but it won't matter any more. She chose that, after all.

CHAPTER 6

Alec treated them to a take-away meal from the Indian restaurant in Dingwall. A festive meal out, even when it was Kate's birthday next day, did not seem quite the thing.

Kate slept till six, then came down bleary-eyed but perfectly well. She had a shower and re-emerged in full make-up dressed as if for a night out, as Alec returned with two brown carrier bags and a smell of curry spices.

Andrew ate hugely, then went out, collected by a friend in a car. Kate picked at naan bread, dipping it in the sauces, and ate a little rice. She said she was going to a party and didn't want to feel full up. To her dismay, Gillian became queasy after a few mouthfuls and had to stop eating.

Frances stopped Kate in the hall as she was leaving. 'You'll never get down the lane in those shoes.'

'I'm not wearing trainers with *these* trousers,' Kate retorted as she pulled on a denim jacket.

'You'd better wear a coat or something.'

'I'm not cold.'

'Can I give you a lift into Dingwall? Where are you going?'

'I don't know yet, we're meeting at the Royal. Maybe Eilidh's house.'

'How will I know?' Frances asked, exasperated. Alec should be dealing with this.

'I'll ring you later if you like.'

Frances had no confidence in this, or that Kate would even answer her mobile. 'Give me the number for Eilidh's house too, so I know I can contact you. Are you staying over?'

'I might.' Reluctantly, she produced the number.

'Come on, I'll run you down to the Royal. You're going to catch your death in that wee jacket.'

'You won't get out of the car?'

'Get *out*?'

Kate looked embarrassed. 'Nothing.'

Frances recognised this: mothers, responsible adults, had to keep a low profile, and preferably out of sight altogether.

On the way back from town she turned along the Strathpeffer road towards Kenny's cottage. As she walked up the path she could hear tentative notes from his guitar.

'Hi there.' He was by the fire. 'Having a wee practice. Geordie Sinclair gave me this tune the other day.'

Frances sat down in the chair opposite his, petting

the dog and easing off her coat. She leaned back and listened while he went through the tune again.

'That's nice,' she said. 'Does it have words?'

'Not yet.' He smiled at her. 'How was the curry? I can smell it from here.'

She laughed. 'Sorry about that. It does cling a bit. I've just been giving Kate a lift to meet her friends and somehow couldn't face going home yet. I've left Gill with Alec.'

'Give her a ring.'

'Och, I'm not staying.' She sighed. 'Some hostess, eh? Desperate to escape.'

He played a few chords then put his hand flat against the strings, killing the sound. 'What would you like to hear?'

'Play the same one again – I liked it.'

She lay back in the chair and closed her eyes, thinking of nothing.

'Not quite there yet,' he said, putting down the guitar. 'Needs a bit of practice. Go on, give Gill a ring and tell her you've come to me in my hour of need. Then we can go to bed.'

Frances sat up and began to put her coat on again. 'Sorry, duty calls.'

He saw her to the door and kissed her. 'See you soon,' he said and went back to his music.

By eleven Kate had still not called. Alec said, getting up, 'Better head for my B & B.'

'*You* should speak to Kate,' Frances suggested. 'Ring her mobile.'

'She'll be fine, they don't like to be checked up on all the time.'

'I don't care whether she likes it or not,' Frances snapped. 'She's barely fifteen – we need to know where she is.'

Alec shrugged this off. 'You do it. She'll take it from you.'

'What do you mean?'

'She's a bit in awe of you.'

Frances flushed. 'Nonsense.'

At the door, Gillian came out to join them. 'Will we see you tomorrow?' she asked Alec. 'Or are you just heading back down the road?'

'I'll call in for a coffee, if that's all right. Say happy birthday to Kate.'

Frances watched the silver car moving down the lane, then went to telephone Kate herself. *Your call cannot be taken at present . . .* It cut out, not allowing Frances to leave a message. She glanced at the hall clock. 'I'll try Eilidh's number. I hope it's not too late.'

'Mother hen,' Gillian said, amused. 'You won't be happy till you've tracked her down.'

'I'm not sure why I'm bothering. She's not my responsibility.'

'Ha.' Gillian shook her head. 'Right.' She waited while Frances dialled, but it was a long time before anyone answered. It was Eilidh's father perhaps, a man at any rate, who had no idea where Eilidh was, let alone Kate.

'I think they've gone to some party. Sorry – can't help.'

Frances turned to Gillian in dismay. 'She said she was going to Eilidh's *house*.'

'I can see it's a bit nerve-wracking, first the mother disappears, then – no, of course not, it can't be that. Sorry.'

'For goodness sake, Gill, I don't think for a minute that she's vanished! How utterly ridiculous. She's young, she's female, and she's going about with these *girls*. I don't even know their families. That man sounded drunk to me. Even Andrew doesn't think much of the company she's keeping, so naturally I'm concerned. Alec brought her here so that we could keep an eye on her.'

'My God, he's got a cheek, eh? She's fifteen, she skives off school, she gets in trouble, and he's expecting you to deal with it.'

'That's what being a mother teaches you. How to worry.'

To her astonishment, Gillian's eyes filled with tears. She put her hand up to her face, turning away. Frances followed her into the living-room.

'What on earth's wrong?' What now, she was thinking, as if I haven't enough on my plate. Guiltily, she perched on the arm of the sofa where Gillian had collapsed, and touched her shoulder. 'What is it?'

Her sister looked up, tearful and pale, and for a few bewildering seconds, Frances saw Kate, then Susan, and was giddy.

'I'm pregnant.'

This was not what Frances had expected. She tried to take it in. 'Are you sure?'

'It was Steve – our farewell shot. So stupid of me. You get so you don't care, but I know I've been really, really stupid. Serves me right. What a *fool.*'

Frances, who was thinking all these things, did not say them. She hugged Gillian who began to weep again, turning her face towards her sister, leaning on her. At first, Frances could not make out what she was saying.

Gillian looked up, tear stained and crumpled. 'I just don't know what to do for the best.'

'Of course you don't. How far—'

'Not so far. I saw the doctor last week.' Frances handed her a box of tissues and Gillian blew her nose, bracing herself. 'I haven't told anyone else. Just the doctor, and the cat downstairs. Cat doesn't count, I suppose.'

'What about Steve?'

'What would be the point in telling *him*?'

'It's his child too.'

'It's not a *child!*' Gillian exclaimed. 'Don't *say* that. It's nothing, a bunch of cells. Not a *person* or anything.' Frances was silent. Gillian scrubbed her face with another tissue, wiping tears away. 'How do you think I *feel*?' she asked.

'Trapped,' Frances said.

She thought of what Gillian had told her that morning about her job, and then of all the times Gillian had called or come to see her, full of angst about her latest unsatisfactory relationship with some man who wanted too much of her, or did not want her enough. Suddenly a terrible weight was pressing on her heart. She wanted to say *don't do it, have the baby, you'll be so glad that you did.* What good would it do, offering her opinion? Gillian must decide for herself. Not my responsibility, Frances thought, truly not, this dilemma, this baby. Yet she could not leave Gillian to make up her mind unguided. If she did nothing how would she feel later, how quieten her own conscience?

'Oh dear, what a thing to happen.'

Gillian seemed calm now, resigned. 'I suppose I'll get through it somehow. In ten years' time, it won't seem so terrible.'

At once Frances saw a ten year old child, androgynous, shadowy, slipping from them. 'Yes it will,' she said. 'That's why you have to be absolutely sure you're doing the right thing.'

'Oh thanks.' Gillian got up and moved away. 'Thanks a lot – for filling me up with guilt before I've even done anything.'

'I believe women have the right to choose, just as much as you.' Frances sighed. 'I think I'll try Kate's mobile again. Pour yourself a drink if you want. Pour me one too. We could both do with it.'

It was going to be a long anxious night. Frances could not reach Kate and could not do anything for Gillian except let her talk and try not to say anything to influence her one way or another.

'The thing is,' Gillian explained, what seemed like hours later, the fire dying, the third drink finished. 'I wouldn't even want Steve's kid. He's a loser, I see that now. If I was choosing a father for my child I'd want someone with more moral fibre. Wouldn't I?'

Surely it was too late to think of such a thing? Some other baby hovered in Gillian's mythical future, carefully sperm matched, perfect, superbaby. All Frances's feeling, as she finished her whisky, warm with it now, caring much less what she said, was for this baby, which was being given no chance at all. She had given up on Kate, who must be at someone else's house, perhaps Eilidh's by now. It was foolish to fret, at least until morning.

Eventually they went to bed and the whisky sent Frances to sleep quite quickly. At five she woke and got up to check Kate's room. It was empty. After that, she could not sleep again and lay waiting for birdsong and for the bright morning light behind the curtains.

Alec appeared just after ten.

'Kate's not here,' Frances told him, 'and Andrew and Gill are still in bed.'

'Where is she?'

'Some friend's house, I think. I've been trying to call her but the mobile seems to be switched off. I can't even leave a message.'

He made light of it: 'She'll be fine. Like I said, they don't want you to keep tabs on them.'

'I'll make coffee,'

They sat in the kitchen in uneasy silence, like two acquaintances who have long since run out of polite conversation but are forced to remain together. The tabby cat prowled, then leapt onto Frances's lap.

'Mimi's lasted well.'

'She's a bit stiff these days.' Frances stroked down the cat's smooth back, feeling the tremor of purring beneath her hand.

'I knew it was her. I've been meaning to say since Christmas.'

'Hec died.'

'I know, Andrew told me.'

'Did he?'

'At Christmas I asked if this was Mimi, and he said Hec got a kidney infection.'

'That's right.'

The clock ticked, the cat purred, Alec cleared his throat. They waited.

'Maybe I should head down the road. I'll leave Kate's present with you.'

'I think you should see her first.'

'I'd like to, but—'

'I'll ring her again. I could try Eilidh's number but it's so embarrassing, having to say I don't know where she is.'

In the hall, she heard a car coming up the lane and went out to look. It turned a little way below the house in a passing place and stopped to let Kate get out. She came slowly up to the house in clothes which were different from the ones she had been wearing the previous night.

'Where have you *been*?'

'What?' Kate looked blank. 'Eilidh's. I *said*.'

'No you haven't. I spoke to someone at Eilidh's house last night – her father? He said you were all out at a party, he didn't know where, and he wasn't expecting any of you to come back there.'

'That was Gary. Her Mum's cousin.' Kate heaved an exaggerated sigh. '*He* wouldn't know. We went back there after the party. I *said* I wasn't sure where—'

Years of teaching had given Frances an instinct for lying. 'I don't think so, Kate,' she interrupted. 'Tell me where you were.'

'I said.' But she would not meet Frances's eyes.

'I cannot see the point in giving me your mobile phone number if you switch it off, and if you lie to me anyway about what's going on.'

'It's a bit funny, sometimes it doesn't work properly.'

'Rubbish, of course it works, you're forever using the thing.'

'Don't believe me then. I don't care. It's not *my* fault you couldn't get through.'

She was like Alec: slippery, out of reach. For the first time in years Frances lost her temper.

'You lied to me. You're *still* lying. That's not going to happen in this house, let me tell you. As long as you're here your welfare is my responsibility. Now, where have you been all night?'

Kate, unable to get into the house without pushing past her aunt, formidable in the doorway, scuffed one foot to and fro on the ground and would not look up.

'Ok, we stayed at Darren's house. So what? That's where the party was, loads of people stayed over, so we thought we would as well, save gettin' a taxi. I thought you'd go crazy if I said I was stayin' at a boy's house, you're so old-fashioned and Andrew doesn't like Darren. Anyway, what does it *matter*? I'm fifteen, I can do what I like.'

'You most certainly can not!'

'Oh shut up, you're not my mother, are you? I never wanted to stay in your stupid house anyway.'

Now she did push past, voice cracking. Frances gave way and Kate ran through the hall and upstairs. Her bedroom door banged behind her.

Frances leaned against the doorpost, shaking. At the same moment, Alec came into the hall and Gillian appeared at the top of the stairs.

'My God,' she said, 'what was that all about?' She made a face, raising her eyes heavenwards, but neither of the others even glanced at her. Instead, they faced each other, speechless.

CHAPTER 7

Alec had gone. Andrew was in the shower, the sound of his radio loud enough to travel to the kitchen, where Gillian and Frances sat at the table. Kate was still in her room.

'Did she speak to Alec? He was with her quite a while.'

'I didn't ask.' Frances said. 'I shouldn't have lost the rag with her, but I was so angry.'

'Like you said – she's not your responsibility.'

'She's under my roof.'

'You were worrying about *her*, not about fulfilling your duty.'

Frances thought about this. 'You're right,' she admitted. I was in a panic in case some awful thing had happened. Not because I'd have to tell Alec, but because I care about her.'

'She's fine though.'

'Boys are so different. I call myself a feminist, but if I'd had daughters, I think I might have treated them differently.'

'Like we were treated? Made to come in at certain times, never trusted out with boys? Look what it did to us. You're a single parent, I'm pregnant and man-less, and as for Susan—' She shrugged. 'Great success our parents made of bringing us up.'

'We can't blame them for everything that's happened since.'

'You're the one who's so keen on parents taking responsibility,' Gillian pointed out.

Frances had had enough. 'How are you this morning, anyway?' she asked. 'You seem better.'

'I'm fine. All this with Kate has made me think. If I did have a child, I'd be well over fifty by the time it was Kate's age. I couldn't cope with teenage trantrums then. When are they grown up, so you can stop looking after them, and getting in a state when something goes wrong?'

'Never,' Frances said. 'Look at what Susan's done to Mum and Dad. It's changed their lives. Dad wasn't always so irritable and Mum's become so diffident, no, *indifferent*, as if nothing much matters any more.'

'Bloody Susan,' Gillian agreed.

'I'm going up to see how Kate is.'

'Do you still want me to have a word with Mum and Dad about Susan's vanishing trick?'

'Oh Gill, you *said* you would.'

'Just checking. I'll go and phone now, and tell them I'll be there by tea-time.'

Upstairs, Frances tapped on Kate's door. When there was no answer she opened it and looked in. Kate had fallen asleep in her borrowed clothes, head flung back, mouth open, in the heavy sleep of the young. Frances stepped back and closed the door.

At lunch-time Kate came into the kitchen flushed and rumpled, her hair awry.

'Are you still mad at me?'

'I'm sorry I shouted at you. I was worried.'

'About me?'

'Of course about you, you silly girl.' She pulled out a chair. 'Sit down.'

'I need a shower, I absolutely stink.' Kate pulled at her cotton top, sniffing and screwing up her face.

'In a minute.'

Reluctantly, Kate sat down and Frances did too.

'You do understand why I got so angry?'

'I suppose so. You didn't know where I was.' She looked up, meeting Frances's eyes. 'I wasn't doing anything.'

'I don't mind where you stay, I just want to be able to reach you if I have to. I need to know you're all right.'

'Sorry.'

'Go and have your shower.' As Kate reached the door, she called her back. 'One other thing?'

'What?'

'Happy Birthday.'

'Doesn't feel much like a birthday.'

'Did Alec give you his present?'

'Money.'

'That's what I've got for you, but I did buy a

202

wee thing as well. Have your shower first though.'

Kate shuffled off and dragged herself upstairs.

Gillian had thought about this, Frances could tell. Her parcel was large and squashy, and turned out to be a black feather boa. Frances, eclipsed, wished she had asked Christine, who would have known what girls of fifteen like. Kate liked the boa.

'Cool!' she gasped, winding it round her neck. Gillian beamed, smug and pleased, though all she had done was buy something she fancied for herself. Frances, shopping at the last minute, between the Post Office and the butcher, had bought a silver chain with tiny glass beads threaded on it. Now she was afraid that perhaps it was too old, too young, not Kate's style.

'Oh!' Kate breathed, her face lighting up in surprise as she opened the little package. 'It's really nice.'

'Is it somebody's birthday?' Andrew asked when he came in and saw the cards and strewn wrapping paper.

'I did tell you – Kate's fifteen.'

'Is there a cake?'

Gillian left them after lunch, left them to tea and cake and a drowsy Sunday afternoon. She left Dingwall in sunshine but the sky was overcast by Nairn, and in Aberdeen a squally shower rushed at her as she came out of the station, looking for her father's car.

They were pleased to see her, while pointing out that she did not come often enough.

'I'm here now. Sorry about the short notice.'

'This is still your *home*, dear.'

It was not. Upstairs in her old bedroom, she looked at the familiar surroundings, upgraded from childhood to adulthood when she became fourteen, as if her taste as a teenager need not be considered because it would not last. She had never liked the peacock blue of the carpet or the fussy swirls on the wallpaper and would rather the nursery print had been kept, and the lampshade with teddies dancing round it. Downstairs, the house closed in on her with its familiar heavy furniture, groups of china figures, and pot plants lush even in February on the broad window sills. Already, she longed to be gone.

In the kitchen she helped her mother get out the tea things.

'I hope you had a proper dinner with Frances, did you? We just have a sandwich on Sunday night. Will I cook you something – an omelette?'

'No, don't bother.'

'No *bother*,' her mother reproved. 'The question is, have you eaten properly?'

Had she? Gillian could not remember. 'A sandwich would do.' She held up a flowered cup. 'You've had these a long time.'

'Twenty five years and only one cup gone, so be careful.'

Gillian carried shortbread and sponge cake to the living-room. The smell of baking was still fragrant throughout the house.

'How is Frances's friend?' Grace asked, when they were settled and she was pouring tea. 'Did you see him?'

For a moment Gillian had no idea who her mother meant. 'Oh – Kenny? No, not this time.'

'He seems very nice. Not that we *know* him, but last summer he called round with some logs for Frances, to dry out for the winter.' Grace sighed. 'It doesn't look as if it's going to come to anything though.'

'Frances will never marry again,' Jim said with conviction. 'I've told you that often enough but you never believe me.'

'She might,' Gillian said, defensive of Grace who looked crestfallen. She did not add not to Kenny, he drinks too much.

'What about yourself?' her father demanded, snapping a piece of shortbread in his strong fingers. 'Have some cake or a bit of this stuff. Your mother's been baking all afternoon.'

'Any boyfriends just now, your father means,' Grace said smiling, holding a plate of cake out to Gillian.

'I'm too busy at work even to think about it,' Gillian said, annoyed, and refusing cake to punish her father. As the only person who minded was Grace, she felt guilty and ate a piece of shortbread instead. 'I might be going to San Francisco later in the year,' she announced. She told them about the new contract.

'Sounds very exciting,' her mother said, glancing at Jim, who remained impassive. He did not believe in Gillian's career, and pretended not to understand what she did.

'Where's it leading, that's what I wonder,' he had said to Grace, sometimes in Gillian's hearing. Now he said, 'and what will you end up *being*, after all this travelling about?'

Grace patted her knee. 'Be sure to send us postcards from all these far flung places.'

Having done their duty, they turned to their own news: church and neighbours, the Rotary Club, a friend in hospital with cancer. There was always some friend or relative who had become ill since the last visit, sometimes several, Gillian noticed, depressed.

They did not ask about Susan. '*I'll* tell them,' she had said to Frances, full of misplaced confidence, believing she was not really part of the old quarrel. They were all part of it: it enveloped them like the furniture, the brocade curtains, the family photographs crowding the top of the sideboard.

'Time for the news,' her father announced, switching on the television. Gillian gave up for the moment, relieved. Later, perhaps even in the morning before they drove her to the station, she would tell them. She would find a way.

Frances drove over to see Kenny as she usually did on Sunday evenings. It was the time Andrew got round to homework, as she reminded him before she left.

'Yeah, yeah, in a minute.'

'Kate, what about you?'

'Haven't got any.'

'I'll see you about ten.'

'Where are you going?' Kate asked, surprised.

'Her boyfriend's,' Andrew said. 'It's Ok – he's harmless. We can trust her to come back and look after us.' Realising what he had said, he flushed. 'You know what I mean. Goin to do some maths.'

He made a face as he passed Frances in the doorway, and a cut-throat gesture by way of apology. She shook her head, half smiling.

'Tact isn't one of his strong points,' she said to Kate. 'Sorry.'

'I'm not bothered.'

'Will you be all right if I go out?'

'Why wouldn't I be? Have a nice time. I'm just goin to sit in front of the TV, and you don't like the stuff I watch anyway.' As Frances went out, she added, 'Thanks.'

'What for?'

'My birthday – the cake and everything. It was nice.'

Frances sat in the car for a moment until the

glow of pleasure and relief subsided. 'Get a grip,' she scolded herself. 'She's only here for a few weeks, all you have to do is get along, make sure she doesn't get in any trouble. Nothing more.'

When she told him about the row with Kate, the apology, the birthday, Kenny said 'Sounds pretty normal to me. Nicky was a real pain at that age.'

'Well,' Frances admitted, '*she* seems to have turned out all right, even though you and June had such a messy divorce, so maybe Kate will survive too.'

'Nothing from Susan?'

'Something and nothing.' She told him Alec's story.

'She's playing a game,' was Kenny's conclusion. 'Playing a game with all of you.'

'A game? Maybe. But with Kate? That would be unforgivable. Isn't it more likely she's got some kind of mental illness? And if that's the case, we ought to try to help her.'

'Beloved Frances,' Kenny said, opening his arms so that she would lean against his chest, 'come here and give me a cuddle. That's better. Don't you think you have enough responsibilities already? Give Susan up. She never did much for you.'

'It's Kate I'm worried about.'

'As if I didn't know. She's not your worry either, when it comes down to it.' Before she could answer he kissed her, putting a stop to argument. Frances pulled away after a moment.

'I'll have to go soon.'

'Not yet.'

'Soon.'

In the background, a Beethoven sonata murmured with the ache of some other sadness.

'What melancholy music.'

'Will I put on something more cheerful?'

'No, it's all right. Suits the mood.' She nestled close again. In front of them, stretched out by the fire, the dog grunted and twitched in his sleep.

'Look at him,' Kenny said. 'Getting old, like me. Don't leave me Frances, stay and be a comfort to me in my dotage.'

She laughed. 'You've got a bottle for comfort. Don't think I haven't noticed it's a different one tonight.'

'Ach, you're a hard woman. I might give up the drink if I had you to look after me.'

'I've more than enough folk to look after without adding you to the list. As you keep reminding me.' She sat up and pushed the pins into her hair more firmly.

'What is it?' he asked, watching her. 'Are you frightened of getting too fond of her?'

He had put his finger on the sore spot of course. She moved away and sat up straighter on the sofa.

'I'll miss her when she goes. I don't want to feel any more than that.' She shrugged. 'You have to protect yourself in my situation.'

'And have you managed that? It seems to me that you love Kate.' He put his large hand over her entwined ones, clasped tightly together between her knees.

'Yes,' she said, 'I do.'

Gillian watched television with her parents all evening. They wanted to see the second part of a thriller they had watched the previous Sunday, then there was the news again, which was exactly the same as the news they had watched at teatime. Gillian dozed in the big arm chair. She was wakened by her father asking her again what time her train was next day. She had thought at first of catching an afternoon one but found herself saying she had to get back early. She still had not told them about Susan.

'What about a cup of tea?' her mother asked.

'I wouldn't mind a drink.' Gillian longed suddenly for Chablis, dry and clean in the mouth. To her surprise her father brightened at the idea, and brought out his whisky and sherry decanters.

Now, Gillian thought, when they had their drinks and Grace her hot milk. Now or never.

'I wanted to tell you something,' she said. 'Frances and I thought you should know.'

They turned to her expectantly, though her mother stifled a yawn, and Gillian could see she hoped whatever it was would not take very long.

'It's about Susan.'

There were nights when Frances would have liked to take Kenny home with her, to sleep sheltered by his comfortable bulk. She supposed that when Andrew had left home it might happen sometimes, but that still seemed a long way off. Besides, by this time on Sunday night she had started thinking about work again, her mind on school and the problems of the week ahead.

She was later than usual coming in and Andrew and Kate were in bed. She spent some time sorting out her bag for school and was setting it down in the hall when the telephone rang. As late as this, it made her heart leap.

'Fran? It's Gill. I'm in bed at Mum's – on my mobile, so I won't disturb them.'

'Have you told them?'

'Sort of.'

'*Sort of?*'

'I said she'd gone away, like you did, on a retreat, then I said she doesn't want to be in touch.'

'They knew that much already.'

'I decided if I told them the whole truth they'd start thinking she'd been murdered or something and kick up a fuss. I thought if I hinted she was off her trolley it would be even worse. You know what they're like about things like that – there's this big stigma about mental illness.'

'So what *do* they think has happened? That she's on a sort of extended holiday?' Frances's voice rose.

'They got hold of the wrong end of the stick altogether. They seemed quite pleased. As if they thought good, this time she's come to her senses, she's getting herself sorted out.'

'*Gill!*'

'You've no idea how impossible it was. How dead it is here, I feel stifled, I can't wait to leave. And now I feel incredibly guilty, and sorry for Mum. He's so bad tempered, honestly, he never considers her feelings, just bangs on and on with his own point of view, never thinking good of anyone. It might have been different if I'd got Mum on her own.'

'So, I assume you didn't tell them about yourself.'

'What?'

'The baby.'

'Stop calling it a baby!'

'Sorry, you didn't tell them about the collection of cells. The accident.' As soon as she spoke, Frances wished she had said nothing. 'Gill?'

But the connection, abruptly, had been severed.

CHAPTER 8

Easter came early, at the beginning of the school holidays. This meant that as well as coping with the busy end of term, Frances had to make up beds and shop and cook for the holiday when her parents would arrive. Jack came home, giving her another hungry person to cater for. He went round the supermarket with her, pushing the trolley and throwing in whatever caught his fancy while she studied the shelves and cabinets, wondering what to have for lunch on Easter Sunday.

She was much too busy to worry about Gillian, yet she did. Counting weeks, Frances realised that if Gillian was going to have an abortion she must have done it by now, or she was leaving it very late. She had not asked, hoping Gillian had changed her mind, not wanting to know if she had not.

'I am really sorry,' she said, calling her sister immediately after Gillian was home from Aberdeen. 'I'm over sensitive about this sort of thing. But I shouldn't have said what I did. I'm sorry.'

'Forget it, I've got to sort this one out on my own, it's not your problem.'

Since then they had spoken only once, about their parents, Kate, work, but not about Gillian herself. This made a change but left a strange gap, and Frances was afraid to ask the question which might fill that gap. Then, with one day of term to go, when she was thinking only about the Infants Easter Parade clearing her desk, Gillian called.

'Can I come up for Easter?' she asked. 'I'll bed down on the floor, I don't mind.'

'Yes,' Frances said, without considering where everyone was to sleep. 'If you're coming by train, remember they'll be crowded.'

'Don't worry, I've booked first class, treating myself. Train gets in just after three tomorrow.'

She was very sure of her welcome. 'I'll get Jack to meet you, Frances said. 'How have you been?'

'I'm Ok. I just want a rest.'

'I can't promise that – not with the boys around and Mum and Dad—'

'Och, you know what I mean.'

'We'll have time to talk, at least.'

'Nothing to talk about now.'

So Frances had her answer. The weight of this loss, that was not her loss, swelled. How heavy such sadness was, dragging everything down with it. 'Take care then,' she said, feeling helpless. 'See you soon.'

In the night Frances dreamed of the baby that was not to be called a baby, the little collection of cells formed to no purpose and now dispersed. In the dream it was not Gillian but Frances herself

214

who was pregnant, and the sister she walked with, talking of whether the baby would be born or not, was Susan. This was a young Susan with shoulder length hair and that light quick way of talking so that you had to listen hard to make out the words. Only her sisters heard everything Susan said, attuned to her from childhood.

Frances did not recognise the garden she was walking in: it was sunny, with flowers shoulder high in deep borders on either side of a narrow path, blooming scarlet, pink and white. She knew it though, knew she was at home there. Some great worry had been lifted: she had decided to keep the baby. Susan was saying yes, it was the right thing to do, it was what *she* had done. Frances woke with a start, wondering where Susan's baby was, not realising it was Kate.

Gillian was awake at five and got up at six, not liking the company of her own thoughts and wanting the day to begin. It would be long: she had a lot of work to clear before she could leave for the weekend. The best way to avoid thinking was to work hard and be with other people, Gillian believed, so she had been working long hours recently. Unlike Frances, she did not dream of babies, or that she was still pregnant.

Just before she left work on Thursday, Richie, who with his partner Rose owned the company, came in to tell Lynn and Gillian that it looked as if the San Francisco contract might fall through.

'There's a problem,' he said. 'One of the major sponsors has pulled out.'

He stayed for a while, perched on the corner of Lynn's desk, explaining the downturn in the US economy, the sponsor's share price falling . . . Neither Lynn nor Gillian was really listening. They tended to listen only to the first five minutes of anything Richie said. After that they drifted off as he digressed and expanded. He was content to have a debate with himself as long as there was an audience.

This time, looking at each other, they raised eyebrows and made despairing faces. No San Francisco, Lynn's expression said, and Gillian's too, though what *she* was thinking was – *I'm free, I'm qualified and experienced* – *I can do anything I like.* When Richie finally drifted back to his own office, Lynn exclaimed,

'Sod that. What's really going on do you think?'

Gillian shrugged. 'Don't know and don't care. At the moment.'

'You coming for a drink?'

'I've got to pack up. Going north tomorrow.'

'Are you Ok? It's a bummer about San Francisco.'

'I'm fine. I didn't really expect it to come off.' Gillian realised as she said it, that this was true.

'You've seemed a bit spaced lately.'

'Tired, that's all.'

They switched off computers, photo-copier and lights, and went out. In his office beside the reception area, Richie was on the telephone leaning back in his chair, long legs stretched out, waving his free hand in the air. 'Yeah,' he was saying. 'You're so right. Absolutely.' Rosie was out, but then she usually was.

Alec was working long hours too. The English schools had broken up a week earlier and the Bistro was full of teenagers during the day, gathering to show each other the clothes and music they had bought, and to spend tiny amounts of money, from Alec's point of view, on cokes and coffees. He saw Kate in the leggy girls and missed her, feeling guilty. He should go and see her, he should bring her home. What was home, now? The silent house gathering dust, the empty wine bottles, the stale smell in the kitchen he could not track down?

He felt disillusioned not just by the dreariness of his home life but by work too. He and Graham bickered, disagreeing about changes of menu, buying equipment and where and whether to advertise. They got nowhere, abandoning discussions in mid-air because they had no will to follow them through. The idea began to creep into both their minds that they needed to get away from each other, and thus of course, from their partnership. Graham was temperamental, like all chefs, Alec thought, but that was not the problem. The problem, as he saw it, was that he was weary of living like this, and of fretting about profit margins or the lack of them. With no Susan to make him long to get to work and be a success *somewhere*, the restaurant became as much a prison as his marriage had been.

There was Lizzie, of course, who was still warm and accommodating, most of the time. Lizzie had worked in the business herself so she never reproached him for working over the weekend. What she objected to was the secrecy of their meetings. Susan had been gone for three months and yet she was not gone. He was not free and never would be, as far as Lizzie could see. After a while a woman wants a little more than bed, she told Alec, kindly enough. She wants to tell her friends, show off her fella, say *this is my partner*, take him to the staff get-togethers on a Friday night. She wants to wear the necklace he's given her and tell everybody where she got it.

'I can't do anything about it,' Alec said. 'I'm married, don't forget.' And Lizzie, raising her beautifully made-up eyes to Heaven, assured him she had not forgotten.

Alec, in limbo, drifted.

The train north was packed, as Frances had predicted. Even in first class Gillian felt crowded. She was surrounded by early season American tourists who ate steadily throughout the journey: sandwiches, bananas, oranges, chocolate. The air was pungent. Just as well I'm not still pregnant, Gillian thought, I'd be throwing up all over the place. She had a window seat and turned resolutely towards the landscape. Through Drumochter Pass there was snow on the fields and trees beside the railway track; elsewhere it kept to the high ground. One or two deer watched from an unafraid distance, Gillian on her way to Inverness.

What she felt was relief. Relief was what had overtaken her when she got home from the clinic. The whole experience had been utterly humiliating, and made her angry. It was unfair; men did not have to endure such indignity for their mistakes. They stood back and got away with it, or worse, did not even know they'd been set free. She had a twinge of longing now and then to tell Steve. Why shouldn't he have at least an attack of conscience, why shouldn't he feel terrible too? He would *never* have to pay for sex like that. An inch long, but so much to go through to get rid of it.

Gillian's face grew hot, remembering. She closed her eyes, shutting out snow-capped pine trees, thick alongside the line, so many they darkened the view. When she looked again, the landscape had opened out and she was gazing along a broad cleft between hills, a river winding through it, glinting like metal as the sun appeared, while on either side the hills were black and bare, scattered with scraps of snow.

The Americans discussed Fort William, Ben Nevis, Loch Ness, the familiar names sounding foreign in their unaccustomed accents. How exotic Scotland is, Gillian thought, how beautiful. Tears welled again, sentimental and foolish, because that was how she was just now. The least thing could set her off. She hoped the farm at Finnerty would not have started lambing yet, since she could not bear to look at lambs. But she was not full of regrets; she was not sorry. This was just her hormones playing up. She had done the right thing.

The car boot was full of food. Jack carried the bags into the house and Frances began unpacking.

'I can remember when everything was closed on Good Friday,' Frances said.

'Was it?' he asked. 'Why was that?'

Frances looked at him in despair. 'Because of the *day*. Good Friday.' He looked blank. 'Didn't you get any religious education at school?'

'Hinduism. Festivals. That sort of stuff.'

Frances's conscience pricked her sometimes about church and Sunday School: when she went back to full-time work she could not spare her precious Sunday mornings any more, and all that part of life lapsed for her and the boys. 'Good Friday is the day Christ was crucified. What you might call a day of great significance in the Christian calendar.'

'Where do you want me to put the rest of these vegetables? The basket's full.'

Frances gave up religious instruction. 'Och . . . just dump the bag in the porch for now. I'll sort it out later.'

'Who's coming?'

'Granny and Grandpa and Gillian.'

'*He's* not coming then.'

'No.'

'Thought he might come and get Kate.'

'It's not that long since his last visit.'

'Is she staying here for good?'

'Certainly not.' She amended this. 'Maybe for a while yet.'

'So she's going back to the Academy after the holidays?'

'Probably. Don't go *on* about it.'

He backed off. 'Sorry. *I* don't mind, I'm not even here.'

Frances had begun washing fruit at the sink. She paused and raised her hands from the cold water. 'Has Andrew said something?'

'What about?'

'Kate, of course. He seems to get on all right with her but you can't really tell. Is there something I don't know?'

'Like what?'

'Jack, pay attention. Has Andrew said anything to you about wanting Kate to go home?'

Jack busied himself with tins of cat food which he had taken out to the porch to stack on shelves. He came back and leaned on the doorjamb, digging his hands in the pockets of his baggy jeans.

'One or two people have been winding him up. Because she's his cousin.'

'*Why?*'

'She's hanging out with a desperate crowd, right?'

221

Frances's heart thudded. Not this, she could do without this. Kate was to be safe here. 'She's not in trouble? Is she skipping school like she did in Newcastle?'

'Not as far as I know. Andy's never said.'

'What then? How do you mean, *desperate*? The girls she goes around with aren't really our sort, I know that, but they seem harmless enough.'

'Mum, they're brain *dead*.'

Boys were callous; she should be used to it. She remembered Andrew and Jack laughing uproariously because one of their friends had a poisoned toe, and someone trod on it at school.

'You're no help,' she said. 'Is there something to be worried about or not? Drugs, drink, that sort of stuff.'

He shrugged. 'You'd better ask Andy.'

'I will.'

Driving slowly and causing considerable annoyance to other road users, Jim concentrated on the A96, acknowledging the soft murmur of his wife's voice with an occasional grunt. His own comments were all on other drivers. 'Bloody idiot! Did you see that, overtaking there? Absolute menace. And what's that maniac up to? Is he coming out of there or not? For God's sake, *bicycles*! Shouldn't be allowed on main roads.'

Sometimes Grace agreed with him; sometimes she went on talking about completely different things. He wasn't really listening but neither was she.

'Cup of coffee at Baxters?' he suggested, veering into the centre of the road well before the white lines indicating the right turn, and braking. A van coming towards them seemed to rock slightly, then it was past. 'Hogging the middle of the road – can't abide that.' Jim turned into Baxter's car park and stopped in a Disabled Parking space, to which, as a perfectly able-bodied pensioner, he considered himself entitled. As he switched off the engine, Grace let out a breath of relief. Jim got so upset these days, driving, but he refused to take the train.

'Put Frances out,' he objected. 'Coming all that way into Inverness to meet us. Working girl. And there's the plants you've brought her. Where would we put all of those on the train?'

They queued for coffee and scones. It was late in the morning, and there was already a meaty smell of game soup.

'We could have some lunch,' Grace suggested.

'Frances has soup and sandwiches for us,' he insisted.

She sighed, giving up. The journey seemed to take longer these days, and they had been late getting away.

'Wonder if that racket's still going on,' Jim said, as they stopped at an empty table.

Grace took their cups and plates off the tray, gave them a napkin each, and sat down with an *ouf* of weariness. 'Och, I'm sure these other people were just visiting. They'll be gone by the time we get home.'

'Should have asked Barbara to look in, keep an eye on the place.'

'Oh, I don't think . . .' She struggled with the lid of her tiny pot of jam. 'These things, they're so stiff nowadays.'

Jim leaned over and took it from her. With his strong old man's hands, faintly bruised and bluish on the backs, he twisted the lid till it opened with a pop.

'Here.'

They spread scones in silence, thinking about their house, left shut up but unguarded. Something upsetting had happened just as they were putting their bags in the car.

'Coffee's bitter,' Grace sighed, adding more milk. Very upsetting. She was trying not to think about it.

They lived in a quiet cul de sac. Behind the back gardens were playing fields, noisy only with the shouts of teachers calling children to order, and Saturday football and hockey matches. It was innocent, healthy noise; Jim approved of it. Sometimes he stood at the end of the garden with the shears or a rake in his hands, gardening forgotten, watching the teams of pupils running about the field, giving a shout of 'well done!' or 'bad luck!' now and again.

There were no wild parties or late-night car doors slamming; no rock music blared from open windows. If an occasional Coke can appeared in the gutter or a crisp packet in someone's hedge, it was always removed and put into a dustbin. Most of the house-owners were retired people like themselves; their neighbours were childless teachers on one side, and on the other was a widower with a small subdued dog, as overweight and elderly as himself. The house beyond Mr Thompson's had lain empty for almost a year after Miss Gibson's death. There was a story about probate, a dispute between her nieces. Then a couple of weeks ago a girl had been seen wheeling a push chair up the path and letting herself in with a key. Mr Thompson, going in at his own gate with the dog, nodded politely but she did not appear to see him. A little later, a van drew up and some boxes were unloaded, and a cot.

The girl and her baby had moved in. No-one knew Miss Gibson's nieces, but she had been eighty-five, and this girl was much too young to be one of them. The neighbours speculated with pleasurable curiosity. Then, as Jim heaved their suitcase onto the back seat of the car, and Grace put the pots of cuttings she was taking to Frances into the boot, a car roared along the street and screeched to a halt in front of Miss Gibson's house. It throbbed with bass rhythm. The music stopped abruptly and two young men got out, followed by two girls. They went straight into the house, the girls calling 'Hiya! Debbie!' Music erupted again, from the house this time.

'What the devil's that?' Jim looked about him, enraged.

When they left about ten minutes later the music was still going on, and two more cars had joined the first. There were now around a dozen young people in the house. Jim drove off in a fury. Grace had restrained him with difficulty from banging on Miss Gibson's door, and indeed ringing the police. 'We're going away,' she said. 'It'll all be over by the time we get back.'

'Doors all locked?' he demanded. 'Windows secured?'

'You checked them twice yourself.'

They drove on, negotiating the heavy traffic on the road north out of Aberdeen.

'I'll tell you what I think,' Jim declared. 'That young woman's one of those unmarried mothers.' Grace looked out of the window, not answering, but he went on. 'No shame. Parties and all the rest of it. How can a lassie her age afford a house like that?'

'She could be one of the niece's daughters,' Grace said, seeing that she must answer eventually. 'That's what I think. She could easily *have* a husband – working offshore maybe. There's plenty young women on their own while their husbands are away on oil rigs.' But Jim only grunted. She tried to turn the subject. 'It'll be nice to see Kate again.' She knew it was a mistake as soon as the words were out.

'What's Susan up to? Tell me that. There's more to this than they're admitting.'

'Who?'

'Frances and Gillian. About that fellow. Why on earth would she go off and leave her daughter with *him?*'

'Alec's her step-father, she's grown up with him. She's at Frances's house now, anyway, at least he had the sense to take her there.'

'One rotten apple,' he said, 'that's all it takes.'
'*What?*'

He backed off. 'The other two never caused us a moment's trouble. Not Frances, at any rate, and Gillian's a good girl. All she needs is a husband to steady her. We did too much for Susan. Look at that girl in Myrtle Gibson's house. Who's paying her rent I'd like to know.'

Even now he could not get over how Susan had let him down, but his anger had nowhere to go except inward, to fester. He had loved her too much and she hadn't deserved it.

They were at Huntly before the atmosphere in the car eased. As the miles went by he vented his anger on other motorists instead. Now, in the pine-tabled restaurant, full of Easter holiday families, Grace wished they could talk of something else, anything else. She kept seeing those young people crowding into the house. She thought of the girl, thin in a tiny skirt and denim jacket, bumping the push-chair up the steps to the front door, the baby, peaky in a blue bonnet, looking out with a bleak, unhopeful expression at the world.

'We didn't do too much,' she said suddenly. He looked at her, puzzled.

227

'What?'

'I think we should have been kinder,' Grace went on. 'Then she might have stayed with us, instead of going to Frances and Alec and all that terrible trouble might never have happened.'

She had gone over and over it, as if by thinking and worrying she could find the first wrong turning. Then she could say *that*, that, was the cause. But what good would it do, to find out? They could not change anything now.

She sighed and pushed away her plate, the scone barely touched.

'Right?' Jim asked, getting to his feet. 'Are we off again?'

Soon they would be in Frances's comfortable house, with their two remaining daughters, their beloved grandsons and Kate, all the family they had now. Grace took heart, and prayed for a quiet road with no tractors.

CHAPTER 9

Kate liked Jack being at home. It took the heat off her, somehow. Andrew stopped needling her and even Frances seemed to chill out a bit. Jack was different from Andrew: he had these mad ideas and you never knew if he was serious or kidding. Mostly kidding, she thought.

'You never lift a finger, either of you,' Frances complained on the Thursday before Easter, as both boys began to slip away before they could be asked to clear up after the evening meal.

'We do,' they chorused, and Kate laughed. Frances smiled at her and for a moment they were in those secret societies: women, men.

'What do you want us to do?' Jack asked, but Andrew hovered near the door, still hoping to escape.

'I shouldn't have to tell you.'

'Go on, give us a clue.' Grinning, Jack picked up a saucepan and gently nudged his mother away from the sink. 'The trouble with you, Mum, is you think there's something morally admirable about work.'

'Well, there is. It's necessary, anyway.'

'Yeah, but it's not necessary for everybody to do it. Look at unemployment: even when it's high, the world keeps going. There's this kind of disapproval of unemployed people, as if they're not doing their bit.'

'They're not.'

He rolled up his sleeves and began to tackle the saucepan. Andrew, seeing his chance, slipped out. Kate wiped over the table half-heartedly, sweeping crumbs onto the floor, listening to Jack.

'Theirs is a useful contribution. They make all the workers feel virtuous. They're probably necessary to the wellbeing of society.'

'The trouble is,' Frances said, struggling to get a few last plates into the dish-washer, 'some people always leave the hard work to others.'

As she straightened up and clicked the door shut, she realised Andrew had gone and Kate was sitting at the table with a dishcloth in one hand and a blank, tight expression on her face.

'Well, that's up to the others, isn't it?' Jack countered as he tipped water down the sink.

Frances didn't bother answering this. 'Are you sure you're all right?' she asked Kate.

'I feel a bit sick. I always feel when I've had something to eat.'

'How long has this gone on? If you will stuff yourself with crisps and snacks at odd hours—'

'I don't eat anything like that now. I don't feel

like eating. Everything tastes weird.' She got up. 'Can I go?'

'Maybe we should make a doctor's appointment for you after Easter. There must be some reason you feel sick.' Frances stopped, aware of Jack.

Kate went out, and soon they could hear a familiar theme tune from the television.

'Don't worry, Mum,' Jack said. 'She's not your problem.'

'Oh, I think she is now.'

'See what I mean? Some people just look for work.'

'Unlike your brother.'

In the living-room, Kate lay on the sofa watching a tense scene between a girl who was expecting her mother's lover's child, and the mother, who had only just found out. The girl's father came in and they all began shouting at each other. Kate switched channels. It wasn't fair, all her usual soaps were spoiled. They had too many mother-daughter scenes. The mothers were all there of course, none of them had legged it, but she couldn't stand to watch any more.

The queasy feeling had faded. She began to think about food, and what she might like to eat. Nothing sweet. Maybe something sort of salty like crisps. No, that wouldn't do either. You'd think with all this giving up chocolate and crisps her skin would be perfect but it wasn't, it broke out all the time and it took ages to cover up the blemishes in the morning before she set out for school. Maybe make-up was aggravating it, she had read that in Frances's *Good Housekeeping*. You had to let your skin breathe, it said.

Her skin breathe! She couldn't breathe properly herself, it was like being squeezed, stifled. She sat at her school desk, making grooves with a sharp pencil in the soft wood, the teachers' words floating over her head. What was she doing there?

'You Ok?' Michelle had asked as they walked down the High Street after the last day at school. Michelle offered her a stick of spearmint gum, but Kate felt her stomach heave just looking at it. 'You're really pale.'

'I feel sick and I've got cramps, I'll be better when I come on. You know.'

'I get all bloated the week before,' Michelle confided, unwrapping more gum. Kate drew away from the blast of spearmint. 'My belly's like, absolutely huge and hard, you wouldn't believe. Mam says drink more water, she's crazy, how could that help?'

'I'm not bloated,' Kate said, feeling her stomach.

Now she lay back on the sofa with her hands on her stomach again. That crampy pain was back, and still no show of blood. Her stomach did seem to be sticking out a bit tonight. She'd just had tea though, that was why.

Wasn't it?

A wave of heat swept through her, erupting in sweat. Every inch of her prickled, fiery, beneath

232

the hair on the back of her neck, between her breasts, under her arms, her thighs, behind her knees. She pressed hard on her stomach, hands damp on the synthetic fabric of her trousers.

'What you watching?' Andrew asked, coming in. 'Can I change the channel?'

Kate got up without a word and left the room. Andrew reached for the remote control.

'You look very well,' Frances said, stacking Gillian's case in the car boot.

Gillian opened the passenger door. 'Oh good.' She smiled, very bright, in case this was some kind of accusation. How else would she look? She hadn't been ill, for God's sake.

'I'm really glad you're here,' Frances said as she drove out of the station car park. It was late afternoon, dry but windy with slaty clouds chasing across the sky.

'When are Mum and Dad coming?'

'Tomorrow. They're driving up in the morning and staying until Tuesday.'

'Are we going to – you know – tackle them about Susan again?'

'*You* can,' Frances said. 'I need all my energy to cook meals and keep everybody entertained.' She sighed. 'Let's not even think about Susan for three days.'

They were out of the city now and crossing the Kessock Bridge onto the Black Isle. Weary with travelling, Gillian was both restless and fatigued.

233

She shifted about in her seat, talked about work, then lapsed into silence.

As Frances negotiated the Tore roundabout and headed up the Dingwall Road, something moved on the back seat behind them – a file from school, probably – but the faint slither sent a ripple of shock through both women, and for a few seconds, speechless, they believed there was someone else in the car. Gillian even half turned her head.

'I've got school stuff in the back,' Frances said.

'Just for a moment I thought—'

Frances gave a puff of laughter. 'Me too.'

'Spooky.'

Silence again: the empty road, the fleeting clouds. Then as the car crested the hill and they began the descent towards the shining water of the Cromarty Firth and the nestled town, its lights winking at them, Gillian said,

'I wonder where she is.'

Frances did not answer at once. When she did, her voice was harder than she intended.

'It seems very odd that we don't speak about her for years, then as soon as she goes off, we can't *stop* talking about her.'

'She seems more *present*. I don't know why.'

'It's having Kate around.'

'Kate reminds you of her?'

'Not really, but Kate being here makes me resent Susan all over again. All those terrible feelings have resurfaced.' Frances's hands tightened on the steering wheel. She had not realised she felt so strongly.

'It's no wonder I suppose. Kate, and then Alec always turning up. It must be awful.'

Frances slowed the car for the Maryburgh roundabout, her driving as steady as ever. 'It's not that. I'm afraid Susan—' Again she hesitated, but not because of the change of gear, the corner smoothly turned as the car sailed calmly along the last mile.

'D'you think something really awful has happened to her? Are you afraid she'll *never* come back?'

'I'm afraid she *will*. I keep thinking one day she'll just turn up out of the blue.'

Frances had never been so frank, or so hostile.

'Even after all this time, you couldn't stand to see her?'

'You don't understand, do you?'

'What?'

'I'm afraid she'll take Kate away. Again.'

Gillian leaned back in her seat. Over her swept the mystery she was never going to fathom now, that she had allowed to be cleared out of her body. Gone, the knowledge and understanding and fear Frances had held within her all those years and which she seemed able now to extend to a sullen girl she barely knew. Motherhood, its smugness and wholeness, and its terrible risk.

Frances extended the dining table to its full length. They would eat family meals here at the weekend, leaving the kitchen clear. At half past seven on Easter Saturday it was still light enough to look out into the garden where a few crocuses had begun to open, clumps of purple and yellow, brave against the cold. Under the apple trees, bunches of snowdrops quivered in a chill wind.

Spoiled by his grandparents, who treated no-one else with such indulgence, Jack made it all easy at first, and there was an almost festive air throughout the house. Everyone but Kate drank wine with the meal on Saturday night, which Gillian was thankful for, and Frances hoped would mellow the atmosphere. Kate did not eat much and said she did not like wine. 'Alec's always drinking red wine, I can't stand the smell,' she told her grandmother.

Grace nodded, approving. 'I just have the one glass myself. White.' She sipped and made a face, smiling at Kate. 'I like it a bit sweeter, but I know I'm out of date.'

Jack caught his mother's eye and winked. Andrew was explaining to his grandfather why he was taking four Highers instead of the five Jack had. Nothing, he thought, hating his brother for a moment, was ever good enough if Jack hadn't done it. It was really himself he disliked, for not measuring up. His grandfather was flushed: he liked red wine, and had had a few glasses. His beaky face, with its strong nose and eyebrows, was set in frowning lines. And yet Frances knew he was enjoying himslef, pronouncing on the boys' future careers, advising, laying down his opinions hard as paving slabs.

She and Gillian flew back and forth with plates of food, opened more wine, stoked the fire, made coffee, stacked dishes, and in the sudden gaps of silence which from time to time froze the whole tableful into a tableau of strangers, found new and innocuous subjects of conversation. Frances knew that by Tuesday morning when she waved her parents away, she would be exhausted. Gillian, leaning on the work surface in the kitchen, waiting for the kettle to boil, was suddenly pale and wilting.

'Help,' she said, 'family life. Thank God it doesn't happen too often.'

'It's not as if we're a big family,' Frances said. 'I don't know why it's such hard work.'

'It's the missing people who make it hard,' Gillian realised. Startled, Frances paused in the middle of setting out coffee cups.

'What?'

'That's where the risk is. The danger. If we were just any old family, there wouldn't be anyone missing. Well, not in the way Alec and Susan are. They'd be here, joining in. Or they'd be somewhere else having Easter with friends . . . or whatever. Do you see what I mean?'

'I think so.' Frances took coffee-making over from Gillian, who was ignoring the boiling kettle. 'But other families must have black sheep. Secrets.'

'I keep thinking Kate's bound to say something

about her mother. Like, *I wish I knew where she was.*'

'Kate hardly mentions her now.'

Gillian picked up the tray of cups and saucers. 'She looks a bit peaky. Spotty. I suppose it's just teenage hormones.'

'Her hormones definitely haven't settled – but that's common in teenage girls.' She followed Gillian out of the kitchen. 'I don't believe she's had a period all the time she's been here.' Gillian opened her mouth to say something, then thought better of it.

Grace was telling Kate about the girl with the baby who had moved into their street. Frances and Gillian had of course heard the whole story already, heard their father's views on the thought-lessness of young people and discussed where the lass got the money to live there. All this had been gone over before Kate and the boys joined them, and Frances had hoped it was set aside for now.

'You feel sorry for her, in a way,' Grace said, cutting a small piece of cheese and balancing it on a cracker. 'Managing a wee one all by herself.'

My God, Gillian thought, does she not remember Frances did it with *two* of them.

'Act of selfishness.' Jim turned suddenly from a football discussion he had been having with Andrew and Jack. 'Bringing a bairn into the world like that. Not the way to do it.'

Gillian couldn't believe her father was going on and on about this. Had he completely forgotten what Susan had done? And in front of Kate. She began to help Frances hand round coffee, trying to think of something to say, anything, that would lead them away from this, when she realised Kate had gone white and was twisting her napkin in her hands, tighter and tighter.

Frances had seen it too. 'Are you all right, Kate? You're not sick again?'

'Yeah, I am.' The girl got up hurriedly. She was wedged between table and window, and had to squeeze behind Andrew and then her grandmother to get out. In a moment she had done it and was gone. They heard her running upstairs.

'Is she coming down with something, Frances?' Grace asked. 'She's hardly eaten a thing.'

'It could be that,' Frances said. 'Some bug or other. I'll go up in a minute and see how she is.'

'Throwing up, I bet,' Andrew suggested. 'She was heaving in the bathroom this morning.'

Beside her, Frances felt Gillian grow alert. Briefly, the two women looked at each other and then away, dismissing the thought as it passed from one to the other. Because it was, of course, unthinkable.

Upstairs, Kate rinsed round the basin, spat, washed her mouth out. She was never properly sick. It would be better if she were.

'Kate?'

It was Frances. Kate splashed her face and wiped it dry with a towel.

'Kate?'

'I'm just coming.'

They faced each other in the bathroom doorway.

'Andrew said you'd been sick today already.'

'What's it got to do with *him?*'

'What's wrong?' Frances asserted herself as aunt, mother, someone who had a right to be concerned. 'You must tell me.'

'It's just a stomach bug, right. Loads of people in my class have had it.'

Frances followed Kate to her room and closed the door behind them. The rest of the household was shut out, the sounds of conversation and dish-clearing faint and faraway, and they were left in quietness together. Andrew's feet thudded upstairs and along the landing. After a moment, they heard music from his room.

Kate sat on the bed with her head bent, gazing at the floor. Frances, on the bedside chair, clenched her hands tight in her lap.

'How long exactly has this sickness gone on?'

'I don't know *exactly.*'

'How long roughly?'

'A couple of weeks.'

'It's not a stomach bug, then.'

Kate bit her lip, not looking at Frances. 'Nothing comes up,' she whispered.

'What?'

'I said—'

'No, it's all right. I got it. Kate—'

'Just leave me alone, right?' Kate swung her feet up on the bed and turned away.

'I do have to know what's going on.'

'I wish everybody would leave me *alone*. It's none of their *business*.'

I could be wrong, Frances thought, frantic suddenly with doubt, and if I am, she'll never forgive me. But Kate leaned forward, hands flat on her stomach as if to press away an ache, and Frances knew she was right.

'You're pregnant.' She laid a hand gently on Kate's arm, slid it down to where the girl's hands folded over her stomach. Kate looked at her at last, eyes dark with terror.

'What am I going to do?' she gasped.

Frances moved from chair to bed and took the girl in her arms. Kate trembled then all at once folded herself into Frances's embrace. Her words, muffled against her aunt's jersey, were clear enough. 'Help me, please help me. I'm so *scared*.'

Grace and Gillian worked companionably together. When the dishes were done and the surfaces clear, Grace found a broom and swept the kitchen floor. Casually, as she emptied the dustpan into the bin, she asked, 'No word from Susan?'

Gillian was caught off guard. 'Not yet.'

Grace squared up to her daughter. She knew perfectly well, Gillian realised, which one to tackle.

'Where is she exactly?'

Gillian took a deep breath. 'We don't know. None of us knows.'

'I see.'

241

'I'm sorry, Mum, we didn't want to worry you and Dad. Nobody's actually seen her since before Christmas. Alec thinks she's all right, though. She's been back for some of her stuff.'

'Let me get this straight.'

This was her mother: not a frail old lady worried about noisy neighbours. It was her mother, calm and quiet and in command. Gillian felt herself grow younger, wrong-footed. Grace set the brush and dustpan aside.

'Susan has left home and no-one has seen her since before Christmas. It's now Easter, and you still don't know where she is. Are you sure *he* doesn't?'

Does she think he's buried her in the garden, Gillian wondered. He could have, he could have, the idea hammered for the first time. *Get a grip here, get back to reality.*

'No,' she said.

Grace seemed to consider this. 'And Kate?' she asked.

'She doesn't know either. Alec thought she'd be better off here because he works such long hours in his restaurant.'

'Frances told us about the restaurant.' In her mother's tone was all the foolhardiness of Alec's life.

'Alec's been worried, of course,' Gillian said, trying to redeem him, 'but he was thinking of Kate. It's worse for her.'

'Do you think I don't realise that? When I

242

consider what—' she stopped, as if words failed her. 'I don't know what to think any more. We did our best, goodness knows.'

She sat down abruptly on a wooden chair, dwindling before Gillian's eyes into old age again.

'I know you did.' She was listening for Frances, perhaps they both were. Why didn't she come back downstairs and get them out of this?

What if Kate *is* pregnant, Gillian thought, appalled, sitting down with a thump beside her mother. How relentlessly families visited their mistakes on the next generation. Look, just *look*, what Susan has done now.

PART III

THE OPEN DOOR

CHAPTER 1

There was something different about Kenny when he came back from his son's house after Easter. Taken up with more urgent preoccupations, Frances did not notice at first. By the time she did, it was almost too late.

Everything was suspended until she could talk to Kate uninterrupted. On Easter Monday her parents left, after an exhausting Sunday night debate about Susan which neither Frances nor Gillian could see had any point at all, except that their parents wanted to make sure every possible avenue for finding her had been explored. All through the discussion, which seemed to circle Susan without in any way explaining her, Frances had the feeling this was a ritual her father needed to observe, and that her mother had tacitly agreed to enact.

Gillian also left on Monday; Frances drove her to the station because she could tell her father did not want to negotiate Inverness traffic and it gave the sisters a last opportunity to talk.

'Is she?' Gillian asked as soon as they were on their way.

'Yes.'

'I knew it.' Gillian put her sunglasses on; the day was very bright and cold, the sky pitilessly clear. The glasses gave her the look of a youthful Audrey Hepburn or Jackie Onassis, a little sharp featured, but younger than she really was. Until they were clear of Dingwall neither spoke again, then Gillian said,

'What are you going to do?'

'What am *I* going to do?'

'Have you spoken to Alec?'

'How could I? House was full of people.'

'Has she seen a doctor?'

'What kind of doctor?'

'Oh God, your doctor, you know what I mean.'

'No.'

Gillian fell silent and began chewing a ragnail on her thumb. After a moment, Frances said,

'Don't tell anyone, Gill.'

'Of course not. Least said, eh?'

Frances realised with a shock that everyone would think as Gillian did. Least said, soonest mended. Keep it quiet. Smooth it over.

'I need to talk to Kate,' she said. 'I haven't even been able to discuss it with *her* properly.'

'Only one option though.'

Frances did not want to utter a word which Gillian could construe as criticism, and yet, as the road fled steadily behind them and they were nearer to parting, she found herself saying,

'Did I ever tell you I lost a baby?'

Gillian took off the dark glasses. 'Lost?'

'Miscarried.'

'Recently?'

'Don't be daft! No, years ago, when Susan was staying with us. I had to go into hospital, and I remember thinking thank God Susan's there to look after the boys for me. Alec was so busy at work he couldn't take time off. That must have been when it happened.'

'What?'

'When he first slept with her.'

'No wonder you don't want her back in your life. As for him – what a bastard.'

'Quite.'

Gillian marvelled that Frances was so cool. Sympathy slipped from her like something smooth and shiny that would never adhere. Gillian longed to have someone at home she could go back to and say, 'I tried, I really tried. But it's too awful, you just feel inadequate.'

'I'm so sorry,' she said after a moment.

'All over years ago. I just wanted you to know why I'm over-sensitive about miscarriage, abortion. It's not anything to do with you.'

Gillian thought about this. 'But you wouldn't want *Kate* to have a baby, would you?'

'Of course not. It's not up to me, though, is it?'

'She's only fifteen!'

'That's not the point.'

Gillian shook her head. 'Remember Susan—'

'She was older.'

'Mum and Dad are very down on single parents. I think Susan having Kate made them worse – or maybe that's the reason.'

Frances sighed. 'Well, perhaps they need never know about this.'

When they reached the station Gillian got out and heaved her bag off the back seat. There were no parking spaces and cars were coming in behind them in the tight turning area.

'I'll just go – you all right?' Frances asked.

'Sure. I'll ring you.'

Jack stayed at home a few days longer. When he went back to Aberdeen Andrew went with him to get a taste of student life. Kenny came home, and Frances said when he rang, 'I'll come over. But not just yet.'

Now Kate was sick every morning and there were dark circles under her eyes. Frances realised she would have to tell Andrew as soon as he came home; even he would guess what was wrong now.

'I've made an appointment with my doctor for you,' Frances told Kate after the boys had left. 'There's a space at four o'clock this afternoon, so I said we'd take it.'

Kate was slumped over a plate of cereal she had not touched. 'I can't even sleep in now,' she complained. 'I wake up at seven o'clock and this feeling comes over me, I'm sweating, and I know the minute I even move I'll want to throw up.'

'I know it's horrible but it does pass.' Why had she said that? It would come to an end soon enough.

Kate suddenly took in what Frances had said about the doctor. 'Why? I mean, why do we have to go to the doctor? They can't give me anything to stop me being sick. I mean, the baby would be deformed.'

'What?'

'If I take any drugs or that.'

'For goodness sake.' Frances sat down beside her.

'I'm sorry,' Kate said, pushing the plate of cereal away. 'I thought I could eat that but I can't. I've got to eat though. I hope I feel better soon – the baby needs me to eat all the right stuff, protein and that.'

'Kate, I don't quite know how to put this, but you don't have to go ahead.'

Kate looked at her, blank. 'How do you mean?'

'You don't have to have the baby.'

Panic flared in Kate's grey eyes, then she turned away with a shrug. 'I'm not having an abortion if that's what you mean.'

Oh God, Frances thought, now what? We've both got to see this through, if she does. Somewhere behind this sweep of dismay, relief flickered.

'That's why we have to see a doctor. So that you can make the right decision.'

Kate faced her, fierce and determined for the first time.

'I told you. I'm not getting rid of it. No way.'

'But think about it, *think*, you're so young, *your body* hasn't finished growing yet, and even if your health is all right, what about afterwards?'

'My Mum will help me.' She folded her arms over her stomach, defiant. 'She'll know what to do.'

Frances sat back, silenced.

'You think she won't come back don't you, she won't come and help me. Well, you're wrong.' Without waiting for an answer she did not want, she rushed on, 'Anyway, it would be murder if I had an abortion. It's killing a baby.'

'Not really, Kate, honestly—' Frances heard Gillian's indignant protest, *it's not a baby, it's a collection of cells.* 'Anyway, first things first.' She could not say anything about Susan, but she could deal with the physical facts. 'When did you last have a period?'

Kate flushed. 'I don't remember.'

'Before you came here?'

A pause. 'Yes,' she admitted. 'Before Christmas. November, I suppose.'

Frances did the calculation rapidly, heart sinking. Kate was at least four months pregnant. With a shock, not realising this had even been in her mind, she told herself *at least it did not happen here.* She had come to them pregnant.

'It was a boyfriend in Newcastle then? Do you want to get in touch with him?'

Kate recoiled. 'No!'

'You're not still in touch?'

'I wouldn't care if he fell into a whole tank full of piranhas.'

No point in pursuing that. They were spared the complication of the boyfriend. It did seem merely a complication; there were more than enough people already who would be drawn into this.

'What about Alec?' Frances asked. 'You'll have to tell him soon if . . . if you're going ahead. Let's speak to the doctor first.'

'You can't make me have an abortion,' Kate said. 'Nobody can.'

'Good Heavens, child!' Frances stopped herself. Keep calm, she thought, Kate must be terrified, she can't think straight, she's nowhere near understanding the implications. 'I'm not trying to make you do anything,' she said. 'All I'm asking is that you see a doctor. You can speak to her on your own, if you'd rather.'

'I don't want to! Will you come in with me?'

'Yes.'

Frances went into the living-room to lay the fire and tidy away newspapers and coffee cups from last night. Morning sunshine lay over the carpet in an arc of light. When she looked out of the window she saw the garden had suddenly filled with colour from crocuses and daffodils, the stirring of a new season. She opened a window and the air that came in was soft and fresh. New life, she thought, breathing in the summer to come, the promise of something she could not imagine yet.

Kate had followed her.

'Don't tell Andrew,' she said. 'Don't tell anybody else.'

Frances put the window on the latch, leaving it open a little, and turned.

'We have to tell the family if you're going ahead. It's not the sort of secret you can keep for ever. The baby will show soon, it's only because you're so young and thin it doesn't already.' Looking at Kate, her long legged girlishness, she thought perhaps there was some change already. How could she have missed it so long?

Kate put her hands over her stomach. 'I'm a bit kind of fat already,' she said. Again, that gleam of panic, and yet behind it pride, astonishment, that this magic should happen to her.

Frances began to tremble. *What on earth are we going to do?* She took a deep breath. 'We have to tell Andrew and we have to tell Alec. At the very least.'

'You tell them.'

Frances wanted to say, if you insist on having this baby you must do your own dirty work. What would be the good? She was barely more than a child and could not be made adult and responsible just because of sex. Frances did not want to speculate on the conception of this unlooked for child. Baby. *A collection of cells.* All at once she understood Gillian's abortion. It was the clean

254

way to end it. Otherwise it did not end, but went on getting worse, much worse, the implications staggering.

'Is it all right to stay here?' Kate asked, following Frances to the fireside, where she was kneeling down and pulling on a pair of old gloves to rake out the ashes. 'Till my Mum gets back.'

Frances sat back on her heels and looked up at her, but before she could speak, Kate said,

'Do you want a hand with anything?'

'Well . . . you could strip Andrew's bed for me. Time I changed the sheets. Just put them straight in the machine.'

I'm a coward, she thought, when Kate had gone. That was the moment to say to her, your mother might never come back. Perhaps Kate had some grounds for thinking she would, perhaps Susan had been in touch. The mobile phone – *that* would be how she would do it. And yet Kate's look had been one of defiance rather than secrecy. Should she ask? No, she decided, we're all right for now, she's confiding in me, trusting me.

She had never been so aware of Kate in the house as she was that day. The girl pursued her, hovering. Perhaps all she wanted was some kind of reassurance, but what reassurance could anyone offer, now?

All day Frances found herself wondering how she could have missed the truth so long. The absence of periods, Kate's heavy breasts, her dreamy look, Frances had attributed to the uneven path to womanhood, and had half envied her seductive, long-legged beauty. Had she and her sisters ever looked like that?

With a jolt, she thought of Susan pregnant, as she had seen her on a visit she and Alec had made to Aberdeen. Susan was staying with her parents, taken care of, if not quite forgiven. The person they were blaming most, openly encouraged by Susan, was Adam. He had abandoned her. *Did he know about the baby*, Frances asked her mother. Grace did not know. *They were living as man and wife. Your Dad says he should have accepted his responsibilities.* But Susan had cajoled her father into a far greater tolerance than he was ever inclined to show anyone else.

Susan had been like Kate in those days, with long legs and slender wrists and ankles, fragile in appearance for all the great bulk of her pregnancy. She had carried it before her with grace like a ship in full sail, the long dresses she wore billowing as she moved. The only time in her life she ever sat still and didn't fidget, restless to be somewhere else. Perhaps that was why her parents were able to accommodate her in their house again. They must have felt protective, as if they were guarding her. As I do with Kate, Frances admitted. As I do, now.

Just as they were leaving the house to drive to the Health Centre, Kenny telephoned.

'Hi,' Frances said, 'we're just on our way out. Can I ring you back later?'

During the school holidays he sometimes called her in his slack spells at work, just to chat. She enjoyed those conversations, caught as she often was in the middle of some domestic task, but she did not want to linger now.

'Sure. Just wondered where you'd got to – have you abandoned me altogether, me and my pooch, in our lonely cottage?'

She laughed. 'Don't be silly. I've just been busy with family stuff. I'll call you later.'

'I'll be waiting.'

She almost stopped at that, something new in his voice, not just humour, but this was not the time to bother with it.

'It was just Kenny,' she said to Kate, as she got into the car. She had never explained Kenny, seeing no reason to do so. Her grown up private life was not shared even with her sons. Not that they minded Kenny. He talked football with them, but kept out of the way on the whole, or Frances kept him out of the way, so that he did not impinge on her family life.

'He's your boyfriend, isn't he?' Kate asked, as they drove down the lane.

'Boyfriend doesn't seem quite the right word,' Frances smiled. 'A friend, I suppose. A good friend.'

Kate looked sceptical. After a moment, Frances asked, 'Are you all right?'

'Yeah.'

They drove the rest of the way in silence.

'We might have to wait a while,' Frances said as they went into the surgery.

Now they had arrived Kate seemed more at ease than Frances, and sat flicking through magazines. They were full of glossy photographs of celebrities in wedding dresses or beside swimming pools, or acres of leather sofa, or holding babies dressed in miniature sportswear. Kate immersed herself in glamour, while Frances studied the equally unattainable houses in *Homes and Gardens*, then gave them up and stared out of the window at the flat stretch of grass behind the Health Centre, and the trees beyond the fence. She realised that the strange sensation in her stomach was what they used to call 'butterflies' when they were young, waiting for a boy to turn up or someone to ask them to dance. Why did she have this feeling, and not Kate?

Kate had stopped turning pages and instead was watching a small child of around eighteen months, walking a little unsteadily, trotting from his mother to the toy box, bringing her back a wooden dog on wheels. His mother showed him how to pull the dog along. He tugged at the string then sat down with a bump in surprise when the toy rolled up to him fast. He laughed, and his mother laughed. Kate turned to Frances and it was as if she had not seen any of this, but was terrified, her eyes dark, her mouth pinched. Frances leaned towards her.

'It's all right,' she said quietly. Kate nodded, biting her lip, and looked away, but not at the child this time.

They went on waiting.

CHAPTER 2

The doctor looked over her spectacles, took them off, and asked Kate,
'Why do you want to have the baby?'
'I just do, that's all,' Kate said, not looking up.

The truth was, she did not. What she wanted was the baby not to exist. For weeks she had convinced herself it did not even though she knew this was crazy, the way to make things worse. She would have told her mother if her mother had been here. It was all their fault. Away from home, there was no-one for her to confide in, she was alone. Who *they* were, she could not specify, or would not. Alec, Frances, her teachers in Newcastle, anyone but her mother.

Susan couldn't help it, everyone knew that, couldn't help her dark moods, any more than she could control her mad shrieking days, frantic with activity, laughing, presents and treats. It was just the way she was. Years ago, when she was little, Alec had told her that when he had found her sitting at the bottom of the stairs crying, Susan nowhere in sight, a pan boiling dry in the kitchen and the back door open, a cold wind blowing through the empty house.

'Where's Mummy?'

'I don't know. She was angry with me because I was the last one out of school.'

He sat beside her, disentangling what had happened, until the smell of burning hissed through the kitchen doorway and he leapt up to turn off the gas. With a whoosh of steam he sank the pan in a basin of water then came back to sit beside Kate again.

'What happened to your knee?' he asked, putting a white folded handkerchief on the graze oozing drops of blood in a criss-cross pattern.

'I fell on the way home. I couldn't keep up with Mummy, she was in a big hurry.'

Alec's face gave nothing away. He said,

'She can't help it, pet. It's not your fault, being late out of school or not keeping up. That wasn't why she was angry. She can't help it – that's just the way she is. You and me,' he went on, lifting off the handkerchief and inspecting the graze, 'we have to understand Mummy. Because no-one else will.'

So it wasn't Susan's fault she had to go, and though Kate had often wished she were different, she had never wanted a different mother. Just to have Susan back, Susan when she was all right was what she wanted, as if by wishing it could happen. That would make it easy to decide about the baby. She wasn't going to let anybody decide *anything*, before her mother came back.

So whose fault was it that she had left it too late

to do anything but have the baby? She was about twenty weeks pregnant, the doctor estimated after examining her. This was a shock to Frances but going home, Kate was the more shaken. As they drove away from the surgery, she muttered between gritted teeth: 'That was *disgusting*.'

'What?' Frances asked, though she could guess.

'The doctor doing that. I never thought you had to do that. Not till the baby was being born.'

'I'm afraid that's one of the things about having babies,' Frances told her. 'Your body's not your own any more.'

'It's horrible.'

'It is necessary. They don't do an internal examination more often than they can help.' She was conscious of Kate stiff with distaste and misery beside her. 'It's such a pity you didn't – we didn't – know sooner. You could still have a termination though.'

'I don't know how you can say that!' Kate flashed out. 'She showed us those pictures – like what size the baby is and that, and how it's got arms and legs. I just don't know how you can *say* that.'

'I'm not sure why she did that,' Frances sighed. She was annoyed with the doctor, and felt let down.

'It has a brain doesn't it, and a heart and *lungs*.'

'Yes.'

'It would die if I got rid of it.'

'Yes.'

'Well then.'

262

'Kate, there's your life too.'

'I could have the baby adopted. There's thousands of people want little babies and there's only big kids with problems or disabled and that for adoption now. I saw a programme on telly about it.'

I wish, Frances thought, as she drew her car up outside the house, I wasn't having this nightmarish conversation. It's mad, I must be mad, or Kate is.

'Let's talk about it later.' She switched off the car engine. 'The first thing, if you've definitely made up your mind, is to call the surgery to confirm you want ante-natal care. You'll have to be booked into the hospital here.'

'I don't want to go into hospital,' Kate said, mutinous, as she opened the car door. 'I want to have the baby at home. My Mum will help me. She's a nurse.'

'Oh, for God's sake!' Frances cried before she could help herself. 'You're fifteen, it's your first baby, and no-one knows where your bloody mother is!'

Kate stopped, rigid with shock. Frances saw the fright in her eyes and was flooded with remorse, at the end of her tether, yes, but ashamed because so was Kate and she should never have let her own feelings show.

'I'm sorry, I'm really sorry. I don't know what got into me. You are only fifteen, I should remember that. I suppose I'm stressed – it's a shock for me too.'

'Forget it,' Kate said. She got out of the car and went into the house by the unlocked front door, which was never secured unless they were away overnight.

We live in a safe place, Frances thought, sitting on in the car, but nothing is safe.

When she went indoors there was no sign of Kate. The telephone was ringing. Frances picked it up not caring how weary she sounded, 'Yes?'

'Mum? Hi, it's me.'

'What is it, Andrew?'

'I just – I thought you might want to know I was all right.'

'What?'

'Mum? What's wrong?'

'Nothing. How's Aberdeen?'

'It's good,' he said. 'I definitely want to come here. The pubs are great.'

'I'm not sure that's what your decision should be based on, actually.'

'The uni is fine too, Jack says, and I'm not gonna go anywhere there's not good clubs and that, am I?'

'How's Jack?'

'I dunno. He might be in bed, still.'

'It's nearly five o'clock!'

'Is it? Well, we had kind of a late night. Mental.'

'As long as you're both all right.'

'We're goin to Glasgow tomorrow for a concert. We'll stay with Rory – remember Rory Mackay that was in Jack's year?'

'Anne and Dougie's youngest? How long will you be in Glasgow? You have to be back here on Saturday.'

'It's Ok, I'll come straight up on Saturday morning. Will you pick me up from the bus station?'

When she had hung up Frances went in search of Kate. She was in her room lying on the bed. With a shock, Frances took in the swell of stomach that still showed when the girl lay on her back. It is real, she thought, as if up to now the baby had been imaginary, a problem but not a presence.

'Are you all right?'

'I'm sorry,' Kate whispered.

'What for? I'm the one who should apologise.'

'No, I mean it.' Kate sat up. 'I'm in the way here, amn't I? I should really go home. You've got Andrew and your job and you're really busy, you don't want me having a baby here. I'll go home.'

Frances sat on the bed near the foot where the tabby cat was lying already, curling over by way of greeting, waiting to be petted. Kate tickled her with one foot, toes rubbing the cat's fur the wrong way.

'She likes sleeping here,' she said.

'Mm. Likes a soft bed.'

They watched the cat for a moment as she showed off to them, luxurious on the soft duvet.

'You don't have to go away anywhere,' Frances said. 'There's absolutely no need.'

'I'm a big enough embarrassment to Andy already.'

'Boys are easily embarrassed.'

'This is kind of more than *usual*, eh?'

Frances smiled. 'I suppose it is. Well, we'll have to tell him. No way to hide it now.'

Kate let out a breath like a sigh. 'I don't have to have an abortion then?'

'Have to? Oh Kate, what do you take me for? It's your body, your decision. What I don't want is to see you go off to Newcastle, with Alec working all hours, and you on your own. I want you to stay here.'

Kate flopped back on the bed. 'Till my Mum gets back.'

'Yes. Then it's her problem, she can deal with it.' She got up. 'I really came to ask what you'd like for supper?'

'I don't know.'

'How's the sickness?'

'The doctor said it could just, like, stop. Do you think it will?'

'Mine did. I didn't ever vomit, but I felt sick with both the boys, especially Andrew.'

'How long did it go on?'

'Till about the stage you are now, I suppose.'

'Good.' Kate smoothed her hands over her stomach, feeling the slight and hardening swell of flesh. 'I feel different,' she said, surprised. 'I feel different even just since we went to the doctor.'

Frances, trying to recall her own young, pregnant

self, understood that. A doctor saying yes, and how many weeks it was, and writing everything down so that there were notes on you, a file: all those things made you somehow much more pregnant by the time you walked out of the surgery. She had been so pleased and excited with a wonderful pure joy. With a surge of pity and tenderness for Kate, she wished for that excitement for her too. The time, the circumstances, the way it had happened were all utterly wrong, but it was her first baby and someone must help her to be happy about it, someone must make everything all right.

'What about plain pasta with butter and a little bit of cheese?'

'Not cheese. Yuck.'

'What then – tuna?'

'Double yuck. No, just pasta with nothing. The kind like shells.'

'That's what I'll make.'

At the door, Frances said, 'We'll talk about it later. Don't fret on your own – you can ask me anything you want to, anything at all.'

'I will.' Kate lay back, one arm stretched out for her i-pod.

While Kate was still upstairs, Frances looked up Alec's home number and dialled. She thought he would be at the restaurant, and meant to leave a message, but Alec himself picked up the phone.

'Frances!' He sounded pleased to hear from her. 'How are you? How's Kate?'

'She's fine, we're all fine. But there's something I need to discuss with you.'

'Oh yes?' He sounded interested and still pleased. 'Hang on – I poured myself a glass of wine. I'll just get it.'

'No, wait – it's not something I can really say on the phone. I know you were up only a week ago, but is there any chance you could you come here? We'd give you a bed. No need for a guest house or anything.'

Before he spoke she knew he was going to misinterpret the invitation but could not think how to prevent that without telling him the truth. Why not after all say it now on the phone, so that when he arrived, as he surely would, he would not be under any illusion about Frances herself. Kate might then be spared the first shock of it.

'I'd love to come, I'm all yours,' he said, and her heart sank. 'As it happens I'm free to come and go now.'

'What do you mean?'

'Sold my share in the business. I'm free, unencumbered. Even got some money in the bank, or I will soon. Bloody great relief, I can tell you.'

'What will you do?'

'Do?' He seemed surprised at the question. 'I've no intention of doing anything in a hurry. I need to take stock first, look around. When do you want me?'

'If you're as free as that,' Frances said, trying to keep the note of irony from her voice, 'then before Andrew comes home on Saturday would be best.'

'Give me tomorrow morning to sort myself out. I'll be with you by ten or eleven at night?'

'That's fine.'

'I'll look forward to it.'

He had not asked what this was about, and although she knew he was making assumptions she wanted to discourage, somehow the moment for making herself clear had slipped past.

'Alec—'

'Yes?'

'Never mind. I'll see you tomorrow.'

Kate had pasta with nothing; Frances had hers with mushrooms and black olives.

'I feel better,' Kate said. 'I don't feel as if I want to throw up, like I usually do.'

'That's something, I suppose.' Frances took Kate's empty plate and stacked it with her own. 'I called Alec,' she said. 'He's coming up tomorrow.'

'That's quick.'

'It seems he's sold the restaurant, or sold his half of it.'

'That's good,' Kate nodded. 'It means he'll be at home more.' She went to pour herself another glass of water, saying as she let the cold tap run, 'Mum hated him being at work all the time.'

'Kate?'

'What?' Kate leaned against the sink, sipping water.

'You don't have any idea where your mother might have gone?'

Kate dipped her head to the glass. 'You never asked me that before.'

'I assumed you didn't know, and I didn't want to upset you.'

'I do, as a matter of fact,' Kate said, setting the glass down carefully on the draining board, 'but I could be totally off the wall.'

'Why on earth didn't you *say?*'

Kate shrugged. 'Like I said, it's off the wall. I just thought if she's, like, Ok, safe and all, I reckon she could be there.'

'Alec checked the Retreat – the sort of Buddhist place.'

'Not that,' Kate scoffed. 'Those weirdos. Na – a different place.' She lit up, her face glowing. 'We could look, right? You and me.'

'Why have you never said anything before?'

'I only just thought of it the other day, if you want to know.' She slumped suddenly, only fifteen, drooping. Then she came back to the table and sat down. 'See,' she said, explaining slowly as if to someone of lesser intelligence. 'I had this dream, and it made me remember me and Mum being there. I was a little kid, but I remember it – it was a really nice place.'

'Right,' Frances said, trying to be patient, trying to hold herself, Kate, this whole impossible conversation in place, so that they would get somewhere at last. 'Where is it?'

'It's called Amble,' Kate said. 'There's a beach, and there was this dolphin. He's gone now, they think he got killed, he disappeared one day, but anyhow it's a beach, and this little, like, harbour. We had fish and chips, when we went there, it was when Mum was in a good mood, feeling happy, you know. Fish and chips in the paper it came in,' she repeated, as if this memory was strongest of all.

'I know it,' Frances said. 'I know Amble.'

When the telephone rang again and it was Kenny, she told him she would call him back.

'Later,' she said. 'Look, things are a bit fraught – can I leave it a day or two? How are you?'

'I'm very well indeed, Frances, *A Ghraidh*. Don't let me keep you from the latest crisis.'

'No need to be sarcastic. What's up?'

'Nothing at all.'

'Oh Kenny, come on, give me a couple of days. Friday?'

'Friday.' He seemed to consider this. 'Why not?'

'Friday evening, then.'

She was uneasy for a moment saying goodbye, but her mind was not really on him or their conversation. Her mind was somewhere else, far back and a long way off.

CHAPTER 3

What Kate did not know was what the doctor had asked Frances, in their few minutes alone together.

'I'd like a word with your aunt – would you wait for her in reception?' Dr Geddes asked, having established that Kate did not want to speak on *her* own. Frances worried about the ethics of this. She had known Dr Geddes a long time and found her altogether wise and trustworthy. Frances, though, was a model patient: respectable, sensible, and rarely ill. She and Dr Geddes had never once had to confront each other over anything more controversial than Andrew's whooping cough or Jack's hay fever.

Dr Geddes wanted to know whether Kate had been raped, though she did not put it quite like that. Was there someone who should be prosecuted? The girl had been – was still – a minor. Frances, with some surprise, found herself on Kate's side rather than the doctor's when it came to discussing this.

'It was some boy in Newcastle, that's all I can tell you. Her own age, I think.' Frances picked up her bag, preparing to leave immediately, but added dryly as she did so, 'Someone she wishes could be eaten by piranhas. No anguished relationship there.'

As if wrong-footed the doctor rose too, spectacles in one hand, the other hovering over the papers on her desk, the new file on Kate.

'Call the surgery and say you want her to be registered for ante-natal care, as soon as you know she'll be having the baby here.' She shook her head. 'This must be quite a worry for you. These girls – you never know how they'll take it. It's always the innocents who get caught, in my experience.'

Frances did not relay this conversation to Kate, who did not ask her about it.

In Aberdeen, Grace had taken the same view as Dr Geddes, defending the girl in Miss Gibson's house to her husband.

'It's the nice girls who get caught with babies,' she said, but he only grunted behind his *Telegraph*. He took a national paper to give him, he said, a broader perspective than the *Press and Journal*, but Grace could not understand how anyone managed to read two newspapers in a day, even in retirement. She preferred a library book herself and was just setting out to change the three she had.

'You want me to run you down there?' He flicked the newspaper aside, looking up at her.

'It's a fine day, I'll enjoy the walk. I might take the bus back up the hill.'

'You could have a look on your way past,' he

suggested. 'See if that nice girl has got any of her pals visiting.'

She saw no need to answer this. There had been cars coming and going but rarely any more loud music. Perhaps one of the other neighbours had complained.

When she had gone out, Jim got up from his chair and went to the window. He caught the last of her, in her camel jacket and tweed skirt, as she rounded the curve of the crescent and disappeared beyond the bushes in Miss Gibson's front garden, overgrown and hanging over the low wall. He went on standing there, brooding.

He knew what she was getting at with her 'nice girls'. It was Susan she meant. She was always too soft with Susan, who had needed firm handling. The girls had grown up in the period when he was busiest at work, with responsibilities which kept him in the office late every night and on Saturday mornings too. Saturday afternoons were for golf, Sunday for church and family. One afternoon a week, he realised too late, was not enough to shape your children's characters. That had been left to Grace.

They all turned out so different, he came to believe character was innate, not created in child-hood or adolescence. He had expected to have sons and was at a loss with girls. After the first surprise he had not minded Frances being a girl. From the start she had the demeanour of an older sister: she rarely cried and was easy-going and sensible, a model daughter. Then Susan, though difficult, was pretty and delicate, a charmer. After Gillian was born, tiny and dark like her mother so that he fell in love again, unable to help himself, Grace said firmly that she thought three was a nice size for a family, and he knew there never would be any sons.

He was not a man who dwelt on disappointment. He was convinced his daughters would, in their different ways, bring him credit. Three Douglas girls, all expected to do well.

No complaints about Frances. He took his newspaper back to the armchair and sat down. Pity she hadn't gone in for secondary teaching though. She could have been head of a big city comprehensive by now, earning good money, someone significant. Not that she wasn't respected where she was, he could see that, but it was a wee place, buried in the country and Frances was capable of much more. Still, she had brought up her boys well. No trouble there. *She* had the sons. Sometimes Grace murmured vague hopes that Frances would marry again. She would have liked all her daughters married, so that she could boast of her sons-in-law as he knew other women did. There was that fellow – Ken? – but it would never come to anything. An ageing hippy, a folk singer, Frances had teased, her guard down for once, and from the Western Isles too, a Gaelic speaker. Jim had been in Stornoway shortly after the war and thought the place backward, hopeless. It probably still was. Frances would never marry him.

He went on thinking about Frances so that he would not think about Susan. Skip to Gillian, less satisfactory but not, as Grace kept telling him, in any way a disappointment. 'You don't appreciate how well she's done. Her lovely flat, and a very good job.'

'Why's she never married then, if she's such a catch?' he had demanded.

'Still looking for the right man.'

Unbidden, Susan drifted into his memories: Susan at twenty five, saying it was over with Adam, he was leaving, could she come and stay at home for a while? He had never thought much of Adam, for all his good looks and easy manners, indeed perhaps because of those things. Soon after that Susan confessed to Grace she was expecting a baby, and her mother, choosing her moment, leaving it as long as she dared, told him. His first reaction was that they must bring Adam back from Canada so that there could at least be a wedding. It was this he and Susan quarrelled over most bitterly, not the pregnancy, a row that reached its terrible peak when she told them Adam was in any case still married to someone else. His reaction was to ignore the pregnancy, refusing to speak of it.

Eventually, of course, he could not ignore it. For the first time in her life Susan was not out every night or restlessly moving from room to room like a prisoner under house arrest. She became suddenly, remarkably still. Through the warm summer of her pregnancy she lay dreaming in the garden, her book or magazine neglected, eyes closed, listening to the low murmur of music from Grace's portable radio. She was still a potent presence, but for a few months the house became an oasis of comfort and peace, as it had never been when she lived at home during her teenage years.

As soon as Katy was born and she had made a swift physical recovery, swifter, Grace told him, than was *natural*, Susan revived and shook off the sleepiness and slowness of the last five months. She took up her old ways and more often than not, Jim saw with increasing irritation, it was Grace who was left to look after the child. He kept himself apart, not caring for babies. He was proud of his grandsons of course, but Frances had conveniently kept all the mess of infancy well away from them in Northumberland. He could not be doing with the smell of nappies and milk, every room steamy with drying clothes, and those terrible wailing cries that sent him straight to his business room, the door firmly shut. When Susan had said she was going to stay with Frances for a while, that Frances was going to help look after Kate so that she could get a job, he was relieved.

Then he discovered he missed her, missed the slow graceful girl who had dozed all summer in his garden, missed the bright child she had once been, so quick to learn. In absence she became girlish again. Thinking of her now, he saw her in the doorway with both hands clasped round the handle, smiling, her hair cut in the old-fashioned heavy pageboy she wore when she was young, and her jeans and loose shirt. That was how she looked when she wanted to coax something out of you, that dimple at the corner of her mouth she'd had since babyhood, her light breathless voice, and the restless way she shifted and turned on her heels, unable to stand still. Susan.

As if in echo of all those old quarrels he felt his heart speed up. Louder and faster it beat in his chest and he leaned further back in his chair, the paper slipping to the floor, pages loose and fanning out. He had that sensation again, as if his head was filling with blood, hot and tight that burning feeling, the beginning of anger. The shrieks and shouting, the slammed doors and final yells, the empty house when she had roared off in her blue Triumph, the only sound Grace weeping softly at the kitchen table. It was always him she blamed, never Susan.

Perhaps he dozed. His daytime naps skimmed the surface of sleep, the senses remaining, however faintly, alert. He thought he heard the front door open and someone come in. Grace would wake him as she always did. *You haven't been sleeping in that chair since I went out, surely?*

No-one spoke and no-one came in. He went on lying back in the big armchair, eyes closed, with the strange sensation that someone was moving softly about the room. There was a scent of some summer flower he recognised – lavender or stocks?

No, nothing so strong, fainter and sweeter even than roses, a young smell, fresh. He shifted in the chair and lapsed into dreaming again, Grace fussing about the church flowers, Susan as a little girl in a red and white frock, running up the garden after a ginger cat.

When the telephone began ringing he struggled free of sleep and heaved himself upright, unable to tell what was happening. The door – no – the phone. A cold air had entered the room and he felt stiff and chilly. Blast Grace, she must have turned the thermostat down again, forever saving on bills, as if they were hard up.

When he went into the hall to answer the telephone, he saw that both inner and outer front doors were wide open.

Bewildered, he snatched at the phone. 'Yes?'

It was Frank, about golf on Friday.

'Just a minute, Frank – with you in a second. Grace must have left the door open – place is freezing.' He shut both doors. There was no sign of Grace. 'Sorry. With you now.'

When he put the receiver down again he knew the house was empty and Grace had not come in. He rubbed his hands over his face. Cup of tea, that was the thing. He glanced at the clock, gauging when his wife might be back. Soon, if she got the bus and hadn't met some crony. Still, he could have his tea on his own and cut himself a slice of gingerbread.

He set about dealing with this, but behind his

methodical preparations, punctuated by grunts as he knelt to get out the gingerbread tin or leaned across the sink to fill the kettle, lay the uneasy sense of something not quite right. He put down the kettle and went into the hall. Silence. No-one had come in while he slept; it was ridiculous to think so. He began to go upstairs, taking his time, listening. Friends living in a nearby street had been burgled while they watched television. Two young men had gone upstairs and cleared out Janet's jewellery drawer and taken Gordon's wallet lying by the bed. Now they all kept their doors locked in the evening.

Cautiously he went into the main bedroom. No drawers had been opened, nothing had been moved. With a sigh of relief he went into the other upstairs rooms but everything was orderly and peaceful. As he stood there telling himself all was well, he became aware of a perfume lingering, faint now, but once heady and sweet like summer flowers after rain. One of Grace's pot plants, he supposed. The house was full of them.

He was in the kitchen making tea when Grace arrived home.

'You left the door open,' he said as she came in and set her basket on a chair, ready to show him her novels and the World War II memoir borrowed for him.

'What?'

'The front door. It was wide open.'

'I shut it after me when I went out. You know that fine.' She put her hand on her breast, suddenly alarmed. 'Jim, no-one's been in, have they?'

'No, you can rest easy. I checked upstairs.' He frowned. 'The door couldn't have been on the latch properly.'

She dismissed this. He had been dozing, she could tell from the way his white hair, still thick round the back of his head, was ruffled. She reached up a hand and smoothed it down.

'You're all untidy,' she said. 'Are you making a cup for me as well?'

'Haven't you had it? Art Gallery tearoom with your pals?'

'I didn't meet a soul down town.'

'We should phone the girls tonight,' he said, handing her a knife so that she could cut the gingerbread.

'Any reason in particular?'

'Keep in touch, that's all. We're the ones with the free time, so we should ring them up.'

'I wonder how Kate's getting on,' Grace sighed. 'Poor lassie.'

'She's in good hands,' he reminded her, carrying the tray to the living-room. 'She'll come to no harm with Frances. Best thing that could have happened.'

'Susan going off for weeks?'

'I meant Alec taking her to Frances.'

They sat down together and he opened the library book she had brought him. Sometimes it was hard to remember the life he had had before retirement. The days meandered by now, unmarked. He thought of saying to Grace, *one of your plants has a very noticeable scent.* Then he decided not to bother. His dreaming and bewildered awakening, the open door, the scent of flowers, seemed less real and he felt confused about what had actually happened.

'That girl,' Grace said suddenly, 'in Miss Gibson's old house. I met her, coming along the road.'

Getting off the bus on the main road opposite the crescent, she had seen the girl ahead of her, in denim jacket and tight black trousers tucked into boots. The high heels thrust her forward, so that she seemed to lean over the handles of the buggy she was pushing. Supermarket carrier bags hung from these on either side, bumping against her legs as she went. She was about ten yards ahead of Grace, who was finding her basket heavy and saw the gap between them widening before they reached home. She would have liked an excuse to say 'hello', to speak to the child perhaps. If she hurried, she would be passing the gate as the girl dragged her pushchair up the steps to her front door.

Just then, unnoticed by the mother, one of the child's shoes, a miniature trainer with blue laces, tumbled on to the pavement and rolled into the gutter. Grace quickened her pace, picked up the shoe and began to trot after the girl, her basket lurching uncomfortably from side to side. A few steps behind, she called:

'Excuse me! Hello? You dropped this.'

It was a moment before the girl realised someone was talking to her. She looked round and saw Grace, breathless, holding out the shoe.

'Thanks. She's always losing them.' As she let go of the buggy, the weight of her shopping tilted it back till she caught it again.

'Let me hold it,' Grace said, 'while you put your wee girl's shoe back on.' She put down her own basket and took the buggy handles. She'd had a big pram for her girls, coach built. You didn't get these flimsy lightweight pushchairs then, but it felt familiar all the same, gripping the handles, looking down on the curls of fair hair, as the mother bent to fit on the shoe. The fair head turned, and the child looked up curiously at Grace.

'Hello,' she said. 'What's your name?' The child gazed, then looked back at her mother.

'Mammy!'

'Look – the lady found your trainer. You nearly lost it, you silly girl.' She stood up. 'Thanks.' She had a crop of copper-red hair with a pinkish tinge. Dyed, Grace decided, not liking the colour or the heavy makeup she wore. Then when the girl smiled her thanks her face brightened and she was almost pretty. Grace picked up her basket and they walked on side by side.

'How old is your wee girl?'

'Twenty two months. Two in June.'

'What do you call her?'

'A nuisance, most of the time!' She laughed. 'She's Lauren, and I'm Debbie.'

'I'm Grace Douglas. We live two doors along from you.'

'I know.'

'Are you settling in now?'

'Oh, we're not staying long. My boyfriend's back soon, he's working in Bahrain. We're getting our own house when he comes home.'

'You're not a relative of Miss Gibson, then?'

Debbie looked blank. 'Who? No, we're just renting.'

This meant, perhaps, a series of tenants. Grace fretted, wondering whether to tell Jim. She held Debbie's gate open while the buggy was wheeled in.

'See ya.' Debbie smiled her wide smile, and the child unexpectedly waved a small hand, opening and shutting her fist. 'That's right, say ta ta to the lady.'

Grace waved back, seduced. Andrew had waved like that as a toddler, fingers opening and closing.

She wanted to tell this story to Jim and did try, but he seemed preoccupied, even dazed.

'Are you all right?' she asked, sharp with sudden anxiety. 'No pains or anything?'

'Pains?' He glared at her, offended. 'Of course not.'

'I wonder if we'll ever have any more grandchildren,' she sighed. Jim picked up his library book again and turned the pages, ignoring this.

Grace sat dreaming in her chair for a few minutes longer, the mug of tea forgotten, thinking of Jack and Andrew.

Shortly after midnight Frances put her book down and was drifting into sleep when someone tapped lightly at her door. It was always ajar and when Frances sat up and said 'What is it?' Kate came in.

'Sorry, didn't mean to wake you. I just wanted to ask something.'

Frances switched on the bedside lamp and pushed her pillows up behind her. 'What?'

'I know the doctor sort of explained, but I didn't listen really. Well, I listened, but it didn't stay in my head, if you know what I mean.'

Frances said with a smile, 'About ninety per cent of conversations with doctors are like that.' She patted the bed. 'Come and sit down.'

Kate sidled up to the bed and sat on the very end of it. 'If I did have an abortion, would I be like, asleep?'

'Asleep?'

'Would they give me an anaesthetic so it would be over when I woke up?'

I should have looked this up, Frances thought, I ought to know.

'I don't think so. We could go back to Dr Geddes and ask her.'

'It doesn't matter.'

'Have you changed your mind?'

With a prickling of apprehension she became

aware that this encounter in the shadowed bedroom was important. What she said, what Kate believed, could make all the difference in the world. To the baby, she realised, to the baby which might become like Gillian's baby, consigned to oblivion, forgotten already. But not by me, she thought, not by me. That another family baby should vanish, become nothing, less than nothing – the very idea gripped her heart with anxiety.

'I don't know,' Kate whispered. 'I'm scared. I'm scared about it being born, you know. It hurts, doesn't it?'

'Yes, it does, but it's soon over – you forget. Memory is treacherous. People would only ever have one child, wouldn't they, if it was so bad? And most of them have two, three, or even more.'

'Yeah, I suppose.'

Backtracking: 'It is up to you.'

'If I have an abortion, would it be *soon*?'

'As soon as it could be arranged. If they could still do it. I don't really know. It would have to be *very* soon.'

'Would it be like a kind of operation?'

This was the moment when Frances might have said something anodyne and reassuring, promising to look it up and refer to the doctor.

'To be honest, Kate, at the stage you're at, it would be more like a very early birth.'

'You're kidding!'

'I'm sorry, I don't know much about it, but I do know that. It wouldn't be so painful or difficult, because the baby is very small. But you would have to go through labour, yes.'

'I'd be as well doing it, then,' Kate said, after a moment. 'Properly.'

'It's not just about a birth,' Frances said, pulling herself up, remembering to be an aunt, conscientious. 'Who's going to look after the baby?'

'Me?' Kate gave a little shrug, half a smile.

'Aye, that's right. You.' Frances smiled back. 'With a bit of help.'

Kate shivered. 'I should have told you, shouldn't I? But I kept thinking it couldn't really be true, especially when I didn't get any fatter, I got thinner really.' She put her hands low on her stomach, pressing. 'But it is true.'

'Go back to bed,' Frances said. 'You're getting cold. Tomorrow Alec will be here and we can talk to him about it.'

'You think he'll totally freak? Go mad at me?'

'Does he ever do that?'

'No,' Kate admitted. 'It's Mum who freaks out. I don't blame her,' she added hastily. 'I mean, I can be quite annoying sometimes.'

'All mothers lose their tempers occasionally.'

Kate's mouth twisted. 'It's more than occasionally.'

'She's like your grandfather. He can be a bit fiery.'

'I'm going back to bed,' Kate said. 'Sorry, I just panicked a bit.'

When she had gone, Frances lay awake thinking

287

first that this was the nearest to an ordinary conversation she had had about Susan for years and then that whatever she had said had probably been the wrong thing to say.

If the baby did come, Kate's life would be spoiled, and the whole thing would never end. Yet if Susan had not had Kate, if she had not come confident and blithe to her parents and said take me in, Kate would not exist. It was like saying Jack or Andrew might not have lived. Unimaginable.

If Kate had not been born, Susan might not have come to stay with Alec and Frances, and she and Alec would never have become lovers. Frances sighed and shifted in bed. So much going wrong because of one act of sex. Or perhaps not. Perhaps the alternative lives they might have lived were lesser lives. She and Alec might have drifted on unhappily for years.

She thought of Kenny's undemanding warmth and kindness, of the job she loved, of how Jack and Andrew, unhampered by a semi-alcoholic father, had grown straight and true. Maybe you did me a favour, Susan, she thought. So let it happen, let the baby be born, and thrive, and be loved and cherished. Why not?

CHAPTER 4

Frances's call had come out of the blue, a godsend, though Alec knew it must be about Kate. He had a faint twitch of anxiety in case she was she skiving off school again, but he shrugged it off in the relief of being on the move, having a purpose. He packed quickly and left early, glad to be on the road.

This meant he arrived in Dingwall in mid-afternoon, so when he got there no-one was at home. He walked round the house and stood in the back garden for a moment. From here, Ben Wyvis lay like a sleeping beast in sunshine, its long back black against blue sky. Below he could follow the firth out towards Invergordon. One or two rigs were visible, like crane flies on the water. It was very quiet. Something brushed softly by and looking down, he saw the old tabby cat strolling on along the path. Absurdly, he wanted to call her back, receive some sign that she remembered him. He associated this cat with Christmas and a row with Frances. Then later, wasn't there an infected paw, a crisis with visits to the vet? She had survived all that into steady old age. I have survived too, he reminded himself, but thought the cat probably more intact.

He returned to the front of the house, and stood in the lane listening for Frances's car. Surely she wouldn't be too long – she *had* asked him to come. It was cold and a cloud drifted over the sun with heavier, blacker clouds in its wake. Perhaps he would wait in the car. The cat had followed him and sat by the front door. It occurred to him to try to open it, just to show her he couldn't let her in, but it opened at a touch and swung ajar. The cat went in, and so did he.

In the silent hall of Frances's house he stood for a moment, smelling coffee mingled with a staler aroma, old carpets, soot from the unlit fire. He was both uneasy and exhilarated, like a boy in the head teacher's study, alone and unseen.

Coats and jackets were bundled onto the hall-stand pegs; there were trainers in a heap behind the door; newspapers were piled on a basket chair. The answerphone sat with its light blinking on a small table cluttered with papers, coins and a couple of pens. He thought he recognised this table from their life together. He wondered if he might make coffee; she wouldn't mind that. But as he moved towards the kitchen, he heard a car in the lane.

Hi,' he said, going out to meet her. 'I've only just got here. Door was open.'

Frances began to take her shopping out of the

boot. 'Could you give me a hand with these? Just put them in the kitchen.'

His cold hand touched her warmer one, taking a cardboard box of groceries from her arms. 'Sorry,' he said. 'Got it.'

He stood watching her unpack till she said, 'Put the kettle on or something, for goodness sake.'

'Where's Kate?'

'Gone to a friend's. I took her over after lunch, then I thought I'd stock up.' She put the last of the groceries away while he made coffee under her instructions. 'Cafetiere's on the window sill – coffee in the blue jar beside the kettle.' She got out mugs. 'Let's take it through to the living-room – the heating's been on so it should be warm enough.'

He did not think it was, but did not say so. They sat down formally, she on a chair near the window, he perched on the sofa. She had her back to the light and he could not read her shadowed face.

'Actually,' she said after a moment, 'I was quite glad when Kate's friend rang. I wanted to see you on my own first.'

'Oh?' He waited, curious and alert. She had been cool so far but that was nothing new. He assumed Kate had been causing trouble but she did not seem annoyed, though she was certainly tense.

'She wants me to tell you,' she went on. 'So I hope you won't mind.'

'Mind what exactly?'

'Just that it's me. That she hasn't told you herself.'

'Is this to do with school?'

'No.'

He really had no idea what was coming but he could see it was serious. A hollow giving-way sensation funnelled down his chest. Frances was still distant, as if none of it had anything to do with her. He resented that. Didn't she care for Kate at all, even now?

'There's no easy way to say this. Well, I can't think of one.'

'Oh dear. Sounds bad.'

'Kate's going to have a baby.'

He went on sitting there, holding a mug of coffee, hearing the words, not believing them.

'You're kidding, aren't you?'

'I'm sorry. I know it must be a shock.'

'What the hell – are you *sure*?'

'Yes – and I'll put you straight on one thing: it happened before she came to stay with me.'

'For God's sake, that's three months – more – what the hell's been going on? How long have you known about this?'

He seemed to her like a man acting indignation and anger. She did not believe in any of it.

'Easter,' she told him. 'You're right, of course, I should have guessed much sooner, but she's a very private girl. I was trying to leave her alone, leave her to come to terms with being here, with Susan going off. I'm not used to girls, I did tell you that.'

'Oh God, Fran, I'm not blaming you!'

'I should hope not.'

'I'm just shocked – stunned. My God.' He put his face in his hands, breathing heavily into the cupped palms. Frances did not believe in this either. She grew icy with dislike, recoiling from him. Who had once been her love, her husband.

She thought he looked different from the last time he had *been* here. Was it only a week ago? She wondered if it was the effect of giving up the business which made him look less prosperous and confident. There was a weary familiarity about his appearance. Young, between jobs, he had looked like this. But then, he had been young and able to carry with style a slight down at heel casualness, a forlorn expression. It did not suit middle age and thinning hair so well.

He looked up, smoothing back the still dark hair. 'What are you going to do?'

'What am *I* going to do?'

She was impatient but not upset. Just as she was remembering precisely how he had once grated on her, he recalled that superior calm of hers. You would bat against it like a moth on a window pane but there was no way in.

'We've seen a doctor, if that's what you mean.'

'She's all right, is she?'

'Her health is fine. She's being sick a lot but that's common. It'll pass.'

'Is she that far on, then? God, she must be. You don't think she should have this baby, do you?'

If anything, she receded farther into shadow. He couldn't make her out.

'It hardly matters what I want, does it?' Cold, she threw him back on himself. 'Kate has to make her own decisions about all of this.'

'She's only fifteen, a kid. She can't have a baby just because some lad couldn't keep his fly zipped. Was that it, was it some lad in Newcastle, did she say? She never even had a boyfriend, that I knew about. But I wouldn't, would I. Christ, if I could get hold of him—'

'It seems it wasn't what you'd call a relationship. Nothing she was keeping secret. Just one night, an accident. There's no point in going on about it.'

'My God, Fran, have you no feelings about it, even after all these months? I admit it was an imposition, but she is your niece after all, surely to God you could help her get an abortion?'

'She's about twenty weeks pregnant.' She saw his shocked look and sighed. 'You said yourself, it's gone on a long time without being noticed.'

'You mean it's too late.'

'Maybe not within the letter of the law, but yes, it is. Soon she'll feel the baby move. It's only because she's so young and slender it scarcely shows. You won't remember, but Susan was like that. Didn't show for months then suddenly up like a balloon.'

'It's too late then. Sorry, give me a minute. I can't seem to get my head round this.'

She sat back, letting him be. After a moment she said, 'I'm really sorry I didn't know sooner, but even if I had, Kate's certain she doesn't want a termination. God knows why but she's absolutely set against it.'

'She's too young to know what she's letting herself in for.'

'I agree with you.' As she leaned forward into the light he saw signs of strain in her face. 'I'm sure there are all sorts of complex reasons why she wants to have the baby. A psychiatrist would have a field day, unravelling them.'

'Let's not get into that.'

'No point,' Frances agreed. 'But we do have to think about this, plan how she can best be supported.'

'You want me to take her home, don't you?' He grimaced. 'My responsibility.'

Before she could answer this, the telephone rang. She closed the living-room door behind her and although he could hear her voice, it was too low for him to make out the words or guess who had called.

Restless, he stood up and crossed to the bookcase to look over, in desultory fashion, what she was reading these days, just so that he could think about something else for a moment or two. The more she retreated from him, the more he wanted to puzzle her out, please her, even though he knew the time had long passed when he could hope for anything better than tolerance. Yet she had helped him out, she had taken Kate in. Now, this. Not one cuckoo but two. He thought back, trying to remember the friends Kate had gone about with at home. It was no good. Most of her telephone conversations were on her mobile phone, or like Frances's one now, behind a closed door. The secret world of fourteen had held her. Fathers, let alone step-fathers, did not have access. Besides, he thought, I was always at work, and when I wasn't, there was Susan. Guiltily, he thought now of how both of them had left Kate to get on with her own life.

He realised he was staring at a row of Scott Fitzgerald novels. So that was where *The Great Gatsby* had gone! Yes, it was the same twenty-year old paperback, worth more now perhaps than the 50p he had given for it in a second hand bookshop in Newcastle. The picture on the cover, from a nineteen twenties photograph, was familiar as an old family snapshot.

He did not think Frances had ever cared for Scott Fitzgerald, and when they divided up the books painfully and quickly on that one terrible visit back home, with black jokes and a sudden deceptive camaraderie, he remembered her saying, 'Here, you have this lot.' She had tipped them into his cardboard box along with Asimov and Heller, Vonnegut and CS Forester. His books. He took the copy of *Gatsby* over to the window and flicked through it, wondering when he had last bought a book and read it all the way through. He did not read now, he drifted. Perhaps his only serious attempt at reading had been during his marriage. He had read hungrily then, the way people do who feel they have missed something important in their childhood.

As the door opened and Frances came in, he put the book back on the shelf, fitting it carefully in the space between *This Side of Paradise* and *The Beautiful and Damned*. He took his time, so that she would notice and might even realise he had found her out. There had been a moment during that visit when she abstracted these books, deciding she wanted them for herself after all. In an odd way he was pleased about this: for once he was not in the wrong, and she was not irreproachable.

'That was Kate. She wants to stay on with Michelle. I told her you were here, but I said it didn't matter, she could stay. She'll see you tomorrow.'

'Does she know you've spoken to me?'

'Yes. I feel bad about that. She ought to talk to you herself. But I didn't want to bring her back tonight. Soon she won't have the freedom to come and go, and stay with her friends. It will all change.' She considered this. 'I wonder if she realises.'

'I doubt it.' As she had sat down again, he did too. Perhaps he ought to insist on Kate being brought back at once, but he shrank from confrontation. What was he going to say?

Frances said, 'You were asking about taking Kate home.'

'I'm not even working now, I could spend the time with her.'

'I think she ought to stay here.'

'*Do* you?'

'She's suddenly started talking about Susan. She says she wants to stay here till her mother comes home.'

'She's not heard—'

'No.' A pause. 'Have you?'

'I'd have told you!'

'No more secret visits to the house or anything?'

'Fran, she's vanished.'

He saw her whiten at that as if the horror of it had shaken her again

'Look, we need to talk this through properly. What'll we do – can I take you out for a meal since Kate's not here. The boys are in Aberdeen?'

'On their way to Glasgow for a couple of days.'

'A curry or something? My treat.' He smiled at her, that old rueful smile.

'I'm not sure.'

'It'll pass the time.' It was going to be a long evening, he realised. Perhaps she did too, since she got up and glancing down at her jeans, said,

'All right. I'd better put on something more respectable. A curry's fine – the place in Dingwall is quite good.'

'I'll bring my bag in,' he said.

'You can have Jack's room. I've made up the bed.'

'You want to go for a drink first?'

'All right. You know where you're sleeping?'

'Oh yes,' he said, going out to the car, 'I know that.'

CHAPTER 5

Gillian was going out with someone new. His name was Paul and he was five years younger than she was. She was self-conscious about this and tended to tell people unnecessarily, forestalling comment. He had never been married, though he had lived with long term girl-friends in London and abroad. He had the glamour of other places and countries about him, and Gillian could not believe her luck. Despite his age, he made her feel young and naïve – those enviable, lost things.

As Alec and Frances were ordering chicken tikka and king prawn passanda in Dingwall, with side dishes Alec considered indispensable and Frances did not want, Gillian and Paul were sitting in a trattoria off Lothian Road. They were still at that uneasy but pleasurable stage of telling each other about their lives and preferences, and trying to make these more interesting and amusing than they usually thought them.

Grace and Jim Douglas had long since finished their evening meal and were watching a wild life programme on BBC2. Jim watched and commented, while Grace kept half an eye on it but paid more attention to the piece of tapestry on her lap. It was destined to be a cushion cover for the Lloyd Loom chair in their bedroom. She had a lamp switched on by her elbow, but it was harder work these days keeping her stitching accurate. She adjusted her glasses, peering.

Kate was at Michelle's house, with Amy. They were in Michelle's bedroom playing music, and had been sending text messages to a boy who said he wanted to go out with Amy. He was working in his father's newsagency and when he finished at eight o'clock he would pick up all these messages. While they waited, messing about with Michelle's long hair, putting it up with sparkly grips then taking it down again, Kate told them she was pregnant.

It was as if, having told Frances, she had opened a door she'd been keeping tight shut. Now there was no reason not to go through, through it and the next one, and the one after that. Whatever Michelle and Amy said, they would not look down their noses at her the way that doctor had done. She was ancient anyway, look at the awful thick tights she wore, how could she understand? She wasn't the sort of person you could tell anything to. Nor, she discovered, was Frances. This was not because she did not trust Frances: she found she did, more and more completely. Frances was worried, you could see that, and Kate felt bad about it, not wanting to give her any more grief than she could help. Frances was straight, she would be shocked by all the stuff that happened, you couldn't tell her the way everybody drank way under age or smoked joints or took Es at parties. She would go spare, she'd think it all meant much more than it really did. Not that Kate was going to do any of that; she was going to be very careful.

For about five seconds, Michelle and Amy stared at her like twins, eyes round and wide, mouths open. Then, 'I knew it,' said Michelle, 'It all makes sense now.'

'What does?' Amy asked. This was a shock.

'Oh everything, like her feeling sick and that. My God, what are you going to do? Have you told your auntie and your step-dad?'

'I told Frances. Well, she sort of guessed. She's brilliant, though,' Kate insisted. 'She wants me to stay till I have the baby and she's going to tell my step-dad. He'll be Ok. I'll see him tomorrow.'

'My dad would go completely mental. They don't want to even think you *know* about sex,' Michelle said.

'You're not going to have it, are you?' Amy was just catching up, her own false alarm well and truly upstaged. She recalled vividly the terrible fright, then her overwhelming relief. The idea of actually *having* a baby was so appalling, she did not imagine Kate could possibly want to, yet there

302

was such an air of drama and excitement about her, the room seemed charged with it.

'I have to,' Kate said. 'I'm about twenty weeks, the doctor says. That's like, more than four months. So it's too late.'

'Oh my God, you're really going to have a baby? When?'

The doctor had given Kate a date which, like a mantra, she had been repeating to herself since her midnight conversation with Frances.

'That's quite soon.' Amy looked surprised. 'What about school? Are you going to leave? You're not sixteen for ages.'

She had not expected them to be so full of questions, nor that she would feel special, as if she were suddenly at the centre of the world.

'What do you think you'll call it?' Michelle asked. 'They can tell you if it's a boy or girl now. My cousin knew she was going to have a boy. She was so depressed, she really wanted a little girl. But she was Ok when Stephen was born,' she added, as if this might reassure Kate.

'I'm not even thinking about that!' It was true, she had concentrated only on pregnancy, not the child to come.

'No, it's too soon,' Amy said, coming in with her own wisdom now. 'Anything could happen. Well, I'm sure it won't, but you know what I mean. My auntie didn't even buy baby clothes till after Kerry was born. She said it was bad luck.' She laughed. 'My uncle had to go rushing out to Mothercare and he'd been up all night because she had the baby at four o'clock in the morning.'

It will be all right, Kate thought, people have babies all the time and it's not the end of the world. It will be all right.

Later, she realised that for all the questions they asked, the thoroughness of their investigation into her symptoms, feelings, action, the future of the still mythical child, they did not once ask, 'When are you going to tell your Mum?' They did not ask because they knew about absent parents.

'Do you think you might get it adopted?' Michelle wanted to know. 'I could never do that, could you Amy, have a baby, go through all that and then give it to somebody else. Imagine, you'd keep worrying was it all right, were the people kind and all that.'

'No,' said Kate, making up her mind in an instant, on the whim of Michelle's words. 'Definitely not. No way am I giving this baby to anyone else. You can look after it yourself nowadays, can't you, they give you help and that so you can go to college. That way I'd get a good job and earn decent money.'

They were silent for a moment as this vision of Kate's future hovered before them.

'You're lucky you've got your auntie,' Amy pointed out. 'To babysit, I mean. You'll still be able to go out.'

Kate, who had till now only been able to think

of being sick and the shame of having to tell people, saw a whole life unrolling in front of her, mysterious and strange. It really would happen. In the other girls' conversation, excited and thoughtless, full of ideas and plans, the baby came to life and was real to Kate for the first time.

In the Indian restaurant in Dingwall, Frances and Alec had also, much more hesitantly, begun to talk about Kate's pregnancy.

'I dread telling people,' Frances said. 'I feel I'm going to spend weeks having a series of incredibly difficult conversations.'

'Oh, that sort of news soon spreads,' Alec said, helping himself to more rice.

Frances sat back in her chair. 'There's not just Andrew and Jack, there's my parents. The school. She's only fifteen, so legally she's supposed to be in full-time education for another year. Maybe they'll provide some sort of tutor, but the budget for that has been cut over and over. I had a primary seven boy with leukaemia and his home tuition didn't amount to much. I used to go and see him myself and arrange work with his mother.'

'Anyway,' Alec broke in, since she seemed to be getting off the point, 'she can't stay at school much longer, can she?'

'The summer holidays I thought, if they'll let her. If she'll *go*.'

'Do you think she will?'

'I doubt it, once the pregnancy is obvious, but it would be better for her than hanging about the house. She's going to need qualifications, goodness knows.'

'We want her to have the best chance she can – and a career eventually.'

They contemplated the improbability of this in silence for a moment. Then Frances said, 'She talked about Susan.'

'You said.'

'She had this idea Susan might have gone to stay in Amble, of all places.'

Astonished, he put his fork down, staring at her. 'Amble? That's barely thirty miles from home!'

'I know.'

'We used to go there, didn't we?'

'On fine summer Sundays when the boys were little. You remember Freddie the dolphin?'

'I think so.'

'She says Susan took her there. Did *you* go?'

He realised she was picturing the same summer Sunday outings, repeated with another woman, another child.

'By the time we moved back north to Newcastle, Kate was five. I was working weekends quite a lot. If we went out it was usually in the city. Susan wasn't keen on anywhere without shops, which makes it all the stranger.'

'She said Susan took her to the harbour to see the dolphins, and they had fish and chips. The

306

same place we went to, I expect.' She reddened. 'Anyway, I just wondered what you thought.'

'The police have all the details and I gave them photographs. If she were in Amble, so close to home, surely someone would have seen her.'

'But will you go and look? Then I can tell Kate you have. She wants me to take her but you're so close, you could just take a run up there, look round.'

'Sure, but I don't honestly think—'

'Nor do I, but I was thrown by knowing the place, having memories of it that are quite separate from anything to do with Susan. I had this sudden picture of her, walking along the sea front near those little terraced houses, past the swing park, the empty pool, to the beach.'

Alec concentrated on refilling his plate, unable to prevent himself seeing this same image. He shrank from the idea of going to Amble to pretend to look for her. Perhaps Frances was seeing the young Susan, the sister she had parted from. He did not.

Briskly, Frances changed the subject.

'What are you going to do with yourself now you've given up the restaurant?'

'Get a job, I suppose. You can always pick something up in catering. People move on a lot.'

'Like you.'

'Oh well.'

'I was wondering,' she said, moving off again as if she had a list of topics to get through with him and was ticking them off. 'If it had been possible for Kate to have a termination, what would Susan have thought? Would she have persuaded her? She would have picked up on it much earlier, I'm sure of that. Being her mother.'

They had both abandoned the empty and half empty dishes in front of them. Alec wiped up some sauce with a piece of nan bread, but left it on his plate.

'Maybe,' he said.

'Were they close?'

'Sometimes.'

Exasperated, Frances pushed her plate away. 'All I'm asking is what would her mother *want*. If she were here. Which she's not.'

'I wish we'd had that bottle of wine you wouldn't let me order,' Alec said. 'Then maybe you'd loosen up a bit.'

She folded her napkin. 'I beg your pardon?'

'Oh come on, Fran, I can't talk to you. This barrier's up, all the time. You've been offended with me for nigh on fifteen years. Couldn't we forget it now, have a normal conversation?'

'*Forget it?*'

He tried again. 'Susan's *your* sister. You must know what she would want.'

'Not now.' She lowered her voice, conscious of other people round them, though the restaurant was quiet. 'She wasn't mentally disturbed when I saw her last. Selfish, self-centred – deceitful. But hardly deranged.'

'You don't understand,' he said. 'It's just the same now. Only more so.'

Frances gave way, weary. 'Sorry. I'm a bit *stretched* just now. Worried to death about Kate.'

Looking at her face, a frown tight between her eyes, he thought, 'she does care for her, she minds for Kate, not herself.' Realising this, he relaxed, knowing there was something in her he could trust that was not just her fierce integrity. There was something vulnerable, open, if not to him then to Kate. He finished his beer and set the glass down.

'Susan would see all this in terms of how it affected her. What I mean is, her response would depend on how she saw it impacting on her image of herself.'

'But surely—'

'You said she was self centred, and I said it was more of the same. Everything centred – centres – on Susan. Would she want to be a grandmother, the mother of a single parent? How would she see that reflecting on her? In one humour, it might be Ok, she would imagine Susan bravely supporting her daughter, getting another crack at bringing up a child without actually having to give birth. Or else—' he hesitated.

'What? What could be worse than *that?*'

'Or else she would be angry and hysterical, and go on and on at Kate, blaming her for being stupid. She would forget, she would simply stop knowing, that she had done the same thing herself.'

For a moment Frances did not answer. When

309

she did, it was a startlingly young Frances he glimpsed, uncertain and sad.

'What you say explains a lot.'

Gillian and Paul ordered a second bottle of wine as they finished the main course. They had talked about mutual friends, holidays and how good it was to live in Edinburgh during the Festival, except that you didn't often get the chance to see much.

'It's our busiest time,' Gillian said. 'We always have two or three things on the go. I don't have more than a few free evenings all the way through.'

'Exciting, though. You must enjoy it.'

'Yes, I do.' She brightened at his understanding. 'This is lovely wine – what is it?'

They talked about wine. The waiter cleared away their plates and brought the menu without asking whether they wanted to see it again. He could tell they would be at the table a good hour yet, settled in for a long evening.

Over tiramisu, they moved on to families. Paul had three older brothers, all working in other countries. This gave them something else in common – both were youngest in the family. Gillian, warmed and softened by good wine and rich food, began talking about her sisters. There was a story there, after all. She was aware, of course, that it was the newness of their relationship made him so attentive. It was always like this at first, when you have not heard each other's stories, or had time to doubt beliefs and aspirations which later may seem to harden into prejudice.

'Missing?' he said, when she told him about Susan. 'That's terrible. When did it happen?'

She did not tell him about Kate. Through the wine-induced haze, something remained clear and hard. She did not want to talk about pregnancy at all. Anyway, Frances would see sense, or Kate would, and it might all be over by now with no harm done.

Jim and Grace watched the news, but Grace dozed off, since it was the same news she had watched at six and heard at one on Radio 4.

'Just see the forecast, eh, then we'll put it off.' She started awake as he spoke and the tapestry slipped from her lap. She caught at it.

'Oh dear, I think I nodded off there.'

'Didn't miss anything. That Tory politician's resigned. The other one.'

'I thought he would.' She tucked her needle in her sewing, safely in the centre, and put it all away in the work bag that leaned against her arm-chair. 'Now then. Cup of tea?'

'Not for me.' He shifted in his chair. 'Think I'll take a turn round the block. You want to come?'

'I sometimes think it's a pity we haven't a wee dog,' she said, getting to her feet. 'It would give you an excuse for your late night strolls.'

'Don't need an excuse. Fresh air's good enough.'

'Put your jacket on then. It's been a fine day, but it is only April.'

When he was ready to go he found her in the kitchen, tidying dishes away.

'You want to come?'

'I don't think so. I'm ready for my bed.'

Later, she was to say, *if only I had gone with him*, but she never did. The evening walk was a habit he had got into when he walked Miss Gibson's dog after she became housebound. About three years ago, the dog had taken a fit and died. She had suggested they get a pet of their own, maybe a West Highland terrier like Jock, but he had said they were too old to start with a dog now. He had been fidgety all day, so the walk would do him good, help him to sleep, dog or no dog. She filled her hot water bottle and went upstairs to bed. She meant to read for a while in peace before he came in.

Kate, Michelle and Amy were watching a video on the television in Michelle's room. The main characters in the film were students at an American college, uniformly good-looking with glossy hair, perfect figures and all-over tans. The girls crowded on Michelle's single bed, eating crisps and drinking coke, since Michelle's mother was in and would find out if they drank anything stronger. Kate said she wasn't going to drink alcohol till after the baby was born.

'I think I'll get a book about it,' she said. 'About the best stuff to eat and drink.'

'My cousin's got one,' Amy said. 'I'll ask her for a lend, if you like.'

Somehow, the balance of knowledge and sophistication had shifted. Kate, for all the drama of her situation, was the one who knew least. The others had cousins, aunts and friends of the family with babies. They were full of good advice. Meekly, Kate accepted it. She was so sleepy she didn't know how she was going to stay awake till the end of the film.

'What about going for a drink?' Alec asked. He paid the bill and Frances did not argue. He owed her the meal, at least. He put his credit card away and stood up. 'Or what about stopping at the off licence to get a couple of bottles of wine? Then we don't have to worry about driving home.'

'I have to admit I wouldn't mind a drink,' Frances said, as the waiter brought her jacket.

The flat was only fifteen minutes away but Paul stopped a cab. Meeting the fresh April air had made Gillian a little unsteady.

'You want to come up?' she asked as the taxi drew to a halt at her door.

'Sure.' He took her arm and helped her out.

'I'm fine,' she said, giggling, letting him hold her, hunting for her key while he paid the fare.

When she opened the front door the Fletchers'

cat slipped out past them and ran along the pavement, close to the railings. Paul kept one arm
round her as they went slowly upstairs. On the
landing, they stopped in an embrace and the kiss
went on a long time, his hands up inside her jacket,
her shirt untucked, his hands cool on bare skin.
Not yet, she was thinking, I'm not ready yet, I
have to be careful. He did not know this, and all
the signals he read in her face, her body, were
telling him to go ahead. They swayed a little,
balanced at the top of the stairs, until she moved
her mouth, damp and hot, away from his.

'Paul—'

'What is it?'

The wine cloud still filled her head and she could
not think straight. 'Coffee,' she said. 'I'll make
coffee.'

Jim marched round the crescent, his pace slowing
as he came down his own street. He found he had
to slow still further, in fact stop for a breather. So
he did, putting one hand on a lamp post to steady
himself. He had had pains in his legs all day and
although he had tried to ignore them as he walked,
they were worse now. Old age, he thought angrily,
old age. There was a tight feeling in his chest and
his head was filling with blood again, hot and
bursting. He put his other hand on the lamp post
too, gripping it.

Debbie was pulling her wheelie bin round the
side of the house. She was just coming down the

path when Jim let go of the lamp post at her gate and slumped forward with a cry. At first she thought, *some drunk*. Debbie was not nervous of drunk men: her father was a great one for booze, and Gary, coming offshore, took a bucket. But there was something odd about the way this man had fallen, the sound he made. She pulled her bin into place on the pavement and looked again.

CHAPTER 6

It was only when they reached home with two bottles of wine that each of them realised they would be spending the night together in the same house, with no-one else there.

Frances rekindled the fire, which had collapsed to a flameless red glow.

'Glasses?' Alec asked.

'In the cabinet.'

'Corkscrew?'

'Kitchen. I'll get it.'

Standing in the kitchen, corkscrew in hand, she wearied, wanting only to go to bed. Let him sit up and drink on his own if he wanted to. What more was there to say?

Alec put a bottle of red down by the fire to warm it, leaving the white Bordaeaux on the table by the window. He asked, 'Do you want to chill that?'

'I'll have red if you are.'

'This is a nice one – lovely nutty aroma.'

'Oh good,' she murmured, not caring.

He stood in the middle of the room warming the glass in both hands. 'This is a nice house.'

Without wanting to know, she asked, 'What's yours like, in Newcastle?'

'Victorian terrace.'

'No garden then?'

'Back yard.'

'Well.' Frances set down her glass, as if that was that, the night was over.

'I suppose we should have a Plan A and a Plan B, shouldn't we?'

'How do you mean?'

Alec refilled his glass, but Frances waved him away; hers was hardly touched. He said, 'What we do for Kate if Susan is here, and what we do if she's not.'

'Is she planning to *come* back?'

'I never know. I mean, I don't know now.' Alec sank onto the sofa and closed his eyes. Frances, with a shock of hurt, saw his young and sleeping face as it had been once, lost and unreachable in dreams, but still beside her where she could wake him with a touch and bring him back. Not now.

Alec opened his eyes and smiled at her. He had not shaved since morning and the dark shadow gave him the look of a man who has been up too long.

'Sorry,' he said. 'Long drive, and a bit of a shock at the end of it. Knackered.'

'We can talk in the morning.'

'I don't think I could sleep. Not without some more of this.'

How often they had done this before, with

Frances going to bed hoping he would come soon and turn to her with his wine-tannined breath, his hands travelling the length of her, pulling her close against him as he had done when they were first married. Abruptly, she got up and stirred the fire, needing to move.

Alec poured himself more wine, feeling there was still no way past the barriers. The years together crowded his mind: marriage, children, the clutter of possessions and Sunday afternoons together by the sea, fish and chips in the car, so that it would smell of them on Monday when he drove to work. Marriage, with its endless meals together, the discussions about money, and lamplight and children's stories when he came in at seven. In his head all these things were jumbled together with memories of earlier days: redecorating their first flat, then their house in Northumberland, the pots of paint stacked in the garage, the ordinariness of life lived in tandem. Suddenly he recalled a pair of her gloves left in his car, lying on the passenger seat unnoticed till he reached the office and took them up, smelling of clean leather, and underneath of Frances herself, her dry warm, sweet-scented hands.

Watching her, as he lounged on her high-backed sofa, chosen and bought without him, he let these memories crowd in, and wondered how the rich tapestry of that life could dwindle to no more than a brittle irritation.

Frances said, brisk again, 'What's Plan A?'

'That's easy. If Susan's here we don't actually have to do anything.'

She raised her eyebrows. 'Let's just hope she turns up soon.'

'I was being facetious. There is only Plan B – we both know that.'

'So Kate stays here till the baby is born.'

'That would be best if you don't mind too much.'

She stared at him. 'You don't understand a thing, do you?'

'Probably not.' He tried a smile but she looked away.

'The real difficulty is afterwards,' she pointed out, taking up her glass and letting him refill it.

'I can help. I am her father, to all intents and purposes.'

Frances laughed. 'You're proposing to look after this infant for her?'

'Well, not exactly *that*. I haven't a job though, so I could be around.'

'Really?' She did not believe him, and anyway did not want this.

'I thought I might sell the house in Newcastle. It's in my name, so there's no problem about that. I'd have a bit of capital to draw on and I could even move up here if Kate wanted to stay in the area. Property prices are much lower.'

'Move here?' *Go away*, she pleaded silently, *I wish you'd go and leave us alone.* After two glasses of wine, she was less guarded. 'Don't you have a life in Newcastle? What would you do here?

Anyway, what if Susan comes home, and you've sold the *house?* You *can't* do that.'

'You don't want me here.' He leaned forward. 'Is there a boyfriend, is that it?'

'That's absolutely none of your business.'

He abandoned this. 'Well, I don't see the point in waiting for Susan. I have waited, quite a long time.'

'I can't believe this.' She set her glass down with a sharp clink on the wooden floor. 'You're giving up on your *wife*, barely four months after she disappears. You said yourself she was ill. She could be in desperate circumstances. Alec, she could be dead.' She stopped, appalled. Only the wine could have made her say this.

'Well, if she's dead, there absolutely *no* point in hanging about.'

'You really are a useless husband.'

'Christ, you've no bloody idea. None at all.'

'Have you gone off her, is that it? How long did it take you to start being sorry, regretting your wild elopement?' Her voice rose.

He did not answer, and in the silence her words echoed.

'I'm going to bed,' she said, trembling. 'I've had too much wine, I'm not used to it, and I'm saying things I really would rather not say.'

His voice was low, but she did not mistake the words. 'Of course I regretted it. What else? But when you've made a decision like that you've got to stick with it.' They looked at each other in silence, then he pushed the flick of hair off his forehead and smiled. 'Fran, you made it impossible. There was no way back.'

'I don't want to hear this,' she said. 'I'm going to bed.'

He watched her go and did not try to stop her. Instead he sat down, finished the bottle and opened the Bordeaux, letting the whole terrible day settle into a cloud of confusion, dimmer now, less painful, nothing hurting except a long way off.

It was awkward, that stage where you knew you were both thinking about it, but you weren't familiar enough yet to say anything. Gillian sometimes thought the best way to deal with it was to get drunk, then you didn't care so much how it turned out, and you could feel less responsible anyway.

Back in the flat, she seemed to wake up, sobered, and went into her tiny kitchen to make coffee.

'Put some music on,' she suggested, but he followed her. The place was so narrow she could not move without brushing against him, so she stood still, filling the kettle. He put his arms round her, and looking down she saw his hands clasped round her stomach, the nails clean but slightly too long, and his gold signet ring.

'I don't want any more coffee,' he said. 'Do you?'

She set the kettle down on the draining board. 'Actually, I'd rather have tea.'

He let her go but he was still there when she turned, and held her again, pushing her against the sink, bending to kiss her. She slid away from him. 'Sorry, must go to the loo.'

In the bathroom mirror her own face looked back at her, makeup gone, skin flushed, a piece of hair sticking up at the back. She splashed her face with cold water, dried it roughly, combed her hair and patched with concealer the blotchy area on her chin. Better.

He was looking along her bookshelves. *Do I want to go to bed with you?* She stared at his turned back, the space on his brown neck between hairline and collar, the specks of dandruff on his jacket, the trousers expensive but a little too tight at the waist, the polished shoes. *You're a stranger.*

He turned and smiled then and she thought, he is very nice-looking, you've got to admit that. We're getting on fine, no need to panic.

They sat on the sofa, Paul with a beer, Gillian with her mug of tea.

'It was a lovely meal,' she said. 'I've only been in that place once and I'm sure it wasn't as good.'

'New owners,' he explained. 'My mate Chris tipped me off. They used to have a place in Glasgow he went to a lot.' He put his arm along the sofa behind her. 'You Ok?'

'Fine.'

'You want to go to bed?'

She laughed, disarmed. 'The approach direct . . . Oh God, I don't know.'

'Best to know where we are, eh?' He leaned over and began nuzzling her neck, so that she gave way and let him kiss her again. Why not, she thought, nothing to stop me.

In the bedroom in the dark, they collapsed in a tangle of clothes half-pulled off, and she gasped, *wait, wait,* helping him, undoing his belt buckle, pulling her shirt over her head. She leaned into him, hands on his warm back, the smoothness of his olive skin, the movement of muscles underneath. This was it, this was the moment, she knew, as she kicked off her trousers, when they would see each other for the first time, and in all the confusion something would be clear at last, that it was right, or wrong, a mistake. His hand came down under her pants, between her legs, warm, cupping her underneath, a finger rubbing, then pushing deeper and she cried out *No!* She grabbed his arm and thrust it away, flinging herself off the bed and away from him, tugging bra straps up, staggering back.

'What the—' He stared at her, then jerked up his trousers, without zipping them, leaving his belt dangling. She could still feel his finger hot inside her.

'I don't want – I don't want you to do that.' She began to cry, tears streaming down, hands over her face, shaking. He waited a moment to see if she would stop, then got off the bed and went back to the living-room, picking up his shirt as he left. She ran to the door and pushed it shut behind him, then lay on the bed till the sobbing died away and she was still.

Silence.

Perhaps he had gone. Well, she didn't care. Let him think she was off her head, frigid, weird, whatever. She didn't care. She sat up and blew her nose, rubbing her face with a clean tissue, then put her dressing gown on, tightening the belt with shaking fingers, damp with tears.

He was sitting on the sofa with a fresh beer, waiting for her.

'Thought I'd better not go till I saw you were all right.'

'That was nice of you.'

'You want to talk, tell me what's wrong? I don't think I misread the signals.'

'No,' she admitted. 'Sorry.'

'You want a drink? Do you have brandy? You're white as a sheet.'

'No, I don't want a drink. Maybe a cup of tea, I don't know.'

She listened to him moving about in her kitchen. He did not once come back and ask where she kept anything, but reappeared in a few minutes with a mug of tea.

'Couldn't find any sugar.'

'I don't take it.'

'So I put honey in. Here, drink it up.'

She could taste the honey, clover sweet.

'I must look terrible. I feel terrible.'

'I can tell.'

He sat beside her while she sipped her tea. 'Don't take this the wrong way, but if you'd like me to stay, I will.'

'Stay?'

'Just stay. Sleep on the sofa, or in bed with you if you want a cuddle. That's all.'

'You must think I'm totally weird.' She leaned against his chest, his arm round her.

'Don't worry about it,' he said.

In Michelle's bedroom, top to tail with Amy on an assortment of blankets and sleeping bags, Kate slept, waking once in the night from a dream about her mother. Susan was in Frances's garden and she wouldn't come into the house, however hard Kate tried to persuade her. Then she said she wanted coffee but when Kate went into the kitchen to make it Frances was there, and she was afraid to tell her Susan was outside. She began lying to Frances, began worrying that if she didn't take the coffee out soon, Susan would have gone. She woke in the hard panic of worrying what to do. Next to her Michelle lay on her back with her mouth open, snoring.

In Balmoral Crescent an ambulance drew up at the kerb, blue light flashing, and a man and a young woman got out. By this time Grace was kneeling beside Jim, afraid to move him, trying to listen to his breathing, which was faint and hoarse. Debbie hovered nearby, wishing she had put a jacket on, but not liking to leave Grace. Maybe he would die. She hoped he would not, since she had never seen a dead person and it would be so upsetting for Grace. The paramedics moved Grace gently out of the way and bent close to her husband.

In the night, Frances's telephone rang on the bedside table. She woke in a fright, heart thumping. Downstairs, Alec heard it but made no move to answer, having finished the bottle of Bordeaux by this time.

CHAPTER 7

Frances left a list of instructions with Alec and called a sleepy Kate at Michelle's house.

Kate muttered, 'it's so *early*, nobody's up yet', and then, taking in what Frances was saying, gasped, 'Are you going *away*?'

She was not frightened for her grandfather, scarcely known; her alarm was all because Frances would not be there.

'When are you coming back?'

'Friday, probably. Andrew will be home on Saturday, so I'll have to be home then. It depends how Grandpa is and how Granny is coping.'

They were not Granny and Grandpa to Kate, but Frances used the names without thinking. Kate lowered her voice,

'Did you tell him?'

'What? Oh yes, he knows. Don't worry, Kate.'

'I'm not.'

Back in Michelle's room, where the other girls, still drowsy, lay wrapped in duvets, she said, 'My Grandad's had a heart attack.'

$\star$ $\star$ $\star$

Frances was on the road by nine. She spoke to her mother before she left, a less frightened and confused Grace by this time, the panic gone from her voice.

'He's stable,' she reassured Frances. 'They think he'll be all right, but it depends on the next few days.'

'I'll be with you by lunch-time. Should I meet you at the hospital?'

'No dear, come to the house and have a bite to eat first. You'll need it after the long drive and we can go up in the afternoon. They'll phone if there's any change.'

'Have you slept?'

'Not really.'

'Go to bed then, get some rest. See you soon.'

Grace sighed. 'Maybe I'll do that. Oh dear, I can't get over it. In the *street*. What a good thing that lassie was there.'

'Have you spoken to Gillian?'

But Grace had called only Frances, because she was the one they turned to, knowing she would take care of everything.

Gillian had slept in after a night of fitful dozing, restless with someone else in the bed. She had forgotten to set the alarm and when Frances called at half past eight, she woke with a start and stumbled out of bed, grabbing the phone on the table beside her. 'Oh God, look at the time – hello?'

Frances was so calm it took Gillian a moment or two to understand just how serious her news was. She turned away from the bed, not wanting Frances to know there was anyone else there, and cradled the phone with a hand over her free ear, concentrating.

'He's going to be all right, though?' she asked, as Paul got up and went into the bathroom. 'What will I do? Should I come up now? I'll go to work first, I have to. Oh God, he's not going to die?' She could not imagine her father submitting to the indignity of a hospital bed. 'Will you call me when you've seen him? I'll come up tonight, that's best. Do you think?'

'Calm down,' Frances said. 'Mum said he was sleeping quite peacefully this morning. He's survived the worst and he's strong for his age.'

'So I'll wait to hear from you?'

'Yes, don't worry.'

Paul was in the shower. Gillian saw him turn, naked behind the screen, and had a spasm of lust, shaming and inappropriate. Too late now. She fetched him a clean towel and he stepped out, taking it from her.

'What's up?'

My father's had a heart attack. My sister Fran is going to Aberdeen this morning. I think I'll go too, maybe tonight.'

'How bad is it?'

'Fran seems to think he'll be all right.'

They faced each other in the steamy bathroom. He put out a finger and smoothed it down the side of her cheek.

'See you when you get back, then. Hope everything works out.'

'I'll call you. Sorry, better get on, I'm incredibly late. Help yourself to breakfast.'

There was something disquieting about how readily he made himself at home in her flat: using the toaster, finding butter and honey, clearing dishes left in the sink overnight.

'You want toast?' he asked.

'I'll just have tea. I don't usually eat breakfast, and I really couldn't face it today.'

'You should try, you've had a shock.' He smiled at her and pushed another piece of bread in the toaster. Gillian gazed at him, not sure what she felt, still stunned by fear and the inexplicable guilt which her father seemed to spark in her.

She was used to being alone in her flat in the morning, and to silence. Paul turned on the radio and sat eating toast and drinking coffee on her sofa. The smell of these things penetrated the whole place too early, too strongly. He leafed through the section of yesterday's paper she usually reserved for morning. How long was he planning to hang around? She couldn't fix her makeup in the living-room mirror which had the best light, while he was there, so she went into the bedroom instead, feeling put out. She straightened pillows on the tousled bed and folded the duvet back, but the room when she left it still had a louche, dishevelled air.

In the street they parted and Gillian walked to

330

work in sunshine. Along the pavement people strode, some with mobile phones already clasped to their ears. The thin trees lining the street were coming into bud and their sparse branches quivered with a haze of palest green. Gillian, setting off in a hurry, turned back to catch a glimpse of Paul at the far corner, not looking back at her.

All the rest of the way to office her thoughts buzzed dementedly between the night just gone and anxiety about her father. She sank into guilty acceptance of what must happen. He would die. Their mother would be on her own and she would have to come and stay more often, needing the company. She pictured her mother bereft and lonely, but somehow that didn't seem true. She might be quite different, Gillian thought as she reached the office and pushed through the glass doors. Free of him she might flourish; she might even be happy. Restless and anxious, Gillian avoided the lift and ran up two flights instead.

Frances reached her parents' house at half past twelve, and her mother, who had been standing by the bay window watching for her, came to open the front door. Awkwardly, since they were not a demonstrative family, Frances hugged her, conscious Grace seemed smaller these days, plumpness dissolving with age.

'Come away in. I've lentil soup heating so we'll have a bite before we go up and see him.'

'How is he?'

'No word since I left the hospital this morning. He was sleeping then, he seemed not so bad.'

When they reached the hospital about an hour later visitors were beginning to straggle in with their flowers and magazines and newly-washed nightwear. A nurse met them at the entrance to the Intensive Care Unit and told them Jim had been moved out. He was in a small side ward with four beds, in Cardiology. One had screens round, one was empty and in the other a skeletal old man lay asleep with his mouth open, nose in the air like a featherless bird.

Frances's father lay in bed with a drip stand on one side, the swivel tray table on the other still bare except for a grey papier mache sick bowl. He was drowsy but awake and raised one hand in greeting. He seemed hardly to be there under the green hospital blanket and white sheet, barely lifting them from the mattress. Frances swallowed her fear: surely everyone felt like this about hospitals, seeing how the people they loved were diminished simply by being there. Jim, though, had a gleam of resentment in his eyes as he watched them approach the bed.

'How are you feeling, Dad?' She bent and kissed his dry cheek, smelling disinfectant and starched linen instead of his own scent, masculine and weathered.

'Very frustrated,' he said. 'They won't let me get up.'

'I should think not.' Grace sat on a plastic chair

on the same side as the drip stand. 'But I see you're not wired up to that machine any more.' She turned to Frances. 'They had him on a monitor, with those lines going across it on a screen.'

'Get yourself a chair.' Jim turned his head and nodded at the bed opposite. 'Take one of those – *he* won't be having visitors.' He meant the sleeper, who had not stirred. For a few seconds Frances wondered if he had actually died, with no-one noticing. 'Down and out,' said her father. 'Nurse told me they had to give him two baths to get him even half clean.'

Frances fetched a chair and sat down. 'You seem fine to me,' she said, 'for somebody who had a massive heart attack last night.'

'Massive, rubbish. Moderate. Nothing to get in a state about. Be home soon.'

'We'll see,' Grace said, looking doubtful. If he's all right, Frances was thinking, I can go home soon. Tomorrow. Especially if Gillian will come and do her bit. Glancing at her mother, that tight pursing of the mouth, the way she sat upright in the hard chair, she was flushed with love and pity and did not want to leave her. All those feelings, she thought, that you have for your parents, always changing, the love all mixed up with resentment and pity and irritation.

As if he wanted to remind them who was in charge here, her father raised a hand again and asked, 'Gillian coming?'

'Sometime today.'

'And what about Susan, did you speak to Susan?'

Frances's heart jolted. What did he mean? Had he forgotten, in the shock of illness, what had happened? She looked at her mother, trying to catch her eye, but Grace was smoothing the bedcover and shaking her head.

'Don't worry about Susan,' she told her husband.

'Worry?' He shifted his legs and moved his head from side to side. 'Ach, hospitals,' he muttered. 'Bloody hard bed.' Then he lay still and closed his eyes.

'Jim?'

He grunted a response but did not speak. Frances and Grace sat in silence, waiting, but the change in his breathing, the way his head sank onto the pillow, arms relaxed by his sides, told them he had fallen into a doze.

'He's not quite himself yet,' Grace said.

They went on sitting there, watchful beside the sleeping man. All at once the old fellow in the bed opposite sprang awake, raised his head, shouted *Get tae fuck!* and fell back grumbling and fidgeting and calling for the nurse. Frances caught sight of one going past the ward and got up to attract her attention.

The nurse tucked the old man in again, more firmly this time, but he went on cursing and grumbling, so she pulled the curtains round his bed. 'I'll be back in a minute, Billy,' she told him. 'You lie still and dinna disturb other folk.'

She raised her eyes at Frances and Grace as she went out. 'Sorry about the language,' she said.

Frances looked at her father but he was asleep, unperturbed. Grace leaned across, whispering, 'They must get all sorts in here. You feel sorry for the nurses.'

As they sat waiting for Jim to wake again, listening to the muttered oaths from the curtained bed, Frances's thoughts jumped to Kate. How were she and Alec getting on? She had an impulse of longing to be with them in her own house, then immediately felt guilty. She looked at her mother, who was watching her husband's sleeping face with an expression Frances could not read. Not anxiety or sympathy, but something else. She is preparing herself for him dying, Frances decided. She thinks she may have to face that. Yet it did not seem her father had even brushed close to death. As a doctor arrived with the nurse, and disappeared behind the curtains of the bed opposite, the slight disturbance woke Jim and he opened his eyes. For a few seconds he was bewildered, but as soon as he saw Grace he knew who and where he was.

'How are you, Dad?' Frances put a hand on the bed to draw his attention.

'I think they've given me something. Keep nodding off.' He looked at Grace. 'Your mother's the one who has the cat naps usually. Not me.'

'You need to sleep,' Grace retorted. 'Get some rest, till you're a bit stronger.'

Jim turned to Frances again. 'What about the boys, where are they?'

'They went to some concert in Glasgow. I've left messages on both their phones.'

'No sense in worrying them anyway.' Jim turned his head to look at Grace. 'You don't have to stay. No need.'

'Well . . .' Grace hesitated. 'Maybe we'll leave you in peace for now. Come back this evening.'

'Aye. You do that.' He was drifting again, his eyes drooping. Quietly, Frances and Gillian got up, replaced chairs and left the ward.

'He'll be fine, Mum,' Frances said as they waited for the lift.

'We've had a fright,' Grace sighed, 'but it could have been much worse.'

It is much worse, Frances thought, you don't know how much worse everything is. They stepped into the lift beside someone in a wheelchair with a nurse, and two other visitors. What could happen Frances wondered, as they descended in silence to the ground floor, so bad that my mother would *not* say it could be worse. Maybe this was it: a pregnant Kate.

When they reached the car and she switched on her mobile phone, there were two messages, from Gillian and Jack. She spoke to her sons first; when she called Gillian the connection was poor with a lot of background noise.

'I'm on the train,' Gillian said. 'People with mobiles are always saying that. I get in at five something, so will you meet me? How's Dad?'

'Out of intensive care. Sleepy, but all right.'

'Thank goodness, what a relief for Mum. Five fifteen, Ok?'

Before Frances could reply the connection broke up and Gillian vanished.

As she drove her mother home, Frances decided not to say anything about Kate yet. It was too complicated and her mother had enough to worry about. I wish I had my old ordinary life back, she thought. But she did not wish Kate away, even a pregnant Kate. Not that.

CHAPTER 8

'What's happening about Kate?'

Their mother had gone to bed exhausted, while Frances and Gillian remained downstairs, having a drink together. Frances would have liked to go to bed too, but Gillian was restless and wanting to talk. They had finished discussing their father. What more could they do except put aside for now their fear that he might die? It looked as if that wasn't going to happen. In the house his presence was still powerful though he was out of it: they saw his jacket hanging in the hall, his business room with the chair pushed back from the desk just as he had left it, papers spread out, a pen laid on top, his diary on the top right hand corner. On top of the bookcase were his golfing trophies and a framed photograph of a rural museum he had designed many years ago.

In the living-room there was more of their mother, less of him. Her plants crowded the windowsill and she had assembled family photographs in pretty frames on the sideboard. Her tapestry bag leaned against her chair and her glasses lay on the table with the lamp. These things, this house, made Gillian restless.

Frances was taking too long to answer.

'Has *anything* happened?' Gillian demanded.

'I can't remember when we last spoke about it,' Frances said. 'I told you about Alec. Andrew's back on Saturday so I'll have to tell him then.'

Gillian flung herself back in the armchair. 'She's still pregnant, isn't she?'

'It was too late for anything else,' Frances protested. 'Anyway, she didn't want—'

'I don't believe this. You're actually letting her have a baby at *fifteen*?'

'It's not a question of *letting* her. By the time we'd seen the doctor, she was twenty weeks.'

'Twenty!'

'I can't imagine what you're so worked up about,' Frances snapped. 'It's not as if it's going to make a blind bit of difference to your life.'

'Of course it will!'

'You're not the one who'll have to support her while she goes through all this. Organise child-minding and help Kate get into college. Have a house full of nappies and all the paraphernalia babies bring with them.'

And then, of course, Frances realised just what she had said. Gillian did not give her time for apology or retraction.

'How can you be so fucking insensitive?' she wailed, springing up from her chair, compelled to move but having nowhere to go except up and down the living-room, kicking a footstool out of the way.

'Sit down. Don't get so – I'm *sorry*.'

Gillian sank into her chair. 'She's got a mother, hasn't she? And a step-father. I don't see why *you* have to make some sort of martyr of yourself.'

'I am really sorry. I didn't mean to hurt you.'

'I asked for it, didn't I? Set myself up for this.'

'You didn't *want* to have a baby. Did you?' Frances's heart sank. 'You're not regretting it?'

'No.' Gillian shrugged. 'Och, whatever. It has quite an effect on your hormones. I'm touchy, emotional. I wish somebody had warned me, that's all.'

'There's no good solution, is there?'

'It doesn't seem like it. At least I'm grown up, I've got a job, a life. Kate's not done anything yet.'

'If it's any comfort, I feel absolutely terrible,' Frances admitted. 'But an abortion at twenty weeks – well, twenty two at least, by the time it happened – that would be awful, wouldn't it?'

'Yes.'

'Was it bad?' Frances wasn't sure she should ask this when Gillian was so volatile, but the words were out, in a tone as gentle as she could manage.

Gillian's eyes filled with tears. 'It was foul.' She looked round for her bag to find a paper tissue, but Frances reached hers first.

'Here.'

'I'm pathetic. I was fine you know, I was over it. I coped very well. All this with Kate – I suppose it's upset me.'

Frances waited while Gillian blew her nose and recovered.

'You're right, of course, about Kate having a mother. And a father of sorts. But who knows when Susan's going to reappear.'

'How did Alec react?'

'Shocked. It's quite a good thing I've left them together, since he's going to have to come to terms with it. He wants to help, somewhat to my surprise.'

'It seems weird to me,' Gillian remarked as she poured them both another drink, 'that you and Alec are fussing round the girl as if she's your daughter and she doesn't belong to either of you.'

Maybe she's not our daughter, Frances thought, but she does belong. Not to us – there isn't an *us* – but we both love her. She flushed, as if Gillian might read these thoughts and sense how much they moved her.

'Anyway,' Gillian went on, more calmly, 'Alec said Susan was all right, she came back for clothes and stuff.'

'That doesn't mean she's all right.'

'Are you sure Alec doesn't know more than he's telling? Look at his life. He's got no job, no business any more, his wife's mysteriously vanished, and now Kate. You'd think it would be hell.'

'I don't know, I can't see him straight. I dare say I'm too hard on him. The past gets in the way.'

'Every time I see him he's anxious, sure, but not what you'd call devastated. Not even at Christmas, when no-one knew what had happened and she could have been in the – what's the river – the Tyne?'

'He wasn't worried because she'd done it before. Gone off, come back,' Frances protested. She was suddenly uneasy.

'So has he got desperate now, after all these months have passed and she hasn't come home?'

Frances thought of Alec saying he would sell the house, move. *I have waited, quite a long time.* 'Not desperate, no,' she said.

'Well then.'

'Alec gives up easily, he always did. Line of least resistance. That's his strong point, you could say.' Frances was thinking about what Gillian had said. 'If he did have some idea of where she's gone he would tell Kate. He wouldn't keep *her* in this awful limbo.'

'Maybe he thinks she's better off without her mother. Or maybe he doesn't want to tell her Susan's never coming back.'

'He doesn't *know* if she will.'

'I think he does know.'

Frances whitened. 'You're imagining things.'

Gillian did not answer, just raised her hands, palms upwards, and for a moment they looked at each other in dismay as Susan hovered between them like a ghost they both longed and feared to materialise.

★   ★   ★

342

Alec and Kate were in Frances's kitchen and she was making hot chocolate. He had cooked a risotto for them both earlier in the evening and Kate, who had now wakened three mornings in a row without nausea, had eaten more than he had.

'I think I'll have toast,' she announced. 'Do you want some?'

'No thanks.' He smiled. 'Glad to see you're eating for two.'

She made a face at him. 'Shut up, I'm hungry. 'I've been throwing up for weeks, I've hardly eaten anything. I need to catch up.' She put two slices of bread in the toaster.

Alec sat down with his coffee, watching her as she stirred her hot chocolate then rummaged in the cupboard till she found a packet of marshmallows. She dropped two on top of the chocolate.

'That looks disgusting. How can you drink it?'

'Easily.'

As she buttered her toast he said, 'Well, this is a fine mess you've landed us in.'

'Stop saying that, it's boring.' She began eating toast and poking at the marshmallows with a spoon as they melted slowly.

Left to themselves they had fallen into their old relationship with its accustomed banter.

'Right then,' Alec said, 'what's Plan A?'

He had forgotten, suggesting his Plans A and B to Frances, it was not something that went back to his marriage to her. It was what he and Kate did, dealing with Susan, or the absence of Susan.

When she was younger it was his device for giving her the illusion they had some control and something could be done. Sometimes it could but not for Susan, only themselves.

'I dunno,' Kate said, her mouth full. 'Haven't got any plans.'

'That seems to be the trouble.'

'Frances has got plans,' she admitted. 'She's got enough plans for everybody in the world.'

'Do you want to come home?'

Kate looked surprised. 'To St James's Street?'

'Well, yes.'

'Mum's not there, is she?'

'You know she's not.'

'Where is she then? Tell me where she is.'

Wearily, Alec rubbed his hands over his face. 'Don't, Kate.'

This was the black side of their easy sparring. He went down into silence, not answering her, however hard she pushed. Whatever he said, she would not believe him.

'You shouldn't have had that row with her.' She had stopped eating, but went on stirring the remnants of marshmallow around in the bottom of her mug. He did not say 'what row', because there was no point. He did not say anything. After a moment, Kate said brightly, 'You know what? Frances gives me a straight answer when I ask her anything.'

'A straight answer about what?'

'Whatever I ask.'

'Is that right. So what are you asking *me?*'

'You know. Tell me where she is.'

He cast his eyes up to the ceiling. 'Tell us where you are,' he murmured, 'for Christ's sake.'

'Don't!' Kate scraped her chair back. 'Shut up.'

'Sorry.' He finished his coffee. 'Drink your cocoa or whatever that disgusting mess is. I can't tell you anything, you know that.'

Kate folded her arms. 'Plan A is Mum coming back and being Ok.'

He nodded, miserable. That was always Plan A.

'And Plan B, I stay here.' She glared at him. 'I've got lots of friends here. You can't move me about like a parcel, you know.'

'I do know. You must stay wherever you're happiest.'

'So what are you going to do?'

'I might move up here to be nearer to you.'

'But what if Mum came home? Then she wouldn't know where we were. Would you leave her a note or something?'

'She could ring your mobile.'

'Oh *right*. She could ring it now, according to you, except she hasn't.'

'I was thinking of a more permanent move. I could sell the house and buy one here.'

'But then she'd come back and somebody else would be living in her house! She'd totally freak. That's not fair, you can't do that.'

'No,' he said, helpless, 'it doesn't look like it.'

'So,' she went on, having gained this point, 'she

comes back, we're not there, I mean, not even our clothes, and she rings my mobile, though she's obviously lost the number, so I don't see how she can, but anyhow, she'd say, tell me where you are, and I'd say, Auntie Frances's house.' She stopped, putting her head on one side, as if she had just proved something and was waiting for him to catch up and understand.

He had had enough of this fantasy. '*Her* clothes aren't there either.'

Kate looked blank. 'What did you do with them?'

'Nothing. She came back and cleared out the wardrobe one day while I was at the restaurant.'

Kate went white. 'When?'

'Before Easter. I told Frances and she thought it was best not to say anything. So maybe she doesn't always give you a straight answer.'

He was sorry he had said that. It was petty.

Kate was struggling with this new, appalling information. 'Mum came home and you never told me?'

'I thought, well, we both thought—'

'We?'

'Frances and me.'

'It's Mum you're married to, not Frances.' She was hot with fury and terror. 'Where is she then, where did she go after she came home?'

'I can't tell you. I never saw her.'

Kate stumbled to her feet. 'It's not fair, why can't she just come home and be ordinary?'

Alec reached out a hand to her then let it drop.

'I don't know Kate, honestly. She can't help the way she is, can she?'

Kate was standing very still. Slowly, she put both hands low on her stomach, and waited. She had moved away from him, from their argument, from the world they were in. Abstracted, her eyes wide, she waited. Then with a cry, she let her hands fly to the back of a chair, gripping it to steady herself.

'I felt something,' she gasped. 'I felt this weird little – *flick*. Oh God.' Mesmerised, she put her hands over her belly again, and whispered, 'there's really something *there*.'

In an instant, the baby had invaded both of them like an incubus, from which there was no escape.

CHAPTER 9

Frances had been away for two days and when she came back, Alec seemed to have moved in. He had few possessions and was not obtrusive, but he had familiarised himself with the kitchen and there were new, foreign cooking smells. The wine rack, which often had as many bottles of beer and Irn Bru as of wine, had been replenished, and there was something different about the way dishes had been replaced on their shelves.

Kate looked different too. It surely wasn't possible that in two days the pregnancy had become obvious but that was what Frances saw. Could Kate go back to school now? It was Friday evening and there was no possibility of doing anything until Monday, when Frances herself would be in her own school for an in-service day. She told Kate she would call the Academy and arrange to see her Guidance teacher.

It was nine o'clock when Kenny called and she realised with dismay that she had completely forgotten her promise to spend the evening with him. Full of apologies, she explained what had happened. 'I'd come over now, but it's quite late and I'm not long home.'

'Don't worry. Come round at the weekend. We should have a wee talk, *A Ghraidh*, for old times sake.'

The Gaelic endearment, which she had always liked, made her feel guilty. *Old times sake?* What did he mean?

'Tomorrow,' she said.

'I'll cook for you.'

She hesitated, thinking of leaving Kate, Alec and Andrew together. 'Look, are you at home tomorrow morning? Let me come then and I'll tell you what's going on.'

'I'll brew the coffee,' he said. 'Nice and strong. Eleven o'clock.'

That was settled, then. No need for anxiety, but a niggling doubt lingered: *for old times sake.*

Andrew called at ten. His bus would reach Inverness late in the afternoon – would she meet him? She would, and somehow on the way home she would manage to tell him his cousin was going to have a baby in September.

Gillian was still in Aberdeen with her mother. They went to the hospital twice on Friday and again on Saturday, afternoon and evening. Her father was at his best in the afternoon, at the beginning of the visit. By the evening he seemed less coherent and lay silent. Gillian and her mother tried to keep some conversation going at first, then they too lapsed into silence. Spring bloomed in the pavement trees and in gardens; visitors brought lilies and tulips for the bedside vases, yellow and white and red. A soft air greeted them as they came out at half past eight on Saturday evening. Even the East coast breeze had fallen.

'I'm sorry, Mum,' Gillian said as they reached the house. 'I have to get a train back tomorrow. I'll come up to the hospital for a while early in the afternoon, then I'll get a taxi to the station.'

'You've got your work, dear, I know that.' Grace manoeuvred into the narrow driveway; after thirty years she still did this very slowly. Once she had scraped a car door on the gatepost and Jim's reaction had convinced her only extreme caution would prevent it happening again.

Gillian saw the evening stretch out in front of her. Not nine o'clock yet and nothing more to say about her father. Before she left, Frances had taken her aside.

'If you find an opportunity please tell Mum about Kate. She had plenty to cope with when I arrived, but it looks as if Dad will be OK. She's the best one to tell *him*.'

Gillian had agreed she would try. It would certainly give them something to talk about. She often complained to Frances, 'I'm stifled in that house, that's why I hardly ever visit. And after a day, there's nothing left to say.' Frances did not understand, since she and her mother always had plenty to say to each other. Gillian supposed it must be having children made that difference, since they talked endlessly about the boys. Frances also had the sort of job her mother understood. Gillian didn't know how anyone could be so interested in the squabbles and triumphs of a pack of little kids.

Now there would be another child for them to discuss. She had a pang of jealousy she could not reason away. Imagine, she thought, as her mother went to make tea, Kate and I could have been pregnant together. What a family scandal that would have been. She began to laugh then found herself in tears instead. All through Kate's pregnancy her own lost baby would float like a ghost beside her, forever amoeba like, unformed, with large head and tiny buds of limbs, its eyes closed, blind, unable to see the future it was never going to have. *Oh, what have I done?*

'I couldn't find that packet of chocolate digestives,' Grace said, as she came in. 'I'm sure I bought one with the shopping yesterday. I wonder where I put it?'

Gillian rustled the paper into folds, looking away, then blew her nose.

'You're not starting a cold, I hope,' her mother asked. 'I always think these hospitals are full of germs.'

'I'm fine.'

Grace put the tray down. 'Never mind, these coconut ones are nice.'

'What?'

'The biscuits.'

'Oh.'

Grace sat down with a sigh. 'Mind, I've no appetite myself.'

'No wonder, it's been a pretty stressful few days,' Gillian said, composed again.

'These things come to us when we get older. He takes ill with it, though, being stuck in there. He'll be better once he's home.'

'Nobody likes hospitals.'

The conversation died. Grace picked up a coconut biscuit and nibbled a corner of it as if the taste might bring her appetite back, then left it on the arm of her chair.

'Mum, I think I'd better tell you something.'

'Oh aye, what's that?' She seemed polite rather than curious, putting on her glasses and reaching for the tapestry bag.

'Frances was going to, but with Dad and everything, she felt she didn't want to worry you.'

This was more serious. Grace put the tapestry down again and looked at Grace over her glasses.

'Is this about Susan?'

So she told her. Like Frances, she found there was no way of dressing it up. Only one way to tell. She went on, clumsily explaining it had happened while Kate was still in Newcastle.

'And Susan – was she at home?'

'I think so.'

'No word from her, I suppose?'

'No.'

Grace frowned. 'I don't know. Susan was always . . .' She seemed to shrug Susan off with a sigh. 'Well, I hope they can do something for Kate. At least it's much more straightforward these days.'

With a shock, Gillian took in what her mother meant.

'You mean an abortion? I wouldn't have thought you'd approve of that.'

'You didn't go through the war.'

'What?'

'The lasses I knew. The fellow would be off, back to his regiment, and there they'd be, in the family way. Sometimes the man was killed before he could even be told. Sometimes, of course, he wasn't interested anyway. It was different during the war. People thought they might never see each other again. It made them careless.'

Gillian could understand that.

'In those days,' her mother went on, 'it was all backstreet ways of dealing with it, and those places were terrible. They paid for their mistakes right enough, one way or another.'

Gillian was so taken aback by this it was a few moments before she managed to say,

'Do you think that's what Susan should have done? When – you know—'

'Instead of having Kate? You forget, Susan thought Adam was coming back and that's what made her think she wanted the baby.'

'Oh it was all over, Mum, that's why she came to stay with you and Dad. She said she never wanted to see him again, remember, she was always saying that.'

Grace looked at her, and Gillian had the sensation of being a teenager again with a sister in trouble, a sister who, it seemed, had told her mother more than she realised. It was not Gillian she had confided in, not Frances.

'Oh I know what she *said*,' Grace scoffed, 'but believe me, she thought Adam was coming back. Despite what her father told her.'

'As far as Kate's concerned,' Gillian said, 'I think she'll *have* to have this baby. She didn't tell anyone until it was much too late for an abortion. Even Frances didn't know.'

Grace sat back and took her glasses off.

'Well, well,' she said. 'The silly lassie.'

'So,' Frances explained, 'that's why I've been neglecting you, that's why things are so difficult just now.'

'I see.'

They were in Kenny's kitchen, smelling of the old Rayburn that kept it not quite warm enough in winter and stuffy hot in summer. On a fine April morning it was a comfortable place to sit at the old Formica-topped table, the sun streaming in and showing up the grime on the surfaces, balls of fluff gathered in the corners of the floor. There was a blue glass vase on the table with daffodils opening, and a stronger aroma even than dust and burning logs – coffee fresh and hot. 'The state of this place,' Frances often complained, scouring the mugs before she would drink from them. For the rest, she left the place alone. Kenny liked it this way and it was his place, her escape. She liked it because it was his.

She watched him pour the coffee. He was the same as ever, his beard still with a gleam of ginger among the grey, his springy pepper-and-salt hair, his old check shirt open at the throat, the cuffs rolled back showing the ginger-brown hairs on his chest and arms. He was substantial, comforting, someone to be counted on for company and sympathy. That was what she wanted this morning.

'So you'll be needing stronger coffee than usual,' he said, putting the mug with flying birds in front of her, a mug he had bought in Ullapool because she liked it.

'What I'd love,' she told him, 'is to get back to where I thought I was just before Christmas. Life was quiet and ordinary with work and home and the boys – and seeing you.'

'Nothing stays the same, *A Ghraidh*', he smiled, sitting down opposite her. 'You can't put the clock or the calendar back a single second.'

'No, I know.'

'So I'm sorry, when you're having troubles, to be adding to them. Or maybe not. You're a very independent woman.'

'What's wrong? You're not ill?' This was the fear she had for him, the way he drank, the lack of exercise, his asthma.

'I'm fine. Better than I deserve.' He stretched an arm across the table and took her cool hand in his larger, warmer one. 'I'm thinking of moving away.'

The shock of it hardly registered, since it made no sense. He had lived here for years, he belonged. How could he leave?

'What on earth are you talking about?'

'I might give up the cottage and go and live near Neil and Catriona and the bairns.' Her hand was inert in his, the fingers did not open or return his grasp. He took his hand away. 'I've been enquiring about severance, see will they let me go with a bit of a handshake and a pension. It seems they will so I've to put in for it and sign the forms. After that, I'd be free to go. Neil's been on at me. He thinks I don't look after myself, living on my own.'

'He's right.' She would not feel guilty about this: how many people was she supposed to look after? 'Kenny, you don't want to live with Neil, do you? In Edinburgh?'

'Midlothian. And not with them, no, but get a wee flat.'

'A flat! You always say they're in suburbia.'

He tipped his chair gently on its back legs, and folded his arms across his chest. 'Frances, I'm tired of the solitude. It's not a thing I ever thought I'd say, but I find myself talking to the dog, the shaving mirror, in a way makes me feel I'm half way to the madhouse already.'

'Nonsense. You're the sanest person I know.'

He laughed. 'You're not always of that opinion. Ah no, it's the drinking, I admit it, aren't you glad I'm admitting it at last? With the family close by and the bairns to look after now and again, I'd drink less, I'm sure of it.'

Frances could not think what this sick, sinking feeling was that turned her into a hollow woman. 'Oh Kenny.'

'What is it? You can come and visit me, sure you can. You're a great visitor.'

'Don't! I said I was sorry, please—'

'You've enough to worry you. It's as well the man himself has turned up again.'

'You mean Alec?'

'I went up the other day to see were you there, but his car was by the house so I didn't go in.'

'But he's married to my sister, Kenny, you know that.'

'This would be the sister nobody's seen for several months?'

'Yes, but—'

'It's good to see you today, at last.'

'But,' she cried with a gasp, the words hurting her to say them, 'I need you here. I don't want you to go away and live somewhere else.' She covered her face with her hands. His chair thudded down on all four legs, scraped back, and he got up and came to her.

'It's only my coffee and the dog you'd miss.'

She took her hands away and breathed deep. 'I'm all right,' she said. 'Sorry.' He hesitated then

357

put his arms round her shoulders. She leaned into him, her cheek against the swell of his stomach, feeling the heat from him, his solid strength.

She would just stay there for a moment, held in the illusion that he would always be there, and she could always come to him.

As soon as Andrew got off the bus and saw his mother, he knew something was up.

'How's Grandpa?' he asked as he heaved his bag onto the back seat of the car and got in beside her.

'Much better. He'll be home in a few days. How was the concert?'

'Magic.' He glanced at her again as she put the car in gear. '*Mum!*'

'What is it?'

'You got your hair cut!'

'You noticed.' She grinned at him, turning her head. How light it was, how airy and light. The long coil of her hair was on the back seat, probably flattened by his rucksack now, in a polythene bag the hairdresser had given her. She did not know why she had taken it with her, this macabre object, cut off from her now like her past. Not like her past. As soon as she got home, she would throw it out.

'Wow, you look really good. When I saw you, I thought something was wrong, you looked so *different.*'

'Well,' she said, as they began to drive out of Inverness, 'something is wrong. So brace yourself Andrew, there are more changes coming than your mother getting her hair cut for the first time in twenty years.'

PART IV

WAITING FOR A SIGNAL

CHAPTER 1

In June, the crying began. At first it was just at night, and Frances would stand outside the bedroom door listening and wondering whether to go in. It was muffled, private crying and it soon subsided. Later, it gathered momentum: it was wilder and harder and not just at night. No-one could ignore it then.

Andrew would stand by his mother's bed late at night or in the early hours of the morning, pleading with her: 'Can't you do something to make her stop? She's off again, it keeps waking me up.'

Frances would rise with a sigh. 'I don't think there's anything really wrong. She's just crying.'

'Is it because she's having this baby or what?' He had gone beyond embarrassment. He wanted to be helpful but was baffled in the face of this. Besides, he didn't really want anything to do with it. If he had to, he would, but on the edge, handing over a box of tissues or holding the car door when Kate, becoming ungainly, struggled to get out. That was his limit. The rest he expected his mother to deal with.

'I'm all *right*,' Kate always said. 'Leave me *alone*.'

Red-eyed, she trudged off to get the school bus each morning, and Frances continued to be grateful she was still willing to go, and the school to have her. She always came home more cheerful. Frances would find her watching television with Andrew, and they seemed quite companionable. Then, after a couple of weeks of this, she began crying one morning at breakfast, soundlessly, tears falling as if she were helpless to stop them, salty tears like fat raindrops, dripping from her chin into a plate of bran flakes.

Andrew set off for the bus alone while Frances called Christine and asked her to take assembly. 'I'll be a bit late.'

'Is everything all right?'

'Well, yes, all *right*, but—'

'Tell me later. Don't worry – we can manage.'

Christine had been appalled when Frances first told her Kate was pregnant: 'Every mother's nightmare.' Later, she recounted the story of some woman she had overheard on a train, talking about her illegitimate grandchild. 'When all's said and done,' this woman had asserted, 'it's a family baby. There's worse things could happen.'

'I agree with her,' Frances said, surprising both Christine and herself. 'It's a family baby. We'll look after the bairn ourselves. It'll be fine.'

Sitting helplessly by the weeping Kate, handing her squares of kitchen towel to mop up the tears, she was not so sure.

'It's your hormones,' she told Kate. 'I promise you'll feel better soon.'

It was not just Kate's hormones that made her cry. Frances, who had unwillingly begun to remember a time when she had cried like this, guessed as much. Frances never cried now. It was as if, having done so much stifled, hidden crying in the terrible months after Alec left, she had no tears left. She recognised the helplessness of Kate's weeping, the rise and fall of it, the hiccups and shuddering indrawn breath when she tried to stop, the useless tears which kept spilling out. She felt helpless, exasperated and full of pity.

'She's not coming back, is she?' Kate said at last.

It was almost July, almost the school holidays, though Kate had not gone to school for the last couple of weeks. Summer had blazed out as soon as the exam season was under way, and they were sitting in the kitchen at eleven o'clock one Saturday morning, a widening triangle of sunshine creeping in at the open door through the back porch. The grey cat lay in this yellow light, his fur-tips gleaming, washing his side with leisurely sweeps of pink tongue. Kate had almost stopped crying. This was the first bout for several days. She was drenched in tears, her eyes heavy lidded, her face white with fatigue. She leaned her chin on one hand, elbow propped on the table. They were alone: the rugby season over, Andrew was still in bed.

Frances understood at once.

'I don't know,' Frances said. 'I'm sorry, that's no help.'

'I wish I knew *where* she was,' Kate sighed. 'I can't sort of picture her, you know?' She sniffed, then took a tissue from one of the boxes Frances kept around the house now, and blew her nose. 'When I was little,' she went on, 'she took me to the hospital where she was working and I saw the ward and everything. All old ladies lying still, kind of creepy. But at least I could imagine it after that, imagine her looking after them. Do you see what I mean?'

'Yes,' Frances said, 'I do.'

'But now, well, where is she?'

'Is that why you thought of Amble?'

'I suppose. I've got to see her *somewhere*.'

For Frances, Susan was still hovering in the past. The girl with the push-chair, walking away across the station concourse. A woman in a red coat, a little overweight, rising past her on an escalator. Or if she thought about Susan for long enough, she saw a girl in school uniform, tie loosened, caught up in a crowd of boys at the Pelican Café. None of those pictures was any use to Kate, of course, or to Frances herself. Years ago, she had had other images of Susan, imagined, but real enough. Susan in Alec's arms, Susan in bed with Alec, Susan and Alec in some flat in Leeds living together, a newly created family with the two year old Kate. She had worked hard to crush those images.

'Sometimes,' Kate admitted, 'I think she's dead.' She said it so matter-of-factly, Frances was taken aback. She had thought this herself, recently.

'Oh no,' she protested, but feebly. 'I'm sure she's all right. She's staying with friends or in digs.' As she spoke she realised Kate too had her terrible visions, images she wanted Frances to render absurd or impossible.

She could not do it. If Susan were still alive, functioning, what was she living on? Alec said she had taken money, but after six months that must have run out. Had she a job, was she living rough? A woman in a red coat, prosperous, her hair glossy with good health, rising on an escalator, or walking swiftly along a busy Edinburgh street, always walking away, leaving them.

'If she's dead,' Kate went on, 'she can't come back, and she's not staying away on purpose. She wouldn't do that. Only if she was ill, and she can't help being ill, can she? Alec says mental illness, people go on blaming you for it, but you can't help it, it's like cancer or whatever, it's not your fault.'

'No of course not,' Frances agreed, inadequate. Kate was right: it was pointless to be angry with a Susan who was mentally ill, or dead.

Kate's eyes filled with tears again. 'I hope she's not dead. Do *you* think she is?'

'Look, I know it's difficult, I know that, but you have to think of yourself now, of the baby.'

'I am, I'm eating all this healthy food.'

'Yes, but you need to rest as well and try not to think of things that upset you.'

'I'm not going back to school.'

'There's not much point now.'

Kate sat up straighter and put both hands over her belly. 'My brain's sort of gone to sleep, you know? I couldn't do any kind of work you had to think about. I feel too fat and stupid.'

Frances was tempted to point out that Kate would feel a good deal fatter and stupider by the time the baby was born.

'I must get on,' she said, rising to her feet. 'Are you all right? Do you want to come to the super-market with me?'

'I can't be bothered. Will you get me a magazine? Michelle's coming over tonight, is that OK? And Amy and Roxanne, I think.'

'Sure.'

'But it's just Michelle that'll be here for tea.'

Was Michelle the one who ate everything or nothing? They came and went like butterflies, Kate's friends, or rather a flock of gulls, descending, squawking, full of shrieks and protests, announce-ments and opinions. When they left the house became still again and felt empty. Frances had almost got used to it. She wondered if they would keep coming after the baby.

Life was divided now into these two unreal parts: before the baby, after the baby. Only last night she had sat on the long sofa between Andrew and Kate, and the pulse of life was so strong it was visible under Kate's baggy tee-shirt. She had felt it, laid her hands on hot tight skin and felt the prod of a foot or hand, there and gone again. *Weird*, Andrew said, not wanting to touch and yet curious. *Hey, he's trying to escape.* Wedged between them Frances thought, there are four of us here, soon there will be four of us visible, breathing. The baby batted at Kate's hard belly, reminding them over and over, I am here, I exist.

In Aberdeen, despite the unaccustomed heat, Grace was knitting tiny jackets and jumpers in white and eau de nil. A cloud of soft wool bulged from the tapestry bag and her fingers flew, in, over, through, out, the slender grey pins flicking to and fro. They sat in their neat back garden on flower pattered padded chairs taken out of the conservatory, and Jim, who had been reading, fell into a doze, the newspaper slipping from his knee, fanning out on the grass. With a dim roar, traffic went past ceaselessly on the Great Western Road, but in the high-walled garden birds sang, and a faint breeze tilted the long buddleia spears, whispered across the purple hebe by the back door.

Alec had taken a temporary job as a bar manager. In mid-afternoon he came home and opened the windows in his stale house, letting air and sunshine in, and stood by the back door smoking. He might as well smoke; there was no-one to mind. The raw taste of the Gauloise soothed him, and he watched the curl of bluish smoke thin out in the windless heat of his back yard. There were weeds flourishing in a corner and a whiff of sourness rose from the dustbin. Above him, the sky was a hard blue. He thought of Frances's shady garden and then, unexpectedly, of the beach at Amble and the sea rolling over pale sand. Perhaps he should have gone there.

In half an hour someone was coming to view the house. Jesmond was a popular area: even uncared for, echoing with emptiness like his, these houses sold quickly. In a few weeks he could be free to move north, find some other job, rent or even buy a flat. As for the furniture, the bulky Edwardian pieces he and Susan had picked up here and there for this house, could all go into store or be sold. Whatever he had the time and energy to manage. Whatever was least trouble.

He liked the idea of starting again with a few bare rooms, a clean slate. The house here weighed him down, oppressive with memories. Even now, when the telephone rang, he had a pang of fear it might be Susan, even while he knew it never would be again. She had done it so often and the calls had come with such relief then, he had rushed to answer.

'I want to come home,' she would say. 'Please Alec, I just want to come home. It didn't work out, you were right.'

Why had he taken her back, time after time? He told himself it was for Katie, who needed her mother, but as the years went by and Susan's affairs became almost predictable, he knew it was because he didn't have the energy to deal with the inevitable fallout. How long before her lovers left her, instead of her leaving them? He suspected it had already begun to happen. 'It didn't work out,' meant 'he dumped me', or at least, 'he couldn't handle it'. That, he could understand.

If Katie hadn't been there he would have ditched Susan that first time, or at least the second. She had the benefit of her beauty, and the proximity of men who worked long hours and succumbed too easily to temptation. They'd all been doctors, except this last one.

He was weak, but he gave himself credit for one thing, in one thing he had been strong. He had never told Kate where her mother was, or who her mother was with. Sometimes he thought she must have guessed or had heard the truth from someone else. She often went silent during her mother's absences and turned away from him, sullen and unhappy. Together they kept up the fiction of Susan's 'illness'. Not altogether fiction, of course. Her violent mood changes had kept them on tenterhooks between lovers.

She had not actually left the first time. The affair was conducted while Kate was at school and he was working; she had managed shift patterns with skill. The next time and all the times after that – at least those he knew about – she disappeared for a few days, a couple of weeks, once as long as a month. Just as he decided he would have to do something, might have to leave himself taking Kate with him, the phone call would come.

He would cover the receiver and turn to Kate aged eight, ten, twelve – all those Kates – and say, 'It's Mum!' and she would dance when she was little, hop down the stairs. *I want to speak to her!* Later, she simply sat there, hunched on those same stairs, waiting while he asked Susan, over and over, *Tell me where you are, and I'll come and get you. Just tell me where you are.*

When the telephone shrilled this time, deep in the empty house behind him, he jumped and his heart thudded with apprehension.

It was Gillian. Her voice was lower than Susan's, but the accent, however faded by time and living in other places, the same.

'Gill, how are you?'

'Alec, I think you should know, I think I should tell you—'

'What?'

'Maybe it's nothing. I don't know.'

It is nothing, he could have reassured her but he waited, and Gill went on,

'I keep getting these strange phone calls. Nuisance calls, the police say. They've advised me to change my number. I might, but then she wouldn't – I keep thinking she's going to say something.'

Now she was getting to the point. 'What is it,' he asked. 'Heavy breathing, what?'

'Just silence, the sort when you know full well there's someone there. Then they hang up, it goes dead.'

'You get the line checked?'

'Oh yes.' She seemed to take a deep breath, as if making up her mind. 'Alec, I know this is mad, but I think it's Susan. I think she's sort of testing me and some day, sometime, she'll speak to me. But it's freaking me out. I thought you should know about it.'

'You should go back to the police. It could be somebody at work or someone who lives nearby. There's not some guy harassing you?'

Gillian attempted a laugh. 'No, that's ridiculous. Anyway it's a woman, I know it is.'

'You could go ex-directory – that would put a stop to it.'

'*You* haven't heard anything, have you – you haven't been getting freaky phone calls?'

'No,' he said, 'and if Frances had I'm sure she'd have told you.'

'I haven't actually spoken to her for a while. The reason I called you is I thought maybe you *had* heard something and you were keeping it to yourself. For some reason.'

'No!' he exclaimed again, startled. She mustn't start thinking like that; he had to make sure she was left in no doubt. 'Honestly, Gill, believe me. Susan hasn't been in touch.' He let his voice drop, warm with sincerity.

'Right. I'll just go ex-directory. I suppose.'

'You haven't spoken to Kate recently?'

'No.'

'She's doing fine – huge, she tells me. I'm hoping to go up when this job finishes at the end of August.'

'What job's that?'

'Just a temporary thing. Management infill.'

He would not say anything about the house. Not yet. It was best not to let Frances get wind of his plans till it was all settled. They talked for a few more minutes then he heard a car draw up. Guessing it was his potential buyers, he rang off with a final word of reassurance.

Gillian put the phone down and crossed to the window. It was not often hot and windless here, but this week she had been unable to sleep for heat, the airlessness of the city stifling her. She should have asked about Kate. She should have ended with something more ordinary, family news. He would think she was hysterical, imagining things which could not be.

She had not wanted to ask about Kate, so had not called Frances for several weeks. As summer emerged from Spring and the waiting months went on, something strange and unsettling had happened to Gillian. The baby she had got rid of had, in some phantom form, gone on growing. It was no longer a collection of cells, a comma, a tadpole, rudimentary life. It had a head, arms, legs, and it floated somewhere just out of reach of her imagination, but there all the same, moving, becoming more detailed (fingers, toes, blind eyes) and more human every day.

In nightmares she caught glimpses of it, as if it drifted under water that was green and clouded. She woke sweating and lay with her eyes wide open, terrified of going back to sleep.

Cut off from Frances, she longed for her and yet longed more for someone else she could tell, someone who would not judge her as she knew Frances would. So she did not call and if Frances left a message for her, she did not return it. Recently, Frances was either too preoccupied to think of her or had given up, since there had been no more messages.

The street was empty. Everyone was out, having gone to the shops, the parks, or into the country perhaps, in search of fresher air. The Fletchers' cat slipped between railings and vanished down the basement steps, looking for a cooler place to sleep.

There had been no more silent messages either. Maybe those phone calls meant nothing, it was just some weirdo who rang up women to scare them. Why had she been so sure it was Susan trying to get in touch?

She knew why. It was because it had happened before.

She was twenty one years old and in the first job she'd really enjoyed, working for a travel agency. She was going to evening classes in

Spanish, and was out with friends every weekend. It was just before she met Michael, who came into the agency to book a skiing holiday a few weeks later. She had been back to visit her parents only once since Susan's return home and the atmosphere was so tense she decided not to go again. 'It will be different when the baby's born,' Frances assured her and she thought, well, I might go then or I might not. Her own life was so interesting she could not bear to leave it for even one night.

She was still in a flat-share in Haymarket, saving for a deposit on her own place. Just three of them by then: Chloe had gone to London to get married.

The first time it happened, Anne answered the phone. 'It's for you,' she said, but when Gillian took the receiver no-one answered, then the line went dead.

'Cut off,' she said. 'Who was it?'

'Don't know. Maybe your sister – same accent.'

When it happened again, Gillian called Frances.

'It wasn't me. How are you anyway?'

The third time she was sure it was Susan, so called her mother's house. Susan was out. It happened again twice, weeks apart. Just after the last time Katy was born and Gillian went to Aberdeen after all, to see her new niece. She meant to say to Susan, 'Did you call me and then hang up? Why? I'd have come if you'd asked me, if *you* wanted me to.'

The birth had been long and difficult, ending in a forceps delivery. Susan looked exhausted and ill.

They were all fussing round, her mother, Barbara, Frances. She remembered Frances saying, 'When you're better, come and visit us.' She said to Gillian privately, 'She really shouldn't stay here. Mum will take over so she'll never be independent. It's a pity about Adam.'

She should have asked Susan about the calls. *It was her then, and I'm sure it's her now.* So, should she have her number changed?

In a few minutes, Paul would be here to take her to a pub in Portobello where they were going to meet some friends of his. She was watching for his car since she had nothing else to do. The phone, ringing again in the quiet flat, made her start. She knew as she went to pick it up that there would be silence at the other end, the silence which was always there, echoing like a buzzing in her ears, the tinnitus of apprehension, voiceless.

'Hello, it's Gillian.' This time, she would not stand for it, would not plead, would not give Susan the satisfaction. 'Susan, I know it's you. Just tell me where you are, Ok? That's all. Are you all right?'

There was only the switch from empty noise to the purr of the dialling tone. With a cry Gillian slammed down the receiver. 'Fuck you, Susan, as if I haven't enough—' She was shaking. The sound of a car, that must be Paul's, stopping in the street, made her take a deep breath and calm herself. He would soon get fed up with her moods and unexplained tears and she would lose him just when she was beginning to think it might be worth something after all, to stay with this relationship. By the time she pressed the button to release the front door she was in control again.

When Frances came back with her Saturday shopping, Andrew appeared to help her unload it, shoving his feet into large loose trainers as he came outside.

'You're up at last, then?'

'Yeah, sort of.' He grinned at her, taking two heavy bags.

'How's Kate?'

'On the phone.'

'All these girls are round here nearly every day. What can they possibly have to say on the phone?'

'It's not any of them.'

'Oh?'

'It's him.'

'What's he saying – did you speak to him?'

'Na. Just Kate. Sounds as if he's planning a visit.'

They began to unpack the bags in the kitchen.

'She's better, isn't she?' Andrew said as he stacked milk and cheese in the fridge. 'Not crying any more. She was mental for a while, eh?'

'I do think a lot of that was because of her mother.' Frances opened the larder and put away cereal, biscuits, dried fruit, flour. How did they get through so much food? At least Kate was eating now.

'What do you think's happened to her, Mum, really?'

378

'I have no idea.' She turned to face him.

'Maybe she's topped herself. You think?' Seeing Frances wince, he added hastily, 'Sorry – she's your sister – sorry.'

'It's all right. Kate thinks the same, or she's beginning to suspect it. The longer this goes on the more likely it seems. I keep thinking *someone* must know.'

'Like a friend or something?'

'Maybe.'

Kate came into the kitchen. 'Alec wants to speak to you,' she said, and began opening a bag of rolls. 'I have one of these? I'm hungry.'

'Go ahead. Is he still on the line?'

'Yeah, I said you were back.'

Frances went to pick up the phone. 'Alec?'

'Hello Frances, how are you? Kate sounds on good form.'

'I suppose she is. The bouts of crying have stopped, mercifully. She was wearing herself out.'

Don't come, she pleaded silently, leave us alone. She realised she wanted the summer with Kenny, unhindered by Alec being around. Kenny had said he might go at the beginning of September, once his redundancy came through. That would be before Kate's baby was born. So far he'd done nothing about selling the cottage or finding somewhere to live near his son. Sometimes she thought it might never happen and they would go on just as usual. In a week Jack would be home, since he had fixed himself up with a job on the Tulloch estate for the summer. Alec would be in the way.

'My job finishes in August,' he told her. 'I thought I'd come up for a few weeks.'

'I'll have a full house,' she warned. 'Jack's coming home, and Mum and Dad will be here sometime over the summer.'

'Don't feel you have to accommodate me,' he reassured.

Irritated, Frances retorted, 'I don't.'

He laughed as if he thought she didn't really mean this.

Sharply, Frances said, 'I don't suppose you've heard anything from Susan? Kate's still hoping. That was what caused so much crying, I think.'

'No.' He came in swiftly, scotching this. 'Kate knows that. She's handling it very well, she's remarkable.'

'I must go,' Frances said, unable to bear this. If he had sat with Kate night after night, mopping up tears, or had to listen, as Andrew had, to that wild sobbing in the early hours of the morning, would he still be so cool? She thought of what Gillian had said, about how calmly Alec seemed to take the loss of his wife. For it was loss, however strange and unfinished.

'I'll call you,' he said, 'let you know when I'm coming.'

'You do that.'

She put the receiver down too quickly, as you do in anger, glad to be rid of him.

In the kitchen, Andrew had put away everything but the fruit, which lay in red and yellow heaps on the draining board, ready to be washed. He was outside kicking a ball against the house wall; she could hear the hollow thud of it. Kate was sitting on the wooden bench which looked down the garden, reading her magazine. Beneath her, the tabby stretched asleep. Frances, coming round the side of the house and finding them, thought, *how peaceful*, and sat next to Kate, leaning her head on the rough house wall and closing her eyes against bright sunlight.

'He's gone all quiet, you think he has a sleep sometimes?' Kate asked.

Frances opened her eyes. 'What?'

'The baby. He's all over the place in the morning when I get up, and when I'm in the shower. At night as well, when I sit down in front of the telly. But now I can't feel a thing.'

'It's a 'he' is it?'

'You can't keep saying 'it', can you? He *could* be a boy.'

'Oh yes.' Frances closed her eyes again. Silence, just bird-song, the turning of Kate's magazine pages, the thud of the football and Andrew's scuffling feet, to and fro on the paving slabs at the side of the house.

'Frances?'

'Mm?'

'It can't die can it, the baby? I mean, even if I can't feel it moving, it's just sleeping, eh?'

Frances opened her eyes and looked at Kate.

'Of course the baby's alive,' she said firmly, sure of this at least. She smiled at Kate. 'Healthy and growing and very much all right. Any minute, you'll feel him playing football inside you again.'

Kate grinned back. 'Yeah,' she said, 'definitely a boy.'

Grace stabbed her knitting pins into the ball of wool and got out of the low chair with a struggle. Jim opened his eyes.

'Cup of tea?' he asked.

'Just going to make it.'

'You still knitting, in this heat?'

'Oh, I've given up. Hands were getting too sticky.'

'You knitted pink, when *you* were expecting,' he said, with a sudden clear memory. 'Pink for a girl.'

'No, I didn't.' She shook her head. 'I'd never have done that. You were so keen on a boy, you thought every one of them was a boy.'

'All the same,' he said, 'I see it's white wool, this time.'

He went on sitting there, after she had gone into the house. His chair was in shade now that the sun had moved round, but it was comfortable, warm enough. He closed his eyes, then opened them again. He was sleeping too much. Time he was active again, busy. He lay listening to the murmur of the radio from indoors, the sound of water as Grace filled the kettle, the chink of cutlery and dishes. A blackbird hopped down from the crab apple tree to the grass below and paused, looking at him with one beady eye.

He did not know what made him think of Susan, except that he was always thinking of her. He did not tell Grace how much or how often. Susan, whom he had loved best and who had hurt and angered him most, would not come back this time. The click of the gate, the light step on the path would always be someone else now, never Susan. He knew that, even if no-one else did.

CHAPTER 2

August was peaceful. The new term did not begin until the last week, so Frances felt more relaxed, and went into her own school only once or twice. She had plenty to keep her occupied at home. Alec called about twice a week but spoke mainly to Kate.

Kate lay in the garden when the weather was fine and in the house when it was not. She could usually be persuaded to wash up dishes or do a little housework, but she had less and less energy as the weeks went on, and was reluctant to go out. Frances drove her to ante-natal clinic and her friends came round, but she rarely went to visit them now, so that meant there were always two or three at Frances's house. She watched them from the living-room window, sitting on the grass around Kate's sun lounger making daisy chains, the shrill of their voices swelling and falling, self absorbed and exclusive. As they moved, their long hair shone glossy in sunlight as they sat surrounded by battered trainers, taken off and flung across the grass. The pages of Kate's magazine fluttered open, turning by themselves in the breeze.

The Academy had sent work home for Kate since she was due to sit exams next year, but she had not completed anything. Half-finished essays and an attempt at a geography project lay neglected in her bedroom where Frances had helpfully put a small desk and chair and a bookcase picked up at the local auction. We've made no plans, she thought, turning away from the window and the chattering girls. Kate will have to buckle down to it next year. Could they afford a nanny perhaps or a good childminder, if Kate went back to school? Sometime, they would have to discuss the whole thing with Alec. As if infected with Kate's lethargy Frances could not bear even to think about all that yet. The summer days would drift by with nothing achieved.

Gillian was working through the summer. When the Festival was over she and Paul would go to Cyprus or Greece, somewhere hot with a beach. She sounded brisk on the phone. She's got over it, Frances decided, because she's met someone else. At least this one wasn't married. Their mother had great hopes of this new relationship.

'Maybe we'll have a wedding, what do you think?' she asked Frances. She and Jim had stopped in Dingwall for a few days before driving to the hotel in Skye they went to every year. Frances had taken her mother to the Station Café for coffee after some shopping in Boots and the old-fashioned ironmonger's where Grace had managed to buy a gadget for stoning cherries. She liked Dingwall shops; the throng of Aberdeen's city centre was too much for her these days.

'A wedding?' Frances asked in surprise at this sudden jump in the conversation. 'I hardly hear from Gill these days, so I can't tell how serious it is.'

'That's a good sign,' Grace said comfortably. 'She must be quite taken up with this Paul.'

'It would be quite a shock, being married, after so long on her own,' Frances mused.

'Nice to see her settled, though.'

'I don't think I could adapt to it myself.'

Grace looked at her, assessing. 'You've a busy life Frances. I hope you're not thinking of taking on this baby as well?'

'What else can I do? Sometimes, when I think of my peaceful life . . . After Jack went off to uni and it was just Andrew and me – he's so easy – it was . . .' She let the words dry up. Had it been peaceful or just empty?

'What about your friend? What does he think of all this?'

'Oh, Kenny. He's supposed to be moving to live near his son but apart from putting in for redundancy at work, he's done nothing about it.'

Grace set her cup down, disappointed. So that was going to come to nothing either. 'Where does his son live? Is it far?'

'Near Edinburgh.'

'You'll miss him,' Grace offered, wondering if this were true. Frances was close, you could never tell. Of all her children it was only Susan who had displayed her emotions, sparing you nothing. Perhaps it was better this way: you could be interested, try to be helpful, but stand back. But she felt excluded from their busy purposeful lives. She was cut off from Susan's too, but Susan had been gone so long she was used to that. Jim still felt it. She sighed, looking down at her empty cup.

'I will miss Kenny if he does go,' Frances said with sudden frankness. 'He's been a good friend. It's selfish, I know, but I'd like him to stay.'

'Your Dad and me,' Grace ventured, since Frances seemed willing to talk after all, 'we thought you would – not marry again – but maybe get together with this Kenny. Once the boys were away.'

'Did you? Goodness.' Frances was touched. She patted her mother's arm. 'Don't worry about me. We're perfectly all right just the way things are.'

'You could do with having a man around,' Grace pointed out, 'now this baby's on the way. If he's going to retire, Kenny could help out.' She ignored Frances's startled laugh. 'It's different nowadays. Men do help with children. Your father of course is from an older generation. He left it all to me. I like to see the young ones together with their bairns, the daddy pushing the pram and so on. It's a good thing.'

Her mother's words caught Frances like the snagging of an old pain. She saw herself at twenty five or six, nursing a teething Andrew, Jack pestering her for a story or just some attention. Alec would be out with colleagues or working late, his odd hours never fitting with hers so that he could take the children and help out. At home, he reached thankfully for a bottle of wine and put his feet up. *These split shifts,* he would say, *I'm knackered.* When they moved to Northumberland he had an office based job and things were better, at least at first. He was still drinking, but he took more interest. The boys were no longer babies and he was able to talk to them and enjoy their company. Then he left me, she thought, without a backward glance at his sons. He left me.

'Are you all right?'

She shook herself back to the present, the little café with its flowered tablecloths and shelves of photograph frames and pottery for sale.

'Sorry, dreaming. We'd better go. Dad will be looking for his lunch.'

There were too many of them in the house. Frances had never minded before because it was always for so short a time: at Christmas, Easter, the odd weekend. It had been too much trouble this time to move everyone around so she had simply given up her own room for her parents, and slept on the pullout bed obligingly dragged to the boxroom by Jack. It barely fitted, so she had a moment of grim satisfaction remembering how she had banished Alec here at Christmas, and on the less comfortable camp bed too.

'I'll sleep in here, Mum, if you like,' Jack had offered.

'No, it's fine. There's enough disruption.'

'You're not kidding,' Jack agreed. 'It'll be worse after September, eh?'

Jack had taken the news of Kate's pregnancy with his usual equanimity, once he managed to believe it was true. He could see a difference in his mother: not just the short feathery haircut which made her seem younger, and the loss of weight, but the tension in her face, her weariness. 'You Ok, Mum?' he kept asking, coming into the kitchen to help her cook, bringing in washing without being asked. She was touched by his concern, but felt guilty that he was worrying about her.

'Guess what I just realised,' he said, when his grandparents left and the house seemed to settle into its familiar state again.

'What?' Frances asked, pleased to have him there, to have both her sons at home and the place to themselves again. They seemed to anchor her to reality, as Kate could not, with all those familiar signs that all was well: their enormous appetites; the scattered trainers in the hall; the late night videos; the empty beer bottles left lying for her to pick up in the morning; Andrew's bedroom throbbing with heavy metal.

'Andy and me – we're going to be uncles.'

'So you are.'

'Magic,' he said, helping himself to an apple, throwing it in the air, catching it in cupped hands.

'Watch you don't drop that.'

'I won't.' He had taken two other apples from the bowl and held them close to his chest. 'See what useful skills you pick up at uni.'

Up went one apple, then another, and the third. His hands crossed, rose and fell, caught and threw. The apples turned in the air. Frances laughed.

'That's wonderful – who taught you that?'

Jack caught the three apples neatly. 'Guy I know. He does it professionally, so if I fail my exams, I could be a juggler. Watch!'

Up the apples went, russet and green in the air, rising, crossing, falling, caught and up again, over and over.

'Amazing! I'm glad you're learning something for all the money it's costing.'

'It's just a knack.' He put two of the apples back in the bowl and bit a large piece out of the third. 'It looks difficult, but it's not really. You want me to teach you?'

'Later,' Frances said. 'I must get my bedroom back to rights.'

'Busy, busy,' he mocked. 'You should relax, Mum, it's the holidays.'

He sat down at the table to read the sports pages of the newspaper while he finished his apple. He was putting on muscle with his outdoor work, and his face and arms were brown. Andrew had a job in the supermarket, which he kept saying was better because he didn't have to work as hard, but Frances could tell he envied Jack and thought himself worse off.

Kate, of course, had no job. She floated through the summer. At least the crying had stopped.

Gillian's nuisance calls had stopped too, now that she had her new telephone number. She and Paul were looking through holiday brochures but hadn't decided where to go.

'We'll get something at the last minute,' he said. 'There are always bargains around.'

He had a friend from New York staying in his flat for a few months, someone working out of Glasgow on a temporary contract, so he and Gillian were usually in her flat in the evenings. Sometimes Paul stayed over; sometimes he had an early start so went back to his own place. When he left she missed him; when he stayed she wished she had the bed to herself. They had their favourite restaurants now, their weekly visits to the cinema, the rudiments of a routine. They were much the same with each other as they had been at the start: enjoying the company and by now the sex, but still a little wary of anything more. Perhaps, Gillian admitted, she was the wary one. There were things she could not tell Paul, that kept her distanced from everyone, even Frances now this other baby was coming.

She woke from dreams of a baby stirring within her body, feeling the solid swell of the pregnancy, dissolving as the dream dissolved and she woke in tears. If Paul was there, she turned her face into the pillow, weeping silently. She had read about this of course, in magazines and helpful books on women's health. It was normal to have some anxiety continue, normal to dream of babies. What dismayed her was that it was the same baby, growing and changing all the time.

At least they would be away when Kate's baby was born. They would be in Cyprus or Greece or Turkey, they would lie on beaches and turn brown, sit by cafes drinking iced beer and growing plump with laziness, swim in blue pools, sleep in a white bed in a white room and make love all afternoon through the siesta. When they came back, it would be different.

Late in August, when term had begun and school-uniformed pupils passed her in groups as she walked to work, Gillian had a call from Frances.

'I'm coming to Edinburgh for an Early Intervention Seminar,' she said, 'and it's a Friday of all days. I wondered if you could you give me a bed for the night? I'll get a train down early on the Friday, come home Saturday afternoon. Is that all right? It'll give us some time together.'

'Yes,' Gillian said, 'of course.' Frances sounded unusually tentative, but there was no question of saying no.

CHAPTER 3

'What would you like to eat?' Gillian asked when she had finished exclaiming over Frances's new hair, growing out a little now, but still a shock after all these years of the heavy coil pinned up daily. She and Frances were still in suits, Gillian's sharper with a short skirt, but office clothes. Frances had arrived with a small suitcase and her folder of seminar papers. Gillian had been home half an hour, time spent energetically tidying the flat and making up the spare bed. 'There's a good deli round the corner, so I could get some stuff there.'

'Let's go out. It's a treat for me, being in Edinburgh in the Festival. We could go down the Royal Mile afterwards, maybe, see what's going on?'

'I'll ring Gianni's. They'll keep us a table if we go quite early.'

'I'll have a shower first if that's OK.' Frances ran her hands through her hair. 'I got the early train so I feel as if I've been up since the middle of the night.'

Gillian followed Frances into the small bedroom, which doubled as her study when she worked at home. Most of the space was taken up by the bed and the computer workstation. 'Sorry,' she said, 'it's a bit cramped in here.'

'It's fine. All I need is a bed.' Frances turned to face her sister. 'How are you anyway? I've hardly spoken to you for weeks.'

'Busy of course, the usual thing. You know where the bathroom is – I'll leave you to it.'

Even at seven, the restaurant was full with theatre suppers, and Frances and Gillian had a table squeezed into a corner.

'This is wonderful,' Frances sighed. 'I feel as if I've escaped, but any minute someone might come and drag me away to make me cook dinner for ten.'

'Time you taught your sons to cook.'

'They can cook when they have to. They're working though. It's Kate who's at home but she shows no interest. No interest in anything really.'

'She's well enough though?' No way out of asking now.

'Getting bigger by the day and very lazy. She's been much better since Jack got home.'

'What was wrong?'

'She cried.'

'Cried? What about?' Me too, Gillian was thinking, it seems you can't win.

'God knows. Everything. Cried and cried. It was exhausting – for all of us.' Frances poured more wine. 'We might need another of these. I hardly ever get the chance to drink and not care if it makes me tipsy.'

'I do like your hair. Your whole image is different, or maybe I just never see you in smart suits. You look younger too.'

'Wish I *felt* younger.' But Frances looked pleased. The waiter came with their pasta.

'When is Kate actually due?' Gillian asked, as they began to eat. She was amused to see how Frances relished the wine and food, her eyes sparkling in candlelight. At the back of the restaurant, with its red walls, the light was dim and romantic. Outside, it was still sunny, a bright August evening.

'They're saying twentieth September, but you never know with first babies, they're unpredictable.' Frances put her fork down. 'There's something I want to ask you.'

'What's that?'

'No, it'll keep. Tell me about Paul, what's happening. Mum was full of curiosity. She's hoping for wedding bells.'

Gillian laughed. 'She'll be disappointed.'

'It's not serious then?' It was the old Frances again, quizzical, sharp.

'Oh, it's early days. Who knows? He's a nice guy.'

'But?'

'But nothing. Like I said, it's early days.'

'He's not married,' Frances pointed out. 'No possible obstacle that I can see.'

'Me,' Gillian said. 'I'm the obstacle.'

Frances waited a moment, but Gillian concentrated on eating.

Outside in the fresh air it was a surprise to find

daylight but Frances, rallying from the heavy meal and too much wine, said brightly, 'Look, night's still young. Could we walk a bit? Maybe go up to the Royal Mile?'

There was a band playing in Princes Street Gardens and couples were dancing on a wooden stage. A lilting waltz followed them as they walked through the holiday makers and Festival-goers thronging the pavements.

The area round St Giles's Church was packed.

'Look – jugglers!'

'You want to stop for a minute?' Gillian asked. She was too used to the open air performances, to musicians from Peru, jugglers and snake charmers from India and elsewhere, to take much notice now. They stood at the edge of the audience circling the jugglers with their coloured balls and sticks, their fire torches and unicycles. Frances said,

'Jack's learning to juggle, but not with flaming torches, I'm thankful to say.'

'Does he dress up for it?'

Frances laughed. 'Not so far – I can't see him in *that!*' The performers were in patchwork pantaloons and satin shirts in jewel bright colours. They wore straw hats they threw from one to the other, till the one at the end had them all, and tossed them expertly above his head, making a spinning wheel of hats, catching them lightly as they fell, flinging them one by one back to their owners.

Gillian, having seen this kind of thing before, too many times, was half-turned away, looking across the crowd. Suddenly she gripped Frances's arm so hard her sister cried out.

Then she let go and was off, pushing through the mass of people between her and the other side of the street, beginning to run. Frances, astonished, started after her. Gillian had begun to run downhill and Frances, bumping into people, apologising as she tried to follow, called after her. But her voice vanished, lost in the noise of the jugglers' drums, the rise and fall of the music of an accordion player on the corner by a pub. About twenty yards away Gillian had come to a halt, and was leaning on a shop window. Frances, slowing now that Gillian had stopped, finally reached her.

Gillian was white-faced. 'I thought I saw Susan.'

They were both breathing hard and for a moment Frances didn't answer, she was so giddy with running. She put a hand on the shop window to steady herself.

'Are you sure? Where did she go?'

'I don't know. One minute she was there on the other side of the road, walking away quite fast. By the time I got through that crowd she was a long way ahead. Then – I don't know – I thought she turned down there, into the close but when I looked, it was empty. She must have gone through a door. I was so puffed, I had to stop.'

'What was she wearing?'

'She had a white shirt with the collar turned up and dark trousers, navy maybe. I followed the white of the shirt. Am I going crazy or what?'

'You really thought it was Susan?'

'I don't know, do I? Your imagination plays tricks and after all these weird phone calls—'

'*What* phone calls?' Frances looked round. 'This is no good, we need to sit down and talk. What about a pub – over there?'

'It'll be crammed.'

It was. The noise meant they could only mouth at each other and there was going to be a long wait before they got near enough to the bar to order drinks.

'Home,' Frances decided, 'to your flat. We might even get a taxi.'

Going down the Mound, they did, and were back at Gillian's flat in ten minutes.

'Are you all right?' Frances asked as Gillian put her key in the door. 'You're terribly pale.'

'Let's get a drink, I need one.'

Frances took over, making coffee, then pouring them a whisky each. She set them on the low table by the sofa, tidying glossy magazines into a pile to clear a space.

'Now, about these phone calls?'

'You know I went ex-directory? That's why.' She gulped some of the whisky and topped up her glass. 'The other thing is, I spoke to Alec, I wanted to ask him about these calls. I've had a feeling for ages that he knows more about where Susan is than he lets on.' She put down her glass. 'I think he *knows* she's never coming back.'

Frances sank back on the sofa cushions and briefly closed her eyes.

'It's his manner,' Gillian said. 'I could be wrong.'

'I don't think you are. When was the last silent call?'

'I went to the police, at least I rang them up, and then the phone company and that was – a couple of weeks ago? Maybe three.'

'Have you told Paul?'

'Just that I was getting crank calls. You think I've been imagining things, don't you?'

'I think it would be good if a man answered now and again. So if it is a crank—'

'Oh, it's a crank all right, but one who happens to be our bloody sister!'

'You can't know that.'

'I know what *you* think,' Gillian snapped. 'You think I've gone crackers because I had an abortion and it's unbalanced me.'

'Of *course* not. I do think you're stressed.'

'And you're not, I suppose? With a pregnant niece and an ex-husband who's angling to get back to you now he's lost his second wife?'

Frances put her cup down. 'This is all out of proportion. Whatever I've done to upset you, I'm sorry. Of course I'm stressed but Alec has absolutely no desire to move back, certainly not with me. It's the *last* thing he'd want.'

'Ask him why he's selling his house then? He

told me he wanted to be nearer Kate, and he's going to look for somewhere in Dingwall.'

'He told you that?'

'Not in so many words, but it was clear enough.'

'It's for Kate, it has nothing to do with being near me.'

'You wouldn't want him back?'

'No!'

'Does he know that?'

'Stop it. I don't even want to discuss him. Drop this. Please.'

'Here,' Gillian said, 'have some more whisky. Bloody Susan – it's all her fault. Why can't she just come home?'

Frances gave a shaky laugh. 'Yes, nothing changes.'

After a moment Gill said, 'In the restaurant, you said there was something you wanted to ask me.'

'There is. Even if Alec does move, I'd still want to ask *you*, not him.'

'What?'

'You said you had some leave to take. Would you come up for a few days when the baby's born and stay with Kate?' She saw Gillian's expression change. 'No, wait. I'll be at work, Jack in Aberdeen and Andrew at school. She'll need someone around for a little while.'

'Why are you asking me? What I know about looking after babies could be written on a second class stamp. Mum's the one you need.'

'She wouldn't leave Dad, which would mean him

coming too and that makes it more difficult.' Frances sighed. 'Och, I thought it might help you as well.'

'You think I might get over having an abortion by having a real baby to look after that's not my own, and never will be?'

Frances gave up. 'Sorry, that makes me sound completely insensitive. I know you're still upset about it, but the world is full of babies and you could still have your own. Maybe you need to think about that.'

Gillian did not answer and silence lengthened between them. Then she said, 'It should be Susan.'

'I know that.'

'Actually, I *do* want to come and be some use and help Kate, be there right at the beginning, so I can see the baby as soon as it's born. Why do I want to do that? I must be mad.'

They leaned back on the sofa cushions in unison, as if something momentous had just happened. Then they found themselves listening to the silence, listening for a phone call, a footstep on the stairs, a light voice calling them. There was nothing, and after a while they began to talk of other things.

CHAPTER 4

As soon as Frances was back in Dingwall she called Kenny.

'Come to supper tomorrow night.'

'Are you sure?' He sounded as if he couldn't believe she had said this. 'What about the family? I thought you had a houseful.'

'I have. I want you to join us.'

She did not say, I want you to protect me from Alec in case he tries to insinuate himself back into my life.

'All right then. Do I bring a bottle, or what?'

'Just yourself. In a clean shirt.'

He laughed. 'Ach, I knew there was a catch.'

She said to Kate, 'Next time Alec phones I want to speak to him.' To all of them she said, 'Kenny's coming over tomorrow night to eat with us.'

Andrew and Jack looked at her, baffled. Kate, intent on the television again, said 'What?'

'Go back to your soaps, dopey,' Andrew told her, and Jack tugged her hair as he went past. 'Pregnancy makes women deaf.'

'Shut up,' Kate retorted, but mildly. Even Jack had lost his glamour with proximity. They behaved like siblings, trading insults or ignoring each other.

'What about a walk?' Frances suggested. 'It's a lovely evening. I need it, after that train journey.'

Jack had disappeared upstairs; Andrew said, 'you don't mean me, I hope,' and sloped off before she could say she did.

'What about you?' Frances asked, sitting on the arm of Kate's chair.

'What?'

'Kate, come on, I bet you've been in front of that TV all day.'

'No, I haven't. I hoovered the hall.'

'Well, come on then, get some fresh air.'

Kate sighed. 'Do I have to?' But the programme had ended, so while the signature tune played she pushed her feet into her trainers, grumbling. 'Where are we going?'

'Just up the hill a bit.'

Out of doors the air was balmy, the sky shadowed by veils of grey-white cloud. They began to walk up the lane towards the farm. The grey cat followed them. He jumped in and out of the dry ditch, slipped under the bottom line of barbed wire into the adjoining field, lay low in the long grass for a moment, then raced out to follow them again.

'He's having his own walk,' Kate said. 'How far do you think he'll come?'

'Just to the farm. When the collie runs out barking he turns back in a hurry.'

Tail in the air, the cat led the way, pleased with

himself. After five minutes Kate stopped for a breather, turning to look back at the slumbering shape of Ben Wyvis, then past the Academy playing fields and the houses spread out on the hillside, to the firth. To Frances it was the dearest landscape she knew; she was surprised and cheered when Kate said, 'It is nice, isn't it?' and added, 'Just as well you're here, or I'd eat all the wrong stuff and never get any exercise.'

As they walked on, Frances asked if Alec had said anything about moving to Dingwall.

'He said he'd come when the baby's born. That's all right, isn't it?'

'Of course it is. But he's not planning a permanent move as far as you know?'

'Oh no. He can't leave the house in case Mum comes back. I mean, it would be nice for me if he lived here, but it's not on, is it?' She brushed her hand along the dry feathery tops of the long grass on the verge. 'I told him he had to stay there.'

'Gillian must have got it wrong then.'

'What about?'

'She seemed to think he was selling the house.'

'No, you can tell her. I made him promise.'

What's that worth, Frances thought, remembering the promises he had made in the past. What Kate needed from other people was some reassurance that they had faith in Susan too. But what was Alec up to?

'I'm tired,' Kate complained. 'Can we go back?'

'Downhill all the way,' Frances said, giving in.

With a high pitched trill the cat turned and raced past them, disappearing into the belt of trees between Frances's house and the farm. She and Kate went more slowly, the landscape below dimmer in fading light. Above them a buzzard wheeled then plunged to earth, no more than a black speck in the distance, too far off for them to see what he had seen, and caught.

Alec's job was coming to an end, but the house sale had been held up because his buyer's own sale had fallen through. He swithered between sticking it out with this buyer, and putting the house back on the market, which would mean spending more money on advertising. If nothing happened with the house he might have to look for another short term contract.

At a loose end on his one evening off work, he stood by his bedroom window looking down into the street and over the allotments which lay between his street and the main road through Gosforth to Newcastle. This road was still busy with early evening traffic. On the allotments old men pottered, digging early potatoes, tying up runner beans, weeding and tidying their plots. It looked peaceful, and Alec wondered idly if he might have been happier in that kind of life, with a regular job and an allotment for weekends. It was Frances who liked gardening; he and Susan had been content with a back yard. Her idea of gardening was to have a cyclamen and a poinsettia in the house at Christmas. By January, she had usually managed to kill them both.

What should he do with the evening? There were friends he could call, or join in one of the nearby pubs. There was Lizzie, though they'd met so little recently he suspected she was seeing someone else. He could go to a film or the theatre. Inertia kept him standing there doing nothing till he made himself move, but only to sit on the edge of the bed. After a moment he lay down on top of the covers, his head propped high on the pillows. Opposite him was the empty wardrobe.

He closed his eyes. Better to think of anything rather than Susan. But he could not stop now, could not prevent another re-run of that last row before she left. He opened his eyes and sat up. Stop, no more. He tried to think of Kate but instead his imagination conjured Frances, Frances in her house. What were they doing there now? Saturday night. The boys would be out or maybe they were all finishing a meal in the bright kitchen. He tried to picture Kate large and slow-moving, but saw only the slender girl he had taken north, full of resentment and misery, last Christmas. Easier to see Frances, her knot of blonde-grey hair slipping a little from its pins. He found he could not visualise his sons.

He was stuck, that was the trouble. Soon there would be no job here. And no house sale. Sod the Wilsons with their bungalow in Sunderland. No wonder nobody wanted to buy the bloody place – *Sunderland*. He rubbed his hands over his face. He needed a drink. Best go out, he thought, not drink here on my own. Call Gerry – he was always willing to go for a pint. He reached for the phone then paused, his hand on the receiver.

Why not go north anyway when the job was finished? Frances could hardly turn him down. For Kate's sake, she would let him come. A few days, a couple of weeks. Why not. He picked up the receiver, but it was Gerry's number he dialled. No point in giving them a lot of notice. Frances might put him off if he gave her time to think of a reason. At any rate, he would get out of this place. It was beginning to give him the creeps. If he sat in the silent house long enough he heard things. Footsteps, whispering. He should put the radio on again, the TV, music. That was what he usually did, the minute he came in. Noise, other people, something happening to prove you're not so fucking *alone*. Better still, to prove you are.

Frances was surprised by how talkative Kate became when Kenny was there.

'What a chatterbox,' he said when he and Frances sat on alone over the rest of the wine. 'I thought you said you didn't get much out of her?'

'I don't usually. She's taken a shine to you.'

'I've a great way with the ladies,' he grinned.

'The boys were fine with you too,' Frances said. 'They've never really had a chance to get to know you, see you in *their* house.'

'Frances, has all this something to do with my imminent departure? So called.'

She could not say no, it's to do with Alec coming back. She was using him to shield her and felt ashamed. He was a good man.

'I suppose I don't want you to go after all. But I haven't the right to ask you to stay, it's nothing to do with me. You want to be near your family and I understand that.'

He put his hands over hers as they twisted her wine glass stem, and stilled the movement, holding her, so that she looked up at him.

'I'll stay,' he said, 'if that's what you want. But you will have to ask me.'

Frances bit her lip. 'I know,' she said.

'Ach,' he withdrew his hands and poured himself the last of the wine, 'you've time on your side, *A Ghraidh*, for when did a Lewis man ever do anything in a rush?'

She laughed. 'That's true enough.'

'Get the wee one here first, safe and sound.'

'Yes.'

They sat on, companionable and peaceful, hearing from the rest of the house sounds just as reassuring as each other's company: Andrew and Kate squabbling over TV channels, and from upstairs, Jack's music, rock guitar, strong and rhythmic. As they listened it was as if they were living another life, one they might have had if they had met years ago, if Frances had gone to the Western Isles on that camping holiday at nineteen with Ruth and Linda, and not to Ullapool, where she had met Alec, backpacking with his friend Joe. The other life took hold for a moment; each dreamed it.

Frances wondered, as she brought herself back to the real life, if Susan might somewhere be living one of her other lives, one she had longed for all the years of being with Alec. *Poor Susan*, she said aloud, seized for the first time with pity. Kenny waited for her to say more but all she said was, 'Oh poor Susan. After all.'

CHAPTER 5

As if it was starting as it meant to go on, causing no trouble to anyone, Kate's baby began the process of being born on a Saturday, when Frances was at home. It was an eager baby, two weeks early. They had bought, or acquired from friends and relatives of Kate's friends, a pram, a bath, a Moses basket and clothes. But they were not prepared.

Andrew was out watching Ross County play Airdrie in a friendly before the season began. Jack was golfing at Strathpeffer with his friend Neil. Kenny was in Midlothian visiting his son and being encouraged to look at properties which seemed to him ludicrously over-priced and crammed together.

Kate and Frances were in Inverness shopping so they were at least close to the hospital. Kate, who once would have shopped for hours on end, could manage less than one these days. They sat on benches in the indoor centre near the great clock with its Noah's Ark of wooden characters which moved round when the hour struck. It was a few minutes to four and a small crowd of parents with toddlers in push-chairs had gathered to watch. 'Look,' the parents said, 'the animals will all move round in a minute.'

Kate and Frances watched too. Kate said, 'I've got these funny cramps again.'

'Braxton Hicks,' murmured Frances, who had been rereading her pregnancy and childbirth books. They were out of date but though fashions change, she had decided, childbirth doesn't.

'It *hurts*,' Kate gasped. 'Ow, oh, oh – oh, it's going, it's stopping.'

There were tiny drops of sweat on her forehead. She was biting her lip, holding her arms round her bump, which seemed lower in the last week or so, weighing her down.

'Wait,' Frances said. 'Sit still, see if you get another one.'

The clock struck, the animals moved, the tiny children clapped and called out and Kate yelled—

'That's it again – yow!'

'Oh Kate, not already, surely not – it *can't* be.

The car was a fifteen minute walk away along the river at Eden Court Theatre. Kate leaned on Frances to help herself up; she was very white, clutching her stomach.

'What if the baby's coming and my waters break – I'll be so *embarrassed*. Can't we go somewhere there's no other people – aie!'

People turned to look. Rigid, transfixed by pain, she gripped Frances's arm. Frances said *breathe, breathe slowly, breathe through it*, but she could

411

hardly breathe herself. Keep *calm* she thought, think what to do.

First labours were usually long, but something in the speed of these contractions told her this could be different. She couldn't gauge the level of Kate's pain since Kate made a terrible fuss if she had a splinter in her finger, but these pains were coming so fast she was alarmed.

'We'll get a taxi.'

In Marks and Spencer, Kate clutching her again, she spoke to one of the older assistants who took them into the staff room and called her supervisor. Frances and Kate sat on green padded chairs and were offered cups of tea which neither could drink.

'My car's in the staff car park,' the supervisor offered. 'Could I take you up to Raigmore?'

'Thank you,' Frances said at once. 'That's very kind.'

'No trouble,' the woman said. 'Poor lass.'

Kate was beyond herself, could not think, could not believe what was happening to her.

'Frances,' she whispered as they edged downstairs, 'do you think the baby's coming?'

'Yes,' Frances said, 'that's what's going on. Never mind, we'll soon have you in hospital'.

'Oh no,' Kate realised, 'people have babies in taxis, I hope *I* don't – what do you do – do you have to take your knickers off in a *car?*'

Frances laughed. 'That would be the least of it, believe me.'

Kate, unreassured, clung still more tightly to Frances. 'You won't leave me, will you?'

'I'm coming too, don't worry.'

'I mean, don't leave me at *all* – promise?'

'I promise.'

It will all be out of my hands, Frances thought, knowing hospitals. Still, first thing was to get her there. In the supervisor's car Frances sat in the back with Kate, but to her immense relief there was a respite from the contractions. Kate relaxed a little and lay back, closing her eyes.

'It's stopped,' she said. 'Maybe nothing will happen after all.'

'We're going to the hospital anyway,' Frances said.

At the main doors they got out, Frances full of thanks for their driver.

'It's very kind of you – we'd better go.'

'I hope it goes well. Good luck.'

Inside, all the drama ceased. No-one was excited by their arrival. Nothing seems to happen fast in hospitals, Frances thought, knowing that could not always be true. No-one rushed Kate anywhere; no-one seemed to think there was any hurry. Eventually they were taken to a labour ward and waited there for Kate to be seen by a doctor. Frances sat on a chair by the bed.

It was a midwife who came.

'Are you booked in?'

'Yes,' Frances answered for Kate.

'I'd better get some details.' As she wrote Kate's name the girl cried out.

'That's it coming again – Frances!'

The midwife put down her clipboard and came round the side of the bed. 'Lie back,' she said. 'That's it.' She drew the curtains round and helping Kate take her trousers and pants off, began to examine her. Frances stayed close by.

'Are you her mother?'

'I'm her aunt. She lives with me.'

'Are you staying with her through the labour?'

'Yes!' Kate gasped.

'Yes.'

'Right, we'll get her down to delivery. She's about four centimetres dilated, and it looks as if things are beginning to happen.' She smiled at Kate, 'Let's hope it's going to be quick, eh? It could all slow down again, it might be hours yet.'

'Hours?' Kate was furious. 'I can't go on having these horrible pains for hours. It hurts too much.'

The midwife exchanged a glance with Frances. 'We'll see how you go,' she said. 'We can give you something to help with the pain if it gets too bad. You put this on meantime. Put her clothes in this basket, Mrs—'

'Douglas.'

'Mrs Douglas – and leave it beside the bed. Right, see you in two tics.'

Kate looked in dismay at the white shapeless garment the midwife had left with them. 'What's *that*?' Resentfully she struggled out of her clothes, trying to keep herself covered up at the same time.

'It fastens up with these ties behind.' Frances said. 'As soon as I can I'll bring your own things.'

'I can manage,' Kate muttered, on the verge of tears. 'It's just I feel so big and ugly and awful.' Mortified, she huddled on the bed.

The midwife brought a wheelchair. 'Now then, let's get you down to one of the delivery rooms.'

Later, looking back, Frances had only an impression of whiteness, and the bright heat of Kate's contractions coming fast again, then slowing and stopping. At six o'clock she realised the boys would be home and wondering where she was.

'I have to call home,' she said to Kate, 'and I can't use a mobile – I'll need to find a payphone.'

'You won't be long, will you?'

'I'll be as quick as I can.'

'Why have they all gone away – the nurses?'

'Because there's nothing they can do. We just have to wait till your baby is ready to be born.'

'Well, hurry up then.'

'What?' Andrew exclaimed when she got hold of him. 'I thought it wasn't due for ages yet?'

'It looks as if the dates were wrong. Or it's early.'

'I suppose I've to get my own tea?'

'I suppose you do. Get some pizza out of the freezer or something.'

'You want to speak to Jack?'

'I'd better go back to Kate. I'll call you later.'

'Tell her good luck. Is that what you say, good luck?'

'It'll do.'

Kate was lying quietly when she got back. 'Another nurse came in,' she said, 'and asked a lot more questions. It's all stopped again though.'

'Why don't you get up and walk about? That'll help.'

'I *can't.* This horrible nightie thing is all open at the back.'

Frances looked round and saw a striped terry-cloth dressing-gown on a hook. 'Here, put this on, then you'll be decent.'

'Yuck. It's worse than the nightie.' She let Frances guide her arms into the sleeves then they walked up and down together, slowly.

'I feel stupid doing this,' Kate said, and heaved herself back onto the bed.

The midwife came and went and so did another nurse, older, in a different coloured uniform. 'You're doing very well,' they told Kate.

'How long is it going to *take?*' Kate wanted to know. 'Ask them, Frances, next time they come in.'

But all they said was, 'You're doing fine. We'll see about painkillers if you need them. Maybe just a bit of gas and air. Let's see how we go.'

'I *want* painkillers,' Kate hissed to Frances.

'They probably mean pethidine or something like that. See if you can manage without – it makes you dopey. I hardly knew Jack was being born, and as for killing the pain—'

Kate lay back again, subdued. 'I thought they might give me some paracetemol. Probably wouldn't work, eh?'

For an hour or so, nothing seemed to happen.

'Maybe it was a false alarm after all,' Kate suggested. 'We could go home.' She sighed. 'It's boring. If I get contractions it's awful, *mega* pain, I'm not kidding. But if I don't, it's boring lying here.'

'Do you want to walk about again?'

'No.'

After a moment, Kate said, 'Kenny's nice. Do you think you and him'll live together when Andy goes away to uni?'

'He's thinking of moving nearer his son,' Frances said, taken aback by Kate's directness.

'Why? I thought you two got on really well. Like you were married, sort of.'

'Did you?'

'Yeah, he really likes you, I can tell.'

'Well,' Frances said, 'I suppose he could babysit, and let you and me go out clubbing.'

Kate raised her eyes. 'Oh ha ha.' She sat up. 'Can I ask you something?'

'Fire away.'

'You wouldn't want to be married to Alec again, would you? You know, if he wasn't married to Mum.'

Frances understood now why Kate was so keen on Kenny.

'You can put that idea out of your head. I don't

want to be with Alec. Ever.' She put too much emphasis on the last word, and Kate noticed.

'What if *he* wanted to?'

'It would make no difference. All that's over. I don't see any point in talking about it. He's married to Susan, he has been for years.' She wanted to explain it better, to convince both of them that her marriage to Alec belonged to another life, as if to another Frances, but was too unused to revealing herself to be able to do it now.

Kate was silent; she seemed to be making up her mind whether to say something more.

'If Mum was – you know – never coming back—'

'Kate, I don't want to be married to Alec. Is that clear enough for you?'

'They had this massive row. The night before she went away.'

Frances's heart jolted. 'Did they?'

'It usually happened before she went away.'

'She'd gone away before? Left you?'

'Yeah, but not for all that long. A couple of weeks, maybe.'

'Where? The Retreat?'

Kate looked blank. 'What? No, Alec said it was a friend, she had a friend.'

'The same friend each time?'

'Maybe. Look, I don't know, do I? They wouldn't tell me anything. And I didn't really want to hear about it, it made me sick.'

'So what happened this time – they had a row?'

'They sort of niggled at each other all day. Then

418

they were in the kitchen and she was supposed to be cooking, only she wasn't, I began to think I'd have to get my own tea again. I was going through to see if we had chips or something in the freezer, then I heard her saying, that's it, I've had enough, you'll never understand. Stuff like that. Suddenly they were both yelling, so I went out. I couldn't *stand* it, they knew that, but it never stopped them. Afterwards they were always like, oh Kate, are you all right, don't worry about us. I couldn't stand it. So I went to my friend Sara's, I stayed over with her. When I went back in the morning, early to get my stuff for school, Alec was making toast. She must have gone already. I never spoke to *him*. He'd put the drawer back, but there was still a few forks and things on the floor.'

Frances thought of knives and shuddered. 'Kate, what on earth do you mean – *forks?*'

'When I went out the front door she was throwing things – I don't know what – then there was this noise like somebody dragging a drawer out. She must have thrown that, the drawer all the cutlery was in. There was an awful clatter.'

Kate's eyes were full of tears. She rubbed them away with the belt of the despised dressing gown.

'Oh Kate, I'm so sorry. It must have been horrible for you.'

She could not think what to say; there was no comfort for this. She remembered Alec coming to her almost nine months ago, saying, 'Susan's missing.' Perhaps he hadn't lied, but he had not

419

told the truth either. She was angry with him and Susan, that they could behave like that with Kate in the house and so carelessly let her come and go. The selfishness of it! My sons were spared that, she thought. We were better on our own.

'Listen,' Frances said, turning the subject, 'did you hear a baby cry there? Someone's beaten you to it.'

'Are there other people having their babies at the same time?' Kate had not thought of this. 'Wow. That's amazing. But I still wish it was tomorrow and my baby was here and I didn't have to wait any more.' She leaned back on the pillows with a sigh.

At eight they were offered food but neither could eat. They had cups of tea and a digestive biscuit each.

'Maybe I am hungry,' Kate said, after this.

'I'll see if I can get you a sandwich. You do need to eat – keep your strength up.'

But as Frances made for the door, Kate yelled, 'Don't go away – it's starting again! Oh – ow – it's *worse*.'

Frances held her. 'Breathe,' she said, 'in – out, that's it, slowly.'

It was different this time, she could see that, the pain escalating, with only a couple of minutes between each contraction. She eased herself away from Kate and went to the door, looking for a nurse. There was no-one, so she rang the bell by

420

the bed. A different midwife appeared, younger than the last, Irish, soft voiced but brisk.

'I think we'll break the waters now,' she said. 'That'll get things going.' She smiled at Kate. 'Here, I'll fix these pillows for you. Lie back now. There you are, that's better.'

It's all right, Frances told herself, they know what they're doing. Babies are safely born every day, every minute. She was stiff with anxiety. This was worse than having a baby herself. Or no, she amended, seeing Kate's face, astonished by so much pain, aggrieved. Not worse. But bad.

Kate waved a hand at her. 'Frances!' so Frances took the hand and held it. 'What are you doing?' Kate asked the nurse in fright, but in a moment it was done, and the warm liquid seeped out and ran down the inside of her thighs.

'Oh my God,' she gasped. 'I'm glad that didn't happen in Marks and Spencer.'

Frances and the midwife laughed, then stopped as Kate cried out,

'Here it goes again!' And then minutes later, 'Something's pushing at me – inside – like – oh God, I've got to *go* – ohh!'

The midwife felt, looked, became brisker. 'Now then, don't push yet, wait a while. Hold on.'

'I can't, I can't help it, it's *coming*.'

Frances remembered that relentless swell of the baby's head as it surged down, pressing, moving its way towards the vagina, towards the outer world and its own life. There is nothing, she could have told the midwife, can stop that.

Kate yelled, tried to breathe, gulped gas and air and gripped Frances so hard she later found bruises on her arm. 'I'm going to burst!' She flung away the mask and tried to sit up farther, her face dewy with sweat. 'It'll never get out – I'll burst – oh nobody *said* it would hurt so much.'

Then the miracle. The dark wet head appeared and Frances, who had borne two children and lost a third, witnessed how birth looks, for the first time. The midwife cradled the head, it seemed to turn a little, and from flesh and blood, from the pulpy distended opening of Kate's vagina, came the slippery pink-blue body of the baby, following her head, the cord coming after, thick and wet, and then the midwife pushed hard on Kate's belly – *one more push, good girl, that's it* – and the great liver-like placenta slid out too, soft and whole.

Kate raised her head and Frances helped her up so that she was sitting higher and could see what was happening. The midwife, swift and careful, had cleared the baby's airwaves and the first cry came like birdcall in the morning, welcome and sweet, thin and high.

It seemed only a moment before the baby was weighed and tagged and Kate held her, wrapped in white cloth, her hair plastered wet and sticky to her head and the dark eyes open.

'Oh!' Kate gasped, but could say nothing more.

Nor could Frances, tears pouring down her face, hardly able to see for tears.

'There now,' said the midwife, 'you've a fine wee girl. Isn't she the perfect baby and a lovely easy birth as well.' She glanced at Frances, wiping tears away. 'It's not so hard on the young ones, they usually have no trouble.'

Trouble enough, thought Frances, knowing how indignantly Kate had greeted the pain. But now it was over, and there they were.

'She's so funny looking,' Kate said. 'Do you think she'll get prettier?'

Frances hugged Kate and baby in the same embrace.

'She's perfect. They all look funny when they've just been born.'

Kate leaned back gingerly holding the baby, as if afraid she might let her go by mistake. 'Oh, I'm so glad you were here. I was really scared.'

'Yes,' Frances said. 'So was I.'

It was almost eleven o'clock by the time Frances left the hospital. Back in the ward, Kate was comfortably in bed, the baby in a Perspex-sided cot beside her wearing a tiny disposable nappy and a white nightgown. Kate's last sleepy words as Frances said goodnight, were 'Bring me something to wear and my make-up and my clean-and-clear lotion, all the stuff I said. Promise?'

'Promise.'

'Oh, and where's my mobile, I've got to text everybody.'

'You can't Kate, you won't be allowed to use it in the hospital. When you're up and about—'

'That's no good, I've *got* to text everybody.'

'Can I call—' Frances hunted in her mind for names (who was the favourite?) 'Michelle or Amy? Then they could text everyone else?' Kate looked mutinous then tearful. It was *her* news. 'Then they can all come and visit.'

Kate gave in. 'Ok then.'

'See you tomorrow.' She leaned down to kiss Kate; the thin arms came round her and, briefly, clung tight.

'Don't let Jack and Andy come in till I've washed my hair and I'm wearing my own clothes, right?'

She turned on her side awkwardly, still sore, and looked at the baby till her eyes closed.

Frances, suddenly remembering her car was still at Eden Court Theatre, was relieved to find a taxi outside to take her there.

It was dark and a crescent moon rode high over the Moray Firth as she drove across the elegant sweep of the Kessock Bridge. She was light headed, exhausted, and sure she would not sleep all night.

CHAPTER 6

Andrew and Jack were watching a film when Frances got home.

'What happened?' Andrew asked.

'You've got a niece.'

'It's a girl?'

'Seven pounds ten ounces.' Frances smiled at their astonished faces. 'Both well.'

'Neat – what's she called?'

'Nothing yet. The tag on her wrist says 'Baby Douglas'.

'She was all for Natalie last week. I told her it was French and she should pick a Scots name,' Jack said.

Frances was surprised. 'She never mentioned names to me.'

'She had them all written down, she kept adding new ones.'

Frances sank into an arm chair. 'I'm exhausted,' she admitted. 'Watching someone have a baby is very tiring.'

'Did she scream, like they do on TV?' Andrew wanted to know.

'She yelled a bit, and no wonder,' Frances smiled.

'It was an easy birth, though, very straight-forward.'

'What's the baby like? Does it look like anybody in our family?' Andrew wanted to know.

'At an hour old it's quite hard to tell. Dark eyes, a wee round face and quite a lot of hair for a newborn.'

'I thought they were bald.'

'You probably think they don't open their eyes till they're six weeks old,' Jack scoffed.

'I do not!'

Frances got to her feet. 'How late is it? I'd better call Alec, I suppose.'

Andrew and Jack exchanged a look. 'He phoned.'

'Alec?'

'Our esteemed, estranged father,' Jack mocked.

'Did you tell him—'

'I said you were at the hospital with Kate and she was having her baby,' Andrew said.

She saw from his expression that there was more. 'What is it?'

'He said could we put him up for a night or two if he drove here tomorrow. I said he had to ask you. He sort of laughed and said he'd take the chance.'

'You should have told him to sod off,' Jack remarked, modifying his language for his mother's sake.

'Don't be silly,' Frances said, getting to her feet. 'There's no need for that. He's bound to be anxious about Kate.'

426

She went out. Jack and Andrew looked at each other.

'She means because her mother's hopped it,' Jack explained.

'I know that, Dumbo.'

They turned back to the television. After a moment, Andrew said, 'You don't think he wants to move back here, do you? Come back to Mum?'

'Mum wouldn't have him. She only puts up with him because of Kate.'

'You think?'

'I know.'

'I suppose she could turn up any time, Susan.'

Jack grinned. 'Na. Topped herself months ago – or Alec did her in.'

'Oh, great, our father's a murderer.'

'Way dysfunctional family we've got,' Jack said, 'Don't know how I turned out so normal. Pity you didn't.'

Andrew kicked him. 'Shut it, I want to watch this.'

In the hall, Frances was speaking to Alec.

'She did very well, I was so proud of her.'

'You'd think she'd passed her A levels,' Alec protested. 'She's all right then?'

'Remarkably so, and the baby is perfect. I'm worn out, Alec, I must go. I haven't called Mum or Gill yet and it's late.'

He seemed reluctant to let her go and she had a pang of pity for him, alone in his house with no Susan to turn to and say 'she's all right – it's a girl'. Of course, if Susan were there, Kate would not be here. And I, realised Frances, feeling the tears start, would not have had anything to do with it. I'd be on the other end of a phone, hearing the news, disapproving, thinking how could they let her, at fifteen, go through all that. The road she had travelled this year had never seemed so long. How far I've come, she thought, and how glad I am Kate's here.

'I'm sorry,' she said to Alec, softened by emotion and pity for what he had missed. 'All this must be so difficult for you. Andrew said you're coming to see Kate.'

'I was packing when you called but you don't have to put me up if you don't want to.'

'Of course we will. Sorry it has to be the boxroom again.'

'The boxroom will do. Thanks, Frances, I appreciate all you're doing. You probably don't realise how much.'

Gill next, but Gill was out, so she left a message. She would call her mother in the morning; it was too late for them now. She wanted to tell someone else, to go on talking about what had happened. If Kenny had been at home she could have told him every detail. That was the only way to absorb the experience and seal it in memory. She had thought it was only their own birth stories women had to tell, over and over, but perhaps there were other stories which had to be made mythical and permanent in the re-telling.

Unable to think of going to bed and suddenly ravenous, she went to make a pot of tea and toast. She was eating a toasted sandwich when the telephone rang.

Gillian had come in just after midnight. She and Paul had gone to a film then to a pub with friends. They were Paul's friends and Gillian felt slightly out of it. She came home glad to have Paul to herself, yet feeling tetchy, wondering if she really wanted him to stay overnight.

He stood behind her as she pressed the 'play' button on the answerphone, nuzzling her neck, hands round her waist then rising to cup her breasts. At the sound of Frances's voice she froze, and sensing the change he released her.

Kate's had her baby tonight, a wee girl. They're fine, both of them. Call me back, even if it's late.

Gillian said, 'Pour me a drink would you? You could open the white wine in the fridge. I have to speak to Fran.'

He went to fetch the wine and when he came in with two full glasses, Gillian was saying, 'We've only just got in. Paul's here.'

He sat down with his glass of wine, and waited. When she finally hung up, she went to sit beside him. 'Fran says it was really straightforward. But poor Kate.'

'How old is she?'

'Fifteen.'

'Ah. I see.'

'Well, no you don't. It's complicated, my family.'

'Is it?'

She had not told him. Now she was only too aware how little she had told him. Before she could decide what to say a great shudder went through her, so that her glass shook and wine spilt. As he took it from her she put her hands over her face and burst into tears.

'Hey – what is it?' He held her, rocking her gently, knowing by now she would come out of it soon enough and this was all he was required to do. Her face was pressed against his shirt, the tears soaking through soft cotton. He stroked her hair. 'Maybe you should tell me what's going on,' he suggested. 'Like this, we're not going anywhere, are we?'

She raised her head. Eye make-up was smudged in dark crescents under her eyes and her hair was sticking up at the front. He smiled. 'Sweet,' he murmured, smoothing it down.

'Where might we be going?' she asked, moving away from him.

'It's kind of hard to get close to a woman who keeps having major emotional traumas and won't tell you what the hell's going on.' He went on smiling, taking it lightly.

'I told you, it's complicated. Kate's my other sister's daughter and it turned out she was pregnant when she arrived at Fran's, though nobody knew that then. And Kate's mother, my sister Susan, right—'

430

'I'm with you so far.'

'You know I told you'd she'd gone off for a while? Well, we still don't know where she is, we don't even know she's still . . . all right. Kate's had a baby and her mother doesn't even know and we can't tell her.'

'That's why you keep crying, because you're upset about your sister?'

'Oh, I don't know why I keep crying . . . it just happens. Maybe that's part of it.'

'I see,' he said, seeing at any rate that this was unlikely to be the whole truth. 'Don't take this the wrong way, but did you want a kid yourself?'

Gillian shook this off. 'Oh for goodness sake, I'm thirty six and single – if it was home and kids I wanted, I've gone the wrong way about it.'

'Thirty six is a terrific age to have a baby. Two of my sisters-in-law had babies in their thirties. Kit was nearly forty.'

'Yes, but presumably they were married to your brothers first.'

'One of them was.'

'Are you making fun of me? Because, quite honestly, I could do without that right now.'

'All I'm saying is, why not?'

'Why not what?'

'Why not have a baby?'

Gillian had found a clean tissue in her pocket and was dabbing at her eyes. Whatever he meant, she wasn't able to deal with it. Not now.

'I said I'd use some of my leave to be around

for Kate when Fran has to be at school. Just for a few days when she gets home from the hospital. I know you said the Algarve has these great bargains, but—'

'Forget the Algarve. It'll still be there next time you have a holiday.' He waited while Gillian blew her nose. 'Better?'

She bit her lip, hesitating. 'Paul, would you – what about coming with me, to Dingwall? If your brothers have all these children you'll know a lot more about babies than I do.'

'I don't even know where Dingwall is,' he confessed, 'but sure, why not. We could maybe do a Highland tour afterwards. I've never been farther north than Perth.'

'In a few days? Or is that too soon for you?'

'Are you taking it back?'

'What?'

'The offer to come and meet your family. That's what it is, isn't it?'

Gillian was silent. He could see her wondering what she was getting into, but he wouldn't offer a way out. He was curious, if nothing else. After a moment she repeated, 'Well, as long as you're sure you want to come.'

Alec lay on his back on the double bed he had slept in alone for nearly nine months. He had a glass of whisky on the bedside cabinet and the bottle lay on the floor beside it. Better not drink too much, since he had a long drive ahead of him next day. He needed a drink, had to have a couple anyway. Wet the baby's head, he told himself, wasn't that what you were supposed to do? He was struggling to remember something, what was it, yes, Susan, why Susan hadn't had more children. Why *they* hadn't had any.

They had never been settled enough to have children, their marriage a fragile guilty thing snatched from all the choices they might have made instead. The life they'd chosen, from all the other lives. She had chosen. Damned if he could remember what he had done. Felt. Meant.

It was dark now but he had not drawn the curtains, and the street lamp sent a white glow through the window so that the furniture made bulky shadows and seemed to loom towards him. He closed his eyes but it was all still there: the wardrobe, the tallboy, the dressing table, all Susan's and all empty of her belongings. Who had come back for her things? Had *anyone*? Perhaps he had dreamed it. One night when Kate was safely gone and he was too drunk to care, he had packed up a whole lot of her stuff and thrown it in the wheelie bin, smelling of rotten vegetables. That could have been any one of many nights.

He sat up abruptly, drained his whisky and poured himself another. *You have to live with what happened. What she did, you did.* Somewhere, she mocked him. He had no answer now, no way to call her back, make her see . . . see something. If only he could sort it out in his own head first.

433

The whisky burned down, numbing. He drank it gratefully and poured another.

Grace woke in the early hours of the morning and rose to go to the bathroom. As she got back into bed, Jim stirred, 'All right?'

She was wide awake. That was old age, she supposed, taking from you the deep sleep of the young and healthy. It seemed she drifted from one doze to another all through the night, never quite conscious but not lost to the world either. She thought she had been dreaming before her bladder woke her. Something about the girls, about getting them off to school? Uneasily, she turned on her side, careful of the left hip which ached all the time and worst at night.

As darkness dispersed and the first birdsong echoed tentatively from tree to tree, she went on lying awake, feeling there was something wrong, something she ought to remember.

'Jim,' she said, knowing by the way he breathed that he was just as wakeful. 'I think I'll phone Frances after breakfast.'

He turned to look at her. 'What for?'

'I just think I'd better.'

He could make nothing of this so turned over again, settling with a grunt. Grace waited for morning and thought of her daughters. 'Here are the three Douglas girls,' Barbara used to say when they went to her house for tea. 'A credit to your parents.'

She said it when they were little, tidily turned out in matching skirts and jumpers. They went outside with glasses of lemonade and biscuits and sat on the bench in Barbara's neat garden, bored. That was what she had dreamed, it was nothing to do with school. Susan in the middle, Susan always the first to get restless and jump up, spilling someone else's lemonade in her haste.

Barbara wasn't so approving when Susan was pregnant or Frances got divorced or Gillian went off to Edinburgh to get a job in an office instead of going to university. No wonder Gillian left, Grace thought, with the atmosphere at home so bad. No wonder she tried to get away from all of us. Susan had hurt them so much in the past, they were numb to it now. Well, she realised, I am numb to it. I don't even worry that she has come to harm, she was always too good at taking care of herself. The others got damaged, not Susan.

Sometimes, looking at Frances or Gillian, she was surprised to find them grown women, responsible adults living separate lives. The children they had been, the young girls they had so briefly become, lived in her mind like teasing ghosts she sometimes longed to see and hold again. Gillian did not seem much different, and Frances always had a grave, self-contained way with her. She had not looked for comfort even as a child, even from her mother.

It was the physical changes which surprised Grace most often, that Frances had grey hairs among the blonde; that Gillian had fine lines around her dark eyes. But they were still young enough to be capable and powerful in ways the old can no longer achieve. I'll never run again, Grace thought, or dive into a swimming pool or get up from sleep feeling rested and fresh. When had these things stopped? She could not say.

Only Susan was not here to remind her that she too was older, with an independent life. She had no picture of a plumper middle aged Susan to counteract the fierce and terrible memories of the last quarrel, the beautiful face twisted with resentment, the young girl leaving with her baby in her arms. Perhaps I am unfair to her, Grace conceded and she allowed, for a moment only, a stab of fear and love to pierce the protective layer she kept between herself and her lost middle daughter. *I may never see Susan again.*

Angry with herself for going down this hopeless path, she turned with an effort onto her other side and gazed at the slow inching of the clock hands. No sense in brooding like this, it never did any good. She wrenched her mind back to the present, to the day ahead. Then she remembered the feeling she had wakened with – that something had happened. She was uneasy all over again. She would call Frances first thing, before breakfast.

CHAPTER 7

The baby opened and closed her pink buttonhole mouth with tiny sucking noises, as if she were tasting something. Her dark eyes seemed to be gazing beyond them all to some far distance only she could see. 'Hello,' said Jack, 'ground to mission control?' and waved at her, but she scarcely blinked.

'She's not focusing yet,' Kate informed him.

'Hey,' said Andrew, 'look at her hands!' The fingers uncurled a little, as if to allow them to marvel at her perfect pinkpearl nails, the damp creases of her finger joints and palm, the skin reddened there, but creamy on the backs of her hands, her arms. Holding her close, Kate touched the fontanelle with one gentle finger. 'You have to be careful,' she told them, 'this bit's still soft, it hasn't all joined up yet, she's too new.'

'You mean you got one that's not properly finished off?' Jack asked, sitting down on a chair by the bed and beginning to eat Kate's grapes, which Frances had brought in along with the make-up and night clothes.

'Don't be stupid,' Kate said. 'They're all like this.'

'Cute,' Jack murmured, putting one of his fingers next to the baby's hand. The tiny fingers opened and curled, holding him. 'Hey, she likes me!'

'It's a reflex,' said Kate, who had been reading Frances's books after all.

'Na, she likes me best already. Favourite uncle,' Jack teased.

'Let me see then,' Andrew said, nudging his brother. 'What's her name? You got a name yet? What about—' He cast around and came up with the name of a singer he liked but Kate didn't.

Kate made a face. 'As if.'

'Is there anything else you need?' Frances had been packing the locker.

'Maybe some magazines. No, don't bother. I can't concentrate on reading, I keep falling asleep. There's not much point reading that sort of thing when you've got a huge stomach and a baby and you're probably never going out with anybody again.'

Frances laughed. 'You will, life's not over yet.'

'Better not be.' Kate held out the baby. 'You want to hold her?'

'I might drop her,' Jack said. 'Crash, right on her head. End of baby.'

'Let Andrew sit on the chair,' Frances said. 'Then he can take her.' For a moment, Jack looked mutinous, but he got up. It was rare for him to feel wrong-footed. Andrew, red with embarrassment (what if he really dropped her?), gingerly cradled the infant, who began to cry.

'Can't stand your ugly face,' Jack crowed.

Andrew ignored him and gently bumped the baby up and down. 'Ssh, ssh.'

The thin wail rose and swelled. Frances had forgotten how it tugs at you, that cry, impossible to ignore. She took the baby from Andrew and putting her on her shoulder, walked up and down. Surprised, the baby hiccuped and stopped crying. Kate watched, half jealous, half relieved.

'Do you want to try feeding her?' Frances asked. Kate went red.

'Not now.'

'Off you go for a wee while, you two – have a coke or something in the café downstairs. I'll be down in twenty minutes.'

'We only just got here,' Andrew protested.

'Yes, but Kate wants to feed her, so—'

'Oh. Right.' They were off, with a hasty wave to Kate. 'See you.'

Kate, watching them, felt she had grown older than both. They could never catch up. 'Did you phone Michelle? When are they coming in?'

'I said to leave it till tomorrow. After that you'll be home anyway. They can all come at once then and you can send all the texts you like.' Kate began to protest, but the baby was fretting again.

'Better give her a feed,' Frances said. 'She's quite wakeful.' At the first piercing cry Kate said, 'All right.'

Frances had bought her a nightdress which fastened at the front. She helped Kate settle the baby at her breast.

'Ouch – it's a weird feeling.'

'I know.'

'I don't have to do it for long, though, do I? We could get bottles when I'm out of hospital.'

'Breast feeding's much better—' Frances stopped. Leave it, she thought, keep that one for another day. Kate would think she was interfering, but how could she help it? Whatever happened, the baby had to come first.

There was no conversation while Kate was nursing. The baby seemed to give up very quickly as if she wasn't getting any milk, and cried, so that Kate was fussed and said it hurt. The rest of the visit was taken up with this. In the end, Frances was glad to hand over to the auxiliary nurse who had been there when Kate was in labour. She got the baby attached at last, and Kate calmed down.

'I'd forgotten how difficult it seems at first,' Frances admitted. 'Never mind, it does get easier.' Kate did not look convinced.

When the baby was back in her cot Kate followed Frances down to the area where she could switch on her mobile and starting calling and texting her friends. Frances gave her a quick hug, feeling dismissed.

By the time she and the boys reached home, Alec had been waiting in the lane half an hour, sitting in his car listening to music and smoking. The smoke curled through the open window.

'You should just have come up to the hospital,' Frances told him. 'I did leave a note pinned to the door.'

'I haven't been here long,' he said, getting out and grinding his cigarette into the earth. He looked at her properly, and his face changed. 'Your *hair!*'

Frances put a hand to the back of her head where the heavy knot had once lain. 'It's much easier to keep.'

They went on standing there after the boys had gone indoors.

'It suits you,' he said. 'You look great.'

She thought he looked terrible. He must be drinking again. She recognised the pallor, the tremor in his hand as he took the mug of tea she made him. The boys had disappeared, leaving them together in the living-room. He looked round, chose a chair and seemed to fold into it, worn out.

'How's Kate?' he asked.

'Doing very well. She's even feeding the baby herself, though I don't know for how long. I keep forgetting how young she is.' She watched him sip his tea. 'Are you all right? You look exhausted.'

'Long drive, that's all.'

'No word from Susan?'

'What? No, nothing.'

'It seems all wrong. She doesn't even know Kate was pregnant, let alone—'

Alec put the mug carefully down on the floor beside his arm chair. 'How would you feel if she *was* here, if she walked in right now?'

'I don't know any more. There's something about newborn babies that *pierces* you, and this one seems so special. In other circumstances, if Susan had been around, she might not even have existed.'

'You don't want to lose her. Either of them.' He stated it flatly, looking for his cigarettes then giving up, remembering no-one smoked in this house.

'Kate and the baby? I suppose I don't, after all this time.'

'I thought so.'

Frances went on hastily, not sure what he thought of this. 'It's up to Kate. It's her future.'

'I've put the house on the market,' he said. 'In fact I thought I'd sold, but it fell through at the last minute.'

'What are you *saying*?'

'I want to be able to go on seeing Kate, and helping her. I don't want to be five hours away by car, I don't want to come up and sleep in your boxroom by your good grace, every now and again.'

'Don't tell Kate about the house – not just now. She thinks—'

'I know what she thinks. I won't mention it yet but the house is in my name, it's my decision. You needn't worry, I've no ulterior motive.'

'I never thought you had,' she said, flushing, annoyed.

'It's just because of Kate and the baby.'

'I know that.'

'We could be friendly. At least.'

She could not say no to that. I should be angry with him, she thought: he's deceiving Kate. He looked frail and thin huddled in the chair, his face hollowed with fatigue and something she might have called grief, if he still loved Susan.

'Kate said you and Susan had a row the night before she left.'

He became even paler, if that were possible. 'Oh God.'

'What was it about?' She held up a hand. 'Sorry, I know it's none of my business, and you can say that if you like, but Kate was very upset telling me about it.'

'What did she say?'

'That you'd been arguing, then it got worse – she said it had happened several times before.'

Alec would not meet her eyes, but he nodded. 'It had. Every time she went off it was triggered by a row.'

'She said something about Susan going to a friend's and I got the impression it was the same person each time, but Kate was cagy and the baby was coming, so I couldn't ask her more.'

'The baby?'

'This all came out while we were waiting in hospital. How you pass the time, I suppose,' she said, with an attempt at humour. Something in Alec's expression dismayed her. She really didn't

443

want to know more, but before she could forestall him he began talking, his voice low, the Scots accent, long made neutral by living in other places, audible again.

'Not always the same friend. Maybe I didn't even know about all of them, but she went as far as leaving me three times, always to be with other men.'

'Oh—' Frances began, but he spoke over her.

'The first guy was married. He went back to his wife, I guess, though Susan's version was that she had made a mistake so she wanted to come back and sort things out with me. Until this time, that's what always happened.'

'Were you so unhappy together? That she kept falling in love with other people?'

'Falling in love?' he mocked. 'She was bored. Marriage bored her, I bored her. Susan liked excitement. When she stopped drinking and I didn't, it wasn't so much fun being with me.'

'She stopped—'

'She got pregnant. She miscarried very early, but never went back to drinking. She found her kicks in other ways. Or her consolation.'

There was so much here, Frances could not take it in. All these lost babies, she was thinking, but he was still talking and she had to listen.

'Then there was Mike, who was married too, but his wife had given up on him and they were living apart. I think Susan had an on-off thing with him for years.' His voice rose. 'I wasn't

444

blameless, I know that. The drinking, the life we had with me working all hours or between jobs, that uncertainty. But I protected Kate, I did do that. She never knew about her mother, she never knew any of this. Don't tell her now.'

'I won't, don't worry.'

'We must both protect her now,' he agreed. 'And the baby.' He fell silent, brooding. After a moment, Frances said,

'So she was never at the place you said – the Retreat?'

'Well, she did go there sometimes.'

'But you never believed she had this time? You lied.'

'There's more to it than that,' he said quietly.

Frances waited, not knowing whether she wanted to hear.

'The row,' he began. 'It started about that, about her going off again. Everything was about Susan, it all had to centre on her. She was incapable of seeing anyone else's point of view or understanding their feelings. This time, I don't know why, this time I lost it. I'd been working long hours, I was shattered, I stopped caring what I said. I told her I wished I'd stayed with you. I said I wished I'd had the gumption to stand up to the pair of you, make you listen, tell her to leave us alone, let us sort out our marriage. I said I wished to God I'd turned her down.'

Frances put her hands over her mouth, appalled. The past welled up and for a surreal moment she and Alec were young again, facing each other over the ruins of their marriage, as if that marriage still existed. Alec, scarcely noticing what he did, fumbled for his cigarettes, took one out and lit it.

'Sorry,' he said.

'Never mind, just smoke. It doesn't matter.' Frances leaned forward, hands clasped round her knees. 'What did she say, what happened?'

'She started chucking plates. Then she got the cutlery drawer out, God knows why, maybe it wasn't closed properly, she just grabbed at it, hauled it out. It was so heavy it fell at her feet and all the bloody forks and knives slid across the floor – the noise they made—' He stopped, drew hard on his cigarette, then got a handkerchief from his pocket and wiped his face. 'Oh God.'

After a moment he went on. 'She said she got the blame for everything. Said if I was so keen on you, why didn't I go back to you?' He paused to sip his cooling tea. He looked round for some-where to tip the ash from his cigarette, then leaning towards the fire, flicked it into the grate. When he began speaking again, his voice was calmer.

'She said I'd be sorry, that if I was so keen to be rid of her, I might get my wish. And then I'd be even more sorry.' He cleared his throat. 'Then she . . . she snatched up this knife and she came at me, she just kind of jumped forward and—' He threw the stub of his cigarette into the grate, and rubbed both hands over his face.

Frances felt her heart thudding in her chest. No, she pleaded, no, please don't let this be true.

Alec looked up, his face clear as if he had rubbed away the worst of the memory. 'I'm no catch, Fran,' he said, 'I admit it. I'm a drunk and I've been a useless husband, as you once told me. But I'm not a violent man.'

'No,' she whispered.

'I tried to get hold of the knife, but she slipped on something on the floor, one of the sodding forks, I suppose, and we were in each other's arms, it was bizarre, and she screamed, so I let her go. I got myself out and I grabbed my fags and I left the house.'

'Was she – had you – ?'

'I walked round the block. I knew if I stayed I'd grab the knife from her and I'd kill her. I didn't want to kill her, Fran, I never meant to hurt anyone.'

'But you went back, you went back to the house, Kate said in the morning you were there and Susan wasn't—'

'Of course I went back. I cooled down and I went back. I walked up the garden path and into the house and it was empty, there was nothing, she had gone.'

'She wasn't hurt, she was all right, oh thank God for that.'

He looked away, not meeting her frightened eyes. 'She was all right enough to pick up her bank cards and a few other things before she left.'

'That was the last time you saw her?'

He shrugged. 'She meant what she said – I'm rid of her.'

We all are, Frances realised, she's gone. 'You checked though with this Mike, you checked she's not with him.'

'Apparently he went to the States a year ago. I've no idea where.'

'So she could be with some other man?'

'Or with him. I have no idea. More likely him.'

'If she's with him the police could find out if she left the country, couldn't they?'

'If she did.'

'You don't think so?'

'No.'

For several minutes, they sat in silence, until the shock of the telephone ringing jolted them into the present.

It was Grace. Frances had had a long conversation with her in the morning but her mother knew she would have seen Kate again by now. She took a deep breath, hoping Grace would not realise anything was wrong. Still, she was trembling.

'I think we'll come up tomorrow,' Grace said, when she was reassured the hospital was up to scratch, the baby was feeding and Kate was coping.

'Oh Mum, I have a houseful just now. Alec's here already and Gillian's coming to help me. It would be lovely to see you but—' How could she say no when it looked as if the rest of the world would be in her house anyway?

'We'll get a B&B. Book us into that nice one in Dingwall Barbara stayed in once – what was their name? Your Dad and I just want to give Kate a wee something for the baby.'

Frances knew her mother wanted to inspect the baby herself.

'My first great-grandchild,' Grace went on. 'I know it's not the way we might have wanted but a baby is a baby, and I've bought a lovely wee suit. I took a chance, and it's a peachy colour, not really pink but nice for a girl.'

Frances had just put the receiver down when there was another call. As she picked up the phone this time Alec went past, heading for the back door. He held up his cigarette packet.

This time it was Kenny. 'I'm home,' he said. 'You'll have great satisfaction in hearing I couldn't stand the traffic and the prices they're asking for poky wee flats are a disgrace.'

'You should have stayed here,' Frances told him. 'You missed all the excitement. I'm a great aunt.'

'You never are. Well, well. So what is it – great nephew or great niece?'

'Niece.'

'Beautiful?'

'Naturally we think so. A red-faced wee mite with a lot of dark hair.' On an impulse she said, 'Come over, come and eat with us.'

'I might do that. Nothing in this place but tins of dog food and a mouldy carrot.'

Putting the phone down, she felt guilty she had not told him Alec was here, but all the old barriers seemed broken now, and if he came, she would feel protected. For the first time, she wanted that protection.

In hospital, waiting for the evening visiting hour, Kate idly picked over names. Michelle's Mum was bringing her in tonight, and Michelle had suggested a whole selection, but Kate wasn't sure any of them suited her daughter. Daughter. She tried the word out, applied it to the smooth sleeping face of the infant in the cot beside her. Her *eyelashes*, she thought, her heart lurching, her wee hands. Already the baby had lost the squashed indignant look of the hurriedly newborn. 'You're so sweet,' Kate whispered, 'when you're not crying. Carly. Juliet. Natalie.'

Alec got there before Michelle and her mother. As soon as he appeared, she said, 'What's Granny's name? Granny Douglas.'

'Grace,' he said, bending to kiss her.

She ignored the kiss. 'You're supposed to look at the baby first.'

'Sorry – hey – you've got a baby here! Where did she come from?'

'Don't be silly.' She leaned over and pulled the wheeled cot closer, edging back the blanket a little. 'She's lovely, isn't she? She was quite ugly to start with.'

'Beautiful,' he said and turned away so that

450

Kate would not see how near he was to breaking down. 'I'll just see if I can get a vase for these flowers.' He had bought the most expensive bunch in the hospital shop, and a large box of chocolates.

'It's like a birthday,' Kate said, pleased, as he dealt with the flowers.

'It is a birthday, just not yours,' he pointed out.

'She's a bit young for the chocolates,' Kate said, opening the box. 'Never mind, my friends will eat them.'

Ten minutes later, Michelle and her mother arrived with Roxanne. More flowers, scented shower gel, chocolate biscuits, and a large teddy bear. The girls bent over the cot, cooing. 'Isn't she *sweet* – aww!' The baby opened her eyes and gazed at them.

'This is great,' Kate said, 'getting all these presents.'

Alec withdrew after a few exchanged remarks with Michelle's mother.

'See you later. Frances sends love and we'll both be in tomorrow to take you and this birthday girl home, I'm told.'

Kate waved him a cheerful goodbye. The baby was awake and they were all taking turns to hold and pet her.

Outside, he lit a cigarette and walked slowly back to his car. He wondered if Frances's boyfriend would still be there when he reached her house.

She'd kept quiet about him for long enough. They had shaken hands with great politeness, but warily. What does he know about me, Alec wondered, glad he was able to escape after the meal on the excuse of visiting hour. A pleasant enough bloke, he supposed, this Kenny. Only a year ago, he would even have liked him and been glad to know he was around.

The house was silent. Everyone was in bed, and probably asleep. Frances was still awake. She was going over again the nightmarish scene with Alec. A few yards away, he was lying in the boxroom. We slept together for years, she thought, but could not imagine that now, could not any longer conjure how it had been. Something was in the way of memory, something obscured her connection with him. Until today, there had always been a connection, however tenuous and unwanted.

What he had told her did not make sense. In her warm bed, she was trembling with cold. *There was a gap. There was something he didn't tell me.* In darkness, it was too easy to imagine terrible things. It's the stuff of those crime dramas on television, she told herself, it doesn't really happen to people like us. She could see the knife gleaming with blood, but she could not see Susan, she could not see what happened in those next minutes. She did not know whose blood it was. He said he went out and when he came back, she had gone.

I don't believe that.

I could make him tell me the truth, she thought, I could get him on his own and *make* him tell me. Then, with a flood of relief, she changed her mind completely. I could leave it, I could just leave it. Why would I want to know more? I don't owe Susan a thing and I don't have to have him in my life any more. But I do have to have Kate and she's the one I must protect. Better for both of us if we just don't know.

'I'm sorry, Susan,' she said aloud. 'If you tell me where you are, I promise I'll do something, I'll find out more. But you have to do that first, you have to tell me where you are.'

In the silent summer night Frances lay waiting for a signal which did not come.

Gillian travelled north in Paul's sleek car. The A9, which had always seemed a long and dreary road (beautiful scenery of course, but you hardly noticed it after all these years), telescoped alarmingly. Blair Atholl already, then they were past Aviemore. She drew her breath in sharply once or twice when he was overtaking.

He did drive very slowly up the unmade road to Frances's house. 'Off the beaten track, this,' he said, negotiating ruts and large stones. He drew up behind three other cars. 'Is there a party going on?'

'That's Mum and Dad's,' Gillian said as they got out. 'And Alec's. Don't know who owns the one in front.'

'Maybe it's broken down,' Paul suggested. 'It's seen better days.'

When they went in they house seemed full of people. Andrew met them in the hall.

'Hi, there. You want a beer?'

'This is Andrew,' Gillian said. 'Andy, this is Paul. Where's your mother?'

'Upstairs, I think.'

Hearing them, Frances was coming down. She and Gillian embraced, Gillian smelling of fresh air and French scent, Frances of the cake she had baked and of baby, milky and sweet.

Frances and Paul shook hands. He looks too smart, thought Gillian. We both do, for the country.

'Come through,' Frances said. 'Everybody's in the living-room.'

The beaten up old car must be Kenny's, Gillian decided as they went in. She had met him only once, but now he seemed to be part of the family. The whole bloody family's here, she realised, except one.

The baby was a week old. Kate was sitting on the arm of her grandmother's chair. Grace held the baby and Jim was taking photographs.

'She's got a name at last,' Frances murmured to Gillian.

'What?'

'Grace.'

'You're kidding? Heavens, Mum must be thrilled.'

'Well, it's turning into Gracie, which she's not

quite so thrilled about, but it could have been a lot worse, believe me.'

Behind the sisters Paul hovered, holding the can of beer Andrew had given him. Gillian bent to kiss her mother and Kate and to admire the baby.

'Come in Paul, and meet everyone,' Frances said. Gillian, turning as her mother did, and her father, thought, oh *why* did I bring him? Look at his city shoes and his signet ring. Do I even *like* him? She turned back to the baby, taking her in this time, with a jolt of anxiety and longing so strong she had to grip the back of the chair for support. Then she looked at Paul again and he was smiling at her, so that she could only smile back and get up and go to him. As she did, all the awkwardness of bringing him into this circle vanished and she had an impulse of feeling for him so strong she knew it must be love. What else? It was as if she were closer to him than any of her family. Did Frances feel this, looking across at Kenny, or had she once felt it with Alec?

Gillian saw no-one now but Paul, the baby, her own rising hope. She put her arm through his. 'Mum, this is Paul.'

Like him, she willed, defying them to do anything else. *Just like him*. As she watched Paul deal with this far better than she could herself, she saw it was all right, and she willed him to like them too.

'Look at this place,' Jack said to Kenny, who happened to be next to him on the sofa. 'It's entirely covered in baby tackle. And look at the size of *her* – how can she take up so much space?' He indicated the baby being held up by Grace for Paul to admire. 'I tell you, I'm glad I'm going back to uni next week. I bet the minute I've gone there's nappies and baby stuff in my room as well.'

'That's the way of it,' Kenny agreed, finishing his beer and holding out the can. 'What about another?'

'Mum told me to put the kettle on – I'll bring you one back.'

In the kitchen he and Andrew speculated on Paul.

'Mint car,' Andrew said, since he had seen them arrive.

'Naff shoes,' Jack commented.

Frances came in with Kenny. 'We'll make tea,' she said. 'Grandpa wants you to take some photos for him.'

He and Andrew went out and Frances caught the sidelong glance they gave Kenny, then the look between them, as they went out. She began to cut cake.

'The baby's coping really well with this crowd,' she said.

'Just you wait. When they've all gone, that's when she'll start waking three times in the night and wanting attention all the time.'

'You would know, would you?'

'Two bairns and two grandchildren to my credit,' he reminded her. 'I'm an expert on babies.'

Together they prepared the tray and he carried it through for her. On the threshold, as she pushed the door open for him, she said,

'Poor wee soul. No father, no grandparents, and a mother who's hardly out of childhood herself. No wonder I feel protective.'

Kenny shook his head at her. 'Oh come on now. Look at this—'

This, was the crowded room, the baby peacefully nestling in Grace's arms, the cat on the window sill pretending to look out at birds, but swishing her tail in annoyance. She knew everything was changed, that nothing would be the way it was, in a house once quiet and undisturbed.

Frances rubbed her cheek against his shoulder. 'What?'

'Do you not think this child has more than enough family to be going on with?'

When the phone rang, Frances was pouring tea and Gillian was nearest the door. 'I'll get it.'

'Hello?' she said, loud and cheerful against the noise from the living-room. But no-one spoke, no-one said, *is that you, Frances?* There was only the silence which is not silence.

Gillian pulled towards her the door between her and her family, to shut out the noise and hear better. 'Hello?' she said again, and could have sworn, in the fading of conversation and rattling cups, the holding of the receiver up to her ear again, she heard someone speak. She was sure, she said afterwards, always said, that a voice faint and faraway, as if from another world, said '*It's me*.'

Gillian took a deep breath, steadying herself with one hand against the wall.

'Susan,' she said. 'Susan, please – tell us where you are.'

She waited, not knowing whether she wanted an answer or not.